She

Drove

Without

Stopping

SHE

DROVE

WITHOUT

STOPPING

a novel by

Jaimy Gordon

McPherson & Company

This edition first published in 1993 by McPherson & Company, Post Office Box 1126, Kingston, New York 12401. [Originally published by Algonquin Books of Chapel Hill, a division of Workman Publishing, New York, 1990.] Publication of this edition has been assisted with grants from the literature programs of the New York State Council on the Arts and the National Endowment for the Arts, a federal agency. Manufactured in the United States of America.
1 3 5 7 9 10 8 6 4 2   1993 1994 1995 1996

Library of Congress Cataloging-in-Publication Data

Gordon, Jaimy.
  She drove without stopping : a novel / by Jaimy Gordon
     p.   cm.
    ISBN 0-929701-36-4 (pbk.) : $14.00
    I. Title.
    PS3557.0668S54   1990
    813'.54—dc20   89-77062

Printed on pH neutral paper.

ACKNOWLEDGMENTS
Sections of *She Drove Without Stopping* first appeared as separate stories (in somewhat different form) in *Ploughshares, Gargoyle, The Missouri Review, and Shankpainter*. The author is grateful to the National Endowment for the Arts, the Michigan Council for the Arts, the Bunting Institute of Radcliffe College, the Washington Project for the Arts, and the Provincetown Fine Arts Work Center for generous assistance while she was at work on this book. She also thanks Shirley Clay Scott, Carolee Schneemann, Stephanie Richardson, and Rosmarie Waldrop for their good counsel. Her thanks and apologies as well to Sherwin Carlquist, whose fine book *Island Life* inspired, but is in no way responsible for, the epigraph from an imaginary *Island Life* in Book III.

For Peter

Boy. And wilt thou make thyself invisible?
Mandrake. Out, out! Who would ever lose sight of herself?
'Tis scarce possible nowadays.

—Thomas Lovell Beddoes, *Death's Jest-Book*

Contents

She

Drove

Without

Stopping

Book I

Love

○
○
● **Murder**

Only later, I began to dream of murder. By then I was living on
a little mountain near Antietam with my dog The Norn. There I
heard about the shooting of Martin Luther King over an old
tombstone-shaped radio that crackled like a rooftop in flames,
but my own life was still as only a season of docile penury can
make it. Even the Buick was dead in the mud road. This was
stillness, complete, temporary stillness—for soon the money I
had borrowed from my father's wife would fizzle out, and I was
going to have to get a job. Long, long before, I had escaped
from a life where nothing could ever happen to me, into a life,
in my twenty-second year, where anything could happen to me.
And it did happen. To recover from that, I had holed up here.

Only now I began to dream of murder. I thought I had killed
someone. Perhaps it was not surprising, for I had more than
dreamed this. I had plotted it. I would picture my father's handsome face growing bigger and bigger in the crack of his opening door. He would blink, for he was surprised to see me, even
apart from the gun in my hand. His eyes went round, his
smoke-blue irises rolled up, his mouth became an O, he is
about to speak, but what can he have to say to me? The skull
flies apart. His blood hangs on the wall as gay as bunting.
Once I looked at this with my eyes open, over and over.

To explain why I wished to kill my father Philip Turner, who was not a criminal, not even a bad sort, I must go back to my first days as a Kaplan and Turner.

I was the happiest of babies. This is evident in certain old family photographs; it has been told me by countless aunts and cousins, both Kaplan and Turner; and remarkably enough, I remember it myself.

A newborn baby who everyone can agree is happy is a phenomenon, and deserves to go down in family history as I did in mine. People say of an infant, "She looks like her father," "She'll have long legs," but never "She looks delighted to be here." For the truth is most babies come into the world looking anything but pleased. Their cramped faces express fatigue, and worry over what will happen next, before what we think of as life has even begun. No doubt time must go by before a baby is weaned of its foreknowledge that the world is a terrible place.

But sometimes a baby is born who lacks this foreknowledge, or else who is so elated to get out of its mother that it forgets all that at the exit. I was such a baby. I was an easy birth, and I have never regretted it. Not even for a visit would I return to the womb. I never sleep in the fetal position, but on my back or stomach, legs flung wide. I stay out of hot dark closets. I choose rooms with windows, full of moving air. I like scattered light, a moon, stars, but will settle for anything, even that greenish glow found nowhere in nature of a Santa Monica Freeway sign. At the thought that I once drew breath through my umbilicus, I want to gag and sputter. Finally, I enjoy my mother sufficiently across a coffee table, and have no urge to grow back into her body.

True, I sometimes find, at large in my sexual humors when they are superheated by the friction of love, an odd and hopeless wish to disappear into my friend's mouth or navel, or even into his anus; and sometimes when I have been lying across his body, stunned and adrift, while the room is darkly glowing, and the curtains tremble as if with pleasure that is never at an end, then I may imagine confusedly for a time I really am inside my lover—inside the body of a male after all, just a male.

But for a woman like me to long to return to the womb of another woman? Why indeed, unless the worst was expected, stay there a moment longer than necessary?

And so I promptly departed the cunnus, my first situation. For I fully expected to be happy. In the earliest photographs, before my facial muscles are developed enough to form a true smile, I wear an expression of pleasure that borders on the idiotic. Without bothering to close my eyes, I have dreamed off, with full trust in the protection of—no, the deep harmlessness of—the company I feel free to ignore.

If sex had had no locus in this infant, the world might have been harmless enough. But in fact its port of entry was rather obvious, pink and soft. It was clear almost at once that, happy or not, I knew a man from a woman with no instruction. This passed, at the time, for innocent, since the man who entered the sunroom, causing my eyes to focus and my first smile to form, was my father, Philip Turner. If I was in love with my father from birth, before I had seen any more of him than his fragmentary picture in my own chromosomes, then it was kind of fate to have made me the happiest of babies, for no one could resist playing with this infant, least of all my father, who was attracted to anything alive that did not remind him the world was a difficult and terrible place. Though a lawyer by calling, he collected queer vegetable life that grew only in places like the Society Islands and Borneo. But at first I was even more persuasive that life could uncurl without friction than *Arthrotaxis*, the pencil pine of Tasmania.

And so, for a time, I had as much of my father's handling as a lovestruck but good-natured baby could desire. My father wandered in and out of the sunroom according to promptings I never thought to question. When he was absent, I rolled around in my playpen. When he entered, I did not reflect upon the difference between this happiness, which my father was causing by zooming me around and around the sunroom like a toy airplane at the ends of his arms, and that other happiness, which dwelt between my ears before he ever came.

The knowledge that love of another person is by nature endangered happiness requires some little geography to wedge itself between desire and satisfaction in the baby's experience. And for this distance to press a locomotive design upon the affections, loss, too, must register as an idea. Someone must be sought, someone must be missed. Now, to this point, I had always been happy and never deprived, happy alone, happy in a crowd of fussing, baby-talking, cooing, cigar-puffing friends and relatives, and happy in the arms of my father Philip Turner.

Then I inherited locomotion from my forebears in the human race. I was given no choice. This was my job. One is a certain age and suddenly grownups are foining you into motion. Cheers for the first crawl, though you beeline for cabinets full of laundry lye, which you will shortly drink. Jubilation as you totter three steps and plunge headfirst into a trashcan. And finally you stagger headlong down the parlor, taking lamps and end tables with you, to deafening applause. Like others before me, I was duped into movement, an occasion for deep depression had I been born, like other babies, with common sense. Instead, for me, that dopey bliss gave way to the thrill of distances, to the fear of fears—that of getting lost entirely. And if one looked closely at this, one saw a liking to be scared, a delight to be scared, even an absolute requirement of it; an instinct to grope in dark places for other living things, to swim in dark elements that certainly could not be mastered.

I became (*in potentia*) an adventuress; or at least certain restful professions were now closed to me—for example, that of a prehistoric Venus on her haunches in a cave, Neumann's model for the female and "vegetable" soul; or that of the moon-white odalisque seen through a peephole by Alexander Kinglake in a Cairo bazaar in 1835, a lady as big as a sofa, kept in a lightless box and fed only milk through a straw, the prize of her dealer, and very expensive.

As soon as I could walk, satisfaction was moved to an ugly and cramped little den down the hall, my father's office. It was not the same as before. When I could toddle to my father's lap instead of having the pleasure of his company only suddenly and mysteriously bestowed upon me, I was receiving a certain power, but not the power to reproduce at will that which before had come only as a gift. That was lost forever. Now it was possible to seek my father, but happen on him when he had a tray of specimens before him, tweezers and cotton ball in hand, nervous sweat fogging his glasses, his fingers trembling slightly.

"You!" he would shout. "Not now! SASHA!" calling for my mother. And my mother would appear and sweep me up, the screen door would slam behind us, and I would find myself wedged between my mother and her friend Sibyl on a bench beside the plastic wading pool, with my hands flattened like two small preserved animals on the silvery picnic table as my mother applied a matchhead-sized droplet of red fingernail polish to each nail. Or she might position me on the kitchen counter beside the sink and, while she worked, allow me some interesting adult food (she was pregnant with Hermine) like pickled herring in cream, which I would soon vomit smoothly into the garbage pail.

I was no less happy. After all, when I got into his den, my father was not always busy. Or, even if he were, quite often he would take me on his knee and blow a loud kiss on my neck as I kicked and screamed with joy. He would say, *Dazyoom?*

(This was baby talk for the question that lovers ask.)

Then he would reach into my cotton underdrawers and squeeze one of my buttocks in a warm, faintly trembling hand.

Am I tattling when I tell you that? If such fondling is improper, still, what an everyday puzzle it was. And for a girl to have noticed so much out loud would not have been everyday, but rather brutally impolite. For my father's part, it was at least absent-minded, this puzzling caress; as absent-minded as the penis falling every morning out of his blue-green boxer shorts, and far less controversial at the time. I will not claim innocence for him any more than I would claim it for myself—any more than I could sham surprise, say, at my dreams of murder.

I masturbated every night from age beyond memory. Really I cannot think when I was myself, Jane, and didn't play with myself, thinking of men, long before I had any sense I was usurping a role or pantomiming a conjunction of far more complex terms. Because I was always sent to bed at fixed hours long before I needed to sleep, it was natural that I would *play* with myself—though by the time I began to come, sex in solitary was my resort from mere play, a way to summon giants, and of course grownups, to my level.

For so many years I was sent into the dark fully awake, night after night. I was not insomniac, really. I never wished for sleep. I did, as I say, other things. Certainly I couldn't allow that sleep was eluding me as though it were something I sought. Instead I waited for it fitfully, hostilely, like a woman who goes to a park hoping to encounter a refractory lover, without admitting she does so even to herself.

I played with myself so often that I got sick of it, and sometimes had to keep on as coarsely and obstinately as any numb-drunk fifty-year-old claiming his nuptial rights, until I did come. And then I would think of much more than men. All the darkest possibilities of sex churned in my mind.

All through my childhood, no one ever told me (as I often

hear women complain of being told) that sex was lewd and animalistic. On the contrary, my parents, Sasha and Philip Turner, took the most modern line on the subject, so that I had to discover these truths by myself: that the body was steamy, swampy, and full of holes you could fall through and never land, and so was only terrifyingly beautiful; and that sex was wicked and dangerous, hence not something to be discussed in carefully everyday tones, front seat to back, on the way to the Lyric Theater for a travelling production of *South Pacific*—which is where I first received sexual instruction.

We were passing Druid Hill Park Reservoir, at night a round black plain strung with small balls of light. (Last year they had been fuzzy pom-poms, but now I had glasses.) I was nine, Carla and I were in the backseat, and one of us must have asked a question. We already knew about the seed planted in the mother's stomach; that explanation had been issued five years before, after Hermine was born. This time we had stumbled on how it was done and who did it. Immediately the sense was in the air, even in the car, of debates by the wan light of my parents' night-table lamp, my mother foraying, her psychiatrist Dr. Zwilling's fatherly yet theatrical face embossed in mid-speech on her shield, my father retreating but smoking his Camel in short resentful puffs. The motor hummed. My mother waited for him to speak. A great headpiece of solemnity rolled over us all, a blue-black glow in the dome of the family Ford, made transparent now and then by passing headlights. I remember my parents' heads hovering in this glow, where the two seemed even better spaced than usual, my father hatless, the deep gouge of obstetrical tongs (a real scar on the back of his neck that I always studied when he was driving) soaked in black shadow, and my mother's smooth dark hair under her little pillbox hat occasionally glinting.

"The man's penis," my father said, "grows bigger . . . much bigger . . . than usual."

How big, we wanted to know.

A long pause. Then, with audible reluctance, "Let's say six

inches long," my father replied. "And three inches wide . . . "

I am sure he meant three inches around—I think he was trying to be, if anything, conservative—but at the time what I saw in my mind was three inches straight across—and I imagined a penis so enormous that it was no wonder a man had to lie down to operate it. I was shocked. Carla and I were giggling nervously in the backseat, but careful not to let our parents hear, and meanwhile, I was packing away the giant erection for study. I suppose such instruction forfended error of a certain kind, but it was not having the clear-eyed sensible effect my parents hoped it was having. And to this day I remember the backs of their two heads—Sasha's little pillbox and the small dark pit of Philip's obstetrical scar—floating above this discussion as sexual semaphores, profoundly bizarre.

I learned the word *rape*, too, at my father's lips. I was ten years old. I first saw it in a newspaper headline.

RAPE SEEN IN SMIGIELSKI DEATH

The body of a sixteen-year-old girl had been found at the base of a B&O railroad trestle, in what newspapers call a wooded area, in Highlandtown, a part of Baltimore where there are steel mills and thousands of Poles (among others) who work in them. Her name was Madalyn Smigielski; her family, first generation Polish, sometimes wrote their name "Smith." The body, the paper said, was blond and nude but for a pink brassiere wrapped around the neck.

I knew no one from Highlandtown. *Highlandtown-Patterson Park* was to me as foreign an expression as Lower Silesia, three words printed across the calm resigned foreheads of certain Number 5 buses and pointed sharply away from my own neighborhood. I had never ridden a bus beyond downtown.

Still I had some sense that such a bus headed towards blocks of brick rowhouses on the other side of the harbor, low, flat, continuous shoals of rose and sand rowhouses, all family houses, south and east of the city. The thought of so many families, all other people's families, always made me anxious. I could already imagine the rank foreign smells of their dinners, their purple and gilt religious bric-a-brac, the snow-capped peak on the calendar from the neighborhood plumbing-and-heating concern, the brand-new crimson set of encyclopedias complete with shelf. The girl who had been raped and murdered came from a house like that.

Oddly, I don't remember the cause of death; probably she was strangled (the pink bra). I recall the high trestle of the B&O; her white yet foreign — *Polish, Catholic* — skin and her blondness; the dirt, twigs, dead leaves of the *wooded area* pressed against the lumpy face (probably a confirmation photo) that had appeared in a box in the papers; the twin surnames, *Smigielski* and *Smith*, with their air of disguise or indecision; the unknown male who had raped and murdered (though I did not understand yet what rape was) and was being sought by police; and above all, the pink brassiere.

I had never even seen a pink brassiere, although I had investigated the subject of ladies' underwear carefully. I knew every garment of my mother's lingerie by heart. I had discovered, on afternoons when my parents were away from the house (never at night for then there would have been a babysitter) exotica that doubtless my mother did not know she had. And I had tried everything on, climbing onto my mother's bed to see myself in the mirror over the bureau, where sunlight filtered through old crinoline like steam: strapless merry widow corselets that, even with nylons stuffed into the cups, stood stiffly away from my flat breastbone like plates of armor; pink silk fingerless gloves that unrolled to the dimple of the upper arm; slips, petticoats and garters; bras with whirlpools of puckered stitching spinning out dizzyingly from the nipple; and even a complete ancient girdle, grayish peach in color like a pig, with sidebones and yards of agleted laces — but no pink brassiere.

Magically, I understood what this meant. Her lingerie was a treasury that ran to ridiculous surplus like a king's. My hands in it were wicked, yet my mother's underwear had a legitimacy, the more so if she never wore a tenth of it. I saw that it was a certain sort of lady's underwear. Here a pink bra was as alien a thing as the word *Highlandtown* printed on the destination signs of buses, for my mother would never own a pink bra, she would look on a pink bra with horror—she wasn't the type. And the difference between types was enough to attract murder. I became frightened, and doubted I could know this much. It seemed to me that I might have seen a pink bra in my mother's drawer after all.

When Sasha left the house the next day, I went to her bedroom and emptied all the lingerie drawers together in the middle of the rug. I dug through the pile, finding nothing pink but the girdle that was really the color of a pig and the beautiful long gloves. Then I heard the screen door slam below, and heard my father's heavy footsteps piling up the stairs. In a panic I shoved the whole heap under my mother's bed and sat down on the edge of the mattress in front of it, assuming a ladylike pose, my hand on the bedpost.

My father appeared in his tennis clothes, gray with sweat. "Hello, Bones," he said, in a not unfriendly voice. I noticed that he was not interested enough in me to ask what I was up to in my parents' bedroom, as my mother would have done. Already he was stripping off his wet T-shirt, then his shorts. Standing before me in his underpants, for a moment he did seem to be staring at me inquisitively. Then I realized he was looking at the tousled bedclothes. "Why is this place such a mess?" he complained. "Things are going to the dogs around here."

Engrossed in my own research, I hadn't noticed that the beds were uncharacteristically unmade. But the drawers, I saw with a cringe, I had left open myself. They were what gave the room its ransacked look.

"You know what?" he said. "Do you know how crazy your mother is? She found a bobby pin in my bed! a bobby pin! and she thinks I had some woman—"

All at once it must have struck him that he was saying the wrong thing to a ten-year-old. I felt this myself—I can imagine the round white plate of shock my face must have become—because he stopped mid-sentence, and wheeled for the shower, when his foot caught in a white garter belt snaking out from under the bed. "Jesus!" he said, lifting the bedspread with his bare toe. He gave the heap of lacy nylon a baffled but impatient kick. "I don't know what's come over your mother, I really don't!"

And he disappeared into the bathroom.

I sat there, holding onto the bedpost. At once I tried to erase his words from my mind, and when they would not rub out, I buried them deep, deep in a crop to one side of memory, which would have found them difficult to digest.

Otherwise the bobby pin was snatched into air and became nothing at all. Whatever words my parents had thrown at each other on the subject by the light of the night-table lamp did not exist for me. I did not hear them argue, because I rarely saw them together at all. My father had just stopped smoking and now was out of the house before the morning sun had hardened the light. He went clumping down the sidewalk in his giant sneakers, T-shirt and shorts. At that time he was the only grown man in the world who ran, and the neighbors peeked out their kitchen windows at him as if he'd gone berserk in his underwear. Sasha never got out of bed until he had gone off again, this time for good, to the office. And when we walked home from school, we only saw the maid. My mother would be marketing, or potting, or, every Monday and Thursday, downtown to see her psychiatrist, Dr. Zwilling. Later her station wagon crunched into the driveway. She would come through the screen door unsmiling, carrying the evening paper.

"Where's your father?"

We didn't know where our father was.

"Come help me with the groceries."

Presently, five shrivelled hamburgers that reminded me of the Black Spot from *Treasure Island* would emerge from the broiler. My father's place was set, but he didn't appear. Sasha said nothing about him. Dinner lasted ten minutes. Carla, Hermine, and I soon tired of swirling red and yellow condiments on our plates and headed for the yard.

Then the phone would ring—then or later—and my mother

would answer it in my father's den, closing the door behind her.

It may well be that my father believed Sasha was telling us more than she was. I suppose she was already collecting his lipstick-stained shirts from the hamper—but of that we had no suspicion. All in all, on the subject of telling the children, Philip Turner was strikingly obtuse as far as his wife's true temperament was concerned. Sasha had principles, and she had Dr. Zwilling to please. There were things you told children, and things you did not. And because I never once saw my mother cry, or get sick, or complain of a headache or cramps, or otherwise physically falter, because her anger had a terrible austerity about it unlike my father's wild swings—because every show of emotion was unusual in her, when Sasha unfolded on the kitchen table *The Evening Sun* that flashed the Smigielski rape in its headline, and caught her breath, sat heavily down, and forgot what she had been saying, I crept up under her arm to see. And there was the word in two-inch capitals: RAPE SEEN IN SMIGIELSKI DEATH.

"What's rape, Mom?"

Sasha folded the paper in half and slid it under the grocery bag.

"Go practice the piano."

"It isn't five o'clock—"

"GO PRACTICE."

I slipped out the screen door on my way to the jungle gym and met my father coming up the walk, briefcase in hand.

"What's rape, Dad?"

"What!" He peered at me.

"Rape."

He shook his head, uttering a little *What next?* sort of laugh. "Look, that's a tough one, Bones. I have to run to a meeting. Ask me later."

After my father's MG left the driveway, I sidled back into the kitchen, hoping to purloin the newspaper while Sasha was cooking dinner. But the paper was on the kitchen desk, still at the front page, and my mother was talking on the telephone, her forehead cradled in her palm.

"My name doesn't matter, I'm only curious . . . for a personal reason, about the time they think . . . I know the date is in the paper, but the time . . . I'd rather not give my name . . . "

She listened for a moment and her hand strayed to her cheek.

"All right," she said in a flat, tired voice. She spelled out our telephone number digit by digit. Then she hung up, and sat there staring at the paper without moving. Suddenly she rose, and the newsprint, flopping over, crackled in her hands.

"Mom, why can't I see the paper?" I asked.

"Because I'm using it. Why aren't you practicing?"

I went to practice.

After dinner, while Sasha was cleaning the kitchen, I took the paper behind the living room sofa, unfolded it on the floor, and read it, on my hands and knees.

My father came home before my bedtime and I caught him on the stairs.

"What's rape, Dad?"

Philip Turner scratched his neck and made a noise with his lips as though he were blowing out a candle.

"You know what sexual intercourse is, don't you, Jane?"

Sasha's little pillbox hat and his dark scar in blue shadow on the way to the Lyric floated between us. I nodded.

"Well, rape is when a man forces a woman to have sexual intercourse without her permission. Do you understand?"

I nodded.

"That's all?" he said, with some relief. He started up the steps.

"Dad?" I said.

He turned three steps above me, his head and shoulders missing in the dark angle of the stairs.

"Why does it kill her?"

He snorted, but not as though anything was really funny. "It doesn't kill her. She may get killed, but *that* doesn't kill her. Where did you get that idea?"

I went to bed, full of the most grotesque imaginings.

My father came home the next afternoon early. Sasha and I were at the kitchen table, she balancing her checkbook, I doing arithmetic problems from school, holding my pencil in two fingers and trying to write my numbers small like hers.

He smiled at me. "Hey, you saw the paper last night, didn't you, Bones?" He turned to Sasha. "She wanted to know what rape was. I didn't know where in hell—"

"I should have explained it to her," Sasha murmured, staring at a pile of pink checks.

"Ten years old and she reads *The Sun*." My father stretched his hand down my back and gave me a squeeze on the buttock.

"Why are you early?" my mother inquired. I looked at her. If she was mad when he was late, why wasn't she glad when he was early?

"Something peculiar happened. Three plainclothes dicks showed up at the office and wanted to know where I was Friday night when that girl, Madalyn whatshername, was—you know, the works." He looked at me and laughed a little. "Oh well, she knows, she reads the papers."

My mother smiled faintly. "What did you tell them?"

"I said I was pollinating all right. They didn't get the joke."

"I don't get the joke either," Sasha said.

"Pollinating *Angraecum sesquipedale* at the Galapagos Club. I offered to show them my specimen. Sixteen inches, I said. They didn't even smile."

"What was sixteen inches?" I said, worried at this figure, but curious.

"I'll explain later," Sasha told me.

"The spur of the orchid," my father said. "They wanted to know if anyone was *with me*." He shook his head.

"Was anyone with you?" Sasha asked.

"Of course. You can't pollinate orchids alone. Then they—"

"Who was with you?"

"A club member."

"Which one?"

My father backed away from the table, looking disgusted.

"Which one?" Sasha repeated.

"Elizabeth. Now don't start!" He walked towards the doorway, waving his hands. "For God's sake, what a day. First the Keystone Cops, now you."

His footsteps clattered up the stairs, two at a time. Sasha stared after him without speaking, as though she had never seen him before, as though midnight had struck, catching the thing outside its casket, exposing its usual discreet metamorphosis. I felt a silvery net creep over my scalp, watching her. Then she said something strange. "I don't know who that man is," she whispered. She continued to stare, but no longer fiercely; rather as you stare at a place on the wall from which a mirror has been removed, startled to see yourself changed into blank space.

Then she remembered I was there, looked at me, and asked softly, "You don't really understand rape, do you, Jane?"

I was afraid to answer her either yes or no.

"I must really be going crazy," she whispered, and lowered her head to the table.

○
○
● **My**

private

life

When I was five I loved my father passionately; hearts flew whenever I saw him. Under the beautiful streetlights, lotus-shaped and still sparked in those days by a city lamplighter, under a purple dusk, jeweled with lightning bugs, he veered to the curb in a sky-blue roadster. He wore a green bow tie. He stepped off the running board with a heart-shaped box of chocolate kisses in his hand. He gave them to me.

When I was seven, my father observed me hanging upside-down on the jungle gym with my spidery fingers between my legs for all the world to see; and doubt overtook him, Philip Turner, the formerly untroubled lover of his daughter, Jane.

We all know it is different when fathers touch daughters than when mothers do. His touch is a world apart from that daily usage of nursing bras and rubber panties and bibs and silver-backed baby hairbrushes—or my mother spitting on her Klee-nex when no one was looking and brusquely rubbing my face clean. When I was eight years old, my father still slipped his hand into my underpants sometimes and squeezed a buttock, but why? At eight I was still in love with my father, but he was no longer in love with me. I embarrassed him. I was odd. I could not amuse him.

My father had a great fear of looking foolish. His own mother had prepared him for a *noble* adulthood, *noble* was her favorite word, with garments that made him look foolish all through his adolescence. One of a handful of Jewish boys on the grounds, craving only to be normal, Philip Turner lived through prep school in black corrective shoes laced to mid-shin for some fancied defect in the classical line of his legs. He was banished from rough sports and muddy playing fields. On his mother's orders he wore rubber galoshes, wool caps as shapeless as the crowns of lichens, huge earmuffs for whatever these caps would not cover. He was proud and self-conscious and did not suffer these indignities lightly.

By the time I knew him, therefore, my father would not put a hat on his head in an era when almost everyone wore hats, for he knew that the edge was fuzzy between a silly hat and any hat at all. My father would never carry an umbrella, for a man with an umbrella in his possession looks fussy and effeminate. What if he should need to stumble into a workingman's bar in a downpour? Where would he hide the thing? My father would not wear rings or stick-pins; he would not wear pajamas because pajamas made one think of a man sick in bed whose wife was standing over him lugubriously with a thermometer in her hand. And pajamas were particularly depressing when they bore a florid machine-scrolled monogram on the breast pocket, as did all the pairs his mother used to send him in packages of three from Saks Fifth Avenue once a year. Giving these to the maid, my father went to bed in blue-and-green striped boxer shorts, although every morning his penis was sure to be falling out of the rumpled fly just as his three daughters trooped noisily into the room, a situation which caused much strife once my mother was instructed that it was pernicious by Dr. Zwilling, her psychiatrist.

In fact Philip Turner was a handsome man, and his daughters soon saw, when they travelled out in the world together, that grownup women noticed him. A strange giddiness came over these ladies and they waited on him sooner than on other people without his having to ask. But for all that, there was something odd in his appearance. It was as though he had a radar unit on top of his head whose job it was to revolve day and night on the lookout for any unmanly article that might approach and try to attach itself to him; and this queer device, like the windmill on a Rootie Kazootie beanie, cast its shadow over the whole careful show.

He was slender, his horn-rimmed glasses seemed a shade too big and too bent and slid down his nose as if perhaps he'd slept on them. He had a barn-green bow tie with yellow and red dots on it—somehow this artifact slipped by the radar unit; he wore it for years. He was thin in the face, and his hair stood up electrically in light-brown waves that made his face seem elongated, shocked and, again, a little silly. His cuffs were loose. His pants bagged a bit more over his shoes than was the fashion. Whenever a photograph of him was taken, no matter how brief the time since his last cautious look at himself in some men's room mirror, somehow his glasses would have slipped, the pocket flap of his suit jacket would have gotten tucked in, the pocket would be sagging down heavily from some mysterious load, and the collar of his overcoat would be folded under on one side. My mother said he looked like a Trotskyite who ought to be searched for a bomb.

This was my father who went to work, a young lawyer, the favorite of women. He had another side where he was the favorite of the girls, his three daughters, and on this side my father surprisingly had no fear of looking foolish at all. He was subject to crazes: for botanical expeditions to which he would drag one of us (Sasha would not go); for throwing the football in the street with his friend Woody; for jokes and toys. When a toy was the object, it was our toy and he would shamelessly hog it—the balsa-wood aeroplane, the pogo stick, the kite. Someone gave us a brown plastic bazooka gun that oinked pleuritically when the trigger was pulled and shot Ping-Pong balls all the way across the street, and until this great toy was broken, we could only trail along behind him anxiously and loyally, like seconds at a duel, while he emptied its barrel into hedgerows and stands of zinc garbage cans, or ambushed Sasha coming out of the screen door.

He was your best playfellow up to the point that he sensed something queer in his connection to you; until someone would say in a certain tone, "Phil, I could pick out these three little girls of *yours* anywhere." What did that mean? For he was not confident of his opinions in the domestic arena. I don't think he had any, really. He recalled, I suppose, what a queer child he had been. It took so little to be completely unlike the others, a condition of failure that could not be concealed, that meant just what it said.

He saw that child-rearing was beyond him, a shadowy duumvirate of mothers and doctors, best left to those two to run so long as his children liked him and (but this was crucial) weren't freaks. So that when he received Dr. Zwilling's doctrine on any article of child care, though always second-hand, through my mother, he never put up any arguments but resolved at once this was law—for a few minutes anyway.

There were times when his enforcement was swift and terrible because our transgression happened to coincide with something that actually got on his nerves, like noise when he was trying to work. "Quit horsing around," my father would suddenly shout from his den, with a menacing violence that we certainly didn't take as a joke; but it was still far away, down the hall and down the stairs, and we would be deep into one of those wars of tickling, pinching and shoving that cannot stop in the middle.

And pretty soon my father's voice would come again, but this time along with his crashing footsteps up the polished wooden stairs: "I THOUGHT I SAID QUIT HORSING AROUND!" And then his arm in an electrically glowing white shirt sleeve would shoot out of the dark hall, fall heavily and slap and grab and, fastening on my upper arm, throw me down the hall—which was terrifying because he seemed to be past all control of himself. And then he would depart, leaving behind that glassy silence that washes in when a person of importance suddenly acts unsound. And we would creep back together, cured of all tension, and in whispers consider the mystery of why our father

Philip Turner always hit me, Jane, in particular, a problem all three of us recognized and discussed in hushed and worried tones like doctors in the anteroom of a patient whose condition was steadily and inexplicably worse.

Now I was nearly ten and my father liked anyone better than me, even the dog. My father and Sasha discussed it too, for after he hit me she would tread white-lipped into his den, closing the door behind her. In the morning Philip Turner would come looking for me with a sheepish yet restless expression on his face; and finding me at the piano, or in the sandbox, or swinging on the jungle gym, "I lost my temper," he would say. "I'm sorry I lost my temper at you last night, Jane, I shouldn't have hit you, but there's one thing that drives me crazy. Why are you playing up to me? Why don't you at least argue with me like Carla and Hermine do? When I tell you not to do something, you always say Okay, okay, Dad, and then you turn around and do exactly what you want."

"Okay, Dad," I'd say, anxious to make his distressed face disappear. And soon it would. For these apologies were hard on both of us. For me they were suffused with a vague physical sense of shame, the way it was getting to be if I should accidentally see or be seen by him naked.

And I am certain my father was suffering genuinely at these moments, since there was about him a profound air of wishing he were doing something else. His handsome face worked over his bow tie; he stammered a bit; his hand trembled slightly as it brushed across the backs of my knees, pried up the moist elastic, and slid into my drawers. And I wouldn't move (it would have been indelicate to do so) though it made me seasick to be touched this way so soon after I had been struck. I waited stiffly for him to take his hand out of my panties, being careful not to meet his eyes with mine, which was not hard. Meanwhile I heard a rustling or whistling about him—his urge to get away. And a minute after I said, "Okay, Dad," he would zoom down the driveway in his green MG (he cleaned out all of our nickel-a-week school bank books to buy that car—years later Sasha made him pay us all back) though no matter how late he was, he'd pause to take the top off if the day was fine.

It is true that all this time I had a rich and inviolate private life, so that it was impossible to be thoroughly unhappy, even though I loved my father with what was now unrequited love. I was not unhappy, for little passed through the keyholes of my privacy from any other person in a form recognizable as influence.

The uninfluenced life was the germ of the adventuress, the place where high spirits sprang up like a propitious wind, the beginning of leaving. The uninfluenced life was in power as often as I was alone—though because I had already been in love, I had some sense that to be alone was a diminished province, life on an island without a harbor, an island from which great ships had been spotted. Still I was not afraid to be alone, and this way I could always be rid of both parents, practicing for the entire loss of them that in time makes an adventurer out of the most timid.

There was nothing dreamy about my private life. It did not compete with society. I abandoned it in favor of my father and even of lesser persons the moment they appeared. True, except for Hermine, there was no child whose company I sought. And once when the others were gone and I was performing some rite I had concocted between the two swings of the jungle gym—a dead mole was involved, and a brick on which he lay in state—my mother came rushing out of the house and took away the mole in a rag, then turned to me and said with a strangely twisted smile: "What a lucky child you are, Jane. You can play with others or by yourself." And though I believe her admiration for this trait was sincere, I saw to my surprise that she thought I had been abandoned—and perhaps I was—and she was consoling me.

As often as I was alone, my private life was there, in the dark, hushed stall between my parents' beds, in all moments of wakefulness while others slept, and whenever I played by myself on the rusty green-and-yellow jungle gym, though this stood in plain view of the kitchen window and screened side door. It must have been the word *jungle* that awakened my privacy. I felt when I played there just as though a million leaves concealed me. In fact the jungle gym showed up starkly against the pale dirt yard where no grass, no trees, no bush grew. I would lie on my stomach over one of its low swings and study the packed earth, its thousands of distinct cracks going every which way, which meant, I believed, that a thousand small earthquakes shook the yard in the dead of night. I would try to drop pussy ants down the tiny ravines, but they struggled against fate like human beings, ran up my arm and would not disappear.

I could easily believe that earthquakes passed unnoticed in the middle of the night. I had often spent these hours awake, watching sparks of meaningless color skid over oily waves of darkness; hours when nothing woke the others up, nothing. In the dark I developed a queer fellow-feeling for machines, since they too at this hour are left to run themselves, with nothing to entertain them but their odd, introverted, infantile ditties,

ssssssssssssssssssssssssss
zum, zum, zum, zum, zum
dottle dottle dottle dottle

—the halfhearted growl of the refrigerator, the faint hiss of the wall clock, the asthmatic dither of the electric fan blindly shaking its head over and over behind its wire mask. These things, like me, all had the air of coming to life without having had any choice in the matter. There seemed something faithful and good-natured in their willingness to live, to repeat themselves, to go on at night when all the others had died in their beds.

I could easily believe I was the only one left; but as soon as I was, everything changed its meaning. There was one place, besides in the dark, that I was always alone: in the bathroom, sitting on the toilet, looking at my genitals, at that quite hairless, moist declivity that until I was nine I could not know shuttered so much as a hole. Here I often had the thought that I was the only real person in the world. The others were in on it, and met around corners suppressing laughter when I had just passed the other way. I never thought them baleful so much as mischievous. But when I sat on the toilet peering at my small cleft, I was so alone that even my father disappeared, and it was impossible for me to be bored or unhappy.

When I was ten, the law came down from Dr. Zwilling:

My father was not to fart in front of the girls.
My father was not to go naked in front of the girls or even inadvertently to let his organ dangle out of his shorts.
My father was not to encourage the girls to fight over prizes and especially not over paper matches.
My father was to try to be a more consistent disciplinarian with the girls and, for God's sake, not to strike Jane.

In the space between my mother's and father's beds stood the night table, upon which was a lamp with a fan-pleated shade, two green glass ashtrays and a pack of Philip Morrises (Sasha's) on the left, of Camels (Philip Turner's) on the right. And matches lay about, black ones, gold ones, ones with cocktail bubbles on the covers, ones splayed inside out like tepees. It was a great thing to the three girls to light the match of our father's first Camel in the morning: every morning there would be a shrill fight over this, pushing, a gruff order of surcease, instructions, the slow scrape of the match.

In her bed my mother rose on one elbow, looked at my father propped orientally in a nest of pillows, at the small daughters crowding around, at the cigarette waving like a tiny wand, the flame approaching unsteadily over the bedclothes, the penis rolling out of the fly of his shorts. At last one morning my father snatched back the matchbook and yelled at us: "Why are you girls always doing this? Get out and leave me alone. Fire isn't a toy." And we stared at him, since we had all four stood in the street, my father, Carla, Hermine and I, gazing into a great fire in a curb sewer, all of us feeling its frantic breath through the grating, all of us sensing its hoarse dry vibration along the blacktop under the bottoms of our feet. This was Hell, we explained to our father, as it had been explained to us by Tommy, the Catholic boy who lived across the street and peed into Coke bottles with Carla in the bushes, which was a sin. "A sin is if you do something bad," Carla told Philip Turner, leaving out about peeing into the Coke bottle, "and after you do enough sins, this devil guy punches through the sidewalk and grabs you down to Hell."

My father stared down the sewer, clearly as thrilled as we were.

"We saw Hell," we told Sasha later.

"Jews don't believe in hell." She looked at Philip Turner without smiling.

"Are we Jews, Mom?" Carla said.

My father snatched his keys up from the table. "You're going to make these children fearful," Sasha told him, but he had already left.

We were always in the street when my father was around, never when he was not. By ourselves we were not allowed to stray from the small parched yard with its swing set and meager fringe of sticker bushes, especially not into the street. The question is why my father always walked in the street instead of on the sidewalk the moment he went outdoors, as though even to him it were still no mean privilege. Perhaps it was because we were sure to follow him into this forbidden and dangerous zone, like a trio of little wazirs following its reckless king. We sat on the curb with our feet in the gutter, occasionally looking over at our house, at its tiny grassless yard, sometimes spotting Sasha standing for a moment in the screen door, drying her hands on a towel, gazing away as though she didn't recognize us, like somebody else's mother. Along the curb we made a row of ragged striped T-shirts, then came my father's white undershirt, full of holes; our faded red hand-me-down camp shorts with waistbands from which all the elastic had vanished; and in the gutter our long line of gray sneakers with toes peeking through the holes, kicking fitfully at bottle caps. It must have been our motherless air that my father prized. As for us, we were proud that we were allowed to be the dirtiest kids in the block—but it was really Sasha (with Dr. Zwilling) who had ruled on that. She had spent her childhood in smocked velvet and silk tulle, never allowed to touch anything dirty.

"Close your eyes and put out your hand," Philip Turner would say suddenly.

"No," we said, knowing perfectly well what he had.

"It's something you're going to love."

"What is it?"

"Something to eat."

"No!"

"No? You girls are going to pass up something terrific. *Would I give you a bum steer?*"

I felt stricken for my father when he had no takers. It seemed wrong to see through even his silliest jokes. At last I would close my eyes and slowly stretch out my hand.

"Now don't say I never gave you anything!" my father would shout. An earthworm, flecked with brown sugary soil, was curled on my palm.

"I knew it was a worm," Carla screamed.

"Say, there ain't no flies on you, sporting life," Philip Turner said admiringly, giving her a slap on the back.

"So did I know," I said.

"Then why did you put out your hand?" said Carla.

"You said it was something to eat."

"Would I give you a bum steer?" my father said. "It *is* something to eat. A lot of people eat worms."

"Yeah, sure," I said.

"The Woruk eat worms," said my father, "*with relish.*"

"What's relish, Dad?" Hermine asked.

"Something you put on hot dogs," Carla shrieked.

"Well, every Woruk would rather eat a big fat worm than a hot dog. A Woruk would rather die than eat a teaspoon of peanut butter." My father had once had a botanical holiday in the Alfred Archipelago, field-collecting among these peculiar people.

"The Woruk didn't wear any clothes, did they, Dad!" Carla said excitedly.

"They didn't wear any clothes, except"—Philip Turner stirred up leaves with a stick—"a little *tutu* made of a shredded pandanus leaf for the girls, and a strip of bark like this"—he drew a small rectangle in air with the twig—"for the boys." I imagined a penis like my father's trying in vain to conceal itself behind such a strip of bark. It was a large penis, even accounting for the toy telescope effect in every child's view of the world. I am in a position to know, for it is not as though my father practiced great modesty, either now or in later years, no matter what rulings Dr. Zwilling sent down on the question.

The earthworm moved in my palm.

"Hey Dad," I said. "Close your eyes and put out your hand."

"Not on your life," Philip Turner said. "You've got to get up pretty early in the morning to put one over on your old man."

Dr. Zwilling wrote a book. My mother was proud of her signed copy. I took *Game with Invisible Men* off the coffee table and lay down on the rug behind the sofa with it, expecting to find her in its pages. She was not there. For Sasha, psychiatry was true romance, but it seemed Dr. Zwilling did not reciprocate. It was, instead, a murderer of women who interested Zwilling. Eddie Q. was of few words until Dr. Zwilling hypnotized him. Then they talked.

Eddie Q.: It said Kill! Kill!

Zwilling: And?

Eddie Q.: I stabbed her with . . . the . . . in . . . her . . .

Zwilling: Her vagina?

Eddie Q.: Yes, there.

I was shocked and relieved; the word *vagina* was not in our dictionary, which had raised the question whether it belonged to the world at all, or was only another euphemism like *tussy*, unintelligible outside of the family. I carried Dr. Zwilling's book up to my room and hid it in the bottom of the closet. I did not like Dr. Zwilling. Doctors, I found, were never far from such things, pain, spying, fingering, the *privates*—they always pretended that their scrutiny was calm and disinterested, that they were, all except their eyes, looking the other way. They were a suspect lot. I knew that my mother found Dr. Zwilling handsome. I did not agree with her. Not that we spoke of such things, but I knew. Dr. Zwilling's upper lip seemed to me to be sewn up tight against his nose by two thick dark stitches of mustache. He had a flirtatious, rubbing voice I found disgusting, and wore a blue striped suit far more shiny and insinuating than anything Philip Turner would be seen in. As Sasha and I would approach Dr. Zwilling's office, she would begin to talk nervously. I could feel her breathless desire to please, to work hard for his sake. I had heard stories from my aunts of the frothy, eager schoolgirl Sasha once had been, but now I could see it for myself. Suddenly she was so excited I feared she too needed parents. And since my mother had every other day the gray stability of pavement, I decided Zwilling was a charlatan, or he would not allow himself to be mistaken for a father.

"Dr. Zwilling says Jane has a powerful sense of the difference between male and female—a little too powerful."

"My God! Any fool could see that," my father exclaimed, pushing his plate away.

"She's aware of men—a little too aware. She's very attached to you."

My father said nothing.

"She is attracted to you," my mother repeated.

"So what! What do you want me to do about it? I'm certainly not going to take her up on it." He banged through the screen door in his torn T-shirt, the football under his arm.

"Do you know what you don't like about Jane?" Sasha, standing in the doorway, yelled after him. "She acts like a girl. She's a girl! She won't hide the fact that she's got a vagina. That's why you can't stand her!"

I was hanging upside down on the jungle gym when my father stopped in front of me. My head was lost in the jungle of my overturned skirt when his big sneakers, each on a pillow of reddish dust, appeared under my nose. "Hi, Dad," I said, pulling myself up, but by the time I was on the ground I had heard the sticker bushes part, and there he was loping down the far side of the street with the football in one hand. "Dad, wait!"

He stopped and waited until I was in front of him. "I'm going to Woody's," he announced. "You can't come."

"I don't want to come."

"What do you want?"

"I wanted to kiss you good-bye." Feeling that I was losing my father completely, I threw myself at his neck and pressed my mouth hard against his. And he gave me a tremendous push, so that I was suddenly six feet away, blinking up at him, holding scraped elbows and feeling the warm asphalt against the backs of my legs.

"Don't kiss me on the mouth! Not on the mouth!" he shouted at me. Then he looked at me very bitterly, and turned and walked away, leaving me sitting there alone in the middle of the street.

○
○
● **The**

adventuress

And so for the first time the adventuress landed in the street on her butt, having been put there by a man, and that man her father, Philip Turner.

Already the street was the forbidden street, the hardened river of popular time, black as the Styx, current as the gasoline engine, warm with the signature of the sun but also with death, with decomposed generations of carboniferous life imprisoned in the asphalt, at this moment heating the undersides of her thighs and making a damp cave of her underpants. Jane stared after her father with half-lowered eyelids and resolved, secretly, to love him less. Contrary to the vulgar notion, this is easily done; though in so doing one learns something about love it is better, perhaps, not to know.

That summer afternoon in the middle of the street did not end their intimate relations. For a short while yet her father, possibly forgetting which daughter he was with, sometimes gave her a squeeze on the buttocks under her skirt as if nothing had happened between them. And indeed, Philip Turner did not seem to notice that anything had happened. Jane knew that something had happened, but the habit of delicacy towards her father died hard.

Die, however, it did, for Jane saw that the more she was Jane, whatever that meant, and she was more Jane every day, the more she got on his nerves. And she had something else to figure out about him, lest she be in danger of supposing that he had a particular taste for her company. Her father hated to be alone. He was not like the fathers of some of her schoolmates, who trooped into bowling alleys in gangs of ten, belching out threats to kill and other cryptolocutions of the sporting life. Philip Turner was never a lout. But when he drove to Pimlico to Read's Drugstore or the newsstand, or stopped by Hopkins to spray a flat of fly-traps at the Galapagos Club, he looked around for somebody to go with him. And that would be a daughter. And the daughter was almost always Jane, owing to peculiarities of her character that were the opposite of his own.

What would happen was that Carla and Hermine were nowhere to be found. But Jane did not like to go to other people's houses. She did not like the sweet, stale nutrimental smell of them, the strange foods that were pushed at her, the foreign manners that prevailed, and above all she did not like the grownups who were always in charge. She played alone. She spent hours in the hammock, frequently leaving her book, even if it was a library book, out in the rain. She had a hideout in some spiraea bushes above the trolley tracks. From here she would spy on the people, mostly black domestics, waiting for streetcars in the little kiosk across the tracks, at a place where a ballast of sky-blue concrete rose almost to the tops of the rails in a rough plate. Inside the bushes she had a missile manufactory underway, slow and painstaking, which required sneaking down to the tracks and balancing limestone splinters from the track bed on the rails, which the next trolley would crush to a pale blue flour. This Jane would collect: at last she rolled the shapely pellets. She never managed to make enough to feel she could spare them to throw at people. In truth, Jane was not hostile until provoked, unlike Hermine who in certain moods would stand on street corners all by herself and heave rocks at cars.

Sometimes Jane ventured down to ask questions of people getting off trolleys, for though inclined to be antisocial, she was not shy. An elderly black gardener in the neighborhood whose hands were enlarged and powdery white explained to her that he'd burned them rescuing two children from a fire, a boy and a girl who lived at the top of a hill, and whose names were Guy and Dolly. These lucky children appeared often in Jane's thoughts. They were Guy and Dolly Madison, but because they lived on a hill they were also Jack and Jill. Together they wandered forth, were delivered from death, and struggled back up the hill, their sloshing heavy bucket between them. Their two heads were not brown and wildly tangled like Jane's, but identically pale, almost white, like the hands of the gardener.

At night Jane often dreamed of the trolley tracks, dreamed she was trapped in the gully where the tracks lay, which was deep, almost a chasm, in the dream. There was a dull mechanical, yet animal, tattoo of something coming down the tracks behind her and she would run along between the rails in panic. Then the tracks lost all their practical familiarity and became something elemental and huge that threatened to sweep Jane away, like a great river in flood. This was a nightmare, and yet because of that deep thrill of geography, invisible during the day, that made them like the Mississippi, she liked the trolley tracks best.

The trolley stop, unlike the backyards and TV dens of friends where Carla and Hermine were hiding, was not out of earshot of the Turner place. Not that Jane was required to stay nearby. Sasha and Philip Turner even bought Jane a small round overnight case. It had a shirred pocket of glimmering blue nylon inside, all the way around its rim, and a mirror in the lid that soon fell off, leaving a cracked island of blackish glue in its place. Jane put pajamas and a toothbrush in it and went to sleep over at her nearest classmate Doreen's.

Doreen was allergic to chocolate, tuna fish, and oranges, three of the few foods Jane would eat. Her father was a doctor, and so she had asthma, as (Jane thought) children of doctors always do. But this afternoon Doreen was also having menstrual cramps (Jane was shocked: they were only ten) and a headache (Jane could not have headaches, because Sasha disbelieved in them: "Children don't get headaches," she said flatly). At supper Doreen's mother suddenly barked at Jane to put her napkin in her lap; this was not a rule at the Turners' ten-minute meals. Afterwards Doreen whispered that her mother had woman troubles that made her mean; when Jane looked blank Doreen added, "Down *there*. In her womb."

Jane slept in an older sister's bed, and the next morning woke before anyone else. All the drapes were drawn, and the walls and furniture, even the toys, had a grainy, dead appearance, as if color had drained out of the world. Doreen slept with her mouth open, making a faint dry noise like paper tearing. The others seemed to breath torpidly through the walls. With nothing else to do Jane slid her feet across the colorless carpet to the sister's vanity table and opened the pots of cold cream, crème sachet, and deodorant one by one, touching each with a finger.

The older sister rushed up to the breakfast table in shorty pajamas and shrieked at Jane. Jane stared at her pajama top, which stuck out like a maternity blouse. The sister had breasts; she was already a grownup, or how would she know that Jane had opened her jars? Doreen's mother asked Jane what sort of rules of personal property were observed in the Turner household. Suddenly Jane felt sick to her stomach, as if all the unseen fluxes of this household were contagious.

As she rode her bike home, she thought gravely that, of all the terrible things that had happened, the worst was opening her eyes to feel the whole house wrapped in a thick gauze of other people's sleep, like waking up in a funeral home. She took the overnight case from her bicycle basket, removed her pajamas and toothbrush and pushed the round case deep into her closet. Then she returned to the bushes over the trolley tracks.

But when she played here her father might summon her anytime, for it never occurred to her to pretend she did not hear him call. She would appear. He would be standing in the driveway in sockless sneakers and khaki shorts, jingling his car keys.

"Come on, Bones, take a ride with me to the store."

She never said no. As they ground out to the street her father would begin: "Hey, why aren't you over at Gutmans' with the other kids?" And then, interrupting himself, not Jane: "Don't say there's nobody your age in the neighborhood. Carla and Hermine find plenty of friends and so could you."

Then he would take his first real look at her, at the T-shirt stiff with lime dust. "What have you been doing? Rolling around in the mud?" He reached over to pluck a leaf out of her hair. "And your posture is terrible. Sit up."

He glanced at her to see if she had complied. Then: "Why are you sitting pushed way up against the door? Are you afraid I'm going to hit you? Why are you sticking your head out the window when I'm trying to talk to you? Why is your mouth hanging open? You're not a dog."

Jane would move her rear end an inch closer to him, still trying, however, to keep most of her head outside in the airstream. She did this summer and winter until yelled at. She rather enjoyed the boiled-milk taste in her mouth after the wind had dried it, and she liked to read the familiar street signs backwards. TIMIL DEEPS. NOITCURTSNOC REGNAD. YAW ENO. POTS.

At last Philip Turner would grasp her by the upper arm and jerk her over sharply, so that she sat, now, a foot away from him.

"I'm talking to you!"

Jane looked at him solemnly, inching unconsciously back towards the window as she did so.

"You know why I get so annoyed at you, don't you, Jane? You remind me of myself when I was your age. I was a bookworm too. I was always walking into things myself. I was left alone a lot. I was the first one to wear glasses and I was absentminded just like you. I shouldn't get angry with you for that, for God's sake! But for some reason you drive me crazy."

Jane had heard this so many times she no longer exactly heard it, not as words. If she listened to the words, they filled her with an uneasiness she did not understand. That Philip Turner had been a queer child himself did not console her. Nothing consoled her, for she really did not know how much she was not enjoying this ride. She pretended to stare at her father's face, as he talked and gesticulated over the steering wheel, and meanwhile she looked beyond him for signs to read backwards through his window. TEKRAM REPUS. YRDNUAL. DAEHA LANGIS. POTS.

When Jane was eleven, she finally said a no of sorts. The Turner family was spending two weeks in July on a lake in Nova Scotia. Their cabin clung to the top of a steep cliff, perhaps fifty rough-hewn log steps up from the lake shore. Behind the cliff was a wide lawn, unnaturally green like florist's tissue paper, and at the top of its long slope, a white Georgian lodge where kippers were served in the morning. Carla and Hermine soon found playmates, and were not seen from one end of the day to the other. Jane, who was a good swimmer, got the solo use of a very small dinghy, as long as she promised not to row too far out of sight.

This was Jane's idea of a good time. She investigated secret coves, she transported cargoes of red salamanders and small mottled frogs in a cigar box from one spit of sand to another, and once when she got out of the rowboat to put it ashore, a water snake slipped in a figure-eight between her legs, causing a thrill of fear that made the trees flash a truer green and the water a truer blue.

Then one afternoon, Philip Turner hired a canoe and looked around for someone to go paddling with him. No daughter could be found except Jane.

"You sit in the back," he said, "the *stern*," correcting himself. "Now that's the really important job because you have to steer while I paddle. Your paddle is like a rudder. Get it? I'm going to do most of the work but you have to *watch and listen carefully.* Ready?"

Jane said she was ready.

"Oh God! Not like that! WATCH!" he shouted at her before they were three yards from shore, as they crashed into a boulder. "Like this! like this!" He wiggled his paddle in the air, looking excitedly over his shoulder at Jane, and they scraped sickeningly over another rock. Soon they were well out on the lake but unable to fix a straight course. "Christ!" he exploded, and duck-walked unsteadily backwards along the ribbed floor of the canoe in her direction. "Why can't you listen? Loosen up! Can't you see what I'm doing?" His large hands swallowed both of hers on the paddle and he dug ferociously at the water. The canoe skidded sideways, threatening to tip, and as he threw himself the other way to right it, letting go of Jane, she dropped her paddle overboard.

"For chrissakes, Jane!"

Grabbing for the thing in a panic, she fell in after it.

In the course of the long afternoon, she actually thought to herself that she might be happier elsewhere, and perhaps she would have tried to sneak off, but there was water around them in every direction. At last they found their rhythm, or at least her father grew tired of yelling at her. The sun was dropping behind tall pines on the shore. And a flamboyant sunset spread over the lower sky and oiled with its colors the small and sedate gray waves of the lake. The canoe, heading slowly landwards, seemed to be always on the point of spearing these colors on its bow and breaking them in pieces, but at the last moment they would clamber backwards over the ripples to safety. It was very quiet. Philip Turner had not addressed a word of any kind to Jane for a quarter of an hour, when she asked him a question.

"Dad, when are we going to sail into them?"

"What? Sail into what?"

"Into the colors."

He twisted his head around and looked at her in disbelief. "You mean it, don't you?" he said, shaking his head. "Can't you see we're never going to sail into them, Jane?" Then he laughed at her. This time he was merely amused, but it cut her to the quick.

They pulled the canoe ashore and turned it over on stanchions at the foot of their cliff. Then they were mounting the steep log steps towards the cabin, Jane in front, her father behind, when he stopped her by the hand and turned her to look at the sky. His feet were one tall stair below hers, so that his face was very close, only a little higher than her own. His arm curled around her waist and in a moment his hand was dipping inside the elastic of her shorts.

"What a sunset!" he said. "Isn't it a beauty, Bones?"

Jane had a fleeting, nauseous sense of the parody they were performing of two lovers against a gaudy twilight, like some picture she had seen on a calendar, not like a father and daughter at all.

She stepped away and said stiffly, "I don't like sunsets."

"You what?" Philip Turner said, baffled.

"I don't like sunsets. They're—" (she sought for a word her parents used) "they're schmaltzy. They're sickening. I hate them."

It was the first time she had contradicted her father, and, significantly, it was on a point of aesthetics with sex lurking unarticulated in the background. She backed up two more steps, looking belligerently into his face, then turned and ran the rest of the way to the cabin. She was afraid, foolishly no doubt, that he would hit her.

Jane was extemporizing, but she was not lying. The adventuress never did like sunsets. She liked the living, tidal dark of the middle of the night, because there she had learned to be alone. And she liked the very early morning, which was the night opening a crack the fist it has closed around her, allowing her to see her way—the funnel of sky between the trees where the track parted them, the white stitches up the center of the road.

Sunsets are for nincompoops to crow over, an austere wit once said, while the wise woman says Tomorrow is another day to die in. Jane now began to understand that was true.

○
○
● **Attack**

of the

fifty-foot

woman

On the back of the Temple, three alleys away from the new house on Pinkney Road, was a school that looked like the blank side of a dime store. Here Jane, Hermine, and Carla sat once a week ignoring attempts to teach them a little Hebrew. The girls did not really care what Jews had believed while they still lived in Russia. Since Sasha and Philip Turner did not believe in God, they were not going to believe in Him either.

Still, Jane puzzled over some of the stories she heard at Baltimore Hebrew, like the one about Jacob wrestling all night with an invisible man. Afterwards he claimed to have seen God face to face and lived, but in the dark he hadn't been so sure. Jane thought his bragging queer; she sensed she wouldn't come off so well in a match with the top dog. *Go fight God about it*, her Aunt Yetta would say. But that meant it was useless to fight.

All the same, at age twelve Jane answered the call. From now on she argued with her father on every excuse. It was no longer easy in that household to locate the rules, but there was one: Jane was to go to bed, at some hour or other she was to go to bed like a normal person. Her father would find Jane reading a novel at two in the morning, when he came upstairs plucking loose the crumpled necktie he had fallen asleep in (and hours ago Jane would have seen him there in the peony-print chair in the living room, his long legs knitted together at the knee, the toes in his polished wing tips seeming to point as if in a dance, one finger touching his temple, the manila pad slid to an odd angle in his lap; and she would hurry by, feeling an irrelevant impulse to pity). Now he would see her. Probably he would not even know it was a novel Jane read—that Jane had not done any schoolwork at all.

He stands in her doorway, blinking to make clear he is having a hard time recognizing her in that gloom. "Why the hell do you insist—?"—*on reading in the dark*, is the rest of the sentence, but it's hopeless; he won't go on. He passes off to the parents' bedroom, his daughter's eyes already as good as ruined.

Why did Jane read in the dark? Though she would begin in a chair like anyone else, it bothered her, as a goldfish in a bowl bothered her, to be stuck in the small yellow pond of her reading lamp. Little by little she would slide out of it onto the ink-stained carpet. By now she was leaning on her elbow (this posture too was going to ruin some part of Jane forever, even her mother said so—one day her shoulder would go) and her book would be crossed by only a fine dusting of light, if that. She *liked* to read in the dark, that was it. Sometimes she pushed her chair close to the windowsill and read by the light of the moon—in which case she would imagine she could feel her eyesight draining away like a fluid, *Yes, she went blind from reading in her youth by the light of the moon*; but on those nights she had the sense to hide her book if she heard anyone coming.

Tonight her father stays. "Why the hell do you insist—" he says, and loses heart, but strength suddenly returns to him. "You never sleep," he points out. "And you look it. What's that on your face?" Perhaps a square of tissue hangs from Jane's chin, attached to some blemish she has molested. Now she hurriedly pulls it away.

Not too long ago her father discovered her sitting at five a.m. in the bottom of the shower stall, memorizing names and dates of battles of the Civil War.

"I have a test," she explained.

"When do you sleep?" he had asked her.

"In French," she said, "ten to eleven," which was true, but this reply exercised her father, as quite possibly she knew it would.

He said, "You look like a runaway. A runaway with venereal disease. Your skin would clear if you got some sleep."

Jane believed him, and though she was not yet at the age when any display of anguish in the body would seem poetic, she knew the grandeur of her sacrifice. She would have done almost anything to repair her skin.

Tonight she glances up at him, suddenly aware that lately, when he stands there grilling her—"And what's that yellow gunk smeared all over your face?"—she is forming the habit of looking at anything but him, so that if he should happen to be balancing a lacrosse stick on his chin as he used to do when she was six, she would never know it.

But he is not balancing a lacrosse stick on his chin. There's a kind of dew shining under his eyes; it collected behind his eyeglasses while he slept, and now spangles the most elegant planes of his face. His hair is no longer the color of clear, strong tea. Its waves that once stood quizzically erect are more evenly mowed now and mulched between them with gray. He does not look so odd as once; he looks like a well-paid attorney, which he is; and Jane, having just snatched the bloody toilet paper from her chin, has the feeling that, as he grows less odd looking, she grows more so, as though his passing out of a certain astronomical phase necessarily pulls her into it. For whether she looks at him or not, he is the weightier heavenly body.

At twelve Jane got the call. She saw she could make him drop a fork with an offhand remark like "Thank God I can have syphilis and live." Once she knew it could be done with her opinions alone, she teemed with opinions, and overnight became as noisy (so her father pointed out) as the old-time socialists and other *luftmenschen* who used to harangue each other day and night at the Workmen's Circle—of whom her mother's father, Jake Rostovsky, had been one.

"It's genetic," Philip Turner would then say. "She's got Jake's hot air in her blood." Jane worried this might be true.

Jake was still alive, a tiny, stringy old man who bickered incessantly with his second wife in a cramped ninth-floor apartment on Ocean Drive in Miami Beach. It would be terrible to end like Jake, who seemed to have been shrunken and hardened in some kind of pickle bath. The girls did not like him because he embraced them ferociously, clapping their faces up tight against his long forelip, which twitched when he kissed them; or they would be transfixed for minutes against the cactus of his cheek while they passed doomed stares at each other over his shoulder. His position in the family was ambiguous. He was the real grandfather, but they sensed that they were not required to love him with full-blown politeness as they must the other grandparents. Yes, it would be a curse to find oneself turning into Jake, who had no idea, none now and none in a long, misadventurous life, how to make anyone love him. He despised his fellow tenants in the Atlantic Arms and spoke to them only with his hearing aid disconnected, and then only to broadcast atheism and other shocking ideas. Long ago he had been a labor organizer; he had gone broke in Palestine in 1926, having failed to organize the tour-taxi drivers between Haifa and Jerusalem, because, he said, the Arab drivers were excitable and fatalistic, the Christian tourists stupid as cows, and the Jewish drivers anarchic on a principle of *sauve qui peut*. Jane understood: even then he couldn't get along with anyone. Nor had he known peace with his first wife, Rosie, back in Baltimore, which is why he had sailed to Palestine to begin with. He had abandoned not only Rosie, who was twenty, but also baby Sasha, after a long night of pushing, shoving, screaming, and willful destruction of household property. The police had been involved. Jane knew it had taken her mother a decade of "work" with Dr. Zwilling to recover her memory of this catastrophic departure. Thus Sasha had better excuses than Jane for her deep reproachfulness towards men.

Jane only knew her father did not like her. She only meant by her belligerence to match, no, outmatch, his dislike, but perhaps, as with Jake—whom even the girls called Jake, since he did not have to be loved as a grandparent—perhaps once she got going there would be no stopping her.

At twelve, Jane was worried about disappearing. She had had a ruptured appendix a few summers before. Suddenly she realized that in any century before this one, she would already have disappeared. Except for the date when she happened to be born, she would have been gone before she had done anything with her life at all, and knowing this gave her a queer feeling of semi-visibility.

Rather than accidentally agree with him on anything, she would distract her father at the dinner table with her taste for vampire movies—that always worked—and for the kind of horror film where a bunch of glassy-eyed undead, advancing with arms in first position *en avant*, always reminded her of her ballet class. By now she had stopped going to ballet class. She did not know how to argue for these lurid tastes with any sort of style, but she sensed that whatever caused Philip Turner's fingers to whiten around his forkful of chicken pie must have a glamorous defense somewhere, if only she could find it. She also felt a need to take positions her father would find ludicrous, and when he waved her away in disgust, to keep at it until at last he turned around and hollered: "Who the hell are you to say that colored people are more generous than white people? You don't even know any colored people but maids."

There was some truth in this. "Well," Jane said weakly, "if I know all the maids in this neighborhood, I know a lot of Negroes."

"Pass the broccoli," her father said, turning, pointedly, to Carla.

"There are two colored girls in my homeroom," Jane said. That was because of Brown vs. Board of Education; their presence was one of the chief differences between sixth and seventh grade.

He ignored this.

"When I get stuck outside Lexington Market without any carfare, who do you think gives me a dime? A maid. Always a maid."

"What are you doing on Saratoga Street without a dime?" Philip Turner inquired sharply.

"At least I know the maids," Jane said. "To you they're just a bunch of humanoids."

"Don't start with the humanoids," her father warned. But then he plunged down that trashy side street himself. "What in hell was the name of that schlock movie you had to watch last night?"

"*Attack of the Fifty-Foot Woman*," Jane said.

Her father snorted his scorn.

"It stunk," Jane said.

"What a surprise!" Philip Turner exclaimed. "It stunk. I like your vocabulary. Did you pick that up in school? *It stunk*," he mimicked her in falsetto.

For some reason it enraged Jane to be mimicked, especially to hear a male baritone stuffed through a pinhole so that it came out this strangled nasal, supposedly female, supposedly Jane's.

She said through her teeth: "You're just like Mr. Manucci!"

Mr. Manucci was their neighbor Gutman's gardener. He was unique in their well-structured neighborhood of Jewish households and black menials: a white man whose clothes were stiff with dirt, missing half his teeth, whose left eye gazed off at a different angle from his right one, who said, "I don't know nutting," and "I seen er half a hour ago." And somehow the kids had discovered he couldn't read very well.

Philip Turner said in a steely voice: "Oh? What do I and Mr. Manucci have in common?"

"Mr. Manucci says, *Aaay, these kids today, buy em books, send em to school, they tear out the pages and eat the covers.*"

Carla and Hermine giggled and at another time Philip Turner himself would have laughed, but now he said, "Mr. Manucci has two boys in the Maryland Penitentiary, so I guess he ought to know."

Silence descended for a moment.

"I know how much Mr. Manucci gets paid," Jane began again.

"I'm not interested!" her father said.

"Thirty-four—"

"Look, how much do I have to know about other people's servants?" Philip Turner said. "You think I should hang around the bus stop with you?"

Jane said: "We pay the lowest in the neighborhood." She had snooped around. Thirty-one dollars a week was rock bottom. "If I were Essie I'd bash in our heads and rob us. In revenge!"

"All right, Jane," Sasha interjected. "Don't be a smart aleck on subjects you don't understand." For Sasha was the one who negotiated these wages.

"Walk down Orleans Street making remarks like that and see how long it takes some kindhearted Negro to bash in your head," Philip Turner said.

"You're such a snob!" Jane said. "Such a small-minded snob!"

"I don't want to hear one more naive, coarse, insulting and stupid word out of you," her father shouted.

And that was quite enough for Jane, for the present. Not once did she feel she had won an argument with her father, and yet she couldn't stop. After their quarrels, Jane felt revolted and unreal in her whole body, a hot pink humanoid manufactured by a B-movie scientist out of radio parts and bubble gum; but at the same time she felt indigestible, hard to get rid of—saved.

One night Jane said at dinner that she liked bad dreams better than good ones.

"Of all the baloney!" her father replied. Then he turned to Hermine: "So how do you like those Colts, sporting life?"

"Good dreams are boring," insisted Jane loudly. She actually did not have any good dreams to judge by, or at least she could not remember any, but woke up with the colors flying away from dreadful nightmares often enough so that she had got somewhat inured to it. She had dreamt she was gazing out her bedroom window into a gaudy sunset, against which she saw the roof of Baltimore Hebrew Congregation like an elevated parking lot, and walking along it a large man, in fact a giant, wooly against the mercurochrome-stained sky. But suddenly he fell through the roof, which caved in tremendously and sent up a rumbling, billowing black cauliflower of smoke. In the dream Jane laughed mechanically at this sight—cackled as though someone had tripped a switch inside her chest, like the one inside the dummy fortune teller in a glass case at Gwynn Oak Park.

"It's not really funny," she thought, but it was too late. The giant rose up again through the collapsed roof even larger than before, and, pointing at Jane, whom earlier he had not seemed to notice—pointing over the roofs of houses straight at Jane he said in a godlike basso: *I'll get you yet.*

It happened to be Philip Turner, working late in his den, who had spotted her wandering about the house after this dream. Actually she was headed straight for the kitchen, however blank the expression on her face, "to dose herself" (as Sasha would have pointed out) "with pure carbohydrates." Already she was deep in a trance at the breakfast table, eating saltines from a tall stack one by one, when two unusual events occurred. Her father entered and inquired what was troubling her. And Jane told him.

Philip Turner listened, and even reflected for a short time before he replied: "Well, Bones, probably you feel guilty about some little thing you did," and then he tried to toss her hair lightly with his fingers, a gesture they had both seen fathers make in the movies, doomed to failure with Jane's coarse brown knots on top of knots. She braced herself and a moment later her father withdrew his fingers with care. Then Jane raised her chin and smiled at him, grateful but troubled. For the "little thing" was not so little. And he would have been her chief scourge, if only he knew.

Some little thing. One day not long before, she and Hermine, who spent hours careening on their bicycles down the hill into the Temple parking lot, had leaned on an unlocked fire door in the school building. They had wandered through it and then, finding themselves in an empty classroom quite like the ones they attended every day, only this one drifting in space and at their mercy—a normal classroom with crayoned pictures of Moses tacked up on the walls, ranks of gray-blond desks in the half-light, a speckled linoleum floor like the eggshell of some giant bird—for some reason Jane and Hermine had, without a word, taken up the boxed games, craft kits, and puzzles piled neatly on the teacher's vacant desk and thrown their millions of pieces all over the floor, and marched about and kicked and stamped on them in a ritual manner. After a time, horror had crawled up their spines and again without a word they had run to their bikes and sped away. They did not even look at each other, embarrassed as though they had found themselves playing doctors, which they had given up some time ago.

This crime (and they had taken no pleasure in it when it was talked about in the neighborhood: talk of these kids today, of *drapes*, which meant teenage hoodlums, never Jewish boys, let alone Jewish girls; talk of anti-Semites, haters of Jews)—this crime went entirely unpunished. Then came that dream, which was one of her worst nightmares ever. It must have been, or she would never have babbled it to Philip Turner in her weakened condition. And now, when Jane said at dinner that good dreams were boring and bad dreams a thrill, Philip Turner said in front of everyone: "So what about that dream you had where a man fell through the roof of Baltimore Hebrew and you laughed? *I'll get you yet*," he mimicked. "Come on, you were scared out of your wits."

"I like to be scared," Jane replied gravely, dissecting the overcooked flounder on her plate.

"That's a delicacy you're tearing apart," her mother pointed out.

"It's fish."

"You don't know what's good."

"You didn't like bad dreams so much that night," Philip Turner said. "Your hair was sticking straight out. Your face was bunched up like an old dried fungus."

This cartooning of the terrified Jane was a sly bid for allies.

Carla laughed. Hermine, Jane could see, wanted to laugh too at the picture of Jane as an old dried fungus, but was too loyal; she stared hard at her crumbling fish and did not even allow her mouth corners to twitch, which gave her a stony, tragic expression.

"Your face was the color of a hunk of snotty Kleenex," Carla improvised.

"You weren't there," Jane said.

"True, but it was, my dear," Philip Turner said.

Jane realized she must have looked more than scared, must have looked beaten and pitiful for her father to ask her that night what the trouble was. Now she consciously composed her face.

"I'll bet if you live through the worst possible stuff in your dreams," she said, "you'll never go crazy no matter what happens."

"I don't see the connection," Philip Turner said. "Why are you so nervous?" he added, as if to dispute the point.

"I'm not nervous."

"Why are you tearing your napkin in little pieces?"

"I enjoy tearing my napkin in little pieces."

"Leave her alone," Sasha said. "You make her nervous, can't you see that?"

"She makes me nervous! She makes everyone nervous!"

That was enough for Jane. "I'm leaving," she said, and got up.

"I'm not nervous," Hermine called after her. Jane waved her thanks without turning around. Although she would never forgive her father for preferring Hermine, Jane in fact liked Hermine better than all the rest of those cornballs herself.

Jane knew that nothing she did would please her father, because even what he said would please him, did not, if Jane was the one who did it. He lamented, for example, that none of his daughters was aping his worshipful posture in the shrine of serious music. Actually, he had reason to celebrate this, since it kept them out of his record collection — except Jane, who stayed out of it only because his records seemed charged with his unseen presence like the walled forest of a sorcerer in certain old tales; that is, she was certain if she touched them, they would tell him about it, like talking trees. (Jane knew herself by now as the Jane who left library books out in the rain.) Jane was in a Schubert phase. She listened to the Great C Major over and over—she owned only five records at the time—and wept, abstractly, for music gave her gift of tears, though nothing else did anymore. She read a sentimental life of Schubert. These practices took place behind the closed door of her room. Still, how could her father know nothing of it?

One evening the Great C came on the radio in his den and Jane heard him humming along with the andante in his soulful but tuneless way. She stuck her head in the door and said: "Hey, Dad. You know Schubert hung around with the maids. I read it in a book."

Her father looked up at her with faint detestation. "He was dead at thirty-one," he said, after a time.

"I know," Jane said.

"Of syphilis." Jane blinked; she knew what syphilis meant. The sentimental biography had said typhus. Also, thirty-one was a significant number. Her father had been thirty-one when she was born. Schubert had had no wife and no children; therefore it was not necessary to imagine him mimicking his snotty daughter through his own nose in a pig squeal. It was as though Schubert had died at thirty-one expressly to avoid collision with this possibility. And all at once it seemed brilliant to have syphilis, to be an artist, and never to have children, especially if you could do all this and not die young.

"Thank God I can have syphilis and live," Jane said.

Philip Turner stared at Jane for a moment. Then involuntarily his eyeballs descended and his newspaper ascended and soon his whole self disappeared behind it, and Jane could hardly help noticing she was not there anymore at all.

About when Jane discovered the first stiff black hair growing in the hollow of her left armpit—only one, true, but looking already as old and queerly autonomous as hair on a corpse —she noticed a change in her father. Before, there had always been a softness for her alive on his face, warring with the itch to zero in, giving him a confused look that made her feel sorry for him, even though he always did zero in. Back when she was eight, nine, ten, if she was a freak, she was his freak, a freak he recognized from his own childhood and thought he might be able to fix. Now, however, that she was eleven, twelve, thirteen, more and more she was granted title to her own peculiar being without having asked for it; or Jake Rostovsky or even her father's own eccentric mother Frieda, empress of the hat shops, might be called in—but mostly he no longer bothered to correct her. Instead he stared at her with, no denying it, distaste, distaste unmollified by kinship, as though Jane had arrived in puberty not from childhood but from outer space.

"You go to extremes!" her father said to her. "What is it about you? Certainly I didn't teach you that." His fork, headed for his green beans, waved at her sententiously. "*Meden agan*, the Greeks said. Nothing too much!" Now that the sissifying exile from the playing fields of his youth was behind him, now that he made a fair showing on the tennis court, now that, without ever saying so out loud, he began to admit physical beauty as a trait a man might properly possess, now, at forty-four, he thought of himself as an Attic type. It was, of course, these pretensions that Jane should have made fun of if she wished to humiliate her father in return. But it never occurred to her to do so.

Funny how, as soon as she saw that black hair in her armpit, she thought of a corpse. She did not want to die, and now it was clear she had better live while she had the chance. People she knew had begun to die: her mother's stepfather Morris, the fathers of two girls at school, Dr. Kramer, the Turners' orthopedist, and then one day her father came home from work and said Old Johnson, the elevator boy from the Mathieson Building, had dropped dead in the lobby. Most died in the unseen interiors of hospitals, like Morris. Jane had never seen a dead person. Once she and Hermine had been striding along the beach at Far Rockaway, kicking through the trash of seaweed at the tide line, playing they were field-collecting in the South Seas, when some people running the other way down the beach shouted at them. Someone had drowned at the jetty! Jane and Hermine turned around and began walking faster; in a moment they were running. "I've never seen a dead person," Jane whispered. "Me neither," Hermine panted back. They forgot about the archipelago in Micronesia. But when they finally reached the jetty, there was no corpse, no crowd, just two old ladies in wedgies and slightly bloodied smocks, placidly fishing. Jane and Hermine flopped dejectedly in the sand—they had almost known it was too good to be true.

Between themselves they felt no need to greet the news that there was a corpse at the jetty with tears, or indeed with anything but violent excitement. But when a grownup delivered this gravest of messages, *So-and-so died*, though there had not been a case yet where Jane knew the dead person much better than she knew the corpse at the jetty, something more was clearly expected of you. And when Jane was twelve an odd thing happened: she got scared that when she heard someone had died, she might laugh. She would try to cry, but it would not work. Cry? She was not even sad. Not that she was without emotion; in fact she was entirely overwhelmed at that report, *Dr. Kramer died*, *Old Johnson dropped dead right in the lobby*, though not with sorrow for the dead or the survivors. However, she did not feel like weeping and was afraid a grownup might find out.

Maybe it started at the swimming pool, where she saw hundreds of her parents' friends in a state of undress. If grownups were the proprietors of sex (and Jane did look on her masturbation as a kind of hasty poaching to be kept secret from those proprietors forever, at any cost) they paid a great price for it, for it showed on them as it never had on Jane. Nothing that differentiated grown women from men stopped at a reasonable size, or if it did it withered on the spot. In the locker room Jane spied on bosoms (she knew this word only in its dubious plural, a woman had bosoms) and concluded it was best to have the kind that never grew at all, but of course you were given no choice in this matter. She was spared seeing the fathers stark naked, but they passed her in their too big or too small bathing trunks, looking even more disgusting than the women (only her father was exempt from this). And all of them walked about with breasts or stomachs hanging down, grizzled, flabby, and talking about politics, money, food, and diseases.

Jane understood what it meant, the first hopeless sight of that black hair in her armpit: she was deteriorating into a grownup. The parentless life was greatly to be desired, so getting older was necessary, but now her sex life was beginning to show on her as theirs did on them.

As it happened, Jane spotted that single but already rank and thriving black hair under her left arm one afternoon as she raised her hand in Mrs. Haskowitz's sixth grade class in "the portables" at Falstaff Road Elementary School. It must have been late in the school year, towards May or June, since she was sleeveless. Perhaps her arm had been up for some time and she was growing bored—in any event, for some reason she examined her armpit. Sick at heart, she lowered her hand immediately. Not that Jane, in that moment, above voices (they had been discussing the burial practices of the pharaohs) that had suddenly become as remote and flylike as the travels of zippers on tracks, had grasped the meaning of death. On the contrary, its abstraction—death as the common lot of humankind—missed her completely. Rather, Jane, age eleven and eleven months, read that black hair as if it were the first unmistakable symptom of a terminal disease. Never mind the others, she was going to die, after a long, visible process of deterioration that had just begun.

It was a hot Baltimore spring. Jane's schoolwork entered upon a steep decline. Not that Jane had a notion what Mrs. Haskowitz meant when she pointed out that Jane's schoolwork was suffering, for Jane had never understood why she should be considered good in school either—these were the fables of grown-ups, developed from abstruse meteorological observations that had nothing to do with anything Jane could recognize as her own effort. However, the case was serious enough so that Sasha was called in. Jane listened uncomfortably to the two women discussing the falling off of her performance. She heard Sasha tell Mrs. Haskowitz, "Her father has rejected her," and was disgusted to see Mrs. Haskowitz's face transfigured with some sort of creamy, mysterious understanding. They looked to Jane at that moment like two crones who had eaten together a satisfying dinner of frogs.

○
○
● **Science**

In the fifties, child psychology became popular science, and parents like Sasha and Philip Turner took pains not to be mad scientists, especially when they viewed their own childhoods as Islands of Dr. Moreau from which they were lucky to have escaped with fangs and tails that could still be hidden under their streetclothes. So Sasha and Philip were all too ready to blame themselves, or better yet, each other, if anything came out funny with the three daughters, and of course it did. Yet, God knows, the parents were working from the start in a dirty laboratory, by open windows, big-city traffic streaming by, and even the agar-agar in their petri dishes came to them already tainted by the predispositions of three private souls.

If only the Turners could have been more like Sir Alexander Fleming, idly making cultures from whatever happened to be sticking to his shoe or hanging from his mustache, and forgetting about them, they too might have discovered penicillin or some other prodigy where yesterday was only a funny-looking child, resistant to every improvement. Instead they were always afraid that things weren't turning out right. And so they didn't. The three girls, healthy and intelligent according to standardized tests, trooped into middle adolescence with dangerous ideas about basic matters, namely sex and money. They thought an honest woman could not have both. Who was to blame? Strange to say, on this point the parents had accidentally come together.

Sasha abhorred a hand stretched out for a handout. Some time after the flight of Jake Rostovsky, her mother, Rosie, had married Morris Kaplan, who was a drunkard but owned a prosperous window-washing concern. Sasha had been the dignified stepchild amid a grasping and vulgar brood, and her stepfather, in his sober moments, had greatly admired her for this: "You were the only one who never had a hand out for money." Morris had given her a good bit of money all the same—more than she ever wanted.

Sasha therefore had no cause to associate high-mindedness about money with actual poverty, although ladylike demurral did not fare so well under the Turner roof. What Philip Turner seemed to be fearful of as his daughters, helpless to do otherwise, grew breasts and pubic hair, was the aptitude for prostitution. He was on the squint for that telltale combo of vanity and greed; even with the bathroom door closed, he knew what went on in front of the steamy mirror, because he was the patsy —for the present—who had to cover those bills and charges that vanity ran up. Not that it had cost him much money as yet, but the whole upstairs was as humid as August with hormones and perfume. How long before the storm broke? And when he could not avoid his daughters, when he ran into them in the upper story, they saw what he was thinking. They felt his knees quivering to flee, as before a pack of dirty bandits, and they knew, when custom obliged him to touch them, that had it been halfway polite, he would have held his nose with his other hand like a boy of eight.

Now that everything, and especially the sight of her father's suspicious face, tended to a hideous embarrassment, Jane rushed through adolescence with her own face averted, without even stopping to get her driver's license. For four years she travelled the seven miles between home and Girls Classical, by ·bus and on foot, with a book propped in front of her face, so that much of this period remains a peripheral blur, and she was lucky not to have died at the bottom of some manhole, but was spared any downfall so early and uncomplicated.

That all three Turner girls were queasy at the prospect of taking money, no matter how respectably, from men, was the last thing their parents intended, and the parents were to be the principal sufferers after the fact. And how will it all turn out? Only the oldest girl, Carla, is going to marry money, and that sullenly, as if in defeat, with every intention of being unhappy about it, after years of wincingly no-account and penurious boyfriends. Meanwhile Jane and Hermine make it clear they will probably never marry at all. Jane uttered a pronouncement to this effect at the dinner table when she was twelve; the parents scoffed, but with little weeds of belief already sprouting between their eyebrows. As for the youngest, Hermine, she had never shown any sexual interest in boys and did not start now.

An idea had taken root among the girls that went something like this: Men were the fountain of money, but this public monument did not represent generosity. It was a bitter, reluctant trough at best. Men might give you money if you were so good they had no excuse not to, but this meant being more good than it was good to be, for to be that good implied a degree of hypocrisy ("playing up") of which even the parents disapproved.

Alas, it was prehistoric, this embroilment of sex with money in the moral faculty. It stretched back behind adolescence into times when sex was not even on the table yet between Philip Turner and the girls, or only diffuse in other subject matters like the starch in a sauce that has yet to thicken. It was present in a fairy-tale notion the girls once shared that went away, but left a set of larcenous fingerprints on all their hearts. When they were small, so unsmiling and minatory were both parents in the dispersal of funds that the girls got the idea their family was poor, poor like Hansel and Gretel, and for any of them to cost an extra penny might land the family in ruin, in the street, in chains. The Turner girls owned a peculiar prestige in their neighborhood because they were made to trudge to school in rain and snow. If they headed for Pimlico they rode their bikes or took buses for five cents. They were never chauffeured by their parents. Their clothes were strange and outmoded. They were often punished. Their parents were famously strict; their allowances were famously small.

Still, the cause had to lie deeper than austere household legislation, had to be something more than the skull-and-crossbones face of justice with which the tiny allowances were handed over once a week, more than the admonitions (always ignored, at least by Jane) to "save up" out of this pittance, more than the speed with which the allowances were snatched away if the girls became through crime or recklessness the occasion of any shame, especially shame that cost money, to the family, as when Jane lost or ruined library books, a constant source of turmoil in the house, or when Hermine's rocks went through the windshields of cars.

It had something to do with the kind of fury Philip Turner could show to the girls—in the flash of revulsion, a hand speeding to guard the wallet, a gesture like that of an outraged john. When Jane was twelve, now and then she would flag at her mission of disputing every word her father said. She would despair, either genuinely or with the innate melodrama of her age. Not on the way home from Nova Scotia but on some other trip not long after, stuck in the back of the family Ford, somewhere along the New Jersey Turnpike, Jane once tried to call a truce.

"How's this, Dad," she proposed. "From now on I'll be polite to you at dinner, I'll even say yes sir, no sir, and I'll stop talking to you the rest of the time."

Philip Turner looked into the backseat and shouted at her: "WHAT DO YOU THINK I AM? YOUR MEAL TICKET? JUST YOUR MEAL TICKET?"

Jane did not reply. She looked down in her lap, her cheeks tight, a feeling of having been scalded in boiling water along the tops of her ears. And she had also registered a kind of electric shock between the legs—not pleasure, with which she was by this time somewhat familiar, but a smothered detonation of the helpless genital rage she sometimes felt at physical objects, pens that wouldn't write but spat ink in all directions, windows that wouldn't open. Why it should be sexual shame she felt at her father's remark, she did not at the time understand.

But soon she began to see, in the air around other people, oily glints as of something whisked quickly away, and she knew that was sex. When she thought of kissing she realized she could not even imagine her parents kissing each other. And yet the presence of the three girls was scientific proof that something more than kissing had been done. Sasha wore the grim mask of the lawgiver, but strangely she was not the missing party here. She was actually pretty, she had a girlish figure, she weighed one hundred pounds, exactly the same as when she was married. Her pale, round Russian face, painted boldly with a line of dark red here, two of black there, had no scars yet; it softened for the purpose of flirting with grocery clerks, insurance salesmen, and gas station mechanics. Jane pictured, queasily, Dr. Zwilling.

Handsome as Philip Turner was (and year by year there was less of the crack-brained botanist, more of the finished man of affairs in his exterior), Jane now wished she could remember him leafing surreptitiously through a girlie magazine in a drugstore, or following a woman's ballooning derrière or great cliff of breasts across a restaurant floor with his eyes, as Jane always did herself if these were stupendous enough, so that she would surely have detected it if her father had done the same. But the perforated lines of their gazes never crossed. To be sure, all of her father's friends pretended they didn't see women in this way, especially when children were present. But Philip Turner was the most polished, or fanatical, at this pretense; he was the only one she never, never caught out perusing the line of a buttock or bosom when he thought no one was looking. And somehow she was not cheered that her father stood this proof.

Philip Turner took Jane along to a CPA's grimy office one Saturday morning where he had to sign some form, a tax document perhaps, and Jane had leaned over the counter that separated the waiting room from the typing pool to stare at the switchboard operator. Her black dress cradled only the bottom halves of breasts that sat side by side like two round scoops of ice cream in a dish; her hair was a sort of pinkish-gold foil, rolled into hardened-looking curls like rose petals on top of a cake. "I have everything ready for you, Mr. Turner," she said, sweeping papers across the counter in such a manner that her breasts swelled to the size of softballs and her pinkish locks almost grazed Philip Turner's chin. Jane popped up between them to get a better look and asked: "Is your hair dyed?" She had heard of such things, but only for movie stars. Philip Turner snatched her away by the upper arm. "Don't ask questions like that out loud," he hissed. "Anyway, can't you see what she is?" What is she? Jane thought uneasily, but had better sense than to ask out loud.

At thirteen Jane realized she could not manage her looks whatever she did, beginning with the uncontrollable explosion of oak-brown hair that her father, since she was six, had insisted must go as soon as it grew two inches (straight out) from her scalp. Her glasses were too heavy for her small face and tended to slide a quarter inch or so down her nose. A cross-eyed view of her father's white index finger approaching this slippage to prod them back into place might be the emblem of their relations at best in this period, for that gesture had replaced the trembling hand in her underpants. She had slightly crooked teeth. A small amount of visible dirt always flew magnetically towards her clothes, just as her nylon stockings reached out to martyr themselves on table legs and trash baskets on the first wearing. She never looked right.

She studied her face at length in the bathroom mirror. She knew all too well what she looked like, though from the mirror she could not get the answer she was looking for—what this might mean to others. Experience told her it was a face that had its uses: the sharp, small but emphatic face of the girl who was always asked to be the witch (and she always was) in the class play. Then again, with her hair cropped close to her skull, and dressed in plain clothes, she could disappear into any crowd and never be missed. That was what her father hoped for her. She could bear being the class witch; she could not bear to disappear, and besides, her father would like her no better if she did disappear, so where was the incentive? It was a high price to pay for his mere relief.

One afternoon she was peering into the medicine cabinet mirror with her nose an inch from the glass. She had removed her eyeglasses in the hope this would improve her face—but of course without glasses on, she was unable to see the difference, if any. All at once Philip Turner appeared in the open door and stared at her with a strange expression. She could see him in the mirror, a blur, but life-size, and for once tragically speechless, as though he saw there was no hope. Suddenly she dared to ask him: "Can I get contact lenses, Dad?"

His eyebrows leaped. "Can you what! You think I'm going to pay *three hundred bucks* to pander to your vanity!"

And he slammed the door in front of him, so that Jane and her smeary double in the mirror disappeared from his view.

This insistence on a price he would not pay to appease Jane's vanity bothered her for days. It was an appraisal of her as a female in monetary terms, and quite low at that, as soon as a little wire of naked sexual hope flickered on in her face. Jane was so sure her father found her unattractive she didn't bother to think it as a thought. She had a sudden intimation of what he feared from her: at any moment, public acts on the model of a French poodle who pumps frantically at the legs of dinner guests. Hadn't she kissed him on the mouth when she was small? She would be boy crazy, she would be fast, she would be as expensive as possible, and she would be a sexual embarrassment. She caught a whiff of his disgust, and in the disturbed air there was also the redolence of quarters and pennies he was snatching away rather than support her proclivities—the smell of money, the strange prison-bar odor of rain falling in summertime on a dusty asphalt road.

Thus it came to pass that squeamishness about money honeycombed the sexual awakenings of all the Turner girls as inseparably as blue-green penicillium runs through a block of Roquefort cheese. The more Carla and Jane succumbed to lipstick and nylons, the more they felt like unsavory misfits in their father's eyes, although the opposite course, it turned out, was not safe either. When Hermine, whom he had always preferred, reached the age of thirteen and her amazonian disuse of males other than as sporting companions did not cease on schedule, she suddenly manifested to Philip Turner as possibly the most freakish of all, and he shrank from her in dumb panic.

Jane was not popular in junior high school. She saw this herself. She was not sought after by boys, but then, few girls were. Most drooped about the gray-lockered halls of Pimlico fully as hidden a lump of fat and bones inside their ugly and faddish clothes as she did, even if they were spared the glasses. The popular girls had breasts well out in front of them and would trail fifteen or sixteen boys to the bus stop. The excited males looked dwarfed and copycat; you could hate yourself without wanting such breasts or such boys.

But Jane was not left out entirely. Now and then a boy called her up on the telephone and asked her to go to the movies, and Jane would accept, even after she knew what to expect: a furtive youth reeking of aftershave, his pale face sporting crimson dots where an underworked razor had decapitated pimples, the two fingers, softer than Jane's, with which he would pick his father's five-dollar bill out of a billfold at the ticket booth and say *Two adults* in a fluty voice, the humid hand-holding and dry kiss goodnight.

It took two years for Jane to grasp all this for the pointless misery it was and to begin to say no. For her parents did not object to such dating—they were more worried when Jane would not go—but they were the reason it had to end. The zone of their witness, which she had to cross over to go in or out of the house with a boy, was as perilous as a moat full of crocodiles, for at that age you can die of embarrassment.

The kiss goodnight normally took place in the front hall. But if her father was still in his den, the long, dark hall ended in that—in Philip Turner in a white shirt with his back to the door, framed in golden light like a god spied on through a keyhole. Then Jane would have to back her date out the front door again for the kiss, her eyes rolling in mortification. One night she stepped back in from the stoop, the front door closed behind her, and her father said without turning around: "Oh Jane, would you come here for a minute?" His voice had gone high and rubbery. Sensing what he was about to say, Jane tried to squeeze her ears shut from the inside. But she heard it anyway. "I hope I didn't, er, *cramp your style*," he said, without looking up from his papers.

Jane stared at his back, thinking: Never again. The sexual part of the boy who had just gone away was as unimaginable to her as if it were stored in a coffer in Tibet instead of right there under the fly of his dress slacks. She hated her father intensely for seeing the two of them in cahoots—Jane and the dazed-looking boy available to her, a human sacrifice who was plainly even farther out in the desert of self-loathing where love did not exist than Jane.

The last date was with a boy named, or at least called, Dagwood Hamburger. When they parked at eleven in front of the house on Pinkney Road, the lantern light from the porch was painting the shiny bushes below a queer lickerish yellow. Jane, peering at this glow, realized no lights were on in the house. She remembered that her parents were at a big party, and then she had the uncomfortable thought that Dagwood's mother and father must be there too, since they were more or less in the same set. The two couples were not great friends, but nothing brings people together like bit parts in the same tragicomedy: Were the four of them sniggering about Jane and Dagwood right now?

Dagwood went to military school as Philip Turner once had done. Jane tried never to think of this for it made her feel sorry for him, a frail, slumping, pink-freckled Jewish boy with fine hair the color of the watery blood that collects in white butcher's paper. Dagwood was so cowed he did not even mumble.

He whispered. She sensed that his parents had sent him to McDonogh to force out his manly qualities. It was her third date with him—three well-spaced trips to downtown movie theaters in his mother's car.

There was something Jane had always wanted to ask him. Had his mother and father really named him Dagwood on his birth certificate? They were Jewish, so he could not be named after a living relative—not *Dagwood*. Were his parents dotty, or heartless? True, Jane would have been flattered if her father had nicknamed her, say, Dragon Lady, instead of the funereal Bones, though nowadays he addressed her by her proper name if at all. But if *Dagwood* had once been a joke, after Dagwood Bumstead, no one smiled at it anymore; it was the only name her date seemed to own.

Standing next to him in the front hall, thinking of their parents clinking vodka martinis together to that comic-book couple, Dagwood and Jane, all at once Jane wanted to know more, anyway a little more, about him, beginning with his name. It seemed worth one of their stilted kisses to be able to find out. She led Dagwood towards the living room, but then caught sight of their two heads silhouetted in a glass picture frame over the sofa. It was hard to tell them apart. Her hair was almost as short as his, his face no larger then her own, though her temples were notched with eyeglasses and his ears stuck out further. Their features were blanked out of the reflection, but she imagined them, his piteously expectant, hers that of the Dragon Lady at work.

Suddenly she wanted only for him to go away. Rather than back foolishly out of the living room, she veered past the sofa, yanked open the door to the patio and sent, almost pushed, Dagwood out into the dark backyard. She stood there squinting through an eyehole in the drapes at his confused face, for she had forgotten to kiss him at all. And he waited, at first patiently, then with a cleft of resentment deepening between his pale eyebrows. Finally he turned his back, moved off slowly on the grass towards the side of the house, and disappeared.

She waited for him to knock at the front door, but a moment later she heard him drive away. She felt stupid, even a little crazy, but she was not sorry. This time, she was sure, she had gotten rid of him forever.

Her two fingers still making a peephole in the woven curtain, she became, in fact, happy, criminally happy—she had a sense of having gotten off for nothing. After all, it was early yet and her parents were not home. Hermine and Carla were out with friends of their own, probably gone for the night. Presently Jane went into the kitchen and piled pretzels on a paper towel, stole a couple of cigarettes from her mother's pack, came back to the living room, laid these provisions on the piano bench and raised the lid of the Chickering baby grand. And she began to play. But somewhere along this route, most likely exactly then, while she was still standing with two fingers in the curtain, and the lid of her self-consciousness beginning to levitate in the dark living room like a hat in a comic strip, she stepped out of her high heels and pinched at the small of her back through her skirt to unhook her garter belt, so that her nylon stockings fell to the floor, as, in fact, they had been trying to do all night.

And this is where they were lying the next morning, two brown nylons in a loose ring, a diaphanous cowpie with the white cotton garter belt snaking over the top. A garter belt, by the way, did not carry the charge of an aphrodisiac appliance in 1959. Or at least it was not credited with such powers by adolescent girls, who wore garter belts to hold up their stockings only until they showed enough behind to justify a panty girdle.

Of course, this maiden unreadiness has a charm all its own in the eyes of some observers. Possibly Philip Turner was more alert to a whole host of messages in feminine undergarments than was Jane at this stage. The next morning he dragged her by the arm from the breakfast table where she had been reading the Sunday funnies, pointed to that spot on the living room floor where nylons and garter belt lay in a dismal heap, and, quite beside himself, shouted at her, though her ear was only an arm's length from his mouth: "What is this? What is this? Goddamn you, answer me, WHAT IS THIS?" He shook her by the upper arm. This time his voice was not rubbery with shyness and sport. It was fatal as a cliff. He leaped over it, dragging Jane.

She said nothing at first. She was remembering Dagwood's perplexed face blinking at her from the dark backyard through the hole she had picked in her mother's drapes. This was what she got for leading him into the living room for a kiss, then exulting that she had gotten off cheap. She recalled how her date had shrunk away silently on the black grass, thinking whatever black thoughts he was left to think about Jane.

Now here was her father trying to shake out of her all he did not know. The lips of his handsome face were drawn back into the skull, so that one saw as in a death's head how oddly large the teeth were and how fragilely attached. He was shouting questions that could not be answered in one day. He knew little about her, because for years he couldn't bear to look at her. And now before she got herself pregnant or so rotten that no one would ever want her, he was after the fearful truth of her sex life while there was still time.

"What do you care?" she hissed at him, her fists curling against her sides. "Are you afraid I might cost you some money?"

Then her father did a strange and wonderful thing. He steered her to the front door and pushed her out to the stoop and slammed and locked the door, which was never locked, in front of her face. And Jane, barefoot, penniless, without even a book in her hand, loitered in the neighborhood telling herself with a kind of queasy rapture: *He threw me out, he threw me out*—a foretaste of homelessness, though it was June and the heaped rosebeds, clouds of viburnum, mounds of sticky peonies in every garden, were hardly austere.

In her last year at home, Jane sometimes wished she were even more invisible than she was. Her parents would come home and find Jane's room blue with cigarette smoke. No, Jane said, she had not been smoking. But when she got in the shower, her father would look in her purse, find the Pall Malls and be unable to bear it: He would come into the bathroom and there he would stand, outside the same clear glass shower stall where he had once discovered her sitting at five o'clock in the morning, memorizing names and dates of battles of the Civil War. Only now Jane was naked, water streaming down, and he, on the other side of the pane, was thundering that's it, not one red cent more, she could forget about her tuition to Harmonia College, the notorious and expensive beatnik school where she was planning to go. Probably he was glad to have some shield, even a glass shower door, between them at such times, since he knew he must not hit her. He was so angry he would not notice Jane's hands hovering as if to conceal, but somehow ashamed to do so, her faintly globed breasts and thin scrawl of pubic hair. She was afraid that any attempt to hide it would only call attention to her nakedness. For her nakedness was invisible to her father, as all the rest of her was invisible to him for days, even weeks, at a time, until she managed to make him angry. Meanwhile her invisibility grew into curious unseen forms, like mold on a slice of raw potato sealed in a jar, and hidden for a junior high school science health experiment in the bottom of a dark closet.

It came into view for a moment the last time he really did hit her. Her parents were out, she was sixteen, she was in her room, reading of coral isles and warm, shallow, shark-infested seas, she was pumping out Magellanic clouds of cigarette smoke. When she heard them drive up, she ran to the shower rather than subject herself to a grilling. But ten minutes later she came out of the bathroom door just as Philip Turner was pushing in from the other side, her Pall Malls in his hand. He dropped the cigarettes and caught her a sharp slap across the shoulders, still humid from the shower, as she passed naked into the hall. She staggered backwards, her eyes on the white cigarettes crisscrossed like primitive stick-writing on the carpet. The door to Hermine's room opened—Hermine, too, though for other reasons, was invisible to Philip Turner by now—and Hermine, in a blue bathrobe, pointed her finger at Jane's chest and said, "Look what he did," as if their father weren't there. Jane glanced down. Splayed across one breast, a little above the nipple, was a rosy palmprint and five long red fingermarks. Surprised, since the blow had not hurt, she looked up at him triumphantly.

He was staring at her, and not only at her breast. He was taking her in, all of her, with a face full of distress, even fear. Watching him at that moment, Jane almost discerned why she had had to become invisible to her father: that it was himself he was in despair of governing. But she stopped short of learning this, for such a perception would have required her to pity him when she most needed to be rid of him altogether. Since for once he was unable to blot her out, she gathered herself up to walk by him, to show him just the gleam of her wet buttocks. But it was as if her invisibility, once let out of its cloak, was too sure of its power to terrify. As she went by him, she thrust out her naked behind, and a jeer, not even a word, came out of her lips.

He jumped back and said: "What do you mean by that?"

Kiss my ass, she was thinking, and her mouth formed those words, though no sound came out.

"Don't," Hermine said. "Don't you dare hit her."

His hands were raised at the verge of Jane's nakedness but could not strike, for the air there was as frangible as hot glass.

"Go put clothes on *right now*," he ordered.

"Nope, you'll have to hit me the way I am," Jane said.

He did hit her, but awkwardly, as if reaching over a fence. She stepped forward as though he had asked her to dance. This time, he swung at her.

Hermine yelled, "Don't." Jane, arms up in front of her face, backed into the bedroom. She did not run. She felt the chenille spread touch the backs of her knees and sat down firmly on the edge of the bed, smiling. She tried to keep a ladylike pose. She hoped her nose would not break. She hoped her father's memory of this event would be as expensive as possible, but she kept reminding herself, You're getting out of here soon. The slaps fell on top of her head, her cheeks and shoulders, and oddly, though her father was shouting and they came in a crazy windmill, they didn't hurt. Either she was past feeling or he wasn't hitting as hard as he could.

He said, "You're devious. You're a liar. Why do you pretend to care what I think of you?"

She grinned up at him fiercely and he clasped her shoulder in one hand and smacked her face with the other.

"You can't be trusted here and now. How can you expect me to pay for you to go to college five hundred miles away?"

You will, Jane was thinking. After this, you surely will. She shut her eyes and pretended to enjoy this encounter. She was sweating and now a reptilian pungency laced the flowery soap that still clung to her damp body like an atmosphere. After he was done she would have to shower all over again. But still she was trying to grin, still he was shaking and slapping her, when Hermine cried, "QUIT IT, DAMN YOU, BOTH OF YOU," in such horror that everything stopped, Jane stood up to cover herself, and her father stumbled away down the hall, down the stairs, and she heard the door to his den slam shut.

Their mother might have told them. Any of their parents' friends might have let some remark slip in front of the girls. The switchboard operator at Turner, Wiener, Blum & Taliaferro, a withered debutante who had once been deserted by a husband, might have been too pointedly sorry for their mother some afternoon when Mr. Turner was out of the office and could not be reached. Or Jane, Hermine, or Carla might have answered the phone one day to a drunken, teary female voice bent on confession and betrayal. But none of this occurred. Three years would pass before Jane remembered the bobby pin, and for now the girls were convinced their father simply loathed women, including themselves, on grounds too embarrassing to contemplate in any detail. Sometimes they took comfort in the idea that their father was obviously a madman, though they guarded this news closely outside of the household where it made sense. But he was not a madman. His suspicion of his daughters, his queasiness at the thought of the loose, grasping women Jane and Carla might easily become, was scientific at its root. It varied in proportion to the amount of money and time and heart's ease he was spending in the pursuit of women who met this description. He knew an adventuress when he saw one, though of course he meant something quite different by this word than the lone drifter in a spangled pink brassiere who was beginning to appear in the dreams of Jane.

Book II

Charity

○
○
● **The**

wayfarer

The rain falls on the roof of the Wayfarer like a million invisible fingers thumping the keys of a million pianos in a million boogie-woogies. It is Jane's nerves these invisible black fingers, which are really raindrops, play upon as she stares into the black dome of the Dodge, parked in a cornfield, unable to sleep. She is too cold to sleep, having stuffed the open window holes on each side of the Dodge with stolen dormitory blankets as the rain poured in. She is beginning to get that scared feeling, that kryptonite green glow around the liver, that seismic puddling between the legs. *No one on earth knows where she is.* She tells herself a little in despair: Now I'll never fall asleep, never. Never, that is, unless she can turn this fertile but dreadful privacy into visitation.

So she does. He's a truck driver, old enough to be her father. Oh easily. And black. Big and stout but solid, growling some country patois. He has picked the girl up on a rainy highway. Coarsely paternal, transparent as a jellyfish down to his rich ulterior designs, he points out she is soaked, shivering. He parks his truck, as long as a cornfield, on the shoulder of the Ohio two-lane, peels off her wet clothes, lays her up in that greasy loft behind the seat of the cab and kisses her goodnight for hours with his invisible fingers between her thighs.

She wakes up at dawn in the jewelled cornfield, the woven frost on the stubble angling the thin sun splat off her windshield, her hands warm at her cunt.

How Jane came to be sleeping in her car: She had run away from the dormitory where nothing would ever happen to her, and arrived at a life where everything could happen to her. She ran away but not far, for it was never school she hated, school which meant books. Books Jane liked, though in her care they were tinged, even brand new, with the melancholy of their early deaths. And it wasn't the papers, the grades, the male professors in their little cubicles. All that stood on the borders of the tolerable. What Jane couldn't stand, not even for one more night, about Harmonia College, was life in a dormitory. But it wasn't easy to get out of the dormitory, for Harmonia needed those dorms to be full. The notorious beatnik college, whose endowment was never in the best of health, needed the money.

And now that she had spent one night freezing under the stars in a cornfield, and lived, *and slept*, she was never going back to that dormitory block with its gray reform-school lavatories where you couldn't get sick drunk and puke in the toilet without a squadron of floormates whom you barely knew trying to mother you. Above all, Jane was through with the roommate —her comfy bathrobe and softly hissing bedroom slippers and the repulsive regularity of her sleeping and waking hours, and all her other habits. Jane always felt like a pterodactyl in a chicken yard, barely in control of the relative violence of her personality at every moment. Jane had never found it easy to go to sleep, but when the roommate was there (Jane never chose a roommate: this was part of her strategy, a wholly unsuccessful strategy, of holding out for off-campus permission) and the roommate's head full of broken pink tubing protruded from the gray cot across the room and her soft snoring filled up the space every night from eleven o'clock on, while Jane clung for dear life to a bubble of light from a desk lamp, then sleep was impossible—and at last she had to get out, so she could get some sleep; it was that simple.

She had to get some sleep. Perhaps it was all the dreadful coffee she drank, and the cigarettes; perhaps it was the habit of twenty years (for she couldn't remember when she hadn't done it) of denying she was tired until sleep all at once swallowed her in its black gorge like a whale. Perhaps it was some neurotic aversion to slipping from control in the presence of a stranger, the roommate, on top of the spotty, teasing, irregular hours Jane had kept ever since she was twelve. By now she felt as homeless as a derelict and at the same time as confined and spied on as a beast in a zoo. She felt she had not slept in three years, that like an amnesiac she had been living nowhere at all, that in three years nothing real had happened to her, and so she hadn't lived. And at last she came to almost an exalted state of exhaustion, full of a restless static charge. She was never, never tired. She had heard that some birds migrate halfway around the world sleeping on the wing. Her bones seemed pocked with air, like a bird's, her mind seemed full of wind, like a migrant bird's; only she could barely think, and her feet were heavy as stones. And when she used to lie down in the afternoon, when the roommate was gone, and try to sleep in this condition, a strange thing would occur. She would fall quickly, too quickly, down a rabbit hole with her nerves still quivering, and suddenly she would be jolted by bizarre electrical sensations that concentrated in her teeth, as though she were in the clutches of a maniac dentist. With all her teeth being drilled at once, neither awake nor asleep, she would struggle to come to her senses. Knowing that only light could save her, she would crawl with immense effort towards the pink pleated shade, faintly glowing in the dark, of a lamp that belonged to the roommate and finally manage to pinch its brass throat between her fingers —and she would wake up in broad day, nowhere near that lamp, shivering and frightened out of her wits.

"So you dream your teeth are falling out," a friend said slyly.

"Being attacked," Jane corrected. For she had already, long

since, in that pastoral era when she still had real dreams, even if they were always bad dreams, dreamed those troubling dreams where your teeth crumble like Roquefort cheese in your fingers, or tear out like paper matches, or flake off like daisy petals.

"Masturbation guilt," diagnosed the friend confidently. "We had that in Psych 250."

But if anything, Jane knew, it was masturbation withdrawal, since that consolation too had fallen to the roommate, to fitful sleep in the afternoons, and to the friendly lockless doors of the dormitory.

Jane had explained this, some of this, leaving out about masturbation, the maniac dentist, and the mind of a migrant bird, to Betty Jean Lucorne, Dean of Student Life. Jane came to hate Betty Jean Lucorne, her air, though she was a single woman in her forties, of perpetual sloppy pregnancy, her grossly relaxed waistline and breasts like yesterday's birthday balloons, her feet in warm scuffies while her black high heels sat parked by her office door. She had a big head and a plain, thick cylinder of a face, like a giant paper cup on which cartoon features had been drawn, and out of this face trickled a very slow, very flat midwestern voice: she was famous for her comfortable voice. She would always say in just that voice: "You seem rather desperate, Jane, for what you say you want, which tells me, Jane, you aren't quite ready for what you think you need."

And though in fact she was a dragon guarding Cappadocia's miserable little pot of gold, she would seem to swell towards Jane, as if to enfold her in the round lines of that perpetual pregnancy, and Jane would give it up and flee—until yesterday.

She had thought that in her fourth year she would finally get off-campus permission, but yesterday a new housing assignment came in the mail: Longfellow 209. Roommate: Shelby Givens, Bristol, Tennessee. Another one of those southern girls with a closetful of taffeta, a shaven-headed boyfriend, and wall-to-wall facial cleansers—and all of them slept ten hours a night. Jane wadded up the housing letter and threw it at the roommate's pink lamp shade and ran as the crow flies across the crabgrass and bald earth (newly seeded: PLEASE KEEP OFF THE GRASS) of front campus to Dean Lucorne's office where she said:

"I'm going to park my car on front campus and sleep in the back."

The dean's eyes widened but she said with perfect mildness: "Now really, Jane, what do you think that would prove?"

"It would prove I'm not in the dormitory."

"You may be arrested."

"That would be very entertaining."

Dean Lucorne gave Jane a long and what is called a searching glance. Something like intelligence sometimes sprang, *sprang* is too athletic a word, washed, slowly washed, over Lucorne's blunt features when she had a moment of deep understanding of you, but Jane was rarely the occasion for one of these epiphanies. Not that Jane was all that hard to follow—rather, she had tried to frustrate this state of exhilaration, mild exhilaration, in Dean Lucorne, because you didn't want to be trapped in a gluey mind like that even for an instant.

But yesterday the dean had been looking at Jane to see if the girl meant what she said. Perhaps she was thinking of the story that might end up in the *Pocahontas City Sentinel*, finding it all too easy to imagine the relishing tone of the article, the photo of Jane's bare feet hanging out the missing window of her fleshpink '49 Dodge.

"You may have off-campus permission since it's so important to you," said the dean.

"Thank you," Jane said, and now she got down to the stony heart of the matter: "I'll need my spring housing money back."

"Of course." The dean smiled a small smile. "Your father will receive an adjusted check in the mail."

That the dormitory fee might be turned over directly to Jane, and at once, was no doubt an absurd hope, but she had dared to hope it all the same, for now she had to telephone her father. She ran back across the newly seeded lawn, ignoring the backsides of the same signs, PLEASE KEEP OFF THE GRASS, to the pay phone in the stairwell of her dormitory, which she told herself she was entering for the last time. She shovelled up a handful of change from the bottom of her purse and called Philip Turner at his office.

"I don't see the big problem," he said. "Why can't you live in a dormitory like every other college girl?"

"Because I can't stand another night of it."

"What can't you stand? You've got no curfew at that crazy school. You're not locked in. They don't give a damn what you do."

"It's giving me terrible nightmares," Jane said patiently.

"So? You used to like nightmares."

"When I was a child I thought as a child," Jane said. "Now that everyday life is a nightmare I don't need any encores when the lights are out."

Her father said: "I'll tell you what's a nightmare. The screwy bills I get from that screwy school. Screwy and big. Didn't I already pay for you to live in the dormitory next semester?"

"They're sending you a check."

"I'll believe that when I see it. And meanwhile I guess you want even more money."

"Just the same money," Jane muttered.

"As soon as I see that check I'll send it. Anyway, the old semester isn't over yet, is it? You can stick it out in the dormitory for a few more weeks, can't you?"

"All right," Jane said. "I'll sleep in my car."

"What? You have a car? You can afford a car? What the hell do you need my money for?"

"I have a 1949 Dodge," Jane said, "with no windows and no backseat."

"Well, that ought to *cramp your style*" —his voice wobbled with mock concupiscence—"even more than the dormitory."

"Nothing cramps my style," said Jane, who had not had a date in six months.

"When are you going to practice a little moderation," her father exploded.

"Moderation does not need me to admire it," Jane said. "It already has too many fans."

"Do you think your excessiveness in everything is a novel idea?"

"No," Jane said, "but between the two, excess needs me more."

To sleep in the Dodge was no cheap threat. It was all she had. All the same, she did have it, the portable boudoir of a thirty-five-dollar auto—something else she owed to Willie D. Usher, The Soul of Commerce, I.P. (in person). Without it, she would never have dared, never have thought about daring, to quit the dormitory without other resort and only fifteen dollars to the good.

And had it been summer, it would be wholly bearable to find a bumpy tractor turnaround in a cornfield every night, or some leafy tunnel of jeep tracks into the Shawnee Woodlands, and to give in to sleep with your nose grazing the steering wheel. But it was not summer. It was cold, and the rain poured in. She could not calm down enough to hang up a flashlight and read. Something had to be done.

Still, she had the Dodge; it was a floor to how far she could fall. The Wayfarer was a one-seater with a huge trunk that ran the length of the enormous ballooning rear end, behind a little round pimple of a roof. Everything she owned fit into it loose when she fled the dormitory. It wasn't quite true that the windows were missing. What was left of two side windows in the tiny top rolled halfway up, no more, and when you played with the window cranks you could hear little pieces of glass tumbling melodiously against each other in the bottom of the door. To make this airy ride tolerable in the winter, Willie Usher had hot-wired a massive red-and-chrome heater under the dash. You could feel like the moon when you drove, your face boiling, your back a glacial unknown.

Some former owner, not Willie, had smeared the Dodge with fleshpink primer end to end. Its albino color even more than its silly shape, but most of all how little he wanted for it, had made Jane back away suspiciously the first time Willie had tried to sell it to her in the empty lot next to his junk store. This was over a year ago, in the fall of 1963.

"Darling, I'm trying to give it away at that price. If you don't take this unusual auto for thirty-five dollars you ought to be helped back to your senses."

Jane slowly shook her head.

"She smell a rat," said Felix, the bartender from the Downtown Recreation Club across the street, who was looking on at these negotiations.

"Don't talk like that. I always liked this car. It's a good car."

"I ain't said it wasn't," Felix said, looking at some disturbance in the empty air over his shoulder. Felix was always mysterious.

"Thirty-five dollars to you, darling," Willie said. "The tires alone is worth that. Why won't you take this car?"

Jane looked at the tires. They were tires all right, with fat black squiggles in all the right places. What did she know? "Because I can't drive," she said in a low voice.

Felix uttered a pleased hee-hee-hee.

"What you mean you can't drive? You shucking?" For only five minutes before, Jane had stuck her head in the Downtown Recreation Club—no women allowed—and asked Willie Usher how much the car was.

"I was thinking of looking for a job in Pocahontas City," Jane said. Actually she had already taken a waitress job in Pocahontas City. Although she was supposed to start in a week, she had not told the manager she had no car, let alone no license.

Willie said: "Poke City isn't but twenty miles. Who's going to stop you?"

"The heat," Felix said bluntly. "That's who."

"Aw, they don't stop no young girls."

"A young girl, all alone at night in that pink junk?"

"It's a good car," Willie said. "It always starts."

"She done told you she can't drive," Felix reminded him.

"Any dimwit can drive. You don't know how?" Willie asked. "Or you ain't legal?"

"Both," Jane whispered.

So they taught her. They set a cooler of beer and Diggs Cream Pop (for Willie, who didn't drink) behind the seat, squeezed in beside her, and went out on the country roads. Jane turned corners at random, Willie pointed out the sights or stopped to see about some piece of junk in some farmer's front yard, and Felix drank beer and ventilated his esoteric reflections. In short, the two of them paid no attention at all to her driving, a reckless omission for which Jane would always be grateful.

By the time she started the job in Pocahontas City, Jane more or less believed she could drive, though she had already flunked her driver's test once, instantly, by going through the stop sign in front of the Department of Motor Vehicles—a concrete-block shack in the middle of cornfields. Willie and Felix, who shunned county officials, had chosen not to accompany her. So she waited till the examiner, shaking his head, went back into the building, then drove home alone.

It may seem queer that Jane of all people should have feared she would never learn to operate a motor vehicle, but that was how it had been. After her sixteenth birthday, Philip Turner had given her one driving lesson in his MG. The family Ford had an automatic transmission, but a real driver ought to learn on a car with a gearshift, he said; to drive an automatic was the next thing to not driving at all. However, to offer his own MG for instructional purposes was a burst of generosity that could not be sustained. Jane was too gingerly with the clutch; her father bit his knuckles as the swift little car hiccupped in first up the steep hill of Old Pimlico Road, Jane's knee bouncing over the throttle. Then she shifted too soon into third and the engine moaned at the abuse; she tried to find second again, died in fourth, and started all over. With Philip Turner clutching his temples, she again started to shift too early. "Not yet, GUN IT, GUN IT," he shouted, and suddenly lay across her lap, grabbed her right foot and pressed it to the floor in the accelerator. The car shot forward. "NOW," he yelled, and grabbed for Jane's hand on the shift lever. The gears ratched sickeningly as her left foot came off the clutch and pounded the brake. Philip Turner, still holding her foot on the gas, lost his balance and pitched upside down between her knees. "Now DRIVE," he yelled, "DRIVE," but Jane pressed the brake with all her might against the hysterical whine of the throttle.

A moment later she was running across backyards towards Pinkney Road, her father calling out the car window after her, "Jane! What the hell is the matter with you? Come back or you'll never get another driving lesson, never."

After four or five lessons from Willie Usher and Felix, Jane ventured out by herself to explore the county roads. First cautiously, then ecstatically; in 1964, that was really all she did, learning every dip, rise, bend, railroad crossing, red barn, hog feeder, silo, and green-gold cornfield on every little road between Xenia and Pocahontas City, the wind sucking at the cracked half-windows, the windshield bejewelled with the ichor of sacrificed bugs. Once two peacocks skittered across a dirt lane in front of her, causing her heart almost to stop with joy. About midyear she procured a driver's license, on her third attempt.

All that long fall when she rode out of Harmonia Springs every day on Pocahontas County Road 601, she had admired a certain house, floating in a sea of unmowed grass some forty feet from the road. It was about four miles outside of town, a plain old deserted Ohio farmhouse with no other house in sight. The place was not a complete ruin. White paint still stuck uncertainly to the clapboards, but wherever these touched sills or cornerboards, dark brown stains seeped into the paint like caries. A porch ran the width of the house, unpainted and sagging almost to the ground. The dirt drive was so overgrown it was hard to see. An enormous willow stood between the road and the porch, making the house look a thousand years old.

Now Jane drove south on 601 to take another look at this house. It was there all right, but it was not quite the same. In the summer, upholstered with so much greenery, it had looked small, protected and hospitable. The riches of weeds and wild vines and unpruned bushes that framed it all around had made the place seem, if anything, freer of its gifts than respectable residences. But now in February it looked defenseless, which it really was, and bigger, now that death had stripped away the green frame, and empty, gnawed by winter from the inside. A lot of the front windows were punched out; she hadn't noticed that before. Still, its ugliness made its affinity with Jane all the clearer. Such a house was like solitude itself: something no one else wanted. And God knows a person couldn't charge you much to live there.

Already in February the willow was full of ambiguous promise. It had no leaves but was strangely glowing; the long tilted branches filled up the space between house and road with a cloud of parallel yellow strings like a mysterious musical instrument or a sorcerer's rain of gold. It was just as well to be scared of the place, not to take to the place too unreservedly. That was how you felt about yourself as well.

Standing by the door of the fleshpink Dodge, before she had even gotten up the nerve to walk up on the porch of the abandoned house and peer in the broken windows, Jane decided to move in. Her gaze swooped up the blotchy facade, and she discovered in the milky twilight a rippling stave of electric wires, dotted with nodes and switches like an unplayed bar of music, that ran from a wooden pole to her house. The place had electricity—she would be able to read. A light snow was beginning to fall; the discolored front seat of the Dodge was powdering up like a teacake with flakes that blew in through the half-open windows. Suddenly Jane was more like other humans than not like them. She worried about cold and the dark, electric light and water, ice, fire, and wind. Broken windows could be fixed, though not by Jane. She had no money to see to such things. In the last three years, she had never at any one time had more than fifty dollars to her name.

But she knew what to do. She turned the Dodge around on Pocahontas County Road 601, and, having escaped twenty-four hours before from the dormitory and the roommate, headed into town to look for someone to live with her in that house.

Or for someone to take her home for the night: Those were more likely the words she put to herself. And did she really find Jimmy Fluharty in the next quarter hour? Such luck from the get-go does not school a girl to look down her nose at chance. She passed Arbuckle's Jiffy Super, crossed an alley—archipelagos of broken glass on fire under a street lamp—opened the door of Baggy's Tavern and peered into the gloom. And there he was, a certain blue-eyed, haggard cowboy she had spotted last week from the street door of the DRC. He had glinted like bullion on Felix's side of the bar. Why did she think cowboy? She really didn't know, beyond his goldenness, the leathery pouches around the eyes, which might have had *Wells Fargo* printed on them, and a certain roughneck grace when he flipped the dishrag. He was washing glasses, a job always reserved by Felix for some sottish princeling down on his luck. Of course the fellow had to have talent too. He must play the harmonica or add up figures fast or something. And now she found him again at a table in Baggy's behind a row of empty shotglasses that glowed red like footlights under his chin. The rosy glamor was borrowed, maybe from the EXIT sign behind his back, maybe from his big red book. As for the book, his nose was in it and he was alone.

Jane wanted her nose in it too. She wanted to know what he was reading in the dark. She slid into his booth, and he looked up at the disturbance with narrow, slightly bloodshot eyes. But when he saw Jane there, pleasure rose in his face. He leaned across the table as she took out a Pall Mall and said theatrically: "Mademoiselle, may I ignite your cigarette?" Then came the ten-gallon sweep of the arm, the tiny lariat loop of the match.

Jane smiled at this naked interest, which was not the local usage. Although hardly older than she, he was nothing like a college boy. He was more distinct in shape, more finely finished than a college boy, but also more corroded. His goldenness was tarnished, his boyish face tired.

"Did you just blow into town?" she asked.

"From New York. I don't strike you as a New York type?" he said. "Well, I'm not. I'm from California. I went to New York to seek my fortune. Until lately, I was a child prodigy," he added, with a sweet smile. "Then I became a bum."

"A harmonica player," Jane guessed.

"A painter." He reached for a smoke himself and Jane sneaked a look at his book, reading upside down and backward. Her eyes widened. THE SEXUAL LIFE OF SAVAGES, said the top of one page, and MOTIVES FOR MARRYING, the other. He had been cartooning palm trees in the margin; his wet black pen lay open in the crack.

"Would I were a mouth organist," he was saying.

"Really? Why?"

"It cost me my last dime to get trucked to this burg with my paintings. I don't know what I'm doing here."

"Lotta stuff, eh?" Jane said slyly, for she was holding a whole empty house behind her back.

"You should see it. I never give a painting away, except to a woman I'm fucking."

He shook his head. And though the point was how many paintings that left in his possession, Jane saw the polygamous spoor of his art spread out like a night burglar's tracks across the apartment walls of the U.S.A., and she tried to smooth the wonder from her face. He really had been around.

"You'll see—I'll show you," he promised, as though he were planning to give Jane a painting soon.

"Another shot, sir?" asked the waitress.

"Not for me. One for the lady." Then he bent over the table to Jane, lifted a golden lock out of his blue-green eyes and confided: "No need to destroy my liver now that I have you. What did you say your name was?"

Jane saw that he didn't want to get too drunk, in case things went well and they— Both of them smiled. "Jane," she said.

Later it seemed queer how even as one eye had told her *This is the one*, the other had said *He's not your type*. He was too handsome, though he hardly seemed to notice this liability himself. He was amorous and wistful as well as corrupt. One thing was certain: Philip Turner would have hated him. Uneasily she asked: "What went wrong in New York City?"

"It was like I wasn't there," he said. "I wasn't used to that. I always expected to be famous."

"That's odd," Jane said. "I always expected to be invisible."

He shrugged. "It didn't seem that hard. My old man owned a Jolly Gas a mile outside of Palm Springs. I used to clean Bob Hope's windshield. Lana Turner peed in our ladies' room. I mean, everybody was famous. Mother played bass in black velvet pedal pushers at the Chi-Chi Club. I won the Palm Springs High School Art Medal and got a hundred dollars for it. Money fell out of the sky, you know? My first job was with Baron Moritz von Rosenwasser, interior decorator to the stars. He wanted to adopt me. My little brother Rex was dating the Pepsi heiress. I hardly even noticed we were broke. I had my own shack behind the house for a studio. One day I set up my paintings in front of a corset shop on Date Palm Drive and Jimmy Durante peeled off five hundred bucks for one of my *Rufous Sierras*. Just like that. I got offered a scholarship at Chouinard. Naaa, I told em, I couldn't be bothered with school. Pete and Ernestine still had their honeymoon car in the garage, a 1942 Buick Flashback Speedster Roadster. I took it over and headed for—What are you staring at?"

Besides his eyes, which in this light glimmered opaquely like turquoise, "Your—self-confidence," Jane said.

"Poo. Don't kid yourself. I'm paying for it now."

"What do you mean?"

"I knew I couldn't be any worse than those fakes," he said. "But in New York I was invisible. Or just a bum. It turned so cold my ass couldn't believe it. I got a job in a building on Broadway and Canal, running the elevator. Watched the roadster collecting tickets until they towed it away. I always meant to go get it back."

"Where were you living?" Jane asked, since now she saw it couldn't have been in his car.

"In a hole on Broome Street. I had to step over the drunks in the stairwell every time I went up there. But I'll tell you what. I liked it. I liked drinking Gallo White Port out of a paper bag with the bums. I liked to go to gallery openings and stand around and fart. I was even drawing a little at night. Want to know why I left?"

"You were invisible," Jane said.

"No! Someone saw me. Someone finally saw me. This Egyptian, anyway he said he was Egyptian, struck up a conversation with me one day in the elevator. Ostovar was his name. Extremely handsome guy. He was interested in my painting. Who did I like? Gorky, I said, and he said, That tragic fire, or something like that.

"He took me out to lunch. Said he represented an older gentleman who liked to help gifted young men. *He has seen you already*, he tells me. The guy was offering a studio, living expenses, artist's materials and five hundred dollars a month."

"Five hundred bucks," Jane whispered. It was a huge amount of money.

"All he wanted was to be allowed to visit me once a month—to talk."

"Wow," Jane said. "So you ran away."

"Oh no, no." Jimmy sat in a swirl of blue smoke. "They gave me time to make up my mind. I had a date to meet the old guy himself in a restaurant on Fiftieth Street. How will I know him? I asked. Ostovar says, *Tell the maître d' that you are Jimmy.* And before this could sink in he says, *We must do something with your clothes. No strings attached. You will enjoy to be dressed by Lodovico* . . . So I went the next day to this tailor on Reade Street and got fitted with a gorgeous suit, shirts, ties, everything.

"I go to the restaurant wearing this suit. I told the maître d' who I was and he led me to a table for two without batting an eye. Then I waited. Ten minutes. Twenty. I ordered a Jack Daniels on the rocks. It was a small place, I could see everyone in it, and no one was looking at me. A half hour went by, forty minutes. I kept telling myself I only wanted a peep at the old guy, but then I thought maybe he had come in, looked me over and changed his mind."

Jane studied the blue-green eyes under their awning of rough gold lashes, the deeply sunny skin. "I doubt that," she said.

"Well, why should I care if he had? I wasn't going to do it. Was I? Then I figured this was all somebody's joke, but there I was in that magnificent suit, bought and paid for.

"I ordered another Jack Daniels. Another one after that. Colors started to glow. I relaxed. That's when it happened."

"What?"

"I realized I'd been expecting this. Expecting fate to save my life. I wanted that money."

Jane was thrilled. Her heart beat in her fingertips.

"I left. I didn't run. I stood up and walked out the door. I passed the maître d'—he said, *Good* night, sir! And that was all."

"Wait . . . " Jane said, unwilling for the story to end.

"I never went back to the elevator. I paid a kid who was dropping out of Pratt to take me and my stuff west in his van. But he was only going to Harmonia Springs."

Jane said: "Maybe there wasn't any old guy. Maybe it was just Ostovar."

"I thought of that, but why wouldn't he come out and tell me? I would have had a hard time saying no to him."

"You mean—"

"He was smooth as silk. He looked like Nefertiti, and his clothes—even I could see he was wearing a fucking fortune. I didn't figure I would be bored."

"You really think you would have—"

Jimmy slowly shook his head. "I don't know. If he had said to me just once, I'd like to look at your paintings. I mean, he knew Gorky. But he didn't. You know, if I was in his position and I wanted to make use of you"—he picked up Jane's hand, playing the ironic, debonair Ostovar, blandishing with the same eyes that were assigning her price—"I wouldn't want to see your paintings either. What if they were terrible?"

Suddenly he burst out laughing, and so did Jane. "I know I should have stayed to get a look at the guy, but I was afraid. I didn't know what would become of me." He sighed and lowered his chin into his palms. A moment later he looked up at Jane again and added ruefully, "Wait till you see my suit."

"I can't wait," said Jane.

They smiled at each other. Jimmy picked up her hand again and pressed it to his lips. He said deliberately: "If I'd had you then, someone like you, I could have risked it. There wasn't a soul in the city of New York who would have missed me."

"My God," Jane said, shocked. "I guess that's possible, that the guy would just—do away with you."

"I don't mean that," Jimmy said. "I mean gotten lost, completely lost. Sunken away. Ruined."

"Oh," Jane said, and stared.

She had found her adventurer, her abandoned housemate, her twin boy—though he was not her type. What he had found in her she was not sure. They slept that night on his air mattress in the unused kitchen of the DRC, walled in by ghostly floor mops and lime-caked buckets, and by Jimmy's seven-foot canvases, turned face to the wall but looming like Dame Nightmares with their bloodstained backs and ragged skirts.

They started patching windows at the house on Pocahontas County Road 601 the next day.

○
○
● **The**

soul

of

commerce

For six more weeks it was cold and Jane and Jimmy took to their bed. On the first of May, the sun came out. The upturned fields across the road began to bake red, and fat clouds loafed across the sky.

As soon as it was good and hot, the friends of the Soul of Commerce convened. This was an educational society. They sat around the porch and told each other what they knew. Jane was in love, for she loved her fellow human with ease from a learning position, which in this case was also a reclining position. Possibly she had not been so happy since the day she was born.

She was on an old plush sofa that had been left behind by the last tenant. She and Jimmy had dragged the thing to the porch for fear something alive might crawl out of it, and no doubt it had.

Felix was at the other end of the sofa, upright, not slumped like Jane. He had been there, except when he went to tend bar at the Downtown, since too early this morning to know when, sitting up big and black and still as a monument to himself, one hand around a bottle of beer, the other spread over a knee as large as a skull, the end of a six-pack parked by his scuffed and backless romeos. He would often be there already in the morning when Jane and Jimmy came down. Sometimes he would not even get out of his car. They would find him behind the wheel of his Plymouth, the car basking in tall grass like a carp in bottom weeds with the motor quietly running, and he would drive away as soon as he saw them.

Today he was on the sofa. His cousin, Officer Rollo, sat on a folding chair with his police chief's hat in his lap. Willie Usher, who had provided the folding chair, also a rusty stoverack on which hot dogs were cooking in the grass, a large electric wall clock that said NEHI across its face, and the lavender toilet seat in the outhouse, was sitting on the edge of the porch where the steps would be if there were steps. His bare feet were lost in deep grass. Next to him were young Fred Blood, a grocery checker at Arbuckle's Jiffy Super, and Roger O. Booth, an actor, not acting at present, Jimmy's childhood friend, formerly Albert Huzzy, of Rancho Mirage, California. Roger had brought the hot dogs, Felix the beer. Jimmy crouched in the grass, pushing hot dogs around with a fork.

Except for the hiss from the stoverack, it's quiet and hot and everyone looks across the blacktop at rows of dark green corn that seem to rush back down the slope towards the watchers, the threads of dark red earth between them giving off heat like a great big toaster. A hawk hangs over the cornfield, then, tipping slightly, begins to roll down the sky. Two blackbirds careen into view from nowhere and chase it off. Just then a car goes by—a convertible crowded with punks from Xenia.

"How them birds can go so fast in this heat?" Felix says. "I wonder do a bird fly faster than a car can drive. Say, Fred!"

"Good fishing weather," says Officer Rollo, fanning himself with his hat.

"Too hot," Felix says. He does not want to go fishing with his cousin, because he can't smoke reefer when Officer Rollo is present.

"Hell no a bird can't fly faster than a car," Willie says. "Can it, Fred?"

Fred Blood, the grocery checker, is a compendium of information, but does not always rise to the occasion. Earlier, before the arrival of Officer Rollo, Fred was trying to teach Jane how to smoke marijuana. Now Jane is unchanged, Felix, who assisted, is unchanged, but Fred's head is down between his knees.

Officer Rollo says reasonably: "Well, what kind of bird and what kind of car do you mean, Willie?"

"Irregardless of the brand, he still can't beat a modern automobile. That's progress."

"Blackbird," Felix says.

"Naw," Willie replies. "Your blackbird only looks fast. He ain't going anywhere. He just flies down to the south end of town in the winter."

"He could beat a car if he wanted to," says Felix.

"He don't want to," Willie says.

Officer Rollo stands up, hat in his hands. "Sure you won't go fishing?"

"Got no bait. Ima go in the morning."

Officer Rollo works mornings. "I heard someplace a buzzard was the fastest bird," the police chief remarks.

"Some birds fly sixty miles an hour," comes a harassed, patient voice from between Fred's knees.

"My stars!" Officer Rollo says. "That's travelling."

"A buzzard isn't one of them."

"See that," Felix says with satisfaction. "That's because a bird don't have no wheels dragging on the road. Pitcher a buzzard with tires. Hee-hee-hee. Sixty miles an hour. I'm sorry I didn't ride no money on it."

"That buzzard is no Fleetwood," Willie reminds him. "And look at a chicken."

Felix says, "A chicken ain't even a bird."

"It ain't! Then what is it?"

Felix is silent for a moment, gazing at the darkening cornfield. "It's a *food*," he says. "Man done made it, just like a hot dog. Like baloney. It's progress."

"Don't tell me about progress," Willie says. "Baloney don't run around a barnyard flapping its wings."

Fred raises his head. His eyes are red and he wears a puzzled expression. "A modern chicken is a man-made bird," he says.

"That young Fred always was a smart young fella," Officer Rollo says. "Just remember, young man, it's never too late to start to college." He puts his hat on his head and steps off the porch, going home to dinner in the sky-blue Ford with *Harmonia Springs Police Department* on the side and CHIEF in smaller letters inside a blue silver star on the door.

"What did he say?" Fred asks, blinking.

"He said you was smart," Felix replies.

"Oh," Fred says, not interested, returning his head to his knees.

Long before anyone put a college there, Harmonia Springs lured a string of utopian founders—Owenites, Nicholites, abolitionists and freedmen, Anthroposophists and organic-egg-raisers—whose descendants now walked the streets on all sides of town. As the son of old Fred Blood, a barber who loathed the teeming whackos and uppity niggers and the Jew-filled college and everything they stood for, young Fred had started out an accomplished hick, good at fixing up old cars, driving them around bends on two wheels, shooting rifles at stop signs, and playing the accordion. Then he penetrated the library of the forbidden college and taught himself entomology and Korean. He was offered a scholarship to Harvard, and almost went, but all at once he renounced books, except for some tracts on Yoga, and kept himself tranquil morning to night with marijuana. (Though well known in Sausage Junction, the black section of town, the moneygreen flower was still rare at colleges, even at advanced Harmonia.) He lived by himself in an empty room on Back Main, right behind the parking lot of Arbuckle's Jiffy Super. He claimed not to have talked to his father in five years, but on the job he sometimes had to add up his mother's groceries. Once in a while Mrs. Blood would load up a cart, pay, and push the full bags towards the checker. Out on PC Road 601, Jimmy and Jane guiltily ate a lot of Bakeless Frozen Pies obtained in this fashion.

Fred had never had a girlfriend and, like Felix, was impossible to picture as half of a couple. But Jane saw how he looked at Roger sometimes. The bleary, artless gaze of the peanut-butter-colored eyes between the coathook ears could only be described as smitten. Roger, who looked like a B-movie star you couldn't quite place, did not seem to notice. All of them knew that Fred was the weakest, the child, the cripple. No one expected to get any important lessons from Fred and yet, besides being a walking encyclopedia, he had once, in a stunning return of the superhick, taken the whole society for a ride after midnight in Felix's big car. He knew the back roads around Harmonia Springs so well he had turned the headlights off and flown them airily, weightlessly over the hills under a full moon, so deftly that nobody was scared.

And Fred must have wanted to teach somebody something, considering the dogged way he stuck to his project of showing Jane how to smoke pot. Many joints were wasted on her before she at last got high, and meanwhile she insulted the intelligence of her benefactor by questioning that such a sensation really existed. One day when Officer Rollo was not expected, Fred squatted beside her on the porch and handed her eight bombers, one after the other, forbidding anyone else to take a single toke. Fred, Willie, and Felix were all coaching her:

"Hold it in, hold it in."

"Not like a gopher. IN YOUR LUNGS."

"I be dogged, lookit her cough like a six grader sneaking a smoke."

Finishing the seventh, Jane was a little dizzy just from holding her breath. "I think I feel something," she said.

"She's stoned. Look at that smirk," Willie said optimistically. Willie had long since given up marijuana, but he wished for Jane to cultivate the habit so that he could soften her with small donations of the stuff.

"Could you read Wigglesworth?" Fred asked her gravely. This was a dense little study of animal courtship that had slipped behind a radiator in Fred's room when he purged his books. When he found it, he had given it to Jane.

"Read Wigglesworth right now? What for?"

"I didn't say, Jane, would you like to read it. I said could you read it."

Jane shrugged. "Sure I could."

"Well, you're not high," Fred said, grimly lighting the eighth joint.

"Good lord! Don't th'ow away no more good reefer on that woman," Felix said. "She some kind of machinery."

At last Fred brought over something that looked like an ounce of baking chocolate wrapped in foil, and a green glass houkah full of scummy water, with a striped tube. Jane took to hashish right away. The houkah belonged to some caterpillar on a mushroom, the hashish was like the amber over which ballet dancers rub their slippers and violinists their bows.

For the first ten minutes, or it might have been half an hour, Jane could not understand English. This was wonderful in itself, but slowly she perceived the reason: Words were sliding back into people's mouths like long pieces of spaghetti, rather than coming out of them. Somewhere an invisible switch had been elbowed; the tape of the day was being played backwards. Jane concentrated on translating the whinnying noise this made back into English words, but by the time she succeeded in doing so, the tape was going forward again. Of the many lessons to be taken from this experience, the first was that she could lose discourse and still be sane. Like the Indian woman who was marooned on Santa Barbara Island for thirty years and then found babbling in a tongue that did not exist, the whole time Jane had understood herself perfectly. Now she saw she could lose the talk that connected her to other people and find it again without going out of her mind. For until now that had always been her definition of madness.

The bed they had taken to, till the cold relented, was there waiting for them. As sexual delight would be for every woman, if nature weren't a miser, Jane thought. It was a white scrolled iron bedstead, small for two on less than friendly terms, rusty and scratched, with painted roses on the headboard and footboard. A frankly sexual bed, pretty and corrupt. Fate had simply left it there for them.

And Jimmy, the boy with whom she found herself in this bed, had the trait she most admired at twenty—the air of a shrewd and golden orphan, one who had been careless enough, as Lady Bracknell put it, to lose both parents. Of course Jimmy was so exquisite that various earthlings, including his biological parents, fell over themselves to suckle him. But this he could take or leave, self-suckler that he was—true, he generally took it.

Of course he had had to grow up among parents like almost everyone else. But he, unlike Jane, had taken over. At sixteen he had driven the Fluharty family out of one of its many sprawling additions, a half-improved plyboard shack a bit into the dunes, once a dream of rental property, with sand blowing under the ill-hung door. He had said *I'm taking over*, and Pete and Ernestine both stepped out of his way, impressed. Jane could imagine how they all had gazed at him, Pete and Ernestine, and brother Rex, who came second, and Roger, who fell in love with Jimmy then and there. Now Jane, too, had seen Jimmy taking over, demoniac but coherent, his fists speared all around with glittering hardware, his gold hair curving in the sun like a winged crown. He was a beauty and a power. And that wasn't all. He could clean and fry catfish, he could boil beans on a hotplate, he had learned how to eat cheap from Pete, and he taught all that to Jane. He showed her how to change the oil in the Dodge, how to glaze windows, how to prime the pump, how to produce a clean white room overnight.

Jane had had lovers before Jimmy, but they could not teach her anything. It was not their fault that they could not teach her. She was obtuse, opaque, for she thought she knew more than she did. Those erotic compositions she had played with her fingers on her own sexual parts were interesting, certainly, but they had at bottom something dispassionate about them—

something like the cold-blooded lust of gods and goddesses who can have whatever they imagine.

Actually Jane had no idea what sex with another person could be. And having never desired with her body anyone in particular, having never been anywhere near the enchanted woods of that hunt where you wander lost, athirst, your arrows all scattered, unable to be tired, desperate for any glimpse or spoor of what you already know to be unobtainable by effort, she was too stupid even to be disappointed.

Now, with Jimmy, she could be disappointed.

He was not her type, but he had a boyishly hairless chest, a grown man's muscular legs, and elegant buttocks covered in tawny lace, the same dark gold that feathered his thighs and framed his erection—which, he pointed out to Jane, was alas the common gnarled and blue venous type, not like brother Rex's perfectly white cock. Jimmy was a fund of this kind of information.

He was wise about sex, wiser than Jane, which wasn't saying much. He almost made Jane feel layered like a rose, almost turned her into the spotted hind in the ensorcelled wood, almost but not quite. Jimmy said sex was truer than art, since it was for everybody and not subject to fashion. He had known this since 1959, when it suddenly dawned on him that his Aunt Junie and Uncle Thedford Fluharty did it too. Jimmy would have thought it ungallant to turn a woman down. One day, climbing the dark fetid stairs on Broome Street, he had encountered his fourth-floor neighbor going unsteadily towards the corner bar where she spent her evenings. A cross-faced, stick-thin West Indian grandmother, who spent her days at a window cursing her daughters in the next building, she suddenly lifted her skirt for Jimmy, said "Come to mama," and there in the dark stairwell he quickly obliged. He had looked for her after that with baffled friendliness, but she didn't seem to know him when she saw him.

And though there came to be nights when he would roll over and go to sleep with barely a sigh if she rolled over first, he never refused Jane. Jane was hypnotized, thrilled, and faintly discouraged by all she was hearing. A kind of abandon she had always hoped might exist in the world was coming true, and yet she felt left out. Jane, what a relief, was not frigid, to use the adjective in mode at the time, that had strayed (not very far) from kitchen appliances into domestic relations. But, no way around it, compared to the creatures she was hearing about, she remained a querulous, parsimonious, self-conscious lover; and in the moment of coming, though it was far better than not coming, she reminded herself less of a libertine than of an envy-bitten charlady stealing the silver a piece at a time. When Jimmy would lie exhausted next to her, purring like a fine engine in his sleep, she stared at the ceiling, wondering if this was as far as she was going to go.

She even began to wonder if it wasn't a sham, this pairing of human women with human men, an expurgated copy of what you were really looking for. Who knew what human was? How did humans happen to perfume their old shoes with the glandular secretions of cats? Why should they share a liver enzyme solely with the shark? Why did they prize a parboiled hue so strikingly like a pig's? Weren't these hints at something unspeakable? And though they pretended to marry for life like wolves and cranes, you could scarcely read a page of Wigglesworth on freaks of animal courtship without being reminded of some human couple in your old neighborhood, Joe and Edith Gutman carrying on like bowerbirds or roebucks or marmosets—so devoid of instinctual guides is everything human.

So maybe it was a big mistake, Jane would think, staring at cobwebs like mouse hammocks on the ceiling as a pair of headlights swooped by on Pocahontas County Road 601, that women are stuck with men. Aren't men merely renovated females? And these made-over, secondhand girlfriends are such a bore that you go into heat and take no notice of them—for every woman knows, doesn't she, thought Jane, in the privacy of her boudoir, that she goes into heat—and then what a sorry excuse a man is for all she had hoped. Isn't it plain that my lover awaits me in outer space? That he left me temporarily to these bumptious stand-ins, but I can get him back? Then she thought of the shape of his prick, and the color of his reptilian wings, and other wild and fruitless ideas.

So while Jimmy slept, between lessons, Jane dreamed of lovers from outer space, but the more he told her of girls he had known right here on earth, the harder it became to resort to such arcana. There were women on earth to whom possibly any human male, but certainly Jimmy, was sufficient. Jimmy had always done well with very rich girls in the far West. These seemed to be so many colonial planters' daughters with lush, equatorial imaginations as well as incessant orgasms and their own convertibles. Above all there was Bernardine. "She would do anything." (Uneasily:) Anything you asked? "Anything you could think of. And then a hundred more things you never thought of."

Bernardine's father owned a factory in the Mojave Desert, along the Mexican border on the American side. He employed two hundred women, Mexican and Indian, to sew canvas boat cushions on heavy-duty sewing machines. Campo is hot, bald desert all around, but the father lived there in splendor among horses, servants, and mistresses handpicked from his two hundred sewing machine operators, as well as a Mexican bride Bernardine's age installed in a new pink hacienda. He was mayor of the settlement and he owned the police.

Bernardine lived mostly at a Santa Barbara boarding school. Jimmy met her at art camp in the Sierras, but that summer Bernardine was not exhibiting anything but her copious vaginal secretions. She drove a new yellow Thunderbird and after a few days, Jimmy, the prodigy, and his instructors had all admired the towering ponderosas from the backseat.

"Maybe she was desperate for friends," Jane said weakly.

"Oh no. She liked it. She had the wettest cunt I've ever seen. She was a good sport, Bernardine. She didn't make a pest of herself. If I was busy, she would find somebody else and drop by again later."

"Maybe she couldn't come," Jane said. "I've heard about girls like that."

"She could come hundreds of times!"

"Maybe she just said so."

"She didn't just say so."

This was the voice of experience, so Jane asked resentfully: "Gosh. How could you let a girl like that get away?"

Jimmy laughed. "You know how it is. Some things are meant for the circus, some things are meant for real life."

But of course you couldn't keep a young woman like that to yourself, so the question had never come up. Bernardine even had a private life of sorts. If she got restless at three or four in the morning, she would drive down from the camp to the San Bernardino Freeway between Beaumont and Banning, when no one was on the road but truckers. She would take off her clothes. And where the freeway starts to pour down out of the mountains, a place of a feathery falling through space into the desert's silvery net of warm air, where the semis really roll, she would give the truckdrivers a show. She would slow down to fifty or so, and when the truckers came highballing down the grade doing eighty, they would sail around her. And suddenly they would be blowing horns, crazily flicking the Christmas tree lights on their trailers, hanging out over the cab door, reaching for her with big arms and shirts sleeves full of wind, throwing cigarettes, styrofoam coffee cups, and money.

"Reckless, eh," Jimmy said with satisfaction.

"She should have been arrested," Jane replied.

"Well, she would have cared less."

"Are you sure she really liked it? She wasn't just crazy?"

Jimmy laughed. "She liked it. She loved it."

"Thank God she wasn't talented," Jane said, "in any other way."

"She wasn't stupid," Jimmy said. "She liked my paintings. She almost got her old man to lay down three hundred bucks for one when he came to see her once. He had his checkbook out and everything."

"What happened?"

"I said to myself, Well, James, this is your big chance, and jacked up the price to 3,000. He put away his checkbook, smiled at me and said, Frankly, young man, I think you've been taken care of far too well already." Jimmy rolled over on his back in the rose bed and folded his hands thoughtfully over his stomach. "Can you imagine? This is a man with two hundred maids and twenty-five mistresses and he thinks I'm spoiled because his daughter blew me a couple of times."

But sometimes Jane thought Jimmy a little spoiled too. Maybe she wasn't rich enough, maybe she lacked the equatorial latitudes, green canopies jewelled with orchids and macaws, where he would be at home. Sometimes she didn't care how beautiful, how powerful—Stop this man, she whispered to herself, before he takes over. She knew she had stumbled upon the sort of unpropertied prince some other girl, some rich girl, would be glad to give her life to. This girl was a wife, and Roger a sidekick to the manner born. But Jane was a democrat who would not give her life even to God.

Besides that air of a changeling suckled by coyotes, since Jimmy had been a child prodigy, he had already had a rise and fall. It was in New York City as he ran the elevator, tipped two bits by touts and shiny-suited shysters even before he encountered the elegant procurer Ostovar, that his fall had begun. He was a little tired. Back in the desert he had felt equal to the landscape he grew up in. He would go out to his shack, would refuse to come in for dinner, would paint the rufous Sierras all night and wait for the schoolbus in the morning. Now he found he had no more energy than other people. He wasn't used to it. He struggled to feel the flatter ground under his feet.

And since there was something splendid in defeat, too, provided the defeat was total, he fell from boy wonder straight to derelict, skipping all the intermediate stages. It was a boy's beauty he had—small wonder a pederast had tried to purchase him, but it was a good thing this connoisseur had never seen him drunk. Four or five shots of bourbon, a few beers, a half quart of white port, and he was transformed into a choleric old wino before your eyes. His cheeks sagged and were covered with whitish grizzle. His nose bulbed and flattened. His eyes bulged with crimson threads like prairie oysters. He was a bespittled coot, beyond redemption.

For that is how a golden changeling goes on a drunk. "I won't *cope*," he promised. He would describe the calculating jackasses who now passed themselves off as artists; and if he was in a bar, and any were on the premises, he hastened to tell them, too, and often had to run for his life or, quite as often, to take a beating. When he reached the bottom he confessed, "I'm an asshole like the other assholes!" Then he passed out and began the long invisible belly-float back to the surface. He could not be aroused, not even by a woman shrieking at him, under these conditions, though he could be dragged from place to place.

Jimmy would not cope. That was his boast, and Jane, a coper since the age of fourteen, currently waiting tables fifteen hours a week at the Haslebacher Family Restaurant in Pocahontas City, did not know what to think. Jimmy said a real artist got over false shame and learned how to bully, hornswoggle and cajole others who were not artists into paying such little bills and charges as arose. Those others had the time to waste on work.

"I'm not an artist," Jane said suspiciously. "Do you think I have time to waste on work?"

"I consider you an artist," Jimmy assured her.

But Jane was not reassured. She believed, almost as much as Roger she believed, in the landless prince behind this protocol, but in practice it was difficult, in fact impossible, for her to make even one long distance telephone call to her father, Philip Turner, to ask him for money.

Jimmy was exasperated. "He's got it. He can afford it. Be a hard nose. Don't let him off the hook."

"It's not worth the grief to me," Jane said. "Besides, he'd say no. I would lower myself and have nothing to show for it."

"Lie to him," Jimmy advised. "Tell him you broke your leg in a car accident."

"He'd say that's too bad, you should drive more carefully."

Jimmy was shocked. "That's terrible. He's your father, flesh of your flesh."

"I'm telling you! He'd be indignant. He'd say if you can afford a car you don't need me to pay for the broken leg. Besides, what is my daughter doing driving around without insurance?"

"Call him," Jimmy said. "Don't be a martyr. Life is too short. Make him pay."

But instead Jane paid, and when he called them in the desert, collect, once or twice a month, Pete and Ernestine paid. They sent moneygrams, cellophane packages of jockey shorts, and a canned ham. Jane was jealous; she was sure her father would feel no guilt even if she starved to death.

And so when the weather turned hot and battalions of May beetles loud as trolleys floated through the unscreened windows, when Jimmy lay asleep and Jane lay staring at the cobwebby ceiling, she was relieved to think that others loved her, not only Jimmy. When she walked out on the front porch in the morning to dump the dustpan of May beetles, still clacking dully against each other, into the skunk cabbages, she was glad to see the mysterious Felix or even the knowing, patient, munificent predator Willie Usher—anyone but Jimmy. Jimmy was too fair—the face of love was always dark. And for all his princely schnorrer's scruples, a bit of moneygreen tarnish soiled his golden crown.

Willie Usher, dark as something moving in the underbrush, looked more like the face of love, but of course, a guy like that was impossible. And why impossible, when there he sat on the porch, guffawing with Felix and Officer Rollo and even with Jimmy in a bluff, careless, cordial manner that was meant to say to Jane: Don't you see your little playmate is inconsequential to me? Because he knew how to vanish into the forest, Willie did, and how to appear out of nowhere; but when he was ready to show himself, he came pounding after her like King Kong —that was why. True, she was the only one who saw his gorilla act. Jimmy never noticed. It made her ears pump heat like two pink radiators. Willie told her too exactly what he wanted.

Willie was a black, very black businessman who refused to try to look respectable, around thirty-five years old, heavily, even sinisterly handsome, Jane thought, with an incipient belly like a shield in front. The Soul of Commerce did well, or anyway the contents of the junk shop would often spill out the front door onto the sidewalk, ANYTHING FOR A DOLLAR, and Willie would be in his element, dickering with twenty people at once in the great sloppy hustle of a one-man bazaar, a fair with one event, until Officer Rollo or his subordinate, Patrolman Dickey, arrived to remonstrate and Willie packed up his boxes again and went indoors.

Everyone is in the junk business now; twenty years later every suburban block has its yard sale every Saturday, its twenty-five fairly new dresses hanging dispiritedly from the porch railing in front of fifteen square yards of broken appliances, being fingered by the neighbor who will hang out her own ugly dresses next week, but Jane would always remember that Willie D. Usher predicted this, and was the first, the premier acte, at a time when most people thought used clothes meant somebody died in it and a junkstore was a place—run by a hobos' mission or a fence—where nice people didn't go, at least not if anyone was looking. At first Willie Usher had called his store Aaabracadabra Antiques, to assure himself front position in the Yellow Pages. But after a short while he had tired of that genteel nomenclature and had one of the kids on Back Main paint raw white over the old sign, and then he mounted a step-ladder himself and painted in: JUNK. *Willie Usher, The Soul of Commerce, I.P.*

He told Jane he didn't care for fussing with antiques, where the ticket was to look for something a person didn't think he wanted and kick up the price so the farmer saw his grandma's old bedstead in your window for ten times what you paid him and felt like a fool. "For that you have to be smart," he said. "There are a lot of smart people in this business, and if you have to be the smartest, you sure to get burned. But a dumb little guy like me don't have to worry."

The philosophy of the Soul of Commerce was simple: Buy cheap, sell cheap, and don't stop. Willie Usher did stop, though, for weeks at a time. For a month he would be there night and day spilling over onto the sidewalk with fifteen ragamuffins discharging his errands up and down Back Main, and then he would disappear. Sometimes he buried himself in the shop's basement with his molds, for he had artistic pretensions, though he did not overestimate their value. He made plaster casts, which he smeared a fecal, vaguely iridescent bronze when they were dry, of the peace symbol, the few astrological signs he had gotten around to copying, the Budweiser insignia, a hand that looked freshly amputated but was making the victory sign (V), and the Great Seal of the United States—something hideous for everybody, as he well knew. This work saved him as long as it lasted from having to answer his phone, which, of course, defeated the purpose of the superfluous A's in his listing in the Yellow Pages, which he hadn't bothered to change. Half the time he let the telephone service lapse for non-payment. He was like this in everything: shrewd and naive, ambitious and go-to-hell, generous but always closing a deal somewhere, honest, in fact blunt, and yet close-mouthed. If he had successes he was innately discreet about them. Jane knew this well, since, you could say, she was one of them.

Willie was appearing daily in some get-up thrown together in the basement of the Soul of Commerce: say, a plaid smoking jacket and blue foil birthday party hat, with a pair of rubber antlers strapped to his forehead. He appeared neglected as well as bizarre, a little overweight, and fifteen hard years older than Jane. He lived on candy bars, milkshakes, and Downtown Recreation Club hamburgers; he hacked and wheezed, belched and farted, and in hay-fever season carried on like a terminal case, but Jane could not remember his ever taking to his bed. True, she did not know where his bed was. No one did.

He was really rather pure. He did not touch tobacco, alcohol, or coffee. When he brushed by you he smelled almost pickled in flowery soap; a lot cleaner than Jane, who went nowadays, not very often, to a big red cold-water pump in a shed out back. He was a straight-standing man with a long, powerful stride, but you remembered him draped in some patient, skeptical pose against a wall of boxes, his big arms crossed, looking you over until you went away. Then you had to look back over your shoulder quick to catch him in motion. Often he would already be gone.

He would go into the Downtown wearing a pair of balloons down the front of a buxom Persian lamb coat.

"Hello, boys!"

"No women allowed," Felix said, reaching across the bar to poke him.

"That'll be fifteen dollars," Willie boomed out.

"Is that all you worth?" the bartender asked.

"That was just a quick feel."

He seemed to have computed his own exact worth, and to be wearing it on his back. Once Jane apologized for taking him away from his work, and he told her flatly: "My time is worth nothing." But if she glanced back quick enough, she might catch him measuring others, his face strangely undeluded and severe. In his shop, if someone kept chipping away at a low price until Willie got bored; or if something he thought he had a claim to was flatly, rudely, denied him. She often saw that face, if she turned around swiftly enough, as she walked away.

She had gotten her typewriter from him—a 1942 Royal newsroom model, heavy and black as a cannonball. Writes real good, he said, and it did, and he offered it to her cheap, very cheap. "Why you so squinty-eyed?" he said when she did not take it right away. "That's seven dollars *to you*, darling. Pull up a crate, try it out, lookit, the *f* and *k* work good." He leaned over her shoulder, rapped out a sentence, and Jane read, *I love you Willie and I am goink to be your freek.*

She stayed away from Aaabracadabra Antiques after that. Aaabracadabra Antiques turned into the Soul of Commerce.

She would see him looking at her over a mountain of junk on the sidewalk. He never stopped talking; five people were trying on fur coats, rooting in boxes, and she would wave and walk by. Then he began to turn up in odd places, especially, uncannily, when she had need of someone—too many times in the last two years. She was standing on one foot in front of the shoe repair shop on Harmonia Springs Avenue, which was closed, dangling a boot with a loose heel from two fingers, when he barged around the corner in a Santa Claus suit. "Go to José on Back Main," he ordered, and told her precisely where. "And tell him I sent you. I'm going to check to see if you tell him."

She told him. "Fifteen cent since Willie sent you," the little man crowed, shaking her hand effusively. And then Willie loomed in the doorway.

"Hey, José! This is my girlfriend."

"Dis da same whose boot I fix before?"

"No," Willie said with a laugh. "This is number two at the sixteenth pole, but moving up fast on the inside."

One day she ran out of gas in the Dodge on a farm road twelve miles from Harmonia Springs, and this time it was truly spooky (she had not seen him for a couple of months) to spot Willie hardening out of the dust cloud at the top of the hill in his fantastic vehicle, his one truly original object of art, the beaten-up Chevrolet station wagon loaded on sides and top to the dimensions of a carnival float with (he said) three rooms of furniture: overstuffed chairs, baby cribs, radio and TV sets, mattresses, lamps, a raccoon in fishing posture, a moose with antlers and a pious expression, a dented tuba, and, on top, a human skeleton he had found in a closet in a condemned I.O.O.F. hall. And underneath, it now appeared, a red gasoline can, full. During these rescues, Jane was never glad to see him, though she always accepted his help.

"Do you have me on some kind of radar?" she would ask peevishly.

"Just keep it in mind, darling, a friend in need is a friend indeed."

Once he had appeared in her dormitory room when she had a particularly despicable roommate, carrying a set of imitation Chinese screens. They were plain gray on Jane's side, but on the roommate's side they had dragon-headed pink phoenixes baring gold and silver teeth on a red ground. She had to laugh.

"Handpicked for my choicy darling," Willie said.

"I can't pay for them."

"I'll make it a loan."

She looked at him narrowly as he fanned the screens out across the room, bustling around like a window dresser. Then he lay back across her bed and smiled up at her. "See how happy you are now that I brought you your screens."

"You're a strange person," she said. "You always work things out so you end up at the center." She plopped into a desk chair and stared out the window, but caught over her shoulder one of those hard, measuring looks.

"You don't think I put you in the center and me on the outside?" he said.

She did not answer, but she saw he had it right: Yes, quite so. It was a matter of getting in, of showing up, whatever the portal. He was perfectly willing to use the tradesman's entrance. It would save him the trouble of improving his appearance.

Whenever he caught her alone for a minute he would ask her: "When you going to be my little freak?"

"I may be a freak but I'm never going to be your freak."

"Why not?" he said.

How did he know, that was the question. *How did he know?* Was it written all over her face? Then why couldn't everyone else read it?

"All that wheezing and belching," Jane lied. "It might be contagious."

"That's just the hay fever."

"You sound like a sick old man."

"Better to be an old man's darling than a young man's fool."

"Well, right now I'm a young man's fool," she said.

"I can wait," Willie said. "Everybody somebody's fool. Just let me know when you ready to be my freak."

Jane said she would let him know.

Jane thought she knew something about love by now, but in truth, if love had been a restaurant, and she had been seated at the best table and given *carte blanche*, she would not have known what to order. A lover from outer space was not on the menu and, anyway, some things are for the circus, some things for the real world. She would have sat there, and when the waiter came back for the third time she would have asked for a good-looking male close to her own age, not fat, afflicted with sensibility and no shorter than herself, as would every other young woman there. Oh, and let him have that changeling, parentless air, Jane would add. *"Ce sera au dernier point comme il vous plaît, mademoiselle!"* the waiter would say, bowing low. He would reappear presently, tray in hand. At first Jane would be delighted with her dish—just what I wanted, better than I could have imagined it. Then she would toy with her food.

Now here is Jane, pedalling an old balloon-tire bicycle laboriously into Harmonia Springs. Be a sport, she is telling herself. How did you get to be such a miser? Just a thirty-five-dollar jalopy after all.

At the same time she is cursing Jimmy. Why, that bossy, spoiled, artistic, self-important little bum! She remembers how the urge came upon her, an urge she had censored right away, not to let Jimmy drive her car. She could see her privacy at the core of this urge, rancid as an old filbert, a dark, mean little hole. Even so she tried to find the words to save her worthless auto for herself, words that would sound right, but there weren't any. Gradually she knew the truth. You have to let your boyfriend drive your car.

So, Jane remembers, growling through her teeth, she did. And off Jimmy drove in the 1949 fleshpink Wayfarer with Roger beside him, to drink away a hot afternoon in the Downtown

Recreation Club. Hours later, out they came, blinking in the slanted light, not seeing all that well anyway. Clambered unsteadily into the Dodge and pulled out into the stream of traffic. The three-quarter-ton hay truck that demolished the Dodge looked about the same before and after. Its driver noticed this with indifference and left. But Jane thought of her Dodge crumpling like the foil from a chocolate kiss and ordered herself to love it no more. Who would have thought it delicate? But it was. Therefore let it go.

But then she had to let the job go, too, since Haslebacher's Family Restaurant was in Pocahontas City, twenty miles away. No job, no car. To lose so little, so fast, and have it seem so much, was comic, but Jane could not fake a laugh. Jane had $5.25. Jimmy had assorted loose change. Jimmy went into his studio to contemplate his half-finished paintings. Jane admired and hated him. She was a coper. She rode her bicycle slowly into town.

Sweat ran into her eyes; her glasses slid down her nose, and savagely she pushed them back into place. Her lovely hair was coiled on top of her head like a cobra in a basket; she felt like cutting it off. Bubbling with curses, she was like a witch who had quaffed her own dirty brew. She was a lowly coper, and it was Philip Turner's fault. This all had to do with the notion of money that had curdled her tissues into cowardly cheese by the age of twenty, so that she had to work for a living. Only charity was a bezoar against that witch's potion. Charity, she counseled herself, charity. She had looked it up in a curious book she had, *The ABC of Jewish Duties*: tsedakah, charity.

It said: Tsedakah is not a question of generous sentiment, but of justice. The man of means has no right to withhold from the poor their share; if he does, he acts like a thief. There it was: If she did not share with Jimmy, she was unjust, and a thief.

But then it said: If reduced to poverty, even a great sage must not disdain manual work, no matter how unworthy of him, in order to avoid dependence on other people. Some of the great sages derived their livelihood from chopping wood, carrying lumber, watering gardens, and asked no help of the community. In short, Jimmy should roam around with a borrowed lawn mower, ringing doorbells. This was part of his greatness.

Moreover, Jane was no longer a man of means. Now she had to justify going to others to beg: Whoever is so much in need of charity that he cannot live without it and yet is too proud to accept it, is guilty of murder and self-murder. So this was pious self-love, her faintly nauseous panic at the thought that she would have nothing to eat. This too was charity. She leaned her bicycle against the Soul of Commerce and peered into the gloom for Willie.

Willie Usher assisted the destitute regularly, from street brats who fetched his milkshakes and kept the change to addled crones like Dora, who slept in his doorway in the winter. He helped them to lay their hands on enough money or stuff so that they could live the way he did, for he lived no better than most of his protégés. And besides going about the streets in the garb of an escaped state-hospital patient and living on hamburgers and Baby Ruths, Willie administered to the unfortunate only in an offhand, joking way, as if his right hand didn't care what his left was doing. Half of those he helped, like Dora, were too far gone to know whom to thank; few of the others could ever do anything for Willie in return.

But Jane could. Therefore she skulked into the Soul of Commerce like a low-down dog.

"What a face," Willie said. "Long as the bus ride home. Your goldfish died. Is that it?"

"I've got no car and no job."

Jane followed him down into the basement. He had his back to her; he was pouring plaster of Paris into the Candleholder of Truth and the Chinese Symbol of Heaven With Hole in Middle. He said, "So you'd do anything for potatoes."

Jane swallowed. "Almost anything."

"Well, do like I do. Sell something."

"I've got nothing to sell."

She heard a scraping; a box turtle was making its way down a canyon of bedsprings towards a small square of open floor.

"There's Reggie," Willie said. He pulled the tied-off balloon end of a hot dog out of his pocket, and a piece of bun stained with ketchup. The turtle approached the heap with ponderous determination.

"See how happy Reggie is now I brought him his dinner."

"He's eating it," Jane admitted.

"So." Willie returned to business. "What you got to sell?"

"Nothing."

Willie leaned against a tower of boxes, his arms crossed. "Listen here, darling, everybody got something to sell. If you don't sell your own you sell the other guy's. You take a piece and everybody makes out."

He pushed a sagging paper carton onto the floor. Its flaps flew up and a red coil of wire bounced out and rolled under bedsprings. The turtle's head disappeared into its shell. Jane looked in the box. It was full of metal hairclips and mousetraps.

"Good stuff," Willie said.

Jane smiled. "You know what's in all these boxes?"

"Roughly," Willie said. Now he had his back to her again and Jane gazed at him. He was wearing a scarlet satin bowling shirt and baggy gray baseball pants. His black feet in flip-flops were scaly, prehistoric, with dust. He stood before the wall of boxes with open arms like a rabbi before the Ark of the Torah.

"Everything for a dollar or less," he intoned. "I'm sick to death of this junk. What say we split five-oh, five-oh."

"You want me to sell your stuff?" Jane said. "I don't think I'd make a very good saleswoman."

"That," Willie said, "is the whole idea of the Soul of Commerce. Never sell nobody nothing, darling. Just put the thing you want to sell out in front of you and look stupid. Make it cheap so the chump thinks he beat you for it. Oh my. Lord have mercy. What a sale we're going to have, a monster." Already he was throwing boxes and loose junk into the tiny bit of open space. "This goes. This goes. At last I'm going to get rid of this. This goes. Hallelujah, everything for a dime."

"But Willie," Jane said. "Say we sold two thousand things for a dime. That would only be two hundred dollars."

Willie was indignant. "Look here, young woman. Don't be greedy. Can't you live on two hundred dollars for a month? I can eat on forty. Anyway, a dime is the last resort. Try for a dollar." He started up the stairs. "Now I'll show you something you'll always thank me for. How to buy a burger and fries on credit. How much you got left, anyhow?"

"Five dollars and twenty-five cents," Jane said gravely.

"Five bucks to the good!" Willie exclaimed. "In that case, how about fronting me two dollars?"

Jane clattered around the corner onto Harmonia Springs Avenue on her bike and saw Roger Booth coming out of Arbuckle's with a bag of groceries. In the mouth of the sack were frozen ravioli, frozen chicken pies, frozen turkey dinners. The garish stack was the calendar, one box a night, of a desolate privacy.

Roger was living in Fred's old room at the Bloods'. He was here in Harmonia Springs only because of Jimmy. This was wonderfully strange, and a little creepy. Jane knew by now that if Jimmy had really vanished into the epicene stews of New York City, somebody would have missed him. For Roger, by then, was living across the river in Teaneck, working in a discount furniture store. Now he was selling radios at Slotkin's in Xenia. Jane pictured him—slinky tallness, shiny black hair, strong if rather meaningless jaw of the male lead in a Classic Comic —killing time in his room at the Bloods' every other night. What did he do with himself? Contemplate the nature of Jimmy, as a monk thinks about God?

"How's my Jimmy today?" Roger asked her, as if to confirm this theory.

"He's okay," Jane said. "Probably hungry."

"In the jungle," Roger said, "a white man grows very lean or very fat. Jimmy Fluharty was of the thin breed. They didn't call him the toughest sonofabitch in the jungle for nothing." Then he smiled.

Jane looked at his movie star face, at this hour covered with a blue relief of beard around the lips and jawline which brought out the handsome desperado in his unemployed actor's repertory. To his credit, he was not vain of his looks. He shone darkly with the completedness of his purpose, and what impressed and disconcerted Jane was his beautiful settledness, which reminded her of the alleged glow of pregnant women. Or of the massive poise you sometimes see in the wives of philanderers, women who have convinced themselves that, compared to the fluff the wind drives by (which their husbands chase) they weigh a million pounds. He was the only human being Jane had ever met who would have disappeared into another person if he could. She was sure he would have been glad to shrink down to a single cell of his dark, handsome self and spend his life navigating Jimmy's veins and arteries; happy so long as he could peer out of Jimmy's eyes, pass through Jimmy's heart, go everywhere Jimmy went, and touch everything Jimmy touched with Jimmy's hands, Jimmy's fingers.

Roger was the real changeling, the truly parentless one, Jane realized with a start. And he was dark, like the face of love. He had annihilated parents at the age of fifteen, by getting a lawyer and changing his name. There had been no father to get rid of. Huzzy was his mother's name, and Albert, as he was then, had shared it with five older brothers, all car thieves by trade, all serving time regularly in one California penal institution or another. Huzzy, Jimmy had told Jane, was a dreaded surname in Riverside County, besides being silly and ugly. Jane wished to like Roger, but so far he wanted nothing to do with Jane.

Only now he was standing in front of Arbuckle's, smiling at her. She suddenly said: "You could do worse than sharing him with me, you know. The next girl might want Jimmy all to herself."

"You do like being one of the boys, don't you," Roger said.
Jane blinked.

He said: "I don't like you because I know you're going to let my Jimmy down."

She tried to smile; this was rather more than she had wanted. "Aren't you hoping I will?"

"Nope. I know you will."

"What makes you say that?"

"Nobody likes Jimmy as well as I do. Did you know Jimmy once shot me in the ass?"

"With a gun?"

"Bird gun."

"What on earth for?"

"For teasing Rex. Jimmy chased me up on the roof of his shack and let me have it with Pete's bird gun."

Jane saw how proud he was, proud of Jimmy for doing it, and proud of himself for taking it. She could imagine the scene, how Roger must have felt, instantly, the triumph of this consummation, how he would have lain in a lover's drowsy nostalgia half an hour later as a doctor tweezed the birdshot out of his ass.

"What did you do?" she asked.

"I laughed. As soon as I was sure he wasn't going to kill me."

"It's true he hasn't shot me yet," she said a little stiffly, "but I like him pretty well."

"Don't feel bad," Roger said. "Don't you know we're all bums except Jimmy? The only difference between me and you is that after it all comes down, I'll still be there."

Jane looked at him. "There've got to be some other differences," she said sharply, pushing off on her bicycle.

In her mailbox at Harmonia, Jane found the letter she had looked for all through April with hope, through May with asperity, and once or twice in June with maledictions. Finally she gave up, and now here it was: a check from Philip Turner, though drastically smaller than she expected—for the mysterious sum of $53.11. There was also a note on Turner, Wiener, Blum & Taliaferro stationery, typed by a secretary, requesting that she call his office upon receipt.

"I finally got a check from that screwy school," Philip Turner said. "I thought you'd changed your mind and stayed in the dormitory."

"No," Jane said, and waited. She wanted her father to imagine her living on day-old Holsum bread for ten weeks, sleeping in her car.

"I know you're not sleeping in your car," he said impatiently.

"No," Jane said, "because I don't have a car."

"So where are you?"

"In a house."

"A house! You can afford a house? It's a good thing you're rich because you won't get far on the money that fishy school sent me back, I'll tell you."

"They sent you $53.11?"

Philip Turner cleared his throat. "That's a first installment."

A pause.

"So why am I worrying if you can afford a house?"

"It's a free house," Jane blurted.

"What do you mean a free house?"

"No one else wants to live there. No plumbing. Roof falling in. Etcetera."

"My God, you're living in an abandoned house like a tramp? A woman alone?"

"Someone else is with me."

"Someone else. Someone else is male, I'll bet."

Jane said nothing.

"You're living with a man *in public*?"

"Well, you know, Dad, the house has walls. It's not made of cellophane."

"You're taking money from this man?"

"Certainly not." Jane felt her eyelids quiver. "He's taking money from me."

A silence, then: "You're supporting him on my money? What kind of bum is he?"

"Your money! This is the first money I've seen from you for months."

"Don't kid yourself, Jane. You're taking plenty of money from me. That crazy school costs a fortune."

Jane quoted *The ABC of Jewish Duties*: "Talmud says, though the father go hungry, instruction must not be interrupted, not even for the rebuilding of the temple."

"Huh? What are you talking about?"

"You'd have died of shame if I hadn't gone to college."

"You could have gone to the University of Maryland like a lot of other people's children. Anyway, I wouldn't die of shame no matter what you did, my dear Jane. Or I would have died long ago." Jane hung up as her father was adding in a loud voice: *"And if you think I'm going to pay for—"* She hurried to the Bursar's Office to cash the check, obviously the last one she would see from Philip Turner for some time.

As Jane rode her bike back to the house on Pocahontas County Road 601, she mulled over the various grades of tsedakah. Her father was right off the bottom of the chart, no, to be just, he had one toe on it, less because he was paying for her education, which for all his complaining he could easily afford to do, than because of that line, *So why am I worrying?* Though uttered in the interrogative, in protest against its own brief existence, it implied that he had, for a moment, worried about Jane.

Willie Usher was at the top of the scale. He had entered into partnership with Jane, saying what's mine is yours if you can sell it; this was the highest grade of tsedakah. Not once had he said: And now, when are you going to be my little freak? But of course this occasion was different from all the others, when she had glanced up from some petty emergency to see his moose-antlered station wagon taking shape on the horizon. This time Jane had come to him.

And then there was Jane. In degree she had to place herself only a little above Philip Turner, for she gave, if she gave at all, in a surly manner, grudgingly and with a gloomy face. But didn't Jimmy fix the windows, cook the beans, and show Jane how to clean fish? What did it matter, in their penny-ante commonwealth, if he paid in cash? It was also true that she would be looking for some miserable job now whether Jimmy was there or not. That habit of mind had its root in some ugly lesson long before Jimmy. Why should she talk to him in Philip Turner's voice? She resolved to be kinder to Jimmy.

But when she got home he wasn't there. Soon he strolled crookedly through the skunk cabbages in front of the house on Pocahontas County Road 601, holding a bottle twisted in a paper bag. No doubt he had felt through the pockets of his clothes and come up with enough nickels and quarters to fetch a quart of white port.

He climbed heavily onto the porch, said "Good evening," and disappeared into the house. A moment later he dragged the painting he had been working on through the screen door and propped it against a porch column. Then he sat down carefully on the couch, the bottle in his lap, to look at it: a squadron of floppy striped cones hurrying through space, a headless figure too luscious to be Jane's, and in front of it all, almost hiding it all, a cirrus curd, a rent mask of clouds, strange weather.

Jane sat on the edge of the porch looking at the road, feeling Jimmy recede behind her into the sweet, oily, synthetic reek of the wine, like an ant into the bell of a giant plastic flower.

In this position Jimmy spent the evening, and on into the night: on the porch, on the couch, sitting rather erect, knees genteelly crossed, one hand holding the bottle, still in its brown paper sleeve, at an odd angle to his knee, eyes closed. After nine o'clock he was dead to all stimuli, still clasping his bottle and facing his painting in the dark, like a monument to his own excesses in the vanished world of appearances. Jane watched the moon rise over the cornfield, thinking about the Soul of Commerce, Jane and Willie, Roger and Jimmy, Jimmy and Jane.

She would never ask a Dr. Zwilling for his judgment. Not for a minute did she believe that Jimmy was an authentic drunk or she herself an authentic tramp. She knew these were merely floor shows whereby each soul made itself visible, rooting up its unspeakable unrest and joining it to a convention the world understood only too well—anything to take on an outward shape. Oh, it could be costly, scarifying. Jimmy might slip up and die a bum, not a painter.

And Roger: Roger would have saved Jimmy from Jane if he could. Jimmy, however, didn't care what Roger thought. Jimmy could not lose Roger whatever he did. Such perfect fidelity inspires one only to be oneself. Roger's poisoned arrows flew over Jimmy's head and stuck in Jane's back. Jane, not Jimmy, feared being lost in a couple.

But Jimmy was not *just a male*. Sometimes, well into changeling drunks like this one, he would corner Jane and ask her exactly that in a deeply melancholy bray, almost a sob, he had at such times: "Do you think I'm *just a male*?" He was not looking for the softest part of his personality (his view of women was not so charitable) but rather the greediest for life. When he was eight, he had wanted, and got, the girl's cowboy suit instead of the boy's—the girl's because it was gorgeous rose satin with rhinestone buttons and white ruffles on the flyless trousers, not sober blue like the boy's. And for a painting smock, Jimmy had taken over a pink nightgown that Sasha sent Jane for her birthday. He did not look feminine in the thing, but like a rococo cherub escaped from some ceiling fresco on an errand of terrible erotic mischief.

Jane had asked him when Roger first appeared on the porch: "Did you—would you ever sleep with Roger?"

"We tried it once. I was afraid I might be missing something, and probably I am, but"—he shook his head—"I seem to be stuck with the procreative variety."

"What about Roger?"

Jimmy shrugged. He didn't know what Roger wanted.

Jane was awakened in the blackness by a crash. The bottle had finally slipped from Jimmy's hand to the porch and broken. It was one or two in the morning. Jane looked above her. No moon was visible, but silver shapes thronged in and out of each other like flanks of pale cattle migrating in the night sky. Jane touched her fingers to her forehead and laughed softly. She had had a dream about Willie Usher.

She had been going somewhere (that was always so in her dreams) at dusk along a winding dirt road, when Willie's station wagon came over a hill in the distance, but the three rooms of furniture and the moose and raccoon in fishing posture had turned into lenses dangling in square frames, a telescope and astrolabe, a scaffoldwork tower of bubbling retorts and alembics, a sundial on top, a giant hourglass in the middle, a beaded abacus on the bottom. Of his usual equipage only the I.O.O.F. skeleton was there, tinkling in the wind. And this time Willie was not coming to her aid, so that this time, strangely, she was thrilled to see him. He was wearing a long sorcerer's robe and was completely absorbed in his study, looking from test tubes to compasses to the stars in the sky, so that he never even noticed her in the crowd where people were whispering his name—not Willie C. Usher, but *Paracelsus*.

This dream left her in a charmed and, yes, a charitable mood. She would have liked to wake Jimmy and lead him gently upstairs, but she knew it would be useless to try. Bending at his feet, she pushed the clinking wine-soaked bag of glass off the porch, dropped a gray blanket over him, and went upstairs to sleep.

Ten minutes later she sat up in the rose bed, wide awake. For some reason she had fought off sleep like a champion as soon as she heard its soft gigantic wing-beats settling. So sleep went away again, and then in that weird cracked eggshell of light that a naked bulb shed on the rough old plaster, something else was there. Something had happened to her. She was feeling a kind of unlimited desire that had never been there before. It was not like the topical genital buzz of her adolescence that she had known at once you should smuggle off to some closet to see to in privacy, with erotic cartoons passing before your squeezed-shut eyes. No, this was something you couldn't do by yourself.

She could see what was coming. This would sweep her off to

the world, which was suddenly altogether compelling and necessary, loaded as it was with human males. She would become a prowler, a raptor, soft-footed down the corridors of cheap hotels, down the twisty paths of city parks, across crowded squares and along country lanes, always looking, only appearing composed. No, she was as composed as she looked, for why should she be distraught? She was a centripetal force, with gravity in all her excentric orbs, the lips, the breasts, the stomach, the buttocks. She would always find what she was looking for —some facsimile, good enough, of the face of love. From now on she would put herself into the hands of men without fear of disappearing, for she was the cunt from outer space.

Jane stood up. Jimmy was still on the porch. And though, when mere charity was the incentive, Jane had despaired of waking Jimmy before she ever tried, note that the cunt from outer space did not give up so easily. Barefoot and naked, with a yellowed sheet wrapped around her, Jane crept back down the stairs.

Eyes closed, still facing his painting, Jimmy was like a well-made sand castle that had slumped and blurred only a little in the heavy dew before dawn. His white hands lay in his lap, each touchingly curled as if holding the two halves of some precious but broken thing until he could think how to repair it.

"Jimmy," she whispered in his ear, shaking him by the shoulders. "Jimmy, can't you wake up?"

He moaned something unintelligible.

She put her two hands on his cheeks and raised his face to hers. "Jimmy!" she said, kissing him on the lips. Without opening his eyes, he kissed her. "Jimmy! Don't you want to come to bed? Don't you want to fuck?"

His eyelids fluttered, the corners of his mouth quivered, and then he said, hoarsely, "Sorry about your car."

"Jimmy!" Jane pressed on, no longer interested in that subject. But Jimmy lurched gently backwards out of her grasp, pulled his knees to his stomach, and rolled sideways to sleep.

⦾ Freaks

The sky-blue patrol car ground onto the shoulder in front of the house on Pocahontas County Road 601. Officer Rollo leaned out the window over his elbow and said: "You, young lady. Call your mama. Call her today."

Jane looked around the porch to see if someone was sitting behind her. She said: "Me?"

"You. Dean Lucorne up the college asked me to deliver you that message."

"My mother called her?"

"I don't have any details."

"But why?"

"I don't read minds, young lady. You just call her."

He shook his head, as if he knew Jane had not telephoned her mother in a long time.

She bicycled into town and called Sasha.

"Your father owes you 950 dollars," Sasha said tiredly.

"What? He does?" Jane could tell that joy would be an unsuitable response.

"From your old Falstaff School bankbook. He borrowed it when he bought that first MG. I've made him promise to pay you girls back but" — heavy pause — "well, now you know. It's up to you to press the issue with your father if you want that money."

Silence.

"Mom, what's going on?"

"I've decided to divorce your father," Sasha whispered, "and he's decided to leave me without a penny if he can."

Jane felt a crawling at the back of her neck. The most grotesque divorce case possible—that would be right for the Kaplan-and-Turners. So this was what had taken them so long. Not to realize that they were natural enemies, that had been quick and easy, but to bring on the occidental money torture, the death grip on every dime, the total banishment of charity and civility—even Philip Turner might have looked into the future and cringed.

"Can he?" Jane said.

"I don't know yet. I don't know if I can find a lawyer in this city to take my case."

"Mom, you know dozens of lawyers. Hundreds."

"Nobody we know wants to get your father mad," Sasha said.

"What will you do?"

"I don't know."

The conversation wasn't over; Jane knew what she should say now.

"Do you want me to come home?" she whispered.

"Could you?" Sasha replied, with such heat, for Sasha, that Jane stepped backwards a little in the phone booth.

"As soon as I can," she said, and hung up.

All at once it smelled a little cheap, even to Jane. In the distance, under a small, hot spotlight, Sasha was alone on a small black stage. She was doing her bad little number for an audience that hated her. Why was she waving on Jane to do her number, too?

Even so, as long as she was at a pay phone and still had a dime, Jane dialed her father, collect.

"I know all about it," he said, as though he didn't believe a word. "It's being taken care of. Among other things."

Jane did not ask what other things. "How is it being taken care of? Not to be pushy, but I could really use that money."

"I can just imagine," her father said. "Well, get in line. Your school bankbook is not high on my list of priorities. You do realize a family event of some weight is underway here? You do know what this means?"

A lengthy pause. It occurred to her, distantly, that in his haughty way her father might be asking her to say something. But what could he want her to say?

Suddenly he observed: "In all my life, only your mother thought I was a really dangerous person."

Now she knew what she was expected to say, but when she opened her mouth, what came out was: "Could you tell me when? I don't mean to press, but I need that money."

For quite a while he said nothing, and then: "I don't have that kind of dough right now. You're going to have to take it in installments."

"Okay," Jane said. "Can you just please tell me when the first installment will be?"

"What is this?" he said hoarsely. "Who do you think you are?" So that Jane had to keep telling herself: He deserves it.

"It's out of my hands," he finally said. "My accountant is handling it, then it goes to payroll."

"Thank you," she said politely.

"Don't worry, you'll be paid." He hung up, and at once she had a terrible urge to call him back and comfort him. But she was out of change and, anyhow, that was not the kind of call you could make collect.

Your little old Poke County dirt farmer, Willie Usher said, since the war he never had it so good. Now give him a shove, the trunk of his car pops open and he turns into a junkman before your eyes. And what does he do when he finally gets shut of that 1949 beehive-model hairdryer and that electric carving knife Grandma got for opening up an account at the bank, and the brand new, never-used ten-gallon aquarium complete with filter, deep-sea diver and treasure chest, and the roofless doghouse from a kit that Dad started to build for poor Queenie, and the rest of it? Come Saturday he jumps in the car with the missus and goes shopping.

This Saturday he came to the Soul of Commerce, I.P., just as Willie said he would. They all did—the Erdmans from Xenia, the Puterbaughs from Circleville, the Proutys from Amosburg, and, as they say in the junk trade, many many more too numerous to mention—and rented ($3), from Jane, in the cowfield behind the house on PCR 601, one of Willie's long shaky metal tables upon which to display their junk. Jane wandered around in a moneygreen daze not quite of disbelief, because she had, after all, made the rounds with Willie, to Xenia, West Xenia, Circleville, Amosburg, St. Elmo, Vandalia, and many many more. How did Willie know so many people? Not only others in the junk business, not only church ladies and den mothers who normally ran bake sales and bazaars, but regular people. "See how happy people are to see me?" Jane saw it, but could hardly believe her eyes. This was still Pocahontas County, and it was not as though Willie dressed up for the occasion, unless you call red-and-white striped pajama top, bermuda shorts and flip-flops dressing up. You could not quite say, Jane concluded, that Pocahontas County had gone color-blind. They simply saw Willie as one of a kind. They were used to him. Jane now knew at least one of his destinations when he vanished from the Soul of Commerce for weeks at a time. He was at everybody else's sales, all over the county, or down in people's basements, or out in the tool shed, buying.

He was buying now. It was Willie who bought the ten-gallon aquarium, the half-finished doghouse, the electric knife, and the Professional Beauty Shop Chair, *ONLY $15*, and other items by the boxful too numerous to mention. He piled this stuff into his freshly emptied-out station wagon, except for the Professional Beauty Shop Chair, in which he sat down to rest after all that buying, pulling the beehive top down over his head to get out of the sun.

The first day they had gone north, to Xenia, West Xenia and St. Elmo. Jane put her bare feet on the dashboard and waited for Willie to bring up his favorite subject. But it seemed to have departed his mind. Instead he talked about how smart they were to have their sale before the fairs started, how gypsies first came to Pocahontas County because of the fairs, which farmers still went to the gypsy to get a spell removed or for a backache, how to cure a backache, how to cure athlete's foot.

Finally Jane hinted: "Were you always a freak? Even when you were a little boy?"

Willie said: "I was like every other black-assed Junction punk whose people never knew where he was. Stealing hubcaps. Robbing crates off beer trucks. Breaking into empty buildings. Smoking that reefer. No visible difference."

"How come you don't smoke now?"

"It don't do nothing for me."

Jane had pictured a solitary child like herself.

"You never got in any real trouble, did you?"

"What is real trouble? As opposed to fake trouble?"

"I mean with the cops," Jane said.

"County Training School, ten months. Is that real trouble?"

Jane was impressed, even a little scared. Only very bad boys went to reform school in Baltimore. She remembered Lenny Frank, who threw a chair at Mrs. Dalsheimer, her sixth grade teacher, bloodying her nose, and who disappeared from Falstaff into reform school. Of course Lenny had been white; the whole school had been white until the following year.

"Wow," Jane said. "What happened then?"

Willie looked at her. "What you see," he said gruffly.

Jane did not press. She was sure she knew something about Willie now that no other white person knew. Felix, Officer Rollo —sure they knew, but they would never say. And Jane wouldn't say either.

"Willie was in training school for a while when he was a kid," Jane told Jimmy that night, when they were lying in bed.

"What for?" Jimmy said lazily, and without surprise.

Jane realized she didn't know. She also realized she was a big mouth, a tourist, and a traitor. But maybe it wasn't too late.

"For—for football," she said. "I think."

Jimmy said: "He was in training school for football? What are you talking about?"

"No, I said he was in training for a while. When he was in school. For football."

But why would this be worth mentioning, thirty seconds after Jane had lifted her face from the gnarled, venous, endearingly common erection?

Jimmy raised his head a little and looked at her peculiarly.

Jane crawled up next to him. "I mean, considering the shape he's in now."

Jimmy closed his eyes. It was too much work to figure out this phase of her delirium. They were getting along well, very well indeed. "What's come over you?" Jimmy had had to ask; and what had come over Jane? Now when they went to bed, she thrashed about as though the world were quicksand and the only hope lay in getting to the ancient column of his prick, which led to the other side, the Antipodes, where up was down. Anyway, she fastened herself to this by every means available, while Jimmy clung to her back, her stomach, her side, half thrilled, half terrified, as though he were kneeling on a magic carpet.

"What's come over you?" he had asked, and she had said, a little crossly, "I don't know." Some things were private. In all candor, she did not think of love at all during this period. Love? —she was like a locust or caterpillar that wanted to eat everything it saw. She had to take hold of every part that stuck out from a man, or could stick out, and put it in her mouth or her cunt.

"Don't you want to kiss me?" Jimmy asked, leaning over her.

"Not right now," said Jane, lighting a cigarette.

Jimmy lit one too.

"He knows everyone in the county," Jane said. "They like him. Why aren't they scared of him?"

Jimmy gave her a long look. "Why should they be scared of him?" he said.

"Because he's different. And powerful. And he's really black.

I mean he's a very dark-skinned Negro. They can't have stopped noticing that."

"What are you telling me? What do you mean, powerful?"

"I mean his overall effect."

Jimmy said: "I see what's going on. If you sleep with him, it's going to be because he's big, ugly, black, and has a completely primitive view of women. Keep that in mind."

"How do you know what kind of view of women he has?"

"It's so obvious. Willie, Felix, Fred, Roger—they all do."

"They never even talk about women."

Jimmy didn't answer.

"I didn't say I wanted to fuck him," Jane said.

"He's the opposite of me, that's why you're attracted to him."

"That's true," Jane said, biting the end of her pinky thoughtfully.

"Don't forget to tell me the exact size of his prick when you get through." Jimmy rolled away from her under the sheet.

"I didn't say I was going to fuck him."

"Uh-huh," Jimmy said.

"Anyway, I don't think Willie's ugly."

"Well, he's certainly not pretty," Jimmy said through his teeth into the pillow. "You do just what you want," he added. "You will anyway, and more power to you."

"I wish you were less pretty," Jane said cruelly.

"So do I," Jimmy said, "so do I."

"I don't think I'm going to fuck him," Jane said. For the moment she believed those words.

"Okay, okay," Jimmy muttered, pulling the sheet up around his ears.

"Would you leave me if I did?"

He would not answer.

"Would you leave me?" she repeated.

"Of course not," he snapped.

The next day Willie and Jane went south, to Circleville and Amosburg. Willie was wearing a white shirt, for a change, and a blue polka-dot neck tie. In Circleville he alarmed her by saying, "Now I want you to meet a genuine freak," but this was another sort of freak he had in mind. He pulled up in front of a tiny red brick building on the main square of town, with an American flag over the screen door and civic-looking geraniums growing in funereal spittoons on either side of the stoop. Inside was a combination bus station, snack bar and pinball palace. "The lady that runs this place is like the north wind," Willie confided. "She's prejudice like you wouldn't believe, but I can handle her—we get on good."

Willie introduced Jane to Mrs. Woodrow Woodford, chairlady of the Circleville First Methodist sisterhood.

"I really doubt my ladies would come on such short notice, Mr. Usher," she said, staring straight at Jane. Jane stared back at her silky black dress and tight helmet of beauty-parlor-blued white hair. On the way out, Willie picked up two Baby Ruths and laid a dime on the counter.

"That will be fifty cents," said Mrs. Woodrow Woodford, or, more accurately, she hissed like iron in a pickling vat. Suddenly Jane could see how she managed to run this low (as well as empty) establishment by herself. She pointed to a sign on the side of the register: *All Package Candy 25 Cents.*

"Fifty cents!" Willie boomed. "Is it legal to charge more than what's written on the package? I'd like a receipt, please, I'm going to have to take this up with my lawyer."

Jane nudged Willie because she saw that Mrs. Woodrow Woodford did not understand the joke. Mrs. Woodford held out a green receipt to Willie with two shaking fingers.

"I have never done anything illegal," she announced. "And now let me tell you something. You Negros have some strange ideas about the world. You can't threaten me. In my opinion the world doesn't owe anyone an apology. Life is hard for everyone. I wouldn't do anything against the law. You can't get away with the pot calling the kettle black here."

Now she pointed one of those very white, trembling fingers at Jane.

"I'll tell you something else. You think you can upset me by coming in here with a white girl. Well, it has nothing to do with me. It isn't prejudice that makes me associate with my own kind. It's nature. Everything really likes its own kind best. Don't you agree? In your heart of hearts?"

Back in the wagon Jane and Willie looked at each other.
"I told you she was a freak."
Jane said: "Personally, I like my own kind least."
They were laughing, and Willie started up the car. It was late afternoon, and hot. On the other side of the street the town green was dotted with catalpa blossoms, like so many perfumed, soiled, dropped lace handkerchiefs. Sunlight splashed the green heads of the soldiers on the Civil War memorial.

"I got another freak for you in Amosburg," Willie said.
But Jane was still dazed by Mrs. Woodrow Woodford. "That dame must be making book or something," she said. "The way she protested her innocence—very weird."
"She's the county sheriff's sister."
"Oy vay," Jane said. She had heard about Sheriff Staples. "Well, same thing."
Willie said: "Never fear, me and the sheriff get on good."
Jane said: "I'll bet."
They drove out of town and found the usual mirage of a hamburger stand wiggling in the heat on the edge of an alfalfa field. You never went hungry when you were with Willie, though of course you ate no better than he did.
"Next freak," Willie said, "is E. B. Biddle, Leading Knight of the Amosburg Elks." He shifted gears with his cheeseburger and they were back on the road.
"Please don't call me a freak in the same breath with these people," Jane said.
"Did I call you a freak lately?"
"No," Jane admitted.
The last houses of Circleville slid by; then zigzags of wild sweet pea piled themselves against a barbed-wire fence, rich and chaotic, like ripped-out embroidery.

"I don't want to meet the Leading Knight," Jane said. "Let's go swimming."

Willie looked at her; he wanted to be sure what this meant.

"Where you want to go swimming?"

"You must know a place."

"You mean like a town pool?"

Jane shook her head.

"You mean like my private swimming hole."

Jane stared at the road, her cheeks getting hot. This was exactly what she meant.

They drove along the highway in silence for a while, still heading south towards Amosburg. Did he know what she meant?

"Take your clothes off, darling," he said in a low voice. Her heart began to bell in her throat—he knew what she meant. She was wearing a green cotton dress; her flip-flops were under the seat. A dusty pickup truck passed them, going the other way.

"All of them?" Jane said.

"Why not?"

She reached under her skirt for her panties. When she brought them up on a finger, Willie's hand disappeared under the folds of green cloth.

"You look good in a dress," he said. "Take it off anyway."

She pulled it over her head. And then she was naked next to him on the seat—a white girl, naked as a cuckoo, with small young breasts, next to a big, fully grown, fully dressed black man. Willie looked like a genuine grownup today in his shirt and tie. Now they were waiting for someone to pass them on the other side of the road. A couple drove by in a newish, very clean car. Jane watched their faces in the windshield go blank with astonishment, their heads turn.

"You really are a freak," he said. "Are you happy to be my freak?"

At last he turned down a dirt two-track Jane had never seen before. It was overgrown with foxgrape vines that lay, starry palms up, on the cracked clay. Through the open windows came a soft, thick, faintly briny fragrance, the pollen of neglected hayfields on the other side of the hedgerows. Now a hickory woods wove densely overhead and at last came the bright skin of water snaking through the trees.

Then they were standing next to the creek, and Jane was staring at his penis defying gravity as penises will. It was bigger than Jimmy's and Jane heard, distantly, *Remember to tell me the exact size of his prick when you get through.*

"It's brown," she observed.

"Well," Willie said, looking down, "what did you expect? Blue?"

It was beginning to dawn on Jane that she need not always say the first thing that came into her head—for instance, in this case, that no white boy's member was ever the same shade as the squire who transported it.

"It's—perfect," Jane said, instead.

The swimming hole was only knee-deep. Willie plopped down in the swirling current and, sitting slope-shouldered like a boy in a bathtub, pulled her down to him.

From under the water, his penis prodded Jane lightly in the belly. It might have been the head of a friendly, befuddled aquatic animal. He rolled her over between his arms and toyed with her breasts, her cunt. Her body was rose in the tea-colored water; Willie's limbs dipped under the surface as black as tree trunks, and, like tree trunks, mysteriously disappeared. Jane closed her eyes.

"Turn me so I can't see the car," she said.

He revolved her straight body, the interrupted current smacking gently at her flanks. When she opened her eyes they could have been in the Amazon.

"My little freak," he said, "tell me how much you want me to fuck you. You love me, don't you."

"I do," Jane said. "Yes."

Then sliding under her back, clasping her hips in his wide-spread fingers, he drew her downwards slowly, carefully, to himself. So it happened at last. Her chin was just above water, her breasts rose and fell like sandy islands with pink tepees at their centers, round clouds traversed the patch of blue torn from the sky to fit the hole in the treetops above her, and the water flowed from green to green as though there were no end to the forest and no road out.

Not that he was tireless—and he was not too dignified to gather his organ into his fist and pump it ferociously if it went flat at the wrong moment—but probably he sensed that he should not give her up too soon, not until he'd had enough, for she would not be his freak for long. Anyway, she suddenly remembered they had other things to do; and Jimmy.

"I don't know what I'm doing here," she said irritably.

133

"You got a short memory," Willie yawned. "Mercy, I forgot you Jewish girls always get an attitude when you're done."

Eyebrows flew up, but only in her mind. She wondered just how extensive his conquests were. She didn't even know where he slept at night!

"Willie, are you married?" she asked him suspiciously.

"With ten kids," he said. They were lying on a mossy bank on the far side of the creek. Willie was decorating the cleft between her buttocks with orange daylilies, one after another.

"If I gave you a dress, would you wear it?"

"Maybe."

"A red dress and a big straw hat. And what about a little girl to play with."

"A what?" Jane said.

"Another little girl for you and me to play with."

Jane sat up, squashing the tiger lilies. "What do you mean?"

"I thought you were my freak," Willie said, disappointed.

Jane, forgetting the couple in the very clean car, fumed at the idea of a witness, never mind a partner. On the other hand, she hated to hear herself say no.

"I wouldn't mind watching you with another girl," she said, in a best-offer sort of voice, "if I could be in a closet."

"Goodness! I wouldn't do something sneaky like that."

"No place to go from here, eh?" Jane said, like a seasoned demimondaine with a few tarnished scruples.

"Oh yes there is and we're going there quick!" A second later Willie splashed across the stream at a gallop.

"What's going on?" Jane said, reaching for her glasses.

Someone was coming, that's what. Two unsmiling men, one of them holding a rifle, stepped out of the woods, and Jane ran after Willie, dropping a trail of blooms like burning lily pads across the water as she went.

It was no worldly courtesan's fib that she loved Willie. Not only did he have charity, Jane thought, spying on Willie through a clump of chokecherry, he was an old outlaw who knew his way, with a hazardous subsidy and a past, and she did not see how he could be defeated or even damaged, certainly not by her.

She admired him. He had just sold the Farm Life & Auto agent, Mr. Jenkins, a plastic lawn chair and a sawed-off umbrella stuck in a length of pipe. Now the fellow was snoring next to his brochures, and Willie was about ready to wake him up and say, "See how happy you are now I sold you a umbrella stuck in a pipe," when someone tapped him on the shoulder.

Jane's eyes widened on a king-sized county law officer whose khaki shirt was so encrusted with badges, pen-and-pencil sets and official insignia that she feared it could only be Sheriff Staples himself. This personage had the Candleholder of Truth in his hands, he was fondling it possessively, saying something about his den, and Jane heard him ask: "I can jew you down a couple bucks, can't I, Willie?"

Willie appeared to search his heart over that rare Candleholder of Truth, of which he had thirty more in his basement. Meanwhile Jane saw him sneak a look at the price on the back—he had told Jane, Sell them for whatever you can get over a dollar.

"Okay, Sheriff," Willie said. "Three-fifty is my special price to you. I can't go no lower."

"But it is three-fifty," the sheriff said, turning it over.

"It is? Lemme see that." Willie scratched out the price with the ballpoint over his ear. "Damn incompetent help," he said. "Okay, now it's four ninety-five, three-fifty to you."

"How about two ninety-five?" the sheriff wheedled.

"Three ninety-five is my low price to you for this Willie Usher original."

"What? It was three-fifty a minute ago."

"Three-fifty is your best offer? Okay, sold."

The sheriff paid and walked away, shaking his head, the Candleholder of Truth under his arm.

All those cheeseburgers with Willie—maybe she hadn't been eating all that well lately. She spotted the farmer from a half mile down PCR 601 who had told her four months ago that no one would care if she moved into this place. Wirz, Wirz was the name—and he was standing next to a flatbed truck decked up mountainously with tilted baskets of fruits and vegetables. Jane kept wandering by, gazing agog at huge tomatoes still golden at the crown and emitting a pungent serpentine perfume, at bell peppers blazed with red and wooden boxes of strawberries, raspberries, and blueberries, each a little blood-stained with rose or purple juice. She hung around containing herself, always a dangerous condition for Jane, until she saw behind the veil of gluttony what fate had provided for her education—the old Wirz family Buick. It had three silver gills glinting on each dark green flank and a sign in its front windshield:

1951 Buick Special
F O R   S A L E
$150 FIRM

Jane put her hand through the open driver's side window and patted the scratchy gray upholstery. Farmer Wirz crept up behind her and whispered in her ear: "Even the lighter works." Startled, she stumbled backwards and caught sight of her blurred and pining countenance in the Buick's perfect enamel.

Then Farmer Wirz was coming around in his muffin-shaped tractor cap to start it up for her. Jane ran away.

Felix manned the barbecue pit in front of the nuptial arena. Here two exhausted-looking apple trees were going to get married during a drama Jane had composed for the occasion. Jimmy was supposed to be dressing the trees but was nowhere to be seen.

"So where is he?" Jane asked Felix.

Felix prodded hot dogs about. His low eyelids fell another notch and his massive chin rose. He puffed up his cheeks and began to whistle, and his face became a perverser and perverser hieroglyphic for keeping one's counsel. Jane stared at him.

"I'll bet he's drunk," she said.

Felix logrolled hot dogs around the grill, whistling "When You Wish upon a Star."

Jane sank into a lawn chair. Uh-oh, Jimmy figured out about Willie, she was thinking. She had been proud of herself for keeping her mouth shut, but who knows what had been spread all across her face? It had been such a—a bounteous afternoon. Her cheeks burned to think of it.

"I ain't saying he is, and I ain't saying he isn't," growled Felix, whom she had forgotten about.

Jane looked at him. "You are saying he is."

"No, I ain't. Because he ain't."

Jane was baffled; Felix, sarcophagus of the world's secrets, seemed to be trying to tell her something. She decided if she concentrated she should be able to read this contorted face. She aimed a terrible X-ray squint upon Felix, and in a moment his eyes rolled up from his work and drew a dotted line to the osage thicket behind the apple trees. Jane saw something blue flickering at its edge.

"I don't believe it! He's with some girl." Jane laughed, but the laugh sounded fake even to her. "What am I going to see if I sneak back there?"

"Why don't you mind your bidness," Felix said to his hot dogs.

Jane started for the osage, but at the same moment Jimmy loped out with a can of beer in his hand. His shirt was all puffed as though he had just parachuted to earth in it. His other hand was trying to settle the flaps in his trousers.

Behind him, also adjusting her clothes, was a girl who, Jane judged, could not have been more than sixteen. No more than sixteen if you looked at her face, that is, for she had the kind of believe-it-or-not figure that Jane would have gawked at in any public place after the age of six. Her waist was small; her white pedal pushers curved like a two-gallon goldfish bowl behind, her breasts were popping open the middle five buttons of a pink sleeveless shirt and Jane saw, or thought she saw, a pink bra behind this weakening trellis. And black ballet slippers on her feet, a style favored by tough white girls—*drapettes*—in Baltimore five years ago.

"This is Cheryl," Jimmy said.

"Are you an artist too?" Cheryl asked Jane.

"No," Jane said.

"Cheryl's been helping me," Jimmy reported. He edged closer to Jane. "What could I do?" he whispered, looking sheepish but not displeased with himself—in fact, he was trying not to smile.

"What *did* you do?" Jane hissed back.

Cheryl backed off discreetly, for a girl of her years, and patted her blond hair. This caused her breasts to rise in the air and wobble liquidly.

"She's such a comic-book sexpot," Jane whispered.

"Sheena of the Jungle," Jimmy agreed. "She did the bride while I was sitting under that tree there resting."

"She works like a dog for you."

"She has real possibilities," Jimmy admitted.

"You're going to get it for this," Jane said.

"I know."

"I'm not kidding."

"I know."

Cheryl was fishing the bride's veil out of the grass, carrying it to the tree.

"You better not dump her now," Jane said. "I hope she asks you for art lessons."

"She already did."

"Good."

Jane started to walk away. She flashed a SO WHAT look at Felix, who pretended to be studying a lump of gray sludge on the end of his cooking spoon.

"Jane," Jimmy called after her.

Jane turned around.

He said in a low voice: "If the boyfriend kills me, I will you my paintings. Look at this guy."

Jane looked where Jimmy was cautiously gesturing and experienced a queer, arctic fluttering around the gills. There were three of them; they were exactly, but exactly, the kind of white boys who had gone to reform school in Baltimore. Never mind Lenny Frank, a Jewish anomaly, violently demented at the age of eleven; boys like this, the size of big men at the age of sixteen, piled off to reform school cheerfully en masse. All three of them had hair slicked back and breaking like the crest of a tsunami over the forehead, packs of cigarettes making lumps in their T-shirt sleeves, and Joe Palooka arms with more tattoos than a cancelled postage stamp.

"Which one?" Jane said faintly.

"Does it matter? His name is Lester." Jimmy laughed a little at the name.

"You dope. You could really get hurt."

Jimmy shrugged. "She was helping me. She didn't mention this clown till five minutes ago."

"Does he know?"

"Beats me. He might have seen . . . something."

"Maybe she'll keep her mouth shut."

"She might," Jimmy said reasonably. "Anything is possible." He was smirking with a sort of blithe hopelessness. "You can go now," he added. "Cheryl is helping me."

Jane drifted back to Willie's junk-ringed station wagon and found herself doing something completely new to her: looking

for something to bang someone over the head with, if necessary. She picked up a huge rusty flashlight, but without batter-
ies it was light as a tin can. "What am I doing," she mumbled to
herself, and threw it down again in the grass. She glanced
around the circle of tables. Sheriff Staples was examining a giant
cucumber from Wirz's truck, and down meadow, Officer Rollo
squatted on his haunches, explaining to a little girl why she
should not hold a cat upside down. So what could happen?
Pow! pow! pow! When Jane whirled around, Jimmy was firing a
staple gun at the groom's striped cardboard trousers, Cheryl
was handing him the painted sections one by one, and the three-
headed boyfriend was smoking under a tree, watching this,
plainly discontented, but throwing no rocks.

The wedding of Bob and Louise

A thicket near Athens. Two apple trees. A cow stream. Enter Nuncio in Jane's pink nightgown.

NUNCIO: Room, friends, room if you please.
Give us room to rhyme.
We've come to marry Bob and Louise
In the good old summertime.

This is the Bride
Known county-wide
For her indescribably large backside.

And, to resume,
Here is Bob the Groom,
Whose heart is going boom-da-da-boom.

Enter Sunburnadeen on a life raft, looking wan in a pink satin bathing suit cut for Jane Russell.

NUNCIO: And come from afar in her yellow rubber
    dinghy
Is she who spins all hearts on her pinky,
Sunburnadeen the Great, Queen of all the
    Summers.
Sing you singers! Hum you hummers!

SUNBURNADEEN: I am Sunburnadeen. Wherever I pass
                 Trees grow like crazy, and also grass.
                 And people get married—except for me.
                 Cobblers go barefoot, and I go free.

                 Now young and old, attention please!
                 Is there a grouch in this group who sees
                 Any fault in the wedding of Bob and
                     Louise?
                 Let him speak now, or hold his peace.

Enter Lionel, in a lion's suit.

LIONEL: Get out the way, you peculiar tart!
                 I am King of the Cold Cold Heart,
                 Lionel! Come from Sausage Junction
                 To discern why I wasn't asked to this function.

                 And now I am hip. For Louise is my daughter
                 Gussied up to get hitched from her veil to
                     her garter.
                 This greenhorn Bob, through craft and art,
                 Has larcenied that poor girl's heart.

                 I told Louise to follow this rule:
                 Be an old man's darling, not a young man's
                     fool.
                 Too bad you got yourselves all overheated.
                 Tsk, tsk! For these nuptials won't be
                     completed.

*Lionel roughs up Bob and spits, ptooie! at his boutonniere. Bob
endures this as if rooted to the spot.*

LIONEL: Nope, I don't cotton to boyfriend Bob.
                 Occupation, fruit! How's that for a job?
                 This boob and his bankbook are both
                     underripe.
                 Would you let your daughter marry this
                     type?

TIRESIAS:	Well, talk up, peoples. Get in the act. Wouldja or wuncha?

"Nosiree bob," Sheriff Staples exclaims. "I would not."

Farm Life & Auto agent Jenkins agrees with the sheriff. "Carry her home and take a strap to her bee-hind," he shouts. The sheriff roars with laughter at this witticism.

Then Hank or Duke or Lester from Xenia yells: "Hey, Sherf. How about running them sambos, fairies, and beatniks out of town?"

Sheriff Staples draws himself up with a pained expression, sidles out of the front row and heads for the tree Cheryl's boyfriend is standing under. The sheriff moves like a rocking barrel, keys and handcuffs jangling liquidly at his belt with each slow sway.

Sunburnadeen stares a moment, then continues:

> The Groom has no dough, the Bride has no
> fear,
> Though famed through the world for her
> beauteous rear.
> Next summer in Reno, godspeed their divorce.
> But let's not put the cart before the horse.
> As a perfect match is a silly myth,
> I propose to wed them forthwith.

LIONEL:	Hands off my daughter, you trollop. Take that!
SUNBURNADEEN:	It seems I must slay this bad-mannered cat.

They fight.

TIRESIAS:	Slash! Boff! Bim! Bang!
	Clop! Bop! Crash! Clang!
	Screech! Yow! Gasp! Groan!
	Whoops! Old Lionel strikes home.
SUNBURNADEEN:	I'm seeing green spots. I'm falling apart.
	I'm feeling queer around my heart.
	I, Sunburnadeen of Modern Romance,

Had a great career going until this mischance.
My prenuptial divorce was almost perfected
When, plop! I died! How unexpected.

Enter Officer Rollo, dressed as usual.

OFFICER ROLLO: A father did this! What could be absurder?
You're coming with me, Pop. And the charge
is murder.

LIONEL: Mercy. What a blow to a lion of my station.
Er—is there a lawyer on location?

Enter Lawyer Nullindeed in robe and periwig, scattering papers in
all directions.

NULLINDEED: I am Lawyer Nullindeed.
I'll write you more briefs than you'll possibly
need.
Lex non scripta? Here's a ton of it.
I whip up contracts for the sheer fun of it.

LIONEL: Psst!—Can you prove this dead floozy's alive
and well?

NULLINDEED: For a fee I can, I must, I shall!

LIONEL: I dig, counsellor. Name your price.

NULLINDEED: Sixty dollars a minute would be very nice,
But since lawyers are so scarce around here,
I'll take a hundred, and a bottle of beer.

LIONEL: When pigs fly, chump! That's far too much.

NULLINDEED: (*Aside*) Can Nullindeed have lost his touch?
Oh well—the old girl isn't looking so hot.
I'll prove she's alive for whatever you've got.
Two bits?—a nickel?—a penny or two?

Lionel gives him a penny.

Okay, it's a deal. Merci beaucoup.

I say, young woman, get up on the double.
You're causing the living no end of trouble.
Hello? Yoo-hoo! Come come, that's enough.
If this winds up in court, I'm going to get rough.
But compromise is the lawyer's art
So allow me to say this ridiculous part:

Hocus pocus elecampane,
The whole truth, the droll truth, the sweet
    novocaine:
Up up, Sunburnadeen, and live again!

SUNBURNADEEN: Where am I? Who am I? Where have I been?
Is the wedding over?

NUNCIO: Let it begin.
Welcome back, Sunburnadeen, from death's
    dark door.
But now, as advertised in your brochure,
The time has come, great saint, if you please,
To proceed to the wedding of Bob and Louise.

Fred plays the Wedding March on his accordion. Suddenly Sunburnadeen forgets her lines. Though the crowd had shuddered when Sheriff Staples rocked across the green to rebuke Hank, Duke, and Lester, and though what he said, he said with meaty hands on hips and the sun careening piratically off the rims of his sunglasses, it now appears it was only a warning. For they're right where they were, smirking, though until the sheriff turned his large back they had looked sad and contrite. Perhaps Cheryl interceded for them. Out of the corner of her eye, Jane had noted her passionate gesticulations. And now Cheryl, Hank, Duke, and Lester are quarreling noisily among themselves just to the left of a Thicket near Athens. Jane hears Cheryl wail, "You're so ignorant, Lester! You're so stupid, mean, and ignorant!" Jane opens her mouth to hurry on with the wedding, even though she can't remember the words, when a great shadow swoops across her brow, as if a bird the size of a sack of meal is passing. She ducks. Uh-oh, it's the Nuncio being borne into the air, too shocked even to curse, on the hands of Duke, Hank, and Lester from Xenia, up over Sunburnadeen's head and down, down, pink nightgown fluttering, into the cowpie-choked creek, kersplat.

This catastrophe, the sight of Jimmy's handsome face be-smeared with muck, his aluminum foil wings dripping globs of the stuff, makes two-fifths of Sunburnadeen want to laugh. The other three-fifths squash this impulse. Hank, Duke, and Lester slouch off; Sheriff Staples stalks up to the creek to glare across it through his sunglasses, and says: "What did I tell you boys! Now that wasn't funny."

Fred is still playing the Wedding March. Sunburnadeen finally utters some mumbo jumbo and Bob and Louise are wed. She has rice along with wads of toilet paper in the bra of her bathing suit but forgets to throw it. People are drifting back to their cars, their tables, saying, "Is it over? What happened?"

Nothing appears to be broken on the former Nuncio. He trudges towards the farmhouse, Jane's pink nightgown glued blackly to his legs. When Jane sees him round the corner of the house a moment later, a bottle has mysteriously appeared in his hand.

Meanwhile Cheryl, in tears, and Hank, Duke, and Lester, smiling behind their hands, are pointed towards their rusty pink and gray Chevrolet Bel Air by Sheriff Staples. The engine comes alive like a machine gun. Sheriff Staples yells something about the muffler. They roll down the grassy slope to the blacktop meekly; then with a roar they disappear down PCR 601. The sheriff watches them all the way with his arms folded, meaning business.

The meadow is in deep shadow; a coolness moves through the air. People are folding up their tables. Cars and pickup trucks crunch slowly downhill, leaving long flat ribbons in the grass.

Now they are back on the porch. Willie, counting their take in the twilight, has just passed two hundred, all Jane's, he says, because he pissed away two hundred this morning. Jimmy's and Jane's, but Jimmy isn't interested. He has drunk half a quart of white port, little red flames show at the bottoms of his eyes, and he has disowned the Soul of Commerce. The other males on the porch are amused but understanding.

"You done the right thing just to set there in the mud or you would have roont the wedding," says Felix.

"You did good," Willie seconds. "Folks thought it was part of the show."

Felix adds: "You just wish you'd of poked somebody."

"That's a lie," Jimmy says gravely. He takes a long, smacking draw at his bottle.

"Gar! How you can drink that stuff," Felix says with a shudder. "It's sick-ning to watch."

"I see it coming," Jimmy says. "I'm turning into a male like the other males. I'm going to break down and get a real job any minute."

"Don't do nothing rash," Willie says, laying down another stack of one-dollar bills.

"I must be getting old," says Jimmy. "I've got to have respect. I want those low-lifes to be afraid to hurt me."

Roger says, with relish: "So what did you think you'd get if you knocked over the sucker's girlfriend in the bushes?"

Fred, who has been dreamily fingering his accordion, looks up in shock. "He did?" he says. "You did? In the bushes? The blonde? Wow, she had the hugest tits I ever saw on a short girl. They were, like, terrifying—how was she, man?"

Felix says. "Will you *shut!*" making a little motion of his finger towards Jane.

"Oops, sorry," Fred says.

"I don't believe this," says Jane. "You guys must think I'm Molly off the pickleboat—where do you think I was?" She lights a cigarette. "Anyway, she wasn't that gorgeous. She reminded me of a pygmy."

This speech provokes cackles and hee-hee's from all around the porch.

"Actually she helped us a lot," Jane says with dignity, seeing her mistake. "I kind of liked her."

"So did Jimmy," Roger says.

"Yeah, but she kissed and told," Felix remarks.

"That hasn't been definitely ascertained," Jane says. "Now look, friends, don't start any hush-hush stuff around me. I'm a woman of the world and don't you boys forget it."

Something about this remark causes the others to collapse in helpless laughter. "I'm a woman of the world, and don't you boys forget it," they repeat in falsetto, over and over. Jane tries to smile. They laugh until they are weak, when they settle down to smoke a joint. Only Jimmy is not laughing. He is no longer part of the group except in body. He fixes his red eyes on a knothole in the roofboards and for a long time says nothing at all.

It is now nine-thirty of a midsummer evening, and the sun, glittering percussively along the poison ivy on the far side of the driveway all the time they have been sitting there, sinks out of sight. A mockingbird sits in the willow off the porch, invisible except for the bobbing of one small branch, and unreels everything he has ever heard, from baby trills to wild alarms. And the sky in the west is equally absurd, boiling up far-fetched colors, trying each one on a different cloud. But Jane, preferring the backside of the sunset, turns to the east, to the unreally green treetops, to the queer mouse-colored glow of the sky and the velvety black of the road. So she sees it first—the pink and gray Bel Air inching along the shoulder, perhaps three hundred yards away.

She stands up, and at the same moment, jarred by her movement, Jimmy lurches to his feet, grabs one of the piles of money and waves bills out in front of him like two green bouquets. "No, thank you!" he shouts, suddenly performing Cyrano de Bergerac. "No, I thank you! And again I thank you!" And he throws the bills into the skunk cabbages.

The Bel Air rolls closer. Roger volunteers to take Jimmy into town, drag him indoors and keep an eye on him. Fred and Roger shanghai the kicking Jimmy into Roger's car, and they disappear down 601. And the pink and gray Chevrolet keeps approaching the house at a crawl along the road shoulder. The garish sunset glints solidly off the windshield; they can't see how many are inside. Finally the car comes even with the house —there's only one. It must be Lester. He gets out.

He wades through high grass and stops a few feet from the porch. A hand comes up and planes along one arc of his improbably modelled hair. Jane watches the muscles in his tattooed forearm moving like the shuttle of a loom. The pearly light in back of him darkens his face, but she sees he has large, soft eyes. Isn't it rococo, she thinks, that a male should go to all that trouble with his hair—and suddenly she's taken with that corkscrew of a forelock. But she has always placed a drape like this completely off-limits.

"Hank, Duke, and me, we shouldn't of messed up your boyfriend," he says.

Jane peers at him.

"Cheryl won't talk to me now."

So Cheryl is behind this.

"That's all right," Jane says. "I'll give him your apology."

He stands there, examining his feet in the skunk cabbages. "I'm sorry," he mumbles, following instructions. But still he doesn't leave. Instead he stomps around in a circle, as if he wonders why he is apologizing. "It tore me up when I saw him kiss my girl," he says heatedly, and folds his arms like Powhatan.

"Well, why don't you kiss his girlfriend?" Jane says.

He looks at her, uncomprehending. She shrugs, as if to say that's how we do things in this neck of the woods. Dawn breaks across his face, but now he looks nervously at Felix and Willie.

"Don't mind them," Jane says.

"Go 'head on," Felix says, looking the other way. "We ain't here."

Jane steps off the porch. Lester gives her a long, wet, grinding kiss, his tongue poking deep in her mouth like an eel, his hardness nudging her belly. Jane doesn't rush him. Finally he backs away with a smirk, finds his car and peels off towards Xenia.

"Goodbye," Jane says to the air.

"That was a brainy move," Felix says.

"We got off cheap," Jane says.

"I'll say," Willie observes, a little disgusted. "Come on, Felix, let's grab a cheeseburg." They climb in the wagon, which creeps to the edge of the blacktop. Willie leans out the window and calls to Jane: "Well, Toots? You coming?"

"I think I'll hang around here," Jane replies. "Thanks for everything."

"My pleasure."

"I'll see you later," Jane adds.

"Like, when?" Willie says.

When she doesn't answer he tells her: "Don't forget to pick those dollar bills out the grass."

At last it's just you and me and the starlight, the adventuress said to her dough. This is Jane, sitting swami-style on the rose bed, star-gazing out the bedroom window with the money between her legs. She is on a raft, alone. She looks for Polaris to guide her. But she has no idea which one is Polaris. There they are, scads of them, clinging to the smoky chute of the Milky Way like sequins on a veil. And here is the demimondaine under the veil, smoking lipstick-stained cigarette after cigarette, alone in the world, pilotless, and she doesn't know a single star by name. But that does not prevent her from throwing invisible cables to the stars and cranking up her spirit on their pulleys.

She leans far out over the sill and the money slides to the floor. In a moment she really has to go and put it in a proper place. Heartless, that is what she is, freakish, rude and heartless not to be with Willie on the very night he has made her (comparatively speaking) rich. But Jane is happy to be alone. For she is not altogether happy. And why on earth not?

She will return to that puzzle in a moment. First, the cash. Where to put it? She is not expecting to be robbed. Still, Jane, drifting anesthetically downward through class, is ever more at one with the moneyless state and its anxieties and consolations. She crouches by her little pile and studies the galaxy that transports her. The Milky Way looks ragged, a long soiled veil hanging from a ghostly demimondaine's pompadour, but somewhere Jane has read it is really flat as a watchface and turning, ever turning, like a roulette wheel. Luck seems as close as that: not too far off to change its mind and snatch the treasure away. Only 228 dollars, but enough to ransom nine weeks of summer, a voluptuous sum by anyone's standards, a virtual subsidy of Demeter, the subterranean gangster's payoff, a bus ticket out of the underworld.

Jane knows just the place. On her reference shelf stands a volume, *Fundamentals of Secondary Education*, by Cork and Drainer, which she and Hermine, as kids, had bought for a dollar at a North Howard Street used bookstore. They had taken it home and carved out all the print with a razor blade, so that it became a coffer whose walls were six hundred empty margins. Aside from the thrill of violating a taboo by operating surgically upon any book at all, at that age Jane and Hermine were always inventing secret repositories for hypothetical contraband—after all, yet a little while, and they would be hiding themselves and their baggage in the whole world. They had nothing, and especially not money, to put in the *Fundamentals of Secondary Education* at the time, so they filled it with corpses of Japanese beetles. But at thirteen Jane had pressed it into service as a hiding place for her ashtray, sometimes with the smoking butts still in it. Its cavity is somewhat blackened from this employment; still, it looks like a normal and certainly a boring book when closed. There she secretes her dough.

Now she can turn to the question of why, despite her good luck, she is somewhat less happy than the day she was born. She descends to the front porch and sits down on the couch to wait. She hates to wait, and that is how she realizes she is doing it. The couch feels wormy and damp against the backs of her legs. A car passes by, dragging a piece of tailpipe along the blacktop. Its noise bounces across her forehead like the zigzag attachment on a sewing machine. She lights up a Pall Mall; it tastes even more terrible than usual and she throws it into the wet skunk cabbages. This reminds her that, owing to Jimmy's outburst, eleven dollars are still at liberty there in the weeds, probably under the porch or out in the cornfield by now. Jimmy. She stirs slightly on her bottom, as though she has found herself sitting on a burr. She has to admit, much as she hates to, that she is waiting for Jimmy.

Not so long ago, in a leap of faith based on having the old Dodge under her ass in case she fell, she blasted out of the dormitories to take up the solo life. Then, for a moment, there she was all solo, navigating lonely roads cut to her fit in a solitary state. Full of fear and elation, she saw she could squat in a throwaway house that faced the highway, where anything could happen to you. That is what she wished, for anything to happen to her. And that quick, before anything could happen to her, what did she do with her fear and elation? She buried them in a boyfriend.

Wait a minute—Jimmy is no poltroon you can ward off with a flash of the beaver but a boy who loves women and does more than half of the housework. A unique male. And she tells herself that if ever she says he is not, she lies. For even now her lips are puckering in that lie. She sees that wishing in this morbid, corrupt way that Jimmy were here is exactly the same as wishing she had never met him. It is a kind of curse on him. And she thinks treacherously: Better no man at all than this suburban stretch of the ocean. Therefore, love him less, which should be easily done, or get rid of him. She cocks her chin defiantly into the tradewinds off the prow of the rat-eaten couch. Then she lowers her forehead into her hands.

So here is Jane in a posture most unusual for her, that of a half-baked adventuress who knows herself to be one. True, she did not invent this custom of burying romantic love in the tomb of a more stable union, as though one naturally followed the other, though in fact the shocking difference between these two states of affairs, so queerly reminiscent of life and death, has often been commented upon by wise women. Jane is almost realizing that even a unique male will be changed from a wizard into a dullard simply by making an excursion into the domestic habit with her. For with Jane, this will prove to be a laboratory result as dependable as the precipitation of blue vitriol from copper sulfate in the presence of water.

She senses that, no, she is not going to leave Jimmy, who has done nothing to deserve being left, but then again, if all goes well, she might drive him away. She raises her head. She feels a sudden odd spasm of pity for Jimmy, for she sees, from now on, how she will be nothing but trouble to the kid. If she does not leave him, she will make him pay. It does not occur to her that maybe she is not fit for love. She is in love, so she must be carried off to the tertiary stages of love. But not wanting to see that far, Jane now does something she almost never does. She pulls on an old nightgown and goes straight to bed, putting her head between two pillows.

○
○
● **Fundamentals**

of

secondary

education

Jane presses her head between two pillows in a big, gray, empty front room, the largest upstairs in the derelict house. For some reason no old wallpaper clings to its walls. There are only cobwebs, unsteady pillars of books, and the metal bedstead under the window that catches moonlight, already shredded by branches, in its twisted sheets. More than the other rooms this one is abandoned. Pearly dust glows from its unfinished floors, walls and ceiling. To one side is a closet door. The closet behind it is large but empty. Jane and Jimmy have forgotten its existence. They have nothing to put in a closet. Besides, it stinks of a dead rat under the floorboards.

For once in her life, Jane goes right to sleep. Sleep, on her, has a thin skin. Light penetrates it, local movement picks at it, voices quickly pry up its edge. At first, far from scaring her, it seems, quotha, the silliest stuff that ever I heard.

"What's this?"

"Is it cunt?"

"It better be."

Laughter, and four, no, five clowns at the end of the bed, stumbling around like some kind of vaudeville act. What angel wakes me from my flow'ry bed? Jane dreams she is reaching for her glasses.

"It better be! Shit fire! I guess he knows what he wants."

"Didn't come but for one goddamn thing."

Moonlight rinses the curtainless room. *Woof*—a column of books topples, and the round ashtray that was on top of them clanks across the uneven floorboards. It stops. The closet door opens.

"Phew. What died in here."

Closes.

"Where's the light in this joint?"

The figures move thickly about, sometimes dancing off into a parade, sometimes bunching into one wooly mass. They are running their hands over the walls, looking for a light switch. The only one is behind the headboard—behind Jane.

"Shit, I guess I know cunt when I see it."

All at once Jane throws a lasso over the edge of sleep and grasps what they have been saying. Her first impulse is to play dead—maybe they will look, sniff the body, pass by. But her eyes won't close and instead her hand goes straight to her glasses. The darkness hardens into compartments. She reaches for the light switch and planes of wall snap up around her. And around them.

"Look at that."

"I said I know cunt."

"I guess you do." They gather around the bed. They look human now, and more her size. She feels better, then swiftly worse, as she peers at the one nearest her, who bends over her and says again: "I guess I know cunt."

He is dark, shorter than the others, with a pinched expression. A day's growth of beard scoops out his already small face. It is hard to tell his age. Twenty-five? Though he stares at her with—for some reason—hatred, he does not look strong. *I could take him*, Jane thinks absurdly. Meanwhile there is something incredible, some unbelievable detail, about him that makes this *not* like a scene from some cheesy black-and-white thriller where she is about to be killed. She realizes she is gazing obliquely, with instinctive tact, if tact is the word, at the oval name patch of a Sunoco gas station uniform—she is looking at his name. *Homer*. She almost laughs.

Behind him, the other four: teenagers, pale-eyed, with soft pimply cheeks of an unhealthy pink, as if they have all been scalded in the same soup. Brothers. One is the oldest, one is the baby, the two in between could be twins. Their hair is thin and pinkish; all are big and pudgy, with arms like sticks. Lost souls, so blurred, incoherent and feckless they make the Xenians of this afternoon look like princes. The Xenians *are* princes in Xenia, but these—they could look out of place anywhere. They are not sure yet what's going on. They stand behind their malignant little chaperone, hardly daring to believe he knows what he's doing; for if he did, why would he want them along? Now they are poking at the rough plaster, eyeing the cobwebs that throw fantastic shadows over the ceiling. They eye the girl in the bed with the hair and glasses the same way.

"Are you sure this is a—"

The dark one says sharply: "It's a cathouse. Like I told you."

The oldest brother looks offended. "Like fun," he mutters.

"You're right," Jane says, encouraging mutiny. "This is my house." He looks at her blankly. She is no authority, just part of whatever went wrong here.

"Where are the whores?" the youngest one blurts.

"Shut up," one of the twins says automatically.

"What do you think *that* is?" Homer says, jerking his finger at Jane. The baby stares.

Jane thinks: Maybe I should get out of bed to put myself in a stronger position. But would it be wise to argue with these guys in a flimsy nightgown? She inches away towards the far side of the bed.

Homer asks her, accusingly, like an office manager trying to save face in front of a squadron of clerk typists: "Where did you put the other broads?"

Jane tries to laugh.

"You know what we're here for, and we want it," he adds.

"I'm not so sure this is a cathouse," says one of the twins faintly.

"What do you know about it?" Homer barks. "I said it's a cathouse and it's a cathouse. There's the girl."

They all five look at Jane, the labile factor of disbelief flowing like a puny electrical current from one of their faces to another. You really couldn't accuse them, so far, of having a good time at her expense. The four brothers suffer dully; they have the irrelevant faces of subjects photographed for exemplary diseases in medical texts. The other, their mentor, is boundlessly irate, a B-movie psychopath. Nobody is happy.

"You made a mistake," Jane tries to say pleasantly. "Why don't you just forget it and leave? This is my house, I live here."

"You're a whore," Homer says. "You got a nightie on, ain't it?"

Jane sees there is no use talking. They are not going to leave. Her heart begins to stroke, stroke, stroke, like some crude, purposeless armature wired up in a science class. That she should be offered as exhibit A in this low-life fantasy of the sex wizard and his apprentices! Suddenly her tact flies out the window.

"Who are you trying to kid?" she says. "Any fool can see this is not a whorehouse. Even those little boys can see it."

His face gathers into a dark knot. Never mind the gauzy nightgown, she needs to be on her feet, and now. She starts to slide off the bed on the other side. His left hand shoots out and fastens on her bicep; his right hand slaps her sharply under the jaw. Sharply, but not hard. Her glasses flop askew but somehow stay on and fall back, more or less, in front of her eyes. She isn't hurt but a green-black wave of depression passes over her. It's this, she's seeing the seriousness of the situation, those five against her alone, her heart starts going a million beats a minute, and she feels the biochemical shock of it, then a deep, deep tiredness. But even so she easily wrenches free of his hand and off the bed.

The four brothers back away slightly at this eruption, looking confused. This is not what Homer promised, something easy, something silky, where at a word from Homer the girl takes care of everything and just like that you have something to brag about.

"That's right," Jane says to the boys. Her shaky voice studies to be wise. "This fellow is going to get you in a lot of trouble, do you know that? Don't you wish you were home right now?"

"I don't think it's a cathouse," one of the twins whispers.

"Get the fuck out of here," Homer shouts at them. "Pussies! I'll take care of her myself. Wait downstairs. Watch the front."

They exit quickly, and he slams the door behind them and turns to face her across the room. She is standing in the small space between bed and window, and now she does something tactical, to her own surprise. She pushes the whole rose-painted bedstead out, out, out to the middle of the floor. There it stands in the empty room, an island she can run around forever if necessary. And now she waits, hunched, as ready as she'll ever be, which is not very ready, aware of her body in the worn cotton nightgown, aware that her nipples and pubic hair are soft dark shadows in its transparency. Not that she feels fetching, only exposed. She can feel the blood bashing rhythmically against the soft membranes in her neck, ears, and stomach, like the mechanical surf of a washing machine. It doesn't seem possible that the body could stand this for long. Therefore, because she must predict an end to it in order to endure it, she thinks: Jimmy will come home.

Now begins the race around the bed. He gallops a few steps at a time, and Jane is always ahead of him; she is barefoot, his mechanic's boots can get no purchase. Besides, he seems scrawny, tired, eaten up by something, maybe a little drunk. He lunges, she slides off nimbly as a nymph in Arcadia. A cartoon cloud of dust flies up in front of the naked light bulb; the powdery floorboards make it easy for her to glide, reverse, twist away.

"C'mere," he keeps saying. "C'mere, I'm gonna pay for it, you damn bitch cunt, c'mere!"

This is not persuasion, Jane realizes, it's epistemology. He repeats his faulty knowledge over and over, chasing the refractory quiddity around the bed to convince them both he will never change his mind. Jane is not immune to flickers of weird bravado. They are like little electrical disturbances along the overworked circuitry. She thinks, if my heart doesn't quit I can stay ahead of him, she thinks, thank God I have big muscles for a girl, she thinks, *I can take him*—but that's so crazy, why does she keep thinking that? And then she tells herself, just hold him off, Jimmy will get home. But in fact it's too late. It must be two-thirty, three, and now there winks, far back in her memory, the mouth of the hole she's in: a ring of brittle sunset, Jimmy stumbling through it with red-rimmed eyes, nine-tenths dead to the world already. Suddenly he's playing Cyrano de Bergerac with frayed nosegays of bills in each hand: *"No thank you! No, I thank you! And again I thank you."* And Roger and Fred hustling him off to town. Dragged to safety by love—Jane could curse him, but no, she blanks the picture from her mind. He must come home, because she can't keep this up forever. She's sure to make a mistake, to weaken.

"The price is coming down, you dumb skirt," Homer says, panting. Jane backs away from the bed, leans against the wall, and stares at him.

"Why did you come here? How did you pick this place?" she asks him. She is not going to argue the point. She wants to know if there is someone to blame for all her troubles.

"I seen it."

"What did you see?"

"I seen it from the road. I seen what was going on."

"What was going on?"

"You know what was going on. Whore! Don't ask me no more questions. I don't want to talk to you. Damn slut bitch cunt. C'mere!"

Now he remembers to try to smash her against the wall with the bed. But he steps on the ashtray, trips and falls sideways into a pile of paperback books, which take off like a fleet of flying saucers.

"Bastard!" He gets to his feet. His face is gray with rage, metallic, dead, his eyelids taut and lowered. His lips hardly move.

"How long you think I'm gonna put up with this?" he says.

It occurs to her that if she makes him any angrier, when he finally catches her, he might beat her to death.

She says: "Listen. It's not you personally. I'm not in this business or you'd be as good as anybody else. Can't you understand I'm not in this business?"

He cocks his shoulders back and screams at her: "I understand all right, cunt. I don't care who you give it to for free." He holds his billfold up, shakes it crazily; it flops open in his hand. "Look! look!" he says. "I didn't take it, I never taken it, I always paid for it. See?" He pulls out some cash, creases it roughly down the middle, and with a jerk of his arm sails it in her direction like a paper airplane. The notes flitter down to the bed: three one-dollar bills.

Something smashes downstairs. The brothers, smashing things—that's more up their alley than sex. There's nothing down there to smash but Jimmy's paintings, his equipment. A new wave of black-green depression rolls over Jane—and she's made a mistake in backing so far away from the bed. Homer springs onto it and, this time, over it. His thick bootsole sinks deep in the hash of sheets and dollar bills and pops out again like a plunger. He bowls through the air and comes down in front of Jane. She's cornered. But he's not good at this either. She gets an elbow in, pushes off his crotch with her bare foot and, when his grip breaks, ducks free. Furious, he sinks his whole hand and fingers into her hair. Jane's hair—when it's braided, you could tow a Volkswagen with it. Stuck, she twists around, opens her mouth wide, and bites his forearm as hard and deep as she can. And though she knows that boys punch, girls bite, she's thrilled to hurt him with the same mouth he wouldn't listen to. As a kid she often practiced biting herself but was always disappointed, for no matter how hard she tried to act like a mad dog, she never drew blood. Now she sees that it is quite another thing to bite some other animal and not yourself, for you don't have to feel the pain. She grinds her teeth until something salty springs into her mouth.

"Jesus Christ you fucking loony tune!" He pushes fiercely off her head to cradle his damaged forearm and—asking herself at the same time why she doesn't just beg his forgiveness and give in to the guy while she's still alive—completely without plan, she bolts to the bedroom door, slips through it and slams it behind her. Although she's looking at the stairs, she can hear the four brothers banging around at the foot of them. Her own room stands open to her right and she steps inside and hides behind the door. Then curses herself: Moron, how obvious can you get. But now she's lucky. As Homer bursts out of the bedroom there is a noise at the bottom of the stairs, something falling over with a crash, and without looking around he pounds down the steps.

"Grab her, don't let her go," he shouts.

It occurs to Jane that the brothers would probably have let her walk right by them.

But now she can proceed to a clever hide-out, like the clever girl she is. True, she has not been particularly brave, because long ago she could have jumped out the window and taken her chances with a fall into the skunk cabbages; but they are chunked with big rocks that a farmer once pried out of his fields, and all she could imagine, when she thought of going over the sill, was supporting a man's pumping weight on top of a broken back. She didn't have the nerve. And she has not been particularly strong, because—really—he's such a wizened, ugly little monkey; shouldn't she be able to take him? Again she pushes that madness out of her head.

Now, however, Jane can be clever, in one of the freaky, solipsistic ways she has always been clever. She was always good, too good, at hide-and-go-seek. She always knew places. For instance she used to hide in her parents' liquor cabinet, which she could get into with the liquor. She would rearrange the bottles in front of her, and by the time she came out again,

Hermine, her disgusted pursuer, would be upstairs watching TV. It took Jane some years to understand she had missed the point of the game. But of course she is hoping for such infidelity, such want of perseverance, now.

She goes back into the bedroom and lets herself into the closet —that long and empty closet, stinking of dead rat. For here, long ago, Jane noticed a perfect hide-out. The closet, unlike the bedroom, still has wallpaper—layers and layers of it, stiff as cardboard—and at the end of the closet where, if you could pass through the wall, you would be floating in air over the landing, the wallpaper is loose, though it looks solid, and behind it is a big hole in the plaster. In a moment, Jane is sitting in the wall, breathing decades of rat feces and plaster dust; and though she never tried this haven before, it falls out better than she could devise. Through a long crack in the other side of the wall, she can just see the top of the stairs. And if she closes her left eye, sees a wedge of her own room, including the work table, where, oh God! the *Fundamentals of Secondary Education* is still lying, stuffed with all the money she has in this world.

She hears them arguing downstairs.

"Aw, let's go," says a fluty, querulous voice. "This ain't no whorehouse." Homer's voice rises over that one.

"I said she goddam well chewed my arm off, the dingaling. Look at this!" Silence. Presumably the brothers inspect the wound. They start to laugh. Homer tramps up the stairs alone. His profile on the landing is furious, betrayed. He goes into the bedroom, pauses, throws open the closet door, pauses, slams it again.

He reappears on the landing, sideways to Jane, and peers into her room. She sees him jerk forward a little as he spots a closet door on its far wall. He disappears; the invisible closet door bangs open. A basket of dirty laundry, an apparition from Mother Goose, sails through the air and explodes into a pastel rain of bras and panties. He comes back into view, walking on panties. Notices a piece of paper in Jane's typewriter and

—exactly as Jane would do in his place—crosses over to read it. Jane winces, for she knows what it says: *My mistress with a monster is in love*

In great disgust he crumples the sheet and throws it on the floor. And now he is looking hard at another object which, like the paper in the typewriter, may need to be heaved across the room. The *Fundamentals of Secondary Education*. He reaches.

What occurs now is not entirely clear. Jane kneels on all fours inside the closet wall, thinking chaotically, wanting someone to blame for all her troubles, someone besides Homer, someone besides herself. *Jimmy*. She feels some sort of psychic TNT blow up all her loyalty to Jimmy along with the last hope that he will ever arrive to save her. She sees him with those green bunches of hard-won money at the ends of his absurdly waving arms and curses him with all the strength of her lying heart. Because he is not here she is on the verge of losing all her dough, her liberty, her summer, her ticket if ever she should want out of this place and away from Jimmy, as, yes, she thinks, I do. I do.

That she should lose that money!—the defense of her, let's put it bluntly, indelibly spotted and inconstant honor dwindles to a caprice before this great cause. But if she goes so far as to will what happens next, if there is an atomic particle of decision at work here, it is lost forever in the mushroom cloud of its consequences. He reaches for the *Fundamentals of Secondary Education*. The better to observe the fate of her bankroll, she yanks herself forward on a rotten lath. Suddenly it cracks, with a loud though muffled *boink*, and half the remaining wall comes down on her. She coughs, sneezes, bangs her forehead on gritty plaster, her knees slide off a joist and she rolls sideways through the stiff curtain of wallpaper back into the world. And into the arms of Homer, now inside the closet. Or rather, into his hands, which lock with unfriendly purpose around her neck.

Here now is a grim and serious pickle. She has not had a breath of whole air since the plaster dust started to fall; her glasses, though still on, are white with dust, and Homer is on top of her, his knee digging into her belly. The summer she was about to lose becomes the whole of her life. The case is dire enough so that she actually thinks to herself: I haven't written a book yet. I can't die. But how long can she live without air?

"You're gonna pay for all your lip, cunt," he says, as though this indemnity is still in the future.

Maybe this man is stronger than she thought. She tears at his hands. She can do nothing. Doubtless there are tricks—*Pull out his eye*, some well-trained ex-Marine would advise her blandly—but by now she is convinced she shouldn't get this fellow any madder. She cannot speak, but waves her arms frantically as if there were two white flags at the ends of them.

Getting the message—and perhaps he doesn't desire her death—he lets go.

"I paid for it, you thieving bitch," he reminds her.

"Well," Jane says. (Her voice is not quite itself yet.) "If you're going to put it in those terms, I'm convinced. Let's waste no more time haggling. How about right here?"

"On the bed," he commands. He stands, she stands, they proceed to the rose-painted bed. He loosens his workpants and she hitches up her nightgown. He falls to, rather joylessly after all this.

"How do you like it, baby?" he asks.

"I don't think you're really my type," Jane says, staring into his face. She sees that if he did not shave, he would have a black tufty beard almost to his eyes. She sees he had a bad case of acne some years back. There's a small white pit shaped like a bottle cap on the left side of his chin. My right, his left, she notes. It's remarkable how little a woman can feel, in fucking; not that this biological ability to play dead mitigates her humiliation. Somehow it completes it. She could pretend, as a private impertinence, that she ordered this drone to masturbate her, but her heart would not be in it. She tells herself to pay attention, for this, like your death, is something unlikely to happen to you twice. And it's true that one like Homer, in a gas station, in a grocery store, in line at the DMV, would normally be invisible to her; but he is not what the cunt from outer space had in mind, in fact nothing at all like what Jane, as mistress of her own dark ceremonies, can imagine, and besides—he's finished. Stands up, zips his green gabardine gas station trousers with a nervous braggadocio smile—the face of a mental patient who has just cheated at a game of gin rummy. He fishes around in the sheets now, looking for those three one-dollar bills. Jane turns her back.

Then he's yelling: "You guys. Come on up now. Look what I got for you. C'mere."

Jane hears the screendoor bang, feet scrabbling across the front porch. It seems the brothers are running away from this opportunity. In a moment, a car horn blares nasally, once, twice, three times. Homer runs to the window and leans over the sill.

"I guess I know cunt," he shouts. "Come on."

There's no answer at first. Then: "Ain't you done yet?"

"You fucking queer punks!" Homer yells furiously. "You little pussy punks. She's ready for you, you punks. Now c'mere."

Silence, then the starter motor whines, *waa-waa-waa*, like a gigantic mechanical babydoll. At last the motor kicks over, idles. A geometric glow rises into the branches outside the window. Headlights.

Now he is angrier with them than he is with Jane. He gallops by her to the door, clatters down the stairs and out the front. And she, she runs downstairs and climbs out a back window. She heads off wildly, stumbling, barefoot, into the cowfield. A moment later she is telling herself: Stupid coward. Why didn't you look? For their tires peel out shrilly on the asphalt, and all Jane sees disappearing down the country highway is a white car.

Book III

Justice

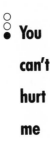

You
can't
hurt
me

Moonshine and Lion are left to bury the dead.
Ay, and Wall too.
—A Midsummer Night's Dream

She pedals toward town, as fast as her spare-parts bike can roll. The house she flees may be a fit resort for tramps, but her destination is strictly middle class. It never enters her mind that her next stop should not be her local police. She went back to the house only long enough to pull on a pair of shorts and a jersey. She did not even look for shoes.

She is alive, and except for a lump on her head that she got when the wall caved in, she is unhurt. As for the worst of it, she tells herself: Given that I lived, it couldn't have happened to a better person. She has never looked on her body as a temple —more like a garage. Her blood is laced with Orthonovum, so that no footloose egg will show an interest in the barbarian intruder. Back in her study, inside the *Fundamentals of Secondary Education*, her bankroll is untouched. (*That* she checked.) And finally, the odds that justice may be done are not bad at all. She can describe the criminal in minute detail, from the bottlecap-shaped scar on the left side of his chin to the surgical condition (circumsized) of his erectile tissue. She may well know his name, occupation, and place of employment. As for her veracity as a witness, thank God she knows the police chief personally. She will not have to stammer out any excuses for the proximity of the old wreck of a house to the country road, the opportunity of night, the ill counsel of a desert place, the lockless front door, since Officer Rollo knows all that already.

Back of these thoughts is the refrain *You can't hurt me*—and yet she pedals the slow bike as hard as she can. She can't believe it's over, that's the problem. The never-feared has occurred, and the erroneous belief, *Nothing like this can ever happen to me*, has been replaced by the idea, *Something like this will always happen to me*. So that, even with only cool night air lifting the hair beside her ears, even with only the crickets, tree toads, and punctual *ratch*, *ratch* of her bicycle chain disturbing the quiet, even with open fields billowing into blue-black infinity beyond the ditches on either side of the dark road, Jane can't quite believe she is free of them. Maybe they'll come back. Maybe they're on their way back right now.

On an old two-lane blacktop through rolling cornfields in southwest Ohio, you first see a spectral glow behind a faraway hump in the road, say a mile off, and then it comes over the crest with an almost audible pop, a pair of tiny headlights whose glow is impersonal, self-absorbed, flat; they hang there a moment, then fall away. Then they are back, larger, rising over another hill, and now you see them move, a muleteam of comets drawing an invisible load, still hieratic and withdrawn until —owing to some coincidence in the angle of the beam and your pupil—all at once they bloom enormous, explode without a sound and cast two perfect clouds of shining pollen into the air they plough. And the air begins to solidify behind them, no longer only light and the absence of light, but pale, solid color, the sheen of gray or light blue metal, perhaps even white metal, a white car.

Jane is never really sure it is that car. *Them.* This one is coming from the east, from Harmonia Springs, and Homer and company drove off to the west, towards Xenia. But they could have circled back on the perpendicular farm roads, nothing could be easier, Jane did it hundreds of times in the Dodge, it is hard not to do it, not to turn aimlessly left and left, or right and right, in that agreeable prison of plane geometry, homing again and again to the scene of the crime, why should a car full of genuine criminals do anything else?

She struggles against panic, tries to concentrate on the pokey, earthbound machine between her legs. But as the headlights come over the next to last hill and sink into the last trough, you have too much time to tell yourself who it is, if you happen to be looking for somebody, to change your mind and change it again, and as soon as Jane sees her own arms and legs whiten in those headbeams, she turns the bicycle off the road —wrenches the handlebars blindly to the right as if the bike can gallop up the bank and across the rugged cornfields. And still peddling crazily she feels the bike sink away underneath her, and she is flying over the handlebars into nothing, then water, then mud. A blind horse heads straight for the ditch —and now she is at the bottom of the ditch, already trying to run with her knees grinding into stony muck and the most peculiar sensation of something alive wiggling out from under her, a frog or lizard, maybe even a snake. She scrambles up the bank with her knees flinging up hot stars and, inefficient fugitive that she is, looks back over her shoulder at the car. And sees in the air above it a pink throne and a silver beehive —Professional Beauty Shop Chair, *ONLY $15*. And those familiar pelvic-bone antlers, the devout and childlike gaze of the moose. The door creaks tiredly, and Willie (Jane had forgotten his existence on the planet Earth) slowly unfolds, in the deconsecrated vestments of some well-fed suffragan, who would be greatly surprised to find his black-faced double standing here by a ditch on Pocahontas County Road 601. But no more surprised than Willie is to see Jane climbing out of the mud, one upside-down bicycle wheel still wobbling in the air between them. His face is troubled, and she can well imagine she looks a fright. But he, blacker than the dark, wearing a crimson surplice over his bare chest and a pair of yellow silk boxer shorts, looks impossible, a vision, an enormous puissant elf or the Red Cross Knight of Africa.

"Mercy," he says softly. "I believe it is my darling, but I can't be sure."

"I believe it is the Bishop of Fort Wayne," Jane says, smiling across the ditch at him. "But I hope it isn't."

"It isn't," Willie replies. "We ain't what we seem."

"Yes, we are spirits of another sort," Jane agrees.

Suddenly she sees something as clearly as though it were spelled out in stars across his forehead. He knows where Jimmy is, or rather he knows where Jimmy is not. Knowing that Jane is alone, the Red Cross Knight of Africa is on his way to her bedroom. But she is not in her bedroom.

Now she would cry, if crying were in her repertory. What can it mean, this episode of her education, in which the one night she lies down alone in a hundred, there comes not the gentle outlaw Willie, who has no charted bed, so that his presence after dark comes only as a gift, but rather a demented Boy Scout leader with his troop of idiots, who forces her, so to speak, to work for a living, and then throws at her for two hours' desperate work the minimum wage?

"Why didn't you come an hour ago?" she says.

Willie blinks at her—what is the meaning of the question?

"Aren't you going to ask me why I rode my bike into this ditch when I saw you?"

Willie says: "I know it wasn't cause you saw me coming. No young woman has to jump in the ditch if she don't want my company. My goodness. Wait till old Mr. Cooper sees that bike."

"I thought you might be somebody else," Jane says slowly. "Some guys, I never saw them before, came in the house while I was in bed and . . . " Her voice trails off. "Just one guy ended up, uh, you know," she amends, not wishing to exaggerate. "I was on my way to the police station. I was afraid they were coming back."

Willie gives her a hand across the ditch, throws the bike on the back. He climbs in the wagon next to her but does not start the car.

"Did he harm you?" he asks, his hands on the steering wheel.

Jane reflects. "Not irreparably," she finally says.

"Who was it?"

She shakes her head. Even what she knows she would not repeat, for fear of conferring some quixotic obligation on a male protector.

After a silence Jane says firmly, disliking to appear piteous: "I'm all right."

Willie asks her: "White or Negro?"

"White."

He sighs, starts up the wagon. "Where to, darling?" he says. "Anywhere you want to go. You really want to talk to the cops?"

Jane looks sharply at him. There has never been any uncertainty about this. That was what you did next, wasn't it? "Don't you think I should?"

Willie shrugs.

"Don't you?"

"If you think you get any satisfaction," he says. He backs around on the shoulder and turns back the way he came; they head slowly towards town. A low line of cream-colored clouds is unrolling along the farthest cornfields to the east like a circus tent going up.

But what would you do if you didn't go to the police, she is thinking. What if there were no police? She would sneak off under that glowing circus tent with Willie, roll with him in the tall grass of some meadow that can't be seen from the road, sleep curled in his lap, let him take and pet her and comb and braid her hair, and bathe her in his private swimming hole and throw away her clothes and fuck her nicely.

But no, she must look on her body as, of all things, evidence. She must carry this humid, fingerprinted section of flesh off to the police in all its nastiness, or a crime will go unpunished. Make no mistake, Jane wants Homer to be punished, and in the worst way—there is no middle-class piety about that. Is there?

"I mean, Officer Rollo is a friend of mine," she says.

Willie says nothing.

"And yours. A friend of yours."

"I got no beef with the chief," Willie says. "He's a hard man if you make a U-turn on Cincinnati."

He means that the police chief of Harmonia Springs is a glorified traffic cop, but Jane thinks, I know his name. I know the guy's name.

On the edge of town, they drive by an old man on a bicycle, his basket full of egg crates.

"I have to do *something*," Jane says.

Willie pulls up in front of the Municipal Building. One of the town's two police cars dozes at a notch in the curb like an underworked ruminant at a trough.

"Well, I don't hold with it," Willie says.

"You don't think the guy should be punished?" Jane says a little testily.

Willie snorts softly and rolls his eyes. He seems to mean that is a silly, naive idea.

"I feel like getting back at somebody," Jane says.

Willie nods.

Jane opens the car door and Willie says: "You sure now, darling. I could take you home with me."

Jane wrenches herself out of the car and starts to pad up the cool sidewalk to city hall on her bare feet. She does not look back, and only as Willie rolls slowly away from the corner does she hear what he said. With me, he said. I could take you home with me. Where to, darling? You know I could take you. Anywhere you want to go. To a place that can't be seen from the road. Or home. Or anywhere you want to go. I could take you home with me.

When Patrolman Dickey—the town's number two cop of three—strolled into the station at eight, sloshing coffee on the floor from a paper cup, Officer Rollo had him drive Jane to County Hospital. Riding in the front seat of the number two sky-blue patrol car, Jane felt like a stool pigeon in a bad movie, which in a way she was. She slouched out of sight behind the dashboard. She sank even lower on the way back, since by now people were on the streets.

Except for that sidetrip, she had been in the town hall basement for six hours now, stuck to an orange vinyl chair that squeaked like a rubber mouse every time she moved. Bored senseless, she stared at the wall, which was painted a pale glossy green found nowhere in nature except in the dreams of a person dying of cholera. No one was in the place but Jane and Officer Rollo. His office said CHIEF. Its door was closed.

Officer Rollo was a dignified man. He was the brown of a brown egg, but wizened. As small and exact as his cousin Felix was large and approximate, he had an air of knowing more than he said. Jane certainly hoped it was true. A long time ago, at 5:08 a.m., he had sat down with her, taken up a mechanical pencil and a yellow legal pad, and made notes in a small and secretive hand.

At the end he said: "I want you to go in the toilet and see do you have any bruises on your neck."

In the long mirror inside the bathroom door, Jane examined herself. She looked like a war refugee, she had a bump on her head and her right knee was puffed and going blue-black. But she had no marks on her neck. It was a long neck, with plenty of room for bruises, and she went over it minutely, but it was not even red. The truth was plain: Save to rape her after first demonstrating the discomforts of death by strangulation, the fellow had barely touched her.

Officer Rollo barked: "You don't have a single mark on you you didn't put on your own self?"

"I was doing a pretty good job of staying away from him until he got me around the neck," Jane said.

"Look at you! I've seen better looking things crawl out of a shell hole on Pork Chop Hill. You might have took a slap or two while you were at it."

Jane sulked and Officer Rollo blinked at her patiently. "Come come, young lady. You didn't just fall off the turnip wagon. I'm only a little small-town police chief and come tomorrow what I think won't count. It's the type of case this is."

"Can't they just test his jism under a microscope?" she blurted.

The chief looked dismayed.

"Look, I'm not going to talk this way in front of strangers," Jane said.

"It might not be a question of whether he did it," Officer Rollo said carefully. "It might be a question of how willing to him the girl was."

Jane had an idea. "Hey, if you catch this guy, check out his forearm. He's got a bruise like a horse bit him."

"A horse bit him?"

"I bit him."

"I thought he couldn't catch up with you."

"Once," Jane admitted, "he grabbed me by the hair, and I got him on the arm."

The chief wrote that down. "Possible contusion on the perpetrator," he muttered.

"So what?" Jane said. "He can't say he raped me in self-defense."

"I just wisht you'd let him pop you in the eye once for appearance's sake."

"I couldn't," said Jane. "I couldn't afford to lose control of the situation."

"Control of the situation!" the chief laughed unhappily.

Jane resolved to shut up. She was wondering who in ancient days had told her to come here, since in the present Willie had sensibly recommended the opposite.

"Only my mother would think it was my civic duty to do this," Jane said. "Why am I listening to her?"

"Now quit talking negative," Officer Rollo said. "Your mama is right. That was a serious crime that boy did. I can't have that kind of acting in my town. If you can't get him on a rape charge, you could maybe nail him on a break-in. He could get one to three for that. If you stick with it."

"One to three!" Hard-hearted Jane was ready to lock him up and throw away the key.

"If you stick with it," the chief repeated. "And I will be very disappointed in you if you back out."

That had been five hours ago. Now Officer Rollo leaned out of his door at last, crooking his finger at Jane. She went into his office and there, standing on the same dinky patch of linoleum with Jane, with Patrolman Dickey's hand on his upper arm, was Homer.

Already, he did not look dangerous—a sickly, unprepossessing nobody, his small face bluish from lack of sleep, anger, and fright, looking past Jane's shoulder as if she too were invisible. Because he had recovered it, that deeply invisible quality. Jane could see it even as he stood there with a policeman's hand on his arm.

"That's him," she said.

"You can definitely identify this as the individual who broke in your house at approximately three a.m., June 26th, and sexually assaulted you?"

"That's him."

"I been home all night," Homer said. "I got witnesses."

"Home is 24 Grotto Court in Xenia?"

"That's right."

"Can you explain what your car, a white 1958 Ford, Ohio plate 35-49OZ, was doing in Arbuckle's parking lot from ten p.m. last night to two this morning?"

"I don't know. My buddy borrowed it."

"Could you give me the name and address of your friend?"

"I forget."

"You forget the name of the individual who borrowed your car?"

"I didn't forget. I never knew it. Just some guy who comes in the station."

"And you lent your car to this unknown individual?"

"I'm a generous person." Trying to smirk, Homer threaded a cigarette with shaking hands between his dry lips. Patrolman Dickey took it away.

"Did you also lend your shirt to this individual? The one from the Sunoco station, with your name on it?"

"Thanks for being as stupid as you are, pinhead," Jane interjected.

"Pipe down," the chief said to her. "Well, Homer, you're in a peck of trouble. I want to remind you to watch what you say, because you don't have a lawyer present and I'm going to book you on this charge."

"She's a whore," Homer suddenly burst out. "I didn't break in nowhere. The door was open. Anybody could go up there."

"Anybody but you," Jane said.

"I ain't going to say I didn't fuck her, but I paid for it. I know a hundred guys who been to her." Homer waved his arms, and the police chief stopped one in midair and drew it forward to show Jane.

She looked. The bruise looked like the Appalachian foothills on a cheap relief map, bumpy and blearily colorful, and up the eastern and western slopes ran two crimson dotted lines, the distinct trails of Jane's upper and lower teeth.

Officer Rollo waved her out of the room. When he joined her a few minutes later he said: "Do you see what good shape he's in?"

Jane looked blankly at the chief.

"You didn't see his wedding ring?"

Jane shook her head. She never noticed wedding rings on men, because Philip Turner refused to wear one. He thought they were sissy.

"You better start noticing. Anyway, he's a married man. He's a twenty-four-year-old married man with four children and he holds down a job."

"Oh I see," Jane said in disgust. "He's a mensch. A pillar of the community."

"He appears to be a rapist," said Officer Rollo.

"I hate that word rapist," Jane hissed. "Pianist, harpist, flautist, rapist. It makes him sound like a goddamn virtuoso. You know, I wouldn't let that guy change a tire for me. What station does he work in? How many Sunocos can there be in a two-horse town like Xenia?"

The police chief crossed his arms and said: "Just don't take on like this in front of the sheriff."

Jane said: "I try so hard to be a bad girl. And this isn't helping."

"What you mean a bad girl?" said the chief. "You know you're not a bad girl."

"That's what you think," Jane said. She had been up to some things lately of which the good policeman had not yet gotten wind. She wished she were doing them right now.

"You know you want me to try and pass myself off as a good girl," she said. "It's degrading to have to act like an outraged virgin for Sheriff Staples. My mission is to shock his kind."

"It wasn't degrading to have that fellow come in your house and bully you into the sex act?"

Jane did not reply.

"Are you going to stick with this case, Jane?" The chief rubbed his forehead wearily. "Here's my advice. Put on a skirt tomorrow and comb your hair. Somebody from the sheriff be out to see you. Don't use any cusswords, and for pity's sake keep that bad girl stuff to yourself."

**Island
life**

By an island, we mean an isolation. An island may offer rare opportunity to the emigrant. But once a species accepts the hospitality of isolation, it is likely to undergo change into something quite unrecognizable to itself, to step into vacant niches and take up variant enterprises its former self never dreamed of. Upon islands, with the passage of time, may be found fishes that cannot swim, moths that do not fly but float passively all their lives on the drafts about a single mountain peak; thistles that have shot up into the palm habit, giant lizards that graze in meadows like sheep, and lettuces whose craggy trunks hold them six feet above the ground. Isolation, moreover, is never perfect. The island encourages these flamboyant experiments, and momentarily they succeed; but a delicate air of doom broods over them like a monsoon twilight, with no going back. —Sherwood Kuckuck, *Island Life*

For a woman who has no fear of being alone, the question may arise: What use is a man to me? *Cicerone* to the ensorcelled isle, oh yes, but beyond that, not protector, not prop, not even allowed to drag home the bacon, for fear a bad habit may be formed of leaning on the fellow. So what good is he at all, she may ask, if one day his spell should weaken. But if he is Jimmy, why should that ever occur?

All the same, say that one day she is sitting or lying around unscared, as is her wont, and an intruder intrudes, and does her harm. She cannot charge Jimmy's beauty with not having kept her safe, for this would be quite unfair! And yet, and so, his spell does weaken, his beauty cloys.

It began when Officer Rollo brought her back to the house. The first thing they saw was the line of broken windows all the way down the porch, which gave the place the cheap look of burst cellophane packaging. But inside, the damage seemed arctic and elemental: The whole downstairs was a shallow glittering sea of broken glass, and marooned on a small army-green island in the middle of it was Jimmy, curled on a sleeping bag, emitting the gurgling rale of a stupendous hangover.

Officer Rollo wrote down the broken windows, the stabbed paintings, the overturned cabinets of paint, the footprints on the bed. He collected Jane's torn nightgown and the three one-dollar bills. Then he left, the wooden screen door banging shut behind him. Jimmy slept through it all.

Jane bent to the arc of icy water under the red pump out back until her hide seemed to toughen, and, heading away from the road and the cornfields, she walked the moneygreen edge of the woods. She looked at moneygreen leaves, thinking that leaves really were money of a kind, vegetable currency trading its million flimsy surfaces for one life, money that spent itself. In April they were dark, polished, crisp, straight from the mint; by the end of May every dollar had a hole in it; by now they were mined by a thousand needlelike feeding tubes, skinned alive to lace skeletons on the branch, rolled into fantastic tumors around insect eggs; they had all, all, given half of themselves away. In human terms, they were the dead skin you papered yourself with, so that experience could be traded for life itself, if you wanted to go on living, and of course you did. You had to be willing that the flesh should be a little damaged. You had to be ready to spend, and so you had to assume the ready, as it was well named, could replace itself.

When she came home, Jimmy was on the porch, on the couch, sitting upright, not drinking. She saw he knew what had happened. The windows behind him were empty of glass, the menacing shards whisked away, the pearly boards of the porch swept spotless. "Oh Jane," he said. "It wasn't as bad as it looked. For me."

"I saw the holes they poked in your pictures."

"You must have looked hard," Jimmy said.

"No," Jane said. The holes had been definite holes in the indefinite loins of six-foot figures who suggested wind in their glittering scales—like mermaids soluble in air.

"They couldn't even find the cunts on those girls," Jimmy said. "Anyway, I can fix them."

Jane sat down beside him. He was not being delicate. He had decided the holes in his paintings were inconsequential. What had happened to her, on the other hand, was violence in the real world of Uncle Thedford and Aunt Junie Fluharty, sex being realer than art, the body being truer than eternity.

But Jane did not like this. It made it too true, what had happened to her. Not a hole in moneygreen leaves that would soon be shucked, not a disturbance in dead skin, but a plunge to the innards, no going back, and once there, the founding of a colony or even a religion. For Jimmy all human transactions ended in a *Pietà*, and maybe they do. But right now Jane only wanted a body to scarify with dispatch.

"Jane. I'm quitting booze. Tell you the truth, I'm glad they got my paintings too."

She stared at him.

"Is that corny?"

"No, I just don't believe in rape on the family plan."

"I want to be with you," he said. "Life's too short."

"Oh?" Jane said. "Well, what if I refuse to go?"

"You're already there."

"That's what you think."

Then Jane, half touched, half disgusted at this offer of his paintings on the altar of a kind of cosmic rape, went into the immaculate house, dropping the screen door shut behind her.

Next day Jane puts on a dress and waits in shoes on the porch, reading *Island Life* (not the Wallace, the Kuckuck), but the day wears into afternoon and there is no sign of Sheriff Staples. By 3:30 Jane understands the cops aren't going to show. In the gauzy distance she sees the sheriff rock across an Elks Club putting green like a walking spray can in an advertisement, or rise to speak at a Daughters of the Eastern Star meeting with all his attached hardware clanking. Nothing could be more pleasant than his neglect, she thinks, though neglect is probably the right word. She drops her shoes over the end of the couch, opens a beer.

Meanwhile the friends of the Soul of Commerce arrive one by one. They all know what happened, but no one says anything about it. Roger brings hot dogs, Felix beer, Willie chicken. Fred is at work till four at Arbuckle's Jiffy Super. Jimmy tends the fire. Everyone pretends not to see the line of empty windows along the porch.

Roger is relating a dream he had last night. One of his teeth hurt—Jane listens closely. He went to peer at the tooth in the medicine cabinet mirror, only in the dream this object was under the sink, among the intestinal-looking pipes. Crouching down with his jaw open wide, he found the problem.

"A ballerina this big"—he opens his fingers to the size of a cockroach—"was turning around and around on my tooth like one of those corny figurines on a jewelry box."

"So what you did?" Felix asks.

"I tried to bite her head off, but she kept popping back down in my tooth like a gopher."

"Hee-hee-hee," from Felix. "You look healthy to me."

"This is a dream I'm talking about. Not a doctor's examination."

"What did it feel like?" Jane wants to know.

"Like a giant dentist's drill. *Zzzz-zzzz-zzzz-zzzz*. Maddening. No let up."

Willie says: "Very inta-resting. Felix can doctor you."

"I don't need a doctor," Roger says.

"Aw, he's only kidding wit you," Felix says. "A dream your tooth is rotted means you done trusted somebody two-faced. Play the 2-50-77."

"What about a ballet dancer?"

"Ain't no ballet dancer in the book." Felix reflects a moment. "There's a waltz," he recalls. "Play the 7."

"How about if you just dreamed of a woman?" Willie inquires. "Never mind what line of work she was in."

"You lost your bankroll, jack. Play 6,10,66, and pray for help." Willie roars with laughter.

"That's strange," Jane says. "People must be losing a lot of money if they go broke every time they dream about a woman."

Willie says: "You know it, darling. A lot of people never even had no money to lose."

Jane turns to Roger and says: "If you want to stop dreaming your teeth hurt, stop masturbating."

"What? Never," Roger says.

"Hey, don't listen to her. You don't get no toothaches from jacking off," Willie says. "Modern science has blew the whistle on that bullshit."

"Nobody said anything about a toothache," Roger says.

"You musta woke up with a toothache," Willie says, always the materialist. "For a toothache you soak a little wad of cotton in campfire oil and pack it in there good. If that don't work, see a dentist. I don't hold with the hoodoo cure."

"The hoodoo cure!" Jane says. "Come on. Let's hear it."

Willie peers around cautiously. "Okay. Top secret and I ain't responsible for the consequences."

"Hee-hee-hee," from Felix.

"Here's my Uncle Herbert from Arkansas's shonuff toothache cure. First you find the skeleton of a mule laying in a field. *Make sure nobody else is looking at you.* That's the key. Now get down on your knees and pick up this old mule jawbone with your teeth. Close your eyes and walk back nine steps and drop it on the ground. Toothache should be gone. If it ain't, somebody was looking at you and you have to start over with a new mule."

"I certainly wouldn't let anybody look at me if I was walking around with a mule jawbone in my mouth," Jane says emphatically.

Felix is disgusted. "That's the uselessest thing I ever heard," he says. "I never run across the skeleton of a mule in my entire life, never mind two in one day. Useless. Let's see one of them Rolling Rocks, Jane. Yo the count."

Felix points off the porch with the neck of his bottle. There's Count Dracula, a redwing blackbird who sometimes perches on the Pocahontas County Road 601 sign across the blacktop and arches out his black satin wings like a vampire's cape when he flutes. They all gaze at handsome Count Dracula for a time as he blows his curious double note, more like a phantom train whistle than a song. They're quiet, except for the popping of bottle caps. The air seems to open in wide circles around the bird, and they see, behind him, the tall green corn ripple like a pond.

Then Felix turns to Roger: "So who did you trust that was two-faced?"

"Nobody," Roger says flatly.

"Old Roger wouldn't trust Helen Keller for a nickel," Willie comments.

"That's right," Roger says. "Especially not Helen Keller. And let's not forget it was you two who trusted that punk from Xenia."

"Shut your mouth," Felix says in a stern and horrified whisper. Jane, who squats in the grass puncturing hot dogs with a fork, feels everyone looking at her back.

"I was the one who trusted him," she says irritably. "And I was right. Lester had nothing to do with it."

"*Lester had nothing to do with it*," Roger mimics, in a prissy falsetto, and Jane struggles with the urge to wing the fork at him. "They were just like my brothers, those guys. They all ought to be lined up against a wall and shot."

"Mercy," Willie says. "Good thing you ain't king."

Just then, Fred roars into the driveway, churning reddish dust into whirlpools at each wheel. Even through the dirty windshield, Jane sees the excitement on his face. A moment later he backs out of the front seat carrying a long, slender object in a camp blanket as tenderly as a baby. The barrel of his old sporterized World War I Mauser peeps out of it. He must have come straight from Arbuckle's, and is an odd sight in checkered shirt, black bow tie, and white apron, with not a bunch of broccoli but a German military rifle in his arms.

As soon as Fred steps onto the porch he is in the bosom of comrades who are not in the habit of criticizing each other too strenuously, and the blanket slips away. Everyone is laughing, everyone finds that gun a joke, including Jane. Fred leans the gun against the wall and flops onto the couch.

Roger says: "Is that thing loaded?"

"Damn straight, and I've got another fifty-five rounds right here." The Arbuckle's apron is bulging. Meanwhile Fred draws a number of fat joints out of his breast pocket, lights one, and passes it to Jane.

Jane takes it but says: "I think you should get that thing out of sight. It's just possible the county cops will show." Already the line sounds querulous, negative, and out of place; and so it is ignored by everyone, including Jane.

"You know, Jane," Fred says, "if you wouldn't be mad at me, I could build you a small but powerful bomb."

"I would be mad at you," Jane says quickly.

"Fred's all ready for World War III," Roger beams.

"I know what I'm doing," Fred says. "Let me explain the nature of these punks to you. It is not the obligation of the enlightened to keep punks like them alive."

"We're the enlightened?" Jane asks.

"Never mind us. They're rocks hurtling over a cliff, man, they're rushing to the bottom as fast as they can. It's nothing personal when they smash you up. You're just where they happen to bounce. Hey, I know these punks like the back of my hand."

Roger says: "What's that funny-looking white thing in your lap?"

Fred looks down. "Huh? What do you mean? Where?"

"Your hand, whiz kid."

Fred says: "I know them, man! I used to be a punk just like

them. You'd be doing them a favor if you gave them a push."

"I don't push nothing but a grocery cart," Willie says.

Fred squints across the cornfield a moment, snatches up the rifle and draws a bead over their heads on a cloud, an airplane or a porch pillar. "Anyway, whatever I do, they'll have to catch me first," he says. "They'll never prove anything, unless somebody talks."

"Is that thing really loaded?" Jane croaks.

Fred lays the gun down and looks around the porch suspiciously. The men's smiling faces satisfy him, but then he fixes his eyes on Jane. "Could she hold up under torture?" he asks.

"Jesus Christ," Jane says.

"Definitely," Jimmy answers for her. It doesn't sound like a compliment.

Willie slides the rifle behind the sofa and asks Fred: "Er, uh, wait a minute, young man. Whatever happened to inner quiet? Whatever happened to going around with a gazelle's mind? Where's that maintaining a peaceful island ek-cetera ek-cetera?"

"Hey," Fred says. "If your enemy attacks, you do what you have to do."

"You need a enemy in your ass," Felix says.

A fifth joint goes around, and Jane, yearning for torpid islands, for equatorial distances, drifts into a deep calm. She sees the porch, afloat in a sea of green weeds, with its ragged balustrade of beer bottles and odd crew, as a ferry that will never land. They're on a tuft of man-made island under a monsoon twilight, and there's no going back.

"I thought this island would make me into a whole new person," she says. "But it didn't have time."

"What island is that?" Willie says.

"The one we're sitting on."

"I don't care where I washed up," Willie yawns. "I'd still know it's me."

"Did you ever smoke so much reefer you forgot who you was?" Felix asks the company.

"Once," Fred says, "I smoked a whole dime by myself. I had a convulsion and ended up with my head in the toilet."

"I think this lifeboat of weirdos is doomed," Jane says.

"Speak for yourself," Willie says. "I don't go in for that doom philosophy."

"Everybody have to go sometime," Felix remarks.

"Every single person turns out to be weird if you really know them," Fred says. "Like my mother, she looks really average, but she won't go out of the house without a few hard-boiled eggs and some gold jewelry in her purse in case there's a bomb or an earthquake and she gets stuck somewhere."

"What's the gold jewelry for?" Jane inquires.

"In case she has to, like, barter with the natives."

Jane bursts out laughing.

"I used to think this was our private world," she says.

"Only crazy people got private worlds," Willie says.

"Jane wants one of those private islands," Jimmy says, "where the women change the men into pigs."

"Jane hasn't turned you into no pig," Felix says reproachfully.

"Then why isn't she speaking to me?"

"I'm just disappointed," Jane says. "Don't take it personally."

Felix says: "Them island women is hard."

"Did you know on an island after a while the animals lose all fear?" Jane says.

"Straight dope," says Felix. "The birds fly in your window and roost on your bed. The trucker is friends with the dress shop. The Catholics party with the Baptists. The dog goes south with the cat."

"I'm going to the islands," Fred says, sucking on a roach so noisily that everyone turns to look at him. His eyes are red, his bow tie hangs sideways, the roach corks his puffed cheeks. "Soon as I liquidate the enemy," he gasps.

Roger says: "Speak of the enemy . . . "

A pink-and-gray Chevrolet Bel Air just like Lester's is rolling over the hills from Harmonia Springs; it even has a bad muffler. It isn't Lester's, but—perhaps it is the hot lull of the afternoon, perhaps the six joints that have made the rounds—it really doesn't matter. Jane stands on the edge of the porch, squinting. "Wrong shade of pink," she says. Which is true, but it sounds like a joke, even to her. Fred pulls the rifle out from behind the couch, leaps off the porch, and throws himself on his belly in the skunk cabbages.

They laugh helplessly, they are watching some kind of crazy circus stunt they wouldn't dream of stopping.

"Heavily outnumbered, Blood stalks the foe," Fred narrates as he crawls. "Blood, the most decorated sharpshooter in the South Pacific, creeps out of deep jungle in the Bataan. The enemy approaches in a motorized vehicle. Blood has surprise on his side. He fingers the bolt."

Crack! Fred fires a shot before the Chevy comes over the last hill. The bullet thrashes through the willow boughs like a crazed cat, sowing the air with bits of green and silver ribbon.

"Blood fires a warning shot."

The car slows as it comes around the bend. Jane sees two men in the front seat, laughing, hands tipping beer cans; and in the backseat, two bouffant hairdos, two blondes, faces invisible. The car is hardly moving. The man on the passenger's side leans out the window over his elbow, yells something not unfriendly, flicks a cigarette butt that spatters its orange coal on the road shoulder.

"Blood breaks out in a suicide charge!" Fred leaps up and runs zigzag, dodging imaginary bullets, towards the road, then sinks to his knees with his rifle barrel high in the air and fires once, again, again, again. Jane watches the smiles evacuate the faces in the car, the eyes go blank, dead, and widen in astonishment. Then the driver guns it. For a moment the car seems to rise in the air. Then, before Jane's eyes, the rear windshield explodes. The Chevy squeals, skids, and jumps forward like a wounded water buffalo, drawing out of range, then rising and falling on the dwindling ribbon of asphalt until it is out of sight.

Jane lurches off the porch, runs to the road and peers after them to see if anyone is dead. She tries to find four heads in the empty frame of the rear windshield. It is too late to make anything out.

From nowhere, Count Dracula shoots up through the treetops and veers in a wide arc down the cornfield, flapping only once or twice before he dives over the horizon, scared even out of his voice.

After Fred disappeared, the society disappeared too. The exploding windshield had cut two women in the face, one of them across the eyeball. By the time the society got wind of this, they knew that Fred had never gone home. But where was he? They expected police, and questions. So they stayed off front porches, alone and together.

As for Sheriff Staples, Jane conceived the furtive hope that he would never come. She was in a twilight world where doing nothing was not her fault. She did know that the green island of the former life was capsized—gone. She had no details, she had no ticket, but she would be leaving soon.

Meanwhile she hid out with Jimmy in that house. The place didn't look much worse in July with no windows than in June with wide open windows. They never thought of fixing them. They were thinking their separate thoughts of going away. Jimmy was going west and he spoke of the rufous Sierras, the snowy glimmer of the desert at night, as though Jane were going with him. Already Pete and Ernestine had sent him a ticket. These days Jimmy never left Jane to go on a changeling drunk. He drank like a gentleman, only to the point of good will. He did not even leave Jane for art. He filled the walls with drawings in which two lovers were clinging together, breasts and mouths and legs, arms and necks and waists and winking sexual parts, vining in and out of each other as greenly, as weightlessly, as seaweed.

Jane was thinking of going away, but not with Jimmy. He was on the green island that had capsized—gone. For these four weeks they were drowning luxuriously together. Willie came around sometimes, but he perceived that he could not get in.

There was a suffocating density between Jane and Jimmy, no more inviting to another human than a pond clotted with lotuses. "You know where to find me," Willie reminded Jane. And maybe she would have; but Jane could not go into Harmonia Springs, because she was hiding from Officer Rollo.

One hot Monday early in August they were in the bedroom, their last gin hand lay on the desert island between them, when they heard a car with a good muffler swishing through Queen Anne's lace, heard the car door chunk squeaklessly closed, and they looked at each other, knowing it could only be a policeman. The knock that followed was polite but loud. Jane peeked out the window over the porch roof, saw the number one sky-blue patrol car, the one marked CHIEF.

"It's Rollo," she whispered. "Should I go down?"

Jimmy shrugged. About justice when there was no money at risk, he was an agnostic. The duty to testify was as alien to him as the urge to tap dance. He only wanted Jane not to get upset.

Jane was considering when the chief backed silently off the porch and there he was, glowering up at her, his squarish chin stubbornly set, his sunglasses flashing.

"I'm ashamed of you young peoples," he said, "laying up in your house like a couple of sick pups. What you scared of? Now you come down here directly."

Jimmy stayed where he was, calmly shuffling. Jane went downstairs and out on the front porch.

Officer Rollo folded his arms. "So. How's your case coming with Sheriff Staples?"

"I never heard from Sheriff Staples," Jane said.

The eyes didn't change, but the long, thin lips began to work busily over some impassioned though soundless vocabulary. Jane realized she had never seen Officer Rollo mad, not even the time she went through five stop signs without noticing his flasher behind her. Finally he exploded: "It's that gol-dern cockamamie county fair is what it is. A person can't get hold of that Staples for an entire month! Well, I take care of that. Tomorrow I put a stop to that."

Now his hands went to his hips. "And you, young lady. When were you going to get around to letting me know?"

Jane looked away. "I may leave," she blurted.

"What you mean *leave*? I hope you're not telling me you're going to quit college."

Jane was silent.

"Well now, Jane, I thought more of you. I really did."

Jane said: "I have enough credits to graduate. I don't know why I ever thought of hanging around this burg for another year. I'm too broke to be stuck here all summer waiting for *this case*."

Officer Rollo said: "If that young man of yours would get a job, you'd manage just fine."

"Why should he be the one to get a job?" Jane said uncomfortably.

"All right," the chief said. "Why don't both y'all get a job? Why don't you two young peoples get married and settle down in a regular house or quit each other?"

Jane smiled ruefully. Now the police chief was putting his foot down everywhere at once. That an erstwhile friend of the Soul of Commerce, even though you never could smoke pot in front of him, should march so frontally, so loaded-for-bear, into the former pleasant republic of *laisser-aller*, right here on the old front porch, signalled how the climate had changed.

Suddenly Officer Rollo snapped at her: "And for pity's sake, doesn't any of you know where Fred is at?"

So Jane finally understood where the trouble was. She was ashamed; she had hardly given Fred a thought in the last four weeks.

"I haven't heard anything," she said. "Has anybody?"

"He phoned me up from I don't know where the day after he shot out that window, and snitched on his own self. And that's the last." Rollo shook his forefinger at her. "None of the rest of y'all had the good sense to do that. He was afraid of leaving you young peoples in some kind of trouble. Don't you know that boy's crazy? Don't you know he tried to kill himself once?

Now he's gone and ran away and none of you did anything to stop him."

SHERIFF DEWEY STAPLES WELCOMES YOU
AND REMINDS YOU
TO BE WARE AT THE FAIR!

"I'm a taxpayer. First we come thirty miles, then we have to pay five bucks to find the guy."

"Cough it up," Jimmy recommended in a low voice. "It's only five bucks. Don't make a scene."

Jane laid down a five-dollar bill at the grille and asked the cashier: "Have you seen Sheriff Staples?"

The cashier was a sweating fat-necked blonde. "Not since the Chicken Flying," she said dully. "He give away the prize."

Jimmy and Jane wandered down the worn grass of the midway, clutching their ticket stubs (GOOD FOR ONE FREE RIDE EXCEPT WILDWIND GORGE OR SCENIC RAILWAY). Jane might have lapsed into her old self, so easily entertained by rinky-dink hoopla of every kind, if she had not had to pay the price of admission. Now she had to get something for her money. Everyone they asked had seen the sheriff only a short while ago, on his way somewhere else. The trooper in the Public Safety Booth behind Swine Hall told them to try the Horseshoe Pitching Courts, so Jimmy and Jane kicked through hot, bleached dirt until they found the Horseshoe Pitch. The attendant of the Horseshoe Pitch had seen the sheriff on his way to officiate at the Frog Jump. But the Frog Jump was already over. Back across the balding meadow to the Public Safety Booth. Now the deputy thought the sheriff had gone to the beef auction to bid on a steer for the F.O.P. ox roast, but inside the Livestock Judging Hall, ten acre-long barns away from Swine Hall, people were bidding on goats and there was no sign of the sheriff. The cashier told them to try the Horseshoe Pitch.

They came out into the dust-laden sunshine as Miss Pocahontas County 1965 was being driven by in a corn-green convertible. Jane was mad. "The idea of making me pay five bucks. And a buck for parking! I was summoned to this event. I had an appointment."

That was not precisely true. The trooper the sheriff had sent by the house on Pocahontas County Road 601 had said anytime tomorrow or Wednesday or Thursday, if she could just get to the fair by herself. Jane didn't want to face the fact that the runaround had happened right then and there on the front porch, even though Jimmy, who had been sitting on the couch next to her when the trooper came, had tried to point this out.

"The sheriff doesn't want to talk to you," he said, "or he'd send somebody to get you or come himself."

But Jane couldn't believe that some official she so little wanted to talk to didn't want to talk to her either. And now she had paid six dollars of real money to get stood up by that buffoon!

"You're getting to be such a miser," Jimmy remarked in disbelief.

"I know," Jane said shamefacedly. "I can't help it."

"He's got to be here somewhere," Jimmy said. "Please don't get upset. Let's ride the Ferris wheel." He showed her the ticket stubs. "It's free."

"I'm too disgusted. Let's go home."

They headed out through a side gate and trudged dispiritedly across the grass parking lot, weaving their way through row after row of automobiles, the endless swells of hoods gleaming distortedly like dime-store wax lips in the hot sun. But cars thinned in the remote corner where they had left Roger's Rambler. Suddenly they saw the sheriff's sedan at the edge of the pasture, on an odd incline with its wheels cocked sideways and its door hanging open. A few yards off was Staples himself, talking to a woman in a link-sausage home permanent and a pink seersucker suit. In another moment he threw himself down into the dusty clover with a tire iron, and his khaki shirt sleeve became a blur as he worked a jack handle up and down.

There was something pornographic about his pointless velocity at this task. Jane edged closer, hypnotized by the sight. The woman's car was soon tilted absurdly high in the air, and the sheriff, lying on his back, spotted Jane. He sat up, sweat varnishing his forehead.

"I've been looking for you since two-thirty," Jane said accusingly.

"Oh, I remember you. The colored junkman's friend. You'll have to hold your horses while I help Mrs. Funk with this tire. She's late for the Cake Decorating. Who's that?" the sheriff barked, noticing Jimmy. He did not recognize the Nuncio without his pink gown and aluminum-foil wings, which was doubtless just as well.

"He's with me," Jane said.

"Not your hubby, is he?"

"No."

"Well, you and me best talk private, third parties not invited. Here, son. Go ride the loop-the-loop. She'll meet you in an hour at the main gate." Sheriff Staples lifted one buttock and drew a half dozen purple strips of amusement tickets out of a back pocket. He fanned them at Jimmy.

"No, I thank you," Jimmy said, pivoted on his heel and walked away. The sheriff, unimpressed, lay back down along Mrs. Funk's tire, and a dust cloud of depression passed over Jane. She realized she had let Jimmy go off in this heat without even a dollar in his pocket for a bottle of beer.

At last they sat down at a picnic table in front of the Methodist Church pie bar and the sheriff told Jane: "I know that Stamm fellow busted in where he wasn't invited and I want you to know I don't like it one bit. But one thing I do not understand. Every weekend I chase myself all over this county from the fanciest de-lux country club barbecue to the lowliest little charity bazaar, all to put my bee-hind, excuse my French, in ten places at the same time, but the minute I turn my back, something like this happens. Now I am puzzled, Jane. Can you explain that to me?"

Jane said that she could not explain it.

"Well, I guess," said the sheriff, "there is so much rank evil in the world, it could happen to anybody at any time."

He said this in a resigned but rather loud voice, and Jane looked around to see if anyone was listening. There were not many people in the enclosure, but every one of them was listening.

"But that's the funny part," the sheriff went on even louder, wagging his finger at her. "It can't happen to anybody. Do you think such a thing could happen, say, to my wife?" He shuddered theatrically. "Only one of your psychopaths with a sick mind who wanted real bad to die would lay a hand on my wife, and even then he couldn't get at her, because she is very well taken care of."

The sheriff dropped his voice slightly; the farmers and church ladies scattered about the surrounding tables leaned closer. "Now, Jane, I'll be frank with you. I have reports you consort with a wide variety of men. *In technicolor.* If a girl wants to carry on like that it's her lookout. In my business I run across plenty of that kind. Some of em do right well. But who's going to get worked up about it if one of these girlies takes it in her mind to bring the law on a gent for not acting quite like he should? Huh? Say, Helen!" he suddenly bellowed. "Bring this lovely lady a Coke! And I'll take a piece of that coconut cream pie if you got any left."

Jane gripped the edge of the picnic table in both hands and whispered: "Do you expect me to sit here like a boob and take that? You're telling me that no matter what some creep does to me I don't have a right to complain."

"Oh, you can complain," the sheriff assured her. "Aren't you complaining? And I personally feel right sorry for a girl like you, because she can get hurt bad if one of these old boys gets way out of line like that Stamm fellow done. But the question is who else is going to feel sorry for a girl like you who carries on just like she pleases without any protection? Mind you, it's not just that I like my wife better. The jury likes my wife better, and frankly, it doesn't think the world of you, Jane."

Jane said: "I bet you don't like your wife one bit."

The sheriff smiled sweetly at her and ate his coconut pie. Then his voice became soft and sugary as well.

"Say, that was pretty good, Jane," he said. "I see you know how to stick up for yourself. That little police chief Rollo told me you could talk. Now, I'm sorry if I hurt your feelings. I wanted to see if you could bear the strain. You're going to have to take worse if this gets to court." The sheriff bent towards her conspiratorially. "Because that fellow Stamm has went and got himself a smart Jew lawyer who's gonna drag you through mud and blood. Now think of it. Whatever you've done in your life and you're an eensy weensy bit ashamed of it, this fellow will drag it out." The sheriff shook his head, saddened at the thought.

"Don't worry about me," Jane said, suspicious again. "I can take it." She peered at the sheriff. "It really doesn't bother you, does it, that this guy might just get off."

"Well, the boy did wrong, but it doesn't seem like he makes a habit of it."

"A habit of it!"

"Now, not speaking for myself personally, Jane, but on how it looks in general, it is his word against yours. He claims most of his friends have been with you and they'll swear to it in court."

"Come on," Jane said. "Even you don't believe that."

"He is a married fellow," Staples said. "With children."

"Honestly," Jane exclaimed. "It's disgusting the way you people equate procreation with virtue. The Boston Strangler had a wife and kids, you know. Jesus was a bachelor."

Sheriff Staples said frostily: "I would appreciate it, ma'am, if you would not mock at my religion, for I do not mock at yours."

Jane stared. How did he even know what religion she was? This put quite a different cast upon his remark about the smart Jew lawyer who would drag her through mud and blood. In fact the sheriff was a type she had never encountered before. He was outsmarting her, and she felt her face redden.

"There is a way we can short-cut around all this who struck John," he said, waving his hand.

"What's that?"

"Well, Jane, I would like for you to take a lie detector test. If your story is true, and it rings true to me, why, you'd have nothing to worry about. The D.A. would get behind you. And of course I'm with you. What do you say? Understand, this can't be used in court. It just shows the rest of us you're in good faith, so to speak."

Jane hesitated.

"I don't know what way I can help you if you won't help us that little bit," Sheriff Staples said.

This could not be a good move, Jane thought, wishing dizzily she were on another planet. A lie detector test—it was degrading and bizarre, but after all, her story was true. And no one would have to know.

"All right," she said.

"That's a wise decision," said Staples, in a hearty voice that made Jane sure the opposite was true.

"Here!" Staples slapped down on the table the half dozen free admission strips he had tried to fob off on Jimmy. "Have yourself a good time." And he rocked to his feet and vanished down the midway.

Jane found Jimmy sitting on a bench near the front gate, watching the people go by. He did not look pleased with what he saw.

"Everyone walks funny, like their legs are screwed on wrong," he said. "And the whole world smells like piss. You're the only beautiful thing in it. I can't believe you took those!" he declared, seeing the purple tickets.

"I can't either," Jane replied.

He gazed at her shyly, unwilling to ask her what had happened. She looked away, for he was one of the people she was not going to tell about the lie detector test. If it was the only thing to do, why did she feel ashamed?

She said: "Let's ride the Ferris wheel until we can't stand it anymore. What the hell, it's free."

The gondola rose by jerky stages until it stopped, still swinging, at the top. The whole geometry of the fair fell into place: sawdusted ovals rimmed with puffs of greenery, loaflike barns and conical tents, the gray cubes of booths and the parched grass, and above all the slow, broken, aimless progress of the people. It was a weekday, the fair was not crowded, but still that human movement, small and spiritless as it looked from this height, was everywhere. Jane leaned out of the gondola to see who they were.

"Isn't it funny," she said, "how they're the ones who get to live in the greenest part of the country? What did they do right?"

Jimmy said: "Wait till you see the desert."

Jane leaned even farther over the side with her hand shading her eyes, the gondola swung furiously, and Jimmy said: "Don't fall out. I love you, Jane."

"Look," Jane said, pointing to the people. "They're nothing but mean, sad ants. And they despise *me.*"

"What do you mean? They don't care anything about you."

"I don't want to live in Ohio anymore."

"Wait till you see the desert at night. The air feels fanned by wings. The sand shines white as snow and moves all night like a living thing."

"Okay, okay," Jane said.

No

one

will

ever

know

Jane flees the Bureau of Criminal Investigations in Xenia, walking as fast as possible. It is hot; the sun shimmers in waves on the tar-blotched concrete road, and her sneakers pound white smoke out of the gravel shoulder. She has twelve miles to go to Harmonia Springs. So much the better. She needs to walk to compose herself. She even turns her face away from the stream of traffic, for fear some motorist, or some cop, will try to pick her up.

An unforgivable mistake! she mumbles out loud, and now she is making up her mind again, as if this were a subject upon which you had to make up your mind every twenty minutes for the rest of your life. She will never, never tell anyone she did this, or rather that she allowed this to be done to her. Therefore no one will ever know, and yet the sense of disgrace only thickens.

For she had gone to have her lies detected—after all, she had said to herself, what could go wrong? She had only been telling the truth. To suppose that the truth would protect her when she had not even thought what that was, or where this simple molecule of truth was hiding—to turn herself over to the sheriff, of all people, whose idea of Jane was clear, clearer than her own, clear but not good, and who was not a man who had her best interests at heart—she was no motherless waif. Could a more reckless trust in men be imagined?

Whom then could she blame? What gull's credulity, based on what P.T.A. code of ethics, endorsed by what maladroit small-town police chief, worrying about what vanished loony grocery clerk, could have made her willingly enter that flat-topped brick building and take a lie detector test? The place, low to the ground, looked like a dry-cleaning establishment; in the background, however, behind an angled barbed-wire security fence, was an enormous hint of what they really thought of you: the state penitentiary. Still Jane went in, not in handcuffs or leg-irons, on her own two feet. And yet a street corner bum would know better than to go among such people and let them ask her any questions they liked. Thinking this as she walks, very fast, down the shoulder of Old 127, her hands fly up to her hair and she howls out loud, since no one can hear her with the traffic whizzing by. For the rest of her life she will have to know that she did this! At least no one else will ever know.

She is seeing the room: A deputy brought her in, sat her down, and said Captain Godfrey would be in shortly. Then left, closing the door behind him. The windowless basement room was pumped full of enough fluorescent light for a small stadium, and when Jane pried open her eyes, she was in the presence of *the instrument*. And time began to go by. And of course you looked at the instrument. The chair on which the deputy had asked her to wait was big and thronelike and black and looped with electrical cords, so of course you thought: Uh-oh, the electric chair. This evil throne was set sideways to the instrument, and so placed that the machine and its operator—the one who would ask you questions, detect your lies—would be behind you and out of sight unless you twisted your neck. She wasn't strapped in yet, but already her neck was getting a crick from her scrutiny of the instrument; and time, twenty minutes, thirty, was going by. She looked at the little ink pots, green, red, and black, and the four slender metal needles, L-shaped and faintly splayed at the tips like the long legs of a water strider. And under them the shiny tissue of graph paper, from a fat roll.

If the machine knew its way to the truth like a robot bloodhound, what was the need of theatrical glare, the long wait and the posterior, Eurydicean placement of the instrument? After twenty minutes, thirty, you began to think, at least if you were Jane, of fiddling with the instrument, of ripping out the inkstained plastic tubes, of giving the delicate controls each a shapeless wrench, of smashing the gracile needles with your fist—but Jane was aware that the mirror on the white wall on her side of the desk was not for putting on lipstick through which to utter your lies. It was a window behind which other persons were sitting, watching you, and keeping an eye on the expensive instrument. When she realized this was part of the treatment, she was getting the treatment, she walked over to the fake mirror and banged on it with her fist.

Then he came through the door, a little, bald, goblinlike man of about sixty, with damp, tensionless skin of no color at all under the fluorescent light, as if he had not left this basement in thirty years. Captain Godfrey, therefore a cop—but Jane would have guessed a shipping clerk in a warehouse, thirty years of checking off columns on clipboards behind him. The floppy short sleeves, clipboard, ballpoint pen case in pocket, the dull yet peering eyes of a pigheaded meticulousness—all the signs of overidentification with the management were there.

"Are you the operator of this thing?" she asked.

"Examiner," he said in a high, spiritless voice. "Instrument."

"What was the point of making me wait?"

He seemed not to have heard her. With small, finical gestures he pulled cords around her chest and fastened them under her arms, attached wired thimbles and a blood pressure cuff, picking at the buckles as though he were loathe to touch her. Then he sat down in the chair behind her.

"Face front, miss," he said, when she looked around. Suddenly the air was busy with ticks, whirs, and a thin, high-pitched, metrical scratching, four interspliced bars of it—the translation of her physiology into a string quartet for mice.

"Get me out of here," Jane muttered to some absent deity.

"Close your eyes, miss," the examiner said.

Jane twisted around and opened her eyes as wide as possible. "In this place? Close my eyes? You must be mad. I mean, does that machine work or not?"

"Instrument," he said. "Face front, miss."

Jane faced front, rolling her eyes, not shutting them. The pins continued their faint, shrill wails over the rolling graph paper.

After a long pause his voice came from behind her: "Answer only yes or no. Are you sitting in a chair?"

This, now, was a question. It made no difference what it was. The shock of his dull falsetto curling upwards at the end of a phrase so she would know a question for a question, the rhythmic mousework in the background, caused her to molt a ripple of something into the air and the machinery. She could feel it escape her, some secret message—she had no idea what it was.

"Miss. Are you sitting in a chair?"

"Yes," she said.

"Are you in Ohio?"

"Yes."

"Is your name Jane? . . Kaplan? . . Turner?"

She felt another electrical ghost of herself crawl out of her skin. She realized all at once she was thronged with these doubles, could populate China with her endless supply, and yet had no notion what they were saying—and one of these traitor Jane Turners was behind her right now, talking to Captain Godfrey. Meanwhile the Jane Turner she knew best was sneering in her ear: They didn't bring you in here at gunpoint, you patsy. So go on, answer the questions.

"Answer yes or no, miss. Is your name Jane? . . Kaplan? . . Turner?"

"Yes."

"Could you use a million dollars?"

She bent around to peer at him, uncertain she had heard right.

"What?"

"Face front, miss."

Jane faced front and said loudly: "Would you repeat that question?"

"Could you use a million dollars?"

Jane felt a wild alarm. This was someone's unfunny joke, Godfrey's, or the sheriff's, but all at once she understood they could ask her anything, anything at all.

"Yes," Jane said, "and no."

"Answer every question yes or no, miss."

"No! I mean, I won't. There is no answer to that question."

A pause, then: "You're supposed to answer yes. Everybody could use a million dollars."

She screwed herself around in the chair to have another look at his face. There was nothing, absolutely nothing, in it. It was white as a mushroom, and some sort of hair oil kept the few etiolated strands on his crown in place as he bent over the graph paper with a ballpoint. She thought, This goblin is offering me a million dollars to be his bride and go live with him under a rock. Trying with all her might to broadcast a thunderbolt into his machine, she said yes.

He was busy with his pen for a time. Suddenly he switched the machine off.

"Look here, miss."

Jane blinked at him over her shoulder.

"This is off the record, miss. Did you take some kind of pep pills before you come in here?" His face was as close to cross as such an empty vessel could get.

"Why, no," she said. "What's going on?"

"What are you so worked up about?" Now he wore an almost injured look. "Have you got a tack in your shoe?"

"No," Jane said.

"Take off your right shoe and give it here."

"I don't see why I should have to do that."

"Give it here."

"You'll be sorry," Jane said slyly. She handed over her stinking sneaker, gray with roaddust; he felt around in the toe and handed it back. Then he sighed and stared at the graph paper, unwilling to go on until he figured out how she was cheating.

"I'd like to see an ID, miss," he finally said.

She showed him her driver's license. He read it, handed it back, and they started over.

"Are you in Ohio?"

"Is your name Jane Kaplan Turner?"

"Could you use a million dollars?"

"What is the meaning of that question!" Jane burst out, but then, tired of the whole thing, she said yes.

"Did you ever pose for naked pictures?"

Jane put her hand to her forehead. She knew the source of this question.

"Keep your arms on the armrests," the examiner said. "Did you ever pose for naked pictures?"

"No, but I wish I had, you troll," she said.

"Answer yes or no."

"I dare you to look me in the face when you ask me that. When are you going to ask me about *this case*?"

"Face front, miss," he said, without lifting his eyes from the graph paper. "Did you ever pose for naked pictures?"

"No." But she was seeing the walls of the house on Pocahontas County Road 601, all festooned with imitations of her flesh more sumptuous than anything she deserved.

"Ooops, I forgot. Yes," she said, and again her heart made a blind leap into his machine, saying God knows what.

"Have you engaged in the sex act with more than ten partners?"

Jane realized she was going to fail this test. She had told nothing but lies all her life, to herself and others. All her complaints about men were lies, since she was always looking for something different from what she had ordered. She would have slept with hundreds by now, if she'd had time.

"When are you going to ask me some questions about *this case*!" she shouted.

"I have all the questions right here," the examiner answered dully.

"Yes, but are any about this case?"

"Have you engaged in the sex act with more than ten partners?"

"A lady doesn't keep count," Jane said. "You have no right to ask me that."

"Answer yes or no. Have you engaged in the sex act with more than ten partners?"

"No," Jane said, losing courage. That might well be a lie. She hoped if she didn't start to count up, it wouldn't be. She stared at her knees, and counted them instead: One. Two.

"Someone's going to answer for this," she said feebly.

"Did you ever take money for doing the sex act?"

"No," she said. But her heart quickened, for was that really true? Don't let me think of Willie, laying his claim by patient increments of services rendered; and finally, how much easier it was, and in a way thrilling, to take that Soul of Commerce money, more, much more, than she'd really earned . . .

The mouse quartet suddenly quit. The glazed graph paper rattled oddly, for it was travelling through the air. Jane, confused, saw Captain Godfrey in front of her, trailing the blue scroll from one arm. He was opening the door.

"What's going on? Where are you going with that sheet?"

"Chart," he said. "That's it, miss."

"That's it? What do you mean that's it?"

"Just set there a minute. Don't get excited."

"Wait! Where are you going? You never asked me a single question about this case."

He shut the door behind him.

"Get these straps off me," Jane shouted after him.

A woman in a flowered smock appeared, some sinister matron in plainclothes, but Jane was already floundering out of the armband, the coils and thimbles and buckles, hoping to break something worth thousands of dollars.

"Don't yank," the woman ordered, but Jane dodged around

her and ran out into the corridor. The long blue chart, the floppy shirt sleeves, were turning a distant corner.

Though dreams of murder were still far from her at this time, farther, much farther, than that pale blue fluttering graph paper, something happened when Jane saw the little man patter around the corner in his black policeman's shoes, trailing that esoteric scroll. She galloped down the hallway after him and wrenched him by the side of his shirt as he was turning a key in a frosted glass door marked DETECTIVE BUREAU. His hand still on the lock, he turned to her a face blank with real surprise.

"You better get your hands off me, miss," he said, dangling the chart as far away from her as his short arm could reach.

"You didn't ask me anything about *this case*," Jane shouted at him. "Not one thing."

"You let go of me or I'll have the boys throw you in a restraint."

"I am not the criminal in this case," Jane continued to shout. "Did you detect any lies or not?"

The examiner looked at her helplessly and even a little stupidly, and Jane thought simultaneously, *I can take him*, and, *Let go this instant before they lock you in jail or shoot you dead.*

Captain Godfrey shifted his eyes away from hers and muttered, "Ink and glue."

"Ink and glue!" Jane yanked at his shirt. "Ink and glue—this isn't a book factory. What are you talking about?"

"Inconclusive," he said a little more loudly.

"After all that!" Jane's hands flew up in the air. "Inconclusive —what in the name of God does that mean?"

But Captain Godfrey had already slipped through the door, and when she tried to go in after him, the knob would not turn in her hand.

She was at the end of a long corridor; the flowered matron was coming from the other end. Fifteen feet farther down was a stairwell with a red EXIT sign, one flight up, let it be unlocked, a steel fire door, then it was easy—she was striding across a spanking new asphalt parking lot toward the highway.

And now she is trudging, very speedily, down the shoulder

of Old 127 towards Pocahontas County Road 601. I'll never forget I did this, she is muttering, never. But at least no one will ever, ever know.

Could you use a million dollars? Of all the questions, that one, to which any answer is senseless, even more than any answer is untrue, sticks in her mind. A log of gray water-soaked newsprint lies on the gravel shoulder and Jane viciously kicks it into the drainage ditch. As it plops into the scummy water, Jane catches a glimpse of its red equator, the thin rubber band that binds the whole thing together, and she realizes it is a complete Sunday paper that some sentient being, in a rare flash of perception, chucked out a car window unread. She should have shouted at the examiner: *I could use a ride home*, while she still could have used one. Instead here she is as usual, paying for lowliness with lowliness, toil for toil. If she cannot trust herself to outsmart the sheriff and his kind, alone in the world as she is, as she chooses to be, having no other choice, the only way is never to talk to such people at all.

○
○
● **The**

moneygreen

Buick

The certifiably mad have an excuse to take an auto for a spiritual instrument. Lunatics detect secret messages in license plates; nuts are sent on secret missions by Chieftains, Roadmasters, and Eldorados; paranoids drive off in magical Plymouths with voices piping forth from their hood ornaments and wills of their own—but Jane? Until Jane bought Farmer Wirz's Buick, a car was only a way to get on the road, and if you were lucky to stay on the road, for 150 dollars or less, you all solo, the road a two-lane blacktop through rural mid-America, humping along like a sea serpent on an old map. And what could a 1951 Buick mean to Jane? In 1951, Philip Turner had been driving the first of the family Fords, a sedan with a budding torpedo on the radiator grille, and to get in this car with Philip Turner was already a misery. A 1951 Buick didn't invoke first grade for Jane, or air-raid drills, Margaret O'Brien paperdolls, or the invention of Dacron. For Jane it invoked nothing at all.

Nothing, that is, until, at the end of her long walk home from the Bureau of Criminal Investigations, she tramps by Wirz's farm and sees again, in that red dirt clearing in the cornfields, the Buick she can exactly afford.

The Buick is Atlantic green, opaque as the shadow under a breakwater, a sealed, gleaming green-black. Suddenly she

knows what she wants. She wants the Buick. She wants to wrap
it around her like money whose ink is also tincture of boiled-
down Atlantic. She wants to ride in a coach of that heartless
color that leaped into her eyes the first time she ever laid eyes
on the ocean. On any ocean, but it happened to be that one,
the Atlantic at Far Rockaway when she was three, that imprinted
her, the one the shade of a cruel million, the color of her new
car.

The seats of the Buick, and there were two of them in this
luxurious automobile, were of that soft gray stuff found only in
automobiles of a certain age. The lighter worked. Even the tiny
hidden bulb of the license plate light was functioning. The window glass was all extant, and the side windows rolled up deep
into the plushy weather stripping. The hood, the entire flanged,
elegant carapace over the engine cavity, was removable, and
could be raised from either side and propped on a folding leg
like the lid of a grand piano. It was not so easy to get it down
again. Jane had to sit on the hood and bounce until something
clicked, and even so the thing would be a little skewed. The
Buick was a carriage alien to Jane in its ponderous maturity, so
that this slight asymmetry of its large snout was reassuring, a
sign that it had not always been so wise, that like Jane it had
gotten into fights in its reckless youth, although that youth was
far behind it now, except for that faintly, inscrutably bent nose.
It was a model of how to carry off injuries with massive style
and without explanation. It cruised at 75 with no strain. But it
had a majesty at twenty—as now.

Jane rolls down all the windows front and back. It is late
afternoon, and the temperature is close to 100 over the cornfields. She drives slowly east of Wirz's farm in her new car, and
then, though she knows quite well this old dirt road hooks
every which way, soon to lose all sense of direction in doglegs
around silos, cow fords, and hay bottoms, she takes the first
turn-off from PCR 601 and is lost for hours, coming out at dusk
in the Shawnee Woodlands, property of Harmonia College, near
the old lime quarry where once upon a time two dolichoce-

phalic skeletons were found of a father and a daughter who sank in the peat bog while *fleeing a yellow-eyed hungry timber wolf, or it may have been a lover pursuing the female, for the girl's skull showed manifest comeliness of features, and this was the age of caveman matings.* Jane has often stared at casts of their small skulls in a dusty case in the Cuvier Building:

ALGONQUIN CRANIAL TYPE
FATHER & DAUGHTER
Her Beautiful Teeth
the Admiration
of all Dentists
who have seen them.

Jane wonders how the daughter's pursuer—unless it was a timber wolf—resolves after ten thousand years, even for the Harmonia College chronicler, into *lover.* For Jane is in her leaving mode, where she believes she has never loved anyone in her life. If she were a landscape, she would be a windswept plain. She is not afraid to be uninhabited. Still, her topsoil would yield human implements.

On the edge of town now, Jane is happy in the Buick. She stops at a red light at the old CCC and St. L railroad crossing at Cincinnati Street, which dead-ends after a hundred feet in Back Main. There is the blank backside of the Soul of Commerce, paper boxes spilling out an open door, and across the intersection with the only yellow blinking light in town is the Downtown Recreation Club. Something large and white crosses the open saloon doorway—Felix's apron. Can she face her friends in the car in which she will leave them? Jane lifts her foot from the clutch and the moneygreen Buick rolls on its idle away from Back Main, over the railroad tracks and up Harmonia Springs Avenue.

She thinks, not of Back Main, but of Atlantic surf spilling over the sand at Far Rockaway. How to describe that infinitely practiced, infinitely fortuitous gesture? Imagines an adventuress in the old sense, a woman who haunts casinos, down to her last hundred, no gulls in view to pry apart from their bankrolls; the lace of the sleeve at her wrist a little dirty, a little torn, black-green velvet and ragged lace, throwing dice cast after cast on the sand, that sleeve, that moneygreen sleeve, over and over, unable to give up chance.

On the western edge of town, she is about to pull into the 66 station when, gazing dreamily at the red light in front of her, she happens to notice another red light in her rearview mirror, going round and round and round.

It's Officer Rollo. He climbs out of the sky-blue patrol car with a fat citation pad in his hand.

"Hi," Jane says.

"Don't *Hi* me, young lady. I'm a police officer and this is not a friendly visit. I'd like to see your license and registration."

Jane hands them over, and the chief studies them for a time.

"Is this a 1949 Dodge I'm looking at?" he finally says. "It doesn't look like a 1949 Dodge."

"It's a Buick."

"A Buick! That's funny. Right here on this registration it says a 1949 Dodge. Somebody must have made a terrible mistake."

"I just bought it today," Jane mutters, "from Clement Wirz."

"Oh, you did." Officer Rollo struggles to understand. "You don't mean to tell me you just slapped the license plate from some old wrecked Dodge that doesn't exist anymore onto this Buick here. Without informing the Department of Motor Vehicles of the state of Ohio. Why, that would be illegal."

Jane chews her lower lip. "It was only going to be for a day," she whispers.

"Miss Jane Turner, I am putting you under arrest."

"What!" says Jane. "For a traffic ticket?"

"Let's say I'm bringing you in for questioning on a number of matters."

"Couldn't I follow you?" Jane asks. She sounds shifty, even to herself. "I hate to leave my new car."

Officer Rollo holds open the passenger door for her and Jane gets in. They head back into town, the police chief and Jane side by side in the front of the sky-blue patrol car with a polite space between them. Jane waits for Rollo to go to work on her about *this case*. But he says nothing at all. Harmonia Springs Avenue rolls by underneath them; it has been resurfaced this summer and seems soft, almost furry, under the wheels, making a faintly tacky sound as if the street had been spread with butter. And the newly painted lane divider is so white it seems to float above the street like so many glowing strips of white paper, so many secret messages the chief's front bumper tears off one by one, reads hastily, and throws away behind them. Because nothing is written in these secret messages.

At city hall, instead of turning left into his parking slot, Officer Rollo makes a right, towards the college. A moment later he goes up a driveway with a prosperous crunch to it. Jane sees a white-painted brick Georgian, a carriage lantern under the porch roof throwing square beams across gleaming rhododendrons.

"Come on, young lady," the chief says, opening his door.

"Where are we?"

"Dean Lucorne's."

Jane groans. "That's a dirty trick. I don't want to talk to her."

"She's a nice lady and she's worried sick about this business. Why don't you want to talk to her?"

Jane says, "I don't trust people who sit through thirty, forty hours of courses in counseling. They should have better things to do."

"She's a good woman," Officer Rollo says. "What you talking about? I'm taking a course in counseling myself up the college. It's very interesting."

Dean Lucorne answers the door, wearing a dark dress, pearls, and bedroom slippers lined with pink fur. The air smells of curry and baby powder. Jane is weak with hunger and thinks, If she annoys me the littlest bit, I'll ask her to feed me.

They sit down in the living room. Officer Rollo says, "Excuse me, ladies. I'm going to step into the dining room and look at the pitchers on the wall." Jane steels herself for counseling.

"I was hoping you would come and see me yourself, Jane," Dean Lucorne begins, in her famous creamed gravel voice.

And then she waits, presumably for an explanation of why Jane did not.

But I do not wish to be healed, Jane is thinking. I wish to be fed. "Do you have anything to eat," she blurts.

"Certainly," the dean says, opening her eyes wide. "What can I get you?"

"Anything," Jane mutters. The dean goes through an archway, and after a moment a kitchen light comes on in the back of the house.

Officer Rollo reappears. "You got the manners of a stray mutt," he whispers.

Jane laughs a little.

"She's a nice lady," he says.

"I'm letting her be nice to me," Jane says. "I'm starving."

"Just a stray mutt won't let somebody close enough to pet you."

"That's right," Jane says. "I don't want to be petted by strangers. Who do they think they are?"

"I guess you can take care of yourself," the chief says. He sits down at the far end of the sofa, his blue hat in his lap, and sets his jaw at her.

The dean returns with a platter of cookies. Jane stuffs her face. The chief clears his throat. The dean waits patiently. When Jane finally looks up at her, Lucorne is smiling, mildness spread across her face like some sort of *glace de viande*.

"No matter what happened," Jane says, "I'm not sorry I moved into that house."

Dean Lucorne's smile turns a little sad.

"It was the best time of my life while it lasted."

The dean says: "I sent for you, Jane, because I know you've had a shattering experience."

"The way I look at it," Jane replies slowly, "it could have been a lot, lot worse. I mean, I'm here. Wouldn't a practical rapist kill you?"

"Nice! Very nice!" the chief remarks.

"What do you mean?"

"You know. Destroy the evidence. Motiveless crime. No connection between killer and killed. All that stuff."

The dean says: "I think we can be glad you're here without feeling grateful to your assailant."

"I don't feel grateful to him either," Jane says. "If I were queen I'd ask for his head. But I'm not queen."

The dean glances at Officer Rollo, with whom she is in cahoots. "I understand you have a difficult decision to make, Jane, about whether to press charges against this man or not."

Jane does not reply.

"Don't you need to discuss this with someone, Jane? Don't you want to talk it over?"

Jane still says nothing.

"No!" Officer Rollo explodes. "She doesn't want to talk it over. She wants to leave county law enforcement to scratch itself, while she goes cruising around the countryside in Wirz's old Buick, whistling 'Jingle Bells' with her arm hanging out the window."

Jane blinks, for that is exactly what she wants to do—well, not exactly. "*Tosca*," she corrects. "Not 'Jingle Bells.'"

"Whatever," says the chief. "Some assorted variety of nothing."

Jane shrugs. A most penetrating view of Jane from the chief, especially compared with Dean Lucorne, who has had thirty, forty hours of courses in counseling.

"You can act tough, Jane, and pretend it didn't happen," the dean continues. "But wouldn't it show a more genuine toughness to face the truth?"

Jane thinks, So the truth is what happened? Say, listen to me, Dean Lucorne. There's someone I'd like you to meet. He's a bald, flabby, colorless little dwarf who runs the polygraph machine at the Bureau of Criminal Investigations, PCSD.

"It doesn't mean I think it didn't happen just because I don't want to talk about it with you," Jane says. "Maybe I can't stand you in particular."

The chief says, "Goll!" to the ceiling.

But the mildness only stiffens on Dean Lucorne's face; Jane can see this is where the training comes in, under what to do when the client goes berserk. Why, why does Jane detest this woman so much? Jane realizes that, far from calming her, it's precisely that glow in one who presumes to nurse her that provokes her to savagery, for not only does Jane have no madonna genes in her own repertory, but she has to wrestle down the impulse to attack this strain in other women whenever she sees it, especially when it's pursuing her for her own good.

"You're badly mistaken, Jane, if you think I want you to do this for me," says the dean.

"You think you have no vanity invested in this? I'd be even more scared of you if I believed that."

Dean Lucorne says: "If you don't do something with your pain now, you may never be able to let it go."

Jane says: "I'm aware I appear crude, but even if you were that much wiser than me, I wouldn't want to talk to you. I want to take care of this myself, no matter how bad a job I do. You can help me if you want but not with that."

"How can I help you, Jane?" the dean says a little wearily.

"You can help me get out of here. I want to graduate. Tonight."

The dean stares at her and Officer Rollo says: "They just had one up the college. You know there isn't but one graduation a year."

Jane says: "I don't care about wearing a board on my head. When I leave here, I don't want to come back ever again."

"I don't know," Lucorne says.

"I have enough hours," Jane says. "You could do it if you wanted to."

"I probably could, if I wanted to." The dean summons up a look of determination; Jane watches it swell under the sheen of mildness like a doughnut in a fryer. "Jane, I will not let you run away from your present difficulties without making a decision."

"What about?"

"About *this case*," the chief barks, from his end of the couch.

"I've made a decision," Jane says, "to run away. You think that's not a decision?"

"Then go tell Sheriff Staples that in the morning. He wants to see you," says Rollo.

"I'll bet he does," Jane says.

"Tell him you're leaving and why," says the chief.

"Sheriff Staples can stew in his red-eye gravy. I want to get out of here. *I want to run away.*"

Bang! Dean Lucorne and Jane both jump—the chief has smacked the end table. A silver candy dish flies up in the air and bounces across the rug. Officer Rollo hastily bends over to pick it up. He's ashamed of himself. He says to Jane: "I knew the county cops would be hard on you. I never thought you'd weaken."

"Well, I did," Jane says. "What's the point? You know I can't get any satisfaction from these charlies."

"There are some things in this life you just got to keep coming back alive until you wear somebody down."

Jane looks at his small, tired face, closes her eyes and tries to think. But she cannot think. Instead she sees old blacktop prodding apart the trees at the end of summer, wandering through their bloused, spendthrift greenery, tunneling under those slow, dark fountains of leaves, not in a hurry, but through a richness that can't last. This is the kind of road you drive along in your Buick until you meet up with some surprising fate, some strange being to whom you wisely give all your money, some fellow traveller in a wide hat. It's time for Jane to get back on the road where only the right thing can happen to you, whatever that is.

And yet she's dragging her feet because this pint-sized mother-father figure in blackface, standing awkwardly on the rug, his blue hat in his hand, is shaming her into it.

Jane says: "No. I'll never talk to the sheriff again. These guys have got nothing like my best interests at heart. I don't even make them nervous."

Officer Rollo looks at the rug. He doesn't want to talk about it anymore.

"The only way I'd go back to the Pocahontas County Sheriff's Department is with a lawyer, and that takes cash. So I've got to quit. I've got no choice. I'm broke and I'm not going to work in some beanery just to push this case. That's final."

The police chief nods.

"Your father is a lawyer, isn't he?" Dean Lucorne inquires.

Jane freezes. "What does my father have to do with it?"

"Did you ever think of bringing this problem to your family? Don't you think they would give you some help with it?"

"It's irrelevant whether they would or not."

"It's not entirely irrelevant. Your father paid for your college education. He has some investment in your successful completion of it."

"My father can't wait for me to get out of the celebrated beatnik academy. You should hear him on the subject of this place."

"You're not inclined to discuss these decisions with your parents?"

"No."

"May I ask why not?"

"Because I don't want them to know anything about it."

"What if I make it a condition of my approval of your *in absentia* status?"

Jane stares at her. This must be revenge, revenge crossed with thirty, forty hours of classes in counseling. "You wouldn't!"

"I think you might get more support from that corner than you realize."

"Really? What corner do you think you're talking about?" Jane says.

"If you called your parents."

"Which one?"

Dean Lucorne gives her a puzzled look. Jane realizes that her file will not mention her parents' pending divorce—too recent. She glances stealthily around the room for this document—but of course Dean Lucorne has more class than to bring a file to their interview—that's what thirty, forty hours of counseling courses do for a person. Jane wonders why she feels so violated by Dean Lucorne's banal and secret diagnostic categories. She is not a Bedouin who thinks her soul goes into a camera, or a counseling file. Still, she sees what the phone call home is about. Dean Lucorne is treating her like a mental patient, a crank who should be discharged into the custody of her parents; that is, into the hands of responsible parties in case of a lawsuit or a mysterious disappearance—"when last seen," "when last heard from," that sort of thing.

It is laughable, but Jane suddenly feels that to talk to her father, no matter how he rants—especially if he rants—will be some kind of relief.

"Suppose I call my father and describe my case."

"You'll graduate next spring."

"Where's the phone?" Jane is in a hurry now; she doesn't want to think about what she's doing. But it's not so easy to find Philip Turner. Her parents have been apart since the middle of June, and Jane suddenly realizes she has no idea where her father is living.

She calls one of his law partners; he says her father is on vacation for a few weeks, he doesn't know where. She tries her Uncle Henry in Far Rockaway, who gives her a Baltimore phone number for Philip Turner but is curiously evasive.

"You can try if you want, but he won't be there."

"Where might he be, Uncle Hank? It's urgent."

"I've got a few ideas. I'll try to find him and call you back."

Jane sits at a counter in the kitchen, staring at her huge and bleary nose in the side of a toaster. The dean leans against the refrigerator, tired, no longer trying to make conversation. Officer Rollo sits in the living room. What if Philip Turner cannot be reached? To call Sasha is out of the question! For Sasha to get wind of even a smoothed-over version of what has happened to Jane, much less the whole megillah, would be to call up Dean Lucorne from the deep, ten times ten of her, the ancestral titaness of her, savage where Betty Jean Lucorne is bland, immortal where she is temporary, and in league with a whole covey of deathless Zwillings. Jane has to be under the same roof with

Sasha in a day. The thought of the black cloud her mother would pull down on top of the two of them, if she were to know, makes Jane shudder.

At eleven-thirty her uncle calls back. The number he gives her is in Mozart, Saskatchewan. Jane hopes the call will cost a fortune, and that Dean Lucorne will have to pay for it herself.

At first the operator has trouble getting through. Finally there's a ringing, or rather a faint buzzing, like the sound of a housefly coming in for punctual landings on a pie. A woman's voice answers, tiny but clear.

"Who is this?"

"Jane." Jane does not ask who she is.

"Oh! Your father is at the lake—wait a minute."

The sound of a wooden screen door banging repeatedly, far-away shouting, static on the line. It takes a long time for her father to come to the phone.

"Jane? What's going on?"

His this-better-be-good voice.

"I'm leaving school, Dad. I can graduate *in absentia*."

"So terrific. What else is new at that screwy school. Is that all you called to tell me?" He must not realize this will save him money, Jane thinks.

"I've been having a problem."

"What is it?"

"You know, I moved off campus. Out in the country."

"With that bum," her father supplies.

"With that bum," Jane says, glancing up at the dean. "One night I was there alone, and five men came into the house, five strange men, and they vandalized the house and one of them"—Jane chooses words—"forced me to sleep with him. Then I went to the police."

A long silence.

"Dad?"

"What! What do you want from me? What did you expect? Living in some kind of hobo haven. Living with that bum in public."

"What do you mean, in public? We weren't camped out in the middle of the county road."

"So? People know what goes on. In a small town like that, it's an invitation. You made your bed, you lie in it. You knew what you were doing. What do you want from me?"

"Dad, the police, the county police—"

"I bet they don't think much of you, do they? They think you're a whore. Big surprise!"

"Dad, I don't know whether to go on with this case or not."

"Why the hell not? Let the whole world know about it. How good do you think your chances are?"

"I'd like to talk to a lawyer."

"Am I stopping you?"

"I'm broke, Dad. I don't have any money for a lawyer."

"So? Lawyers give credit."

Jane hangs up the phone. Dean Lucorne looks at her, concern rising on the wide forehead like bumps on a pickle.

"He says lawyers give credit," Jane says.

Then a strange thing happens. Jane starts to cry. She could not have anticipated this, for generally her anger, unlike blood, is entirely insoluble in brine. Besides, Jane never cries.

The dean says, "Jane!" and through the blur Jane sees her coming, but between the wallphone and the refrigerator there is no escape. Then her softness, since she is a large woman, comes all the way around Jane, who pushes her away—politely—and struggles to get control of herself. She pretends not to see the proffered Kleenex, turns her head away and wipes her face on the shoulder of her jersey. Then, blinking, she takes one last look at Dean Betty Jean Lucorne.

The dean's weariness has evaporated, her mildness has been transfigured into the bloom of pure generosity. She has been waiting for this all night.

Jane says: "I'm leaving now."

Dean Lucorne nods. "Don't worry about your standing. I'll see to it."

In the living room the chief takes up his hat, and he and Jane drive away.

Dean Lucorne accomplished her mission the moment Jane's tears appeared, but Officer Rollo, even in the deep blue shadow under the dome of the sky-blue patrol car, looks defeated. Jane is skunk enough to press her advantage. For she understands something she wants, without knowing why.

"Do me a favor. Don't tell Sheriff Staples anything," she says. "You never saw me. You don't know I left town."

"I can't do that," Rollo says. "I can't lie to a fellow officer."

"Well, don't offer any information. Don't call him. Do that for me."

The chief pulls up in back of the moneygreen Buick.

"Let me just disappear," Jane says.

When the police chief drives away, at least he hasn't said no.

Book IV

Shame

*Let a man throw
himself into a blazing
furnace rather than
shame a fellow man
in public.*
—Talmud

○
○
● **The**

ex-queen

Maybe I'm not the girl for this mission after all, Jane is thinking, although it will be nothing new to sit across the kitchen table and hear her mother's story. But as she drives into Baltimore on Route 40, the old broken and tar-splotched National Road, and lets herself get lost on sand-bagged detours of the half-built beltway, she can't help noticing she is in no hurry. Her father—she will be safe from her father, for there Jane has severed relations. She won't call Philip Turner at all. But then she thinks of her mother, her mother's face, and recalls that this too is a dangerous climate, black fog, visibility zero. And this time—though no one will ever know—Jane comes home packing real dread, hides in her old purse new doubts of her own savvy. This time, she wonders if she can come out of there alive.

They will sit, as always, at the kitchen table. Cigarettes, ashtrays, black coffee, Sasha picking a tooth with a paper match. Sasha's sugar spoon clinking slowly around her cup, a sound at once lulling and anciently tedious. Sasha is a slow story-teller, very slow. Jane will look at her mother's face across the table for the ten-thousandth time, wading over it with a hidden, terrible impatience disguised as patience, for this is heavy clay, this is deep swamp, her mother's face, and only because she has crossed it ten thousand times can Jane contain her terrible impatience.

There are what traffickers in ladies' cosmetics call good bones under Sasha's face. She comes from long-lived women. The pretty Russian girl with her square-cut bangs should have lasted, and the hair, like black lacquer, is the same as it always was. But the face has been cheated out of lasting. Sasha's judgment of its shortcomings, of all shortcomings, is written in the flesh on top of its bones. These are no forty-five-year-old woman's few wrinkles, but real scars, wine-red gorges or shiny trenches where pigment is wholly missing. Jane used to observe her mother coming quietly out of the bathroom, would see the pink Band-Aids over the wounds that would turn into these scars without even blinking, so familiar was this ritual. Sometimes it still goes on. And on top of it lies a mask to cover the damage, not the lamentable clown's face that some former beauties put on, lopsided half-dollars of rouge and the rest. A good job, this mask, a noble and dignified restoration.

So that one can see three Sashas at once, if one is looking for the ten-thousandth time. One sees the girl who was going to be more than pretty. One sees the ravaged stratum, not that one can make sense of it. One sees the finished Sasha on top of these two, seated across the table.

Jane thinks of her as an ex-queen locked up in a tower, living on reparations. And does Sasha really have the vanity of a woman who, to save what is left of her beauty, prefers to be seen only from a distance, to be only a white face, red lips, black hair, in a high window? Jane would say yes, as long as she has one person who will come up into the tower from time to time and listen to her, hear her long story. Jane. Jane was always going to be this person. Why. Why Jane.

Driving into Baltimore in less and less of a hurry, Jane sees one good reason she sat through all that privileged talk that was also durance, all that harrowing exegesis of her mother's scars. That she could listen to her mother for hours made it appear that of the three daughters, Jane had all the lenity for the crime of motherhood, that she was the most humane judge.

But Jane knows she was in fact the harshest, for her sufferance, even her love, of her mother was rooted in believing that she would be nothing like her. True, Jane was also her mother's child because her father couldn't stand either one of them. But this didn't make one Gorgon flesh of Sasha and Jane, or did it? Jane always knew she had wriggled clean of the ex-queen's darkly local fate, until now.

Now she avoids Pinkney Road and ends up, of all places, in Druid Hill Park. The Buick stops at the Reptile House, where as a child Jane always tried, always in vain, to get the alligators asleep on a bed of wet pennies to look up at her, so they would be at least a little terrifying. And from here she gazes down the big hill, and it occurs to her that they must have been chauffeured more often as children than she usually admits, for thousands of times her mother drove the girls home this way from downtown. It was this hill Jane would picture at the age of seven or eight when she wondered anxiously if she knew her own way home yet from the city. For what if she should get lost downtown without any carfare? Jane vowed to learn the route by heart every time the family Ford plunged down the steep hill towards Druid Hill Parkway, and always forgot the vow again as soon as they were at the bottom. She could never be sure.

Sometimes she lay in bed at night trying to reconstruct the way beyond the park, but as soon as Druid Hill and the red light at its foot were behind her, the physiognomies of all corners were equally familiar and she was lost in a maze of possibilities. And when she finally drove a car alone through Baltimore city for the first time, at the age of nineteen, she was amazed to find there were no turns at all until one was deep in the old neighborhood, on streets she had explored long since on foot. But by then she was trying to be lost as hard as she could.

All the stories showed that Sasha had been an extremely good girl, pretty but much, much more than pretty. And at first, being good made her all the lovelier. In the wedding pictures she really was a beautiful girl, eighteen years old, in a shining page-boy like the Breck shampoo advertisement, clear-eyed, high-minded, and serene.

Before that she had been popular, unimaginably popular to Jane, who heard the stories, not only from Sasha, and saw as well those monotonously blissful photograph albums—waffle-edged snapshots in black corners with cute captions in white ink, Sasha in tennis skirts, sweater-girl sweaters, smart suits and hats, Sasha with beau after smiling beau, at beaches, star-light band concerts, in leafy parks, and on rocks by Edenic waterholes God knows where, for these places are unknown to Jane and yet Sasha has never left the city where both she and Jane were born. Which is why Jane used to hear those stories at weddings, lawn parties, and bar mitzvahs, when some sales-man or dentist in his cups would corner Jane and crow: "Your mother! If you could have seen your mother!" But he wouldn't say everything, the dentist. He would look at Sasha now, and look away.

Sasha had been more beautiful than any of her daughters. She had been far more beautiful than money, though of money she had always had more than she needed, even to go to col-lege in the middle of the Depression. But still, before she could pose in shorts and halter-top, smiling a closed smile, calm and wise beyond its years, by a shining pond in woods no longer extant, she had had to drag her stepfather Morris out of the hall, had to get the rich but drunken window-washer up the stairs and out of sight before her date came. For Sasha was a good girl, cheerful, high-minded, and true. And besides being, as Morris observed, the only one who never had a hand out for money, she was the one who finished college. She got out of Goucher when she was just eighteen. For her graduation Mor-ris, not quite grasping the protocol of the affair, bought her a big diamond ring.

Then she married Philip Turner. An apprentice lawyer was poor in those days, but Sasha could deny herself, for this was a way of being good. Only gradually she slipped into the middle term, the ravaged stratum between the girl who was more than pretty and the ex-queen on top.

Presently goodness was not buoyant anymore. Now it had a stone face and an air of deep gloom, like a temple waiting to be sacked. This was Sasha the missing link, when Sasha had given birth to Jane. Sasha was only a little older than Jane is now. There came Carla, then Jane, and then Hermine. And one day when Hermine was parked like a bag of cement in a playpen in the living room, and Jane, impervious creature, was banging away at a xylophone on the sunporch, and Carla was sullenly making her way home from kindergarten, Sasha found herself staring coldly into the girls' toy box, at a wad of dirty white satin in one corner. Her wedding gown. What sort of woman gives her wedding gown to three plundering dwarfs as a toy? She had already had to take Carla to Dr. Finkelstein for stuffing the satin pea buttons up her nose. Sasha told herself: Something must be wrong here, very very wrong. And so dragged herself down to the Latrobe Building for the first time to see Dr. Zwilling.

There it is, Jane mutters: Sasha must have managed to ask Philip Turner for money for this, if not for a car or a dress. And Philip Turner saw something in her face and forked it over. That is the trouble, Jane thinks, and a bubble of terrible impatience moves in her craw: that putting herself in the hands of a psychiatrist was high-mindedness reasserting itself in Sasha from the beginning, so that she could even brave collecting the very considerable tariff for this from her young husband week after week. For there was a divine logic to it, that the faulty male should pay for the services of the goodly male. After that there were two men in Sasha's life and thousands of those trips up Druid Hill and down again. Always the ex-queen had listened to too much counsel.

One afternoon when Jane was about five and on the way downtown with Sasha, Jane noticed that Sasha wasn't sneezing, had no cast on her arm or patch over her eye. Why was she going to the doctor again? Because I have an appointment, Jane, every Monday and Thursday, you know that. No, *why* do you go to Dr. Zwilling? Are you sick? Sasha said carefully: Because I want to be a better mother. And at a red light she spat on a piece of Kleenex and roughly wiped something off Jane's nose.

Hold it, don't blame me, Jane is thinking, fifteen years later. I never wanted you to be a better *mother*.

The house on Pinkney Road is for sale.

Sasha comes up the basement stairs. She wears heavy makeup even to pot in, but looks like herself through the mask.

"How are you holding up, Mom? You seem all right to me."

"Did you expect a nervous breakdown?"

Of course not. She isn't the type. With such a mother you can hardly believe out-and-out madness happens in the world. Hieroglyphics on the face are one thing, incapacity quite another.

"I don't know what I expected," says Jane.

Sasha says: "I don't miss your father, if that's what you mean."

Jane opens the refrigerator, gazes at a beaten-up pint of sour cream, two jars of hot peppers, and half a lemon. "Don't you have anything to eat?"

"I live alone now," Sasha reminds her drily.

Jane closes the refrigerator and tries the bread box.

"Your father is with Elizabeth Marcus."

Jane stops foraging for a moment. "What does that mean—is with her?"

"Oh Jane. They've been having an affair since the invention of the wheel. At least I think they have. Your father denies it and nobody else tells me anything."

"What makes you so sure now?"

"He's living with her," Sasha says flatly. "When I need to talk to him I call her apartment. He's never at his apartment."

"You call him up at Elizabeth's?" Jane asks in disbelief.

"Well, there's a divorce case going on here. I call, she, quote, gives him the message. And he calls back. Take my word for it, your father is living over there. You know he can't stand to be alone." There is contempt in this observation, for Sasha can stand to be alone. And so can Jane.

"He's living with Elizabeth Marcus *in public*?"

Sasha looks at Jane peculiarly. "Well, they aren't hanging out billboards. She doesn't live in a zoo."

"Next thing I'll hear he's got contact lenses," Jane mutters.

"Are you joking, Jane? Or do you just keep your head in a hole in the ground? Your father's had contact lenses for five years."

Pensively, Jane opens the loaf she found in the bread box and begins folding the slices into lumps and eating them one by one.

"It's incredible, Jane, how you dose yourself with carbohydrates. Don't you want some butter?"

"Nope." Jane is imagining Elizabeth Marcus. This is a big woman, agreeable looking, heavier boned than any Kaplan female in history, broader beamed, slower moving, deliberate and unexcitable in all her gestures, with a big smile, neatly outlined in lipstick. She lacks any sign of what are vulgarly known as nerves. She is not bookish. She lets other people be the artists. She is the farthest thing from a femme fatale. She is hospitable, philanthropic, Jewish, a lady—convention at its most requiting.

Moreover, she won't cost Philip Turner any money. She has lots of dough from her late husband, an airplane-parts manufacturer and collector of lemuroid fossils of Madagascar, who dropped dead in his thirties. Therefore, she has not even had a divorce to add any question marks to her name. Around Elizabeth you know it is reckless of you not to have arranged an income for yourself by now. You can try to despise her as obvious in her terms, something like a big philodendron in the lobby of a bank. And once at a reception she pushed Jane at Philip Turner and said: "Talk to your father while I get the admiral a drink. You two are the ones with the brains." Which made Jane sweat, since all night in the rack with electrodes attached to her private parts would not have dragged such deference out of

Sasha, and it seemed disloyal not to sneer. Still, it's not possible to dislike Elizabeth, even if you loyally try.

On the other side of the table, Sasha must be wandering over the same piece of track, since she suddenly says tiredly: "She's perfect for your father. And now you don't have to worry that your father might marry some gold digger your age."

"My age?" Jane says uncomfortably.

"Though Elizabeth is only thirty-five."

"She must be one of those grownup types," Jane says. "They never look young, even when they are." Then she realizes what she has heard. "He's going to marry Elizabeth?"

"That's what they say."

"I thought nobody told you anything."

"*That* they tell me."

Jane looks up furtively at Sasha. Her mother's small forehead is draped with black cloud, and Jane thinks of Elizabeth's steadfast smile, her contract to show unvarying good nature, signed in red lipstick that never smears. "She isn't sexy," Jane says, trying to be comforting.

Sasha sighs. "She doesn't need to be sexy."

"Why not? Because she has money?"

"Because she's thick-skinned. Everything rolls off her. She could make a deal with your father. I'm sure she has."

Sasha clinks her spoon around and around the black well of her coffee. Then she says, and it is not a question but a prologue that makes the small hairs stir on the back of Jane's neck: "Do you have the ghost of an idea, Jane, how jealous I've been all these years?"

Jane thinks: Oh, no. The bobby pin. But what could the bobby pin have to do with Elizabeth Marcus, whose name popped up for so many years in connection with a thousand respectable functions of the Galapagos Club that Philip Turner wished to attend and Sasha Turner did not wish to attend? Philip Turner would say: *Don't be ridiculous, Elizabeth is not that type, Elizabeth is a super-efficient hostess with time on her hands, Elizabeth is in fact the transmigrated soul of Martha Washington.*

"But Elizabeth isn't the type," Jane says.

"No," Sasha agrees. "She's not the type. Do you want me to show you, Jane, why she doesn't have to be sexy?"

Jane suddenly wants to see nothing more sexy than Mickey and Minnie Mouse dancing the Charleston. However, she is too far in to back out now. She follows her mother upstairs and down the hall to the parents' bedroom. Sasha vanishes into the walk-in closet and Jane thinks desperately of other times. Inside that same long closet with its double parade of empty sleeves, racked shoes, and glancing plastic bags, Jane once had, not one of the truly great hideouts, but a classic type—in a silky midnight blue clothing bag reeking of mothballs, whose zipper was turned to the wall. It was a good hideout, a decent hideout, but Hermine had come straight to the closet and walked the length of it, punching every hanging thing indiscriminately. So it was a hideout that had been used only once.

Sasha reappears with an armload of rumpled shirt linen, which she dumps on the bed. And now her mother holds up a man's dress-shirt collar with two fingers. Lipstick. "I know what a cliché it all is," she apologizes. "I collected these for years."

"Evidence," Jane says.

"But this is not Elizabeth. Elizabeth is not the type."

"Her lipstick never smears," Jane says. This must be her cue to say, Who was it, who was the type, but something, perhaps some rudimentary loyalty to the genus of loose women (for Jane at least aspires to this nomenclature) prevents her. She tries to imagine her father, that self-proclaimed nothing-too-mucher, out feverishly chasing skirts, but the hackneyed, doggish picture of him it conjures, square in the middle ranks of *Coniunx vulgaris*, the common husbands wringing bourbon out of their neckties and shamefacedly checking their collar points for lipstick in hotel lobby mirrors, makes her turn her face away. In one of her stories, Sasha told Jane that Philip made love to her nowadays maybe every six months, and Jane had wished it were absolute zero, no sex at all, rather than be left to wonder what combination of guilt, alcohol, and sentimental fumbling might trigger this twice-yearly mating and shape its modus operandi.

But at least this means one of her parents doesn't do without sex altogether. Jane is a woman of the world now; she can't let herself wax too indignant about this news. Sasha, however, has the privilege if she wants it. And she wants it.

"Jill. You remember her. She was very young. And Peggy, too, I think. And both the Barbaras, one after the other. And Rae Ellen Cook, a little blonde? She used to call him here. He fired her. And the Negro stenographer, Victoria. You know what your father said to me about her when I found out? How could I be jealous?—she was a colored girl, for God's sake, who wore a hairnet with pearls on it over her pompadour."

These were secretaries, every one. Which is worse than Jane had thought. At least the bobby pin had raised the possibility of, say, a door-to-door cosmetics saleswoman with lips, fingers, toenails all dipped in the same bleeding carcass, a painted shocker with plunging neckline and stainless steel eyelashes who would raise sexual ideas like summer thunderheads out of the level inner plain of the stolidest burgher. Or, say, a batty, pretty, zealous collector for cerebral palsy, thick auburn hair piled skyward in Edwardian coils with half a hundred bobby pins, neglected by her husband and obsessed with the idea of donation, would also have done very nicely, but all the secretaries! All that poignant overtime, taking dictation on glare-cutting steno pads from the distinguished senior partner with trembling fingers, knees pressed together; then a late supper, hearts flying on the slippery backs of credit cards through the humid air of Baltimore after dark, and then—and then the inevitable coming in for a landing with a jolt, the girl sent swiftly packing, with sincerely warm-hearted recommendations, as soon as her replacement could be found. This is worse and worse. Jane tries again to get a fix on Philip Turner as a salty dog, but her father has always been so hounded by puritanical disgust it won't come clear. She has to work to see him eyeing the battalions of typists through sparkling new contact lenses and taking a repetitious delight in knocking over female serfs, girls who make a thirtieth of what he makes, a differential he is not ashamed to squeeze like an investment. Or maybe he is ashamed, was ashamed. But imagine how long a run this scenario had in her father's everyday life, how long it was the only show in town there on the dark side of his moon, which Jane never saw.

"Where was Elizabeth all this while?" Jane asks.

"Your father always had time for Elizabeth," Sasha says with startling bitterness, for throughout the compendium of secretaries, she has been so derisively matter-of-fact. And after this outburst her eyebrows tilt plaintively up at Jane. They make an odd scene, Jane realizes: her mother perched squeamishly next to the pile of pink-smeared shirts, as though testing the bed in a dingy and disreputable hotel; and Jane, leaning against the closet door, arms crossed, seeming by this accident of stance to be Sasha's referee. Sasha's look says: I only appear to be a debased hag, conjuring blackmail from the stumps and parings of a marriage doomed from the start. Tell me I am excusable.

And Jane feels that terrible impatience again at the sight of her mother begging her approval. I never wanted you to be a better *mother*, Jane thinks. Why can't you stand to be a bad girl like me?

"So why did you stay?" Jane says.

"Sometimes I thought I was crazy," Sasha says.

"But for twenty years, Mom."

"Look at the life I've been leading. Just look." Sasha ploughs a hand through the pile of lipstick-smeared shirts.

"I can't see feeling crazy with jealousy when you don't even love somebody," says Jane.

"What makes you think I didn't love your father?" Sasha says.

Jane stares at her incredulously. "If that was love, Mom, I am the Thing from Planet X."

Her mother begins to sob.

"I thought you stayed married because of the children," Jane says feebly.

"I wish I could say that was true."

"Well, don't. I thought it was a ridiculous reason."

Sasha cries no more often than Jane. Therefore, she doesn't know how to cry with any sort of style. She quakes all over her torso, hiccups every second or two like a frog in an amorous emergency, and holds a hand over her face, not to wipe away tears but to hide the visage she accurately guesses is not pleasant to look at. Jane is glad for the underlying physical reserve between her and her mother. In a real crisis, they wouldn't think of throwing arms around one another, but stand apart gravely and quietly to allow the other to recover some dignity with her real grief, instead of wringing it out like a kitchen sponge.

Finally Jane says: "But Mom. Why now?"

Sasha stands at the bedroom window, her back to Jane. "Your father started to see more of Elizabeth," she says, "okay? And keep in mind that through all those years of the secretaries, when I'd never see him till he crawled in bed at three in the morning, he still made it over to Elizabeth's once a week. Every Friday night. As if nothing were wrong in the world! I thought, Well, Philip can be charming, but if she only knew what a Dr. Jekyll and Mr. Hyde he is—your father couldn't sit through that movie, it made him so nervous, did you know that, Jane?

"So I did a terrible thing. I went to a sisterhood lunch at Baltimore Hebrew where I usually wouldn't be caught dead. I got Elizabeth in a corner and told her everything. Everything I just told you. Can you imagine! But she stopped me. She put her hand on my arm like this and said, Sasha, everybody can have what they want. What's so *geferlich* if he runs around a little? Keep a pleasant ambience and he'll come home.

"You know what happened then? I jumped in my car and got lost on Park Heights Avenue. I've lived in this neighborhood for fifteen years! First it came to me I hadn't told her anything she didn't know. She knew all about your father. I could hear him telling her his escapades, not to amuse her, she's not the type, but to pour out the terrible troubles he was having with his wife. And she would give him an unconditional pardon. *What's so geferlich if he runs around a little?* That's the deal they have, you see, Jane. She can be so above it. *Everybody can have what they want.* Is it really true that everybody can have what they want? And I ended up with this? Then I'm beaten. I wasn't even angry at Philip, I just wanted never to see him again. And this time when I threw him out he went to Elizabeth."

Sasha is quiet. The story must be over.

"So Mom. How did she explain all those visits? Those Friday nights?"

"She didn't have to explain it. Don't you see, Jane! That's why she doesn't need to be sexy. Those were shabbos dinners, positively luminous with decency. Flowers and candles and chopped liver. Catered pirogen at five dollars a dozen."

"Keep a pleasant ambience," Jane says.

"Not only that. Pious, too."

So Philip Turner gets an unconditional pardon, and like a Jewish pasha is still allowed, at least theoretically, to call in the dancing girls when the mood overtakes him. Jane is depressed.

"Mom, did you, what's the expression, put a tail on Dad? Have him tailed? How did you know all that about where he spent his time?"

"He's trying to leave me without a cent, Jane! I could hardly get a lawyer to take my case. I had to do something."

"I'm not accusing you," Jane says mildly. "I'm just asking."

"You are accusing."

"I'm not. Go ahead. Tell me about the private eye. Did he look like Bogart or was he a little weasel in a J.C. Penney suit like I always imagined these guys would be in real life?"

"I never saw him, Jane. He was just somebody who worked for Mr. Bungy."

"For Mr. Bungy," Jane says.

"My lawyer." Jane peers at her mother uneasily, for *My lawyer* is said in the voice from the black cloud.

"If you can call that a lawyer," Sasha adds, as if it goes without saying that any lawyer she could draw would be someone Philip Turner would laugh at. And the black cloud swirls outward from her temples like the engineered fog of a low-budget horror movie, flittering under the door, quenching the gay chandelier spoke by spoke, screams, panic, and the world of 3514 Pinkney Road fallen once again under siege by the evil one. For the ex-queen cannot be purloined from the seat of her power, whatever her power is, so long as she clasps this fog of worry around her tight as a corset.

"He means well. He just doesn't have a yiddishe kop," Sasha goes on.

"So? The weasel got the goods on Philip Turner, didn't he?" Jane says irritably.

"Oh Jane! You know how long these cases take. Mr. Bungy is negotiating with Donald. Donald Wiener!" Sasha puts a hand to her forehead, for Donald Wiener is a real lawyer, Philip Turner's original partner in Turner, Wiener, Blum & Taliaferro. "Donald had to call me up. He couldn't even find Mr. Bungy's office. It's a hole in the wall under Pikesville Hardware. Mr. Bungy is a nice man, he's doing his best. He's not going to bring it up about the shirts and the rest of it unless he has to."

Whose girl is she now, the girl who was going to be more than pretty? So Mr. Bungy will never replace the two male eminences whose conflicting permissions once chased the ex-queen up and down her court, as if it were a basketball court. For Dr. Zwilling left Baltimore a year ago. He was going to the West Coast, to join Whole Message, a new therapeutic institute based on the encounter group, whatever that is. When Sasha asked him for a referral, Dr. Zwilling told her to wait a while. He had become "somewhat disenchanted with classical psychoanalysis as a clinical tool."

And now Philip Turner is gone as well. Jane thinks: So much the better! Let the entire tribe of her grand viziers vanish from the face of the earth.

But Sasha says: "I'm scared to death, Jane. Not scared of being alone. When it was all done, I didn't miss Philip Turner for five minutes. I don't even wonder what he's doing." She flips a hand once more through the lipstick-spotted shirts. This time it is a gesture of wise leniency, of quittance. *Take these and dispose of them according to their merits.* Nevertheless, Jane observes, the shirts do not back out of the royal chamber, tucking their offending collars inside themselves as they go. They stay where they are.

"So it's funny, isn't it," Sasha continues, "when he's got a woman and I'm alone, that he's dead set on leaving me broke. I raised his children!" (Jane has reason to think Philip Turner may not be unconditionally grateful for that service.) "He's got this super balabosteh who tells him he's the most fascinating man that ever walked, and who's loaded besides. Why would he want me to end up with nothing? There are no men in my life except my bridge partner," Sasha says, "and he's a fairy."

Jane stops listening. She's hearing something else, a ghostly voice, a scrap of text she locked away long ago in the same cul de sac of unthinkables with the bobby pin. And now the bobby pin has given up its secrets and been thrown onto the garbage. And here lies the other, unclassifiable.

She was eleven or twelve. It was a summer night, hot and sweet; the bed seemed soaked with sticky poison. Too hot to sleep or to get up, she lay on her side staring without glasses at the fogbound whirlpool of the window fan, which pushed no air at all, and thought about swimming pools smeared that neon blue-green found nowhere in nature. Then she got caught in a nightmare. She had jumped off a diving board, balled into a somersault, and was rolling forever in the air without hitting the water.

She got out of bed with a lurch and came as far as the banister. Now she heard her parents' voices rising in the stairwell. They were arguing, but not after their usual fashion, Sasha a whirling typhoon, Philip an arctic silence and then mile-wide ice floes breaking up with a roar. Both voices were strangled, ghostly, disconnected. Jane could not make out the words, and then she heard her father say very distinctly: *I came to you on my knees, and you turned me away.* Jane wheeled about at once and returned to her bed, where she lay in the dark in the numb wobble of the electric fan refusing to ponder these words.

Instead she was cutting slowly and smoothly across the dark waters of some northern lake, all alone, fearless over the distance.

"I'm not scared of being alone," Sasha is saying. "I'm scared to death of being broke. Don't judge me too fast, Jane! I'm not spoiled. Your father gave me so much a week, no more. I don't know what he used to do with all that money he was making. Women couldn't have cost him that much.

"But we didn't even have to be speaking. I could be sick, I could turn blue, I could stay down in the cellar for a week talking Pig Latin to myself and never go near that wheel. On Friday the money would be there. Now if tomorrow I can't stand the sight of clay—and believe me it could happen, it's happening already—I know I won't starve, but I don't want to live in a house that's not painted once in ten years. Don't sneer, Jane. I couldn't live like you."

"I'm not sneering," Jane says.

"Don't give me funny looks. I wouldn't be able to stand it if everything got shabbier and shabbier. If it's going to be just what I make out of potting when checks crawl in from shops —I've never been poor like that. Don't look at me that way, Jane!"

"What way?"

"I couldn't get used to it," Sasha says.

And without exactly believing her, Jane, who had severed political relations with her father the instant she hung up the telephone in Dean Lucorne's kitchen, suddenly arrives back in his power with a thud. Who does he think he is! (And she expunges that unclassifiable message, *I came to you on my knees, and you turned me away,* from the evidence.) It would be one thing to bully and chastise women with money or the lack of it if he had come into his present wealth after a childhood of wearing patched knickers, ransacking trash barrels for loose crusts and looking for nickels in street gutters. But he had had even more money than Sasha! Neither of them has any idea what it means to be poor.

And Jane remembers something else. Her father owes her money. He owed her money all the while they talked on the telephone. If she had demanded payment, probably he would have wiggled out of it as before—My accountant is handling it, that sort of thing—but she would have been spared begging him for a plain handout. She had simply forgotten. She's a hopeless incompetent, a booby.

"How broke are you, anyway, Mom?"

"I've figured it out. I can just make ten thousand a year from potting if I work all the time, every day, grit my teeth and repeat repeat repeat until I turn into a machine."

Ten grand a year! This sounds like a queen's ransom to Jane in 1965. And all at once Jane envies her tragic mother, who is good enough at something she taught herself to do to make ten thousand thankless bucks a year, even though she threatens to crumple or go mad long before she turns into a machine.

Only, such a mother does not go mad. She is not the type. Sasha sighs again. "If only Mr. Bungy can get me the house," she says. And now she is touching her face, fingering those ten-year-old welts and craters under the white mask, as though they appeared the day before yesterday.

"I think I've developed an allergy to clay," she is saying.

Oh

Jane

September 15, 1965

Dear Dad,

A few weeks ago I called you on the phone at some spa in the Arctic Circle to which you and Elizabeth must have been flown in by bush pilot at fabulous expense. I told you I was having a little problem and needed to talk to a lawyer. You said lawyers give credit, a line I hope you'll always be proud of, since you'll read it soon in my life story.

Why didn't I just ask you to pay me back the money you owe me? By now I should have had six monthly checks for $79.16. Will you kindly mail these to me right away c/o Sasha Turner? You know the address. I guess you didn't realize that if I graduate from Harmonia in absentia, I will save you around 3000 bucks in tuition. Since I noticed some time ago you stopped sending me money for food and shelter on the suspicion I would share them with that bum, I expected you to be pleased. Since I will not marry @ $5000* nor undergo a year of psychoanalysis @ $5200*, I hope to remain,

Your cheapest daughter,
Jane

*(The two figures represent bequests of unprecedented generosity from Philip Turner to Carla and Hermine, of which word had travelled fast over the Kaplan-Turner grapevine. Probably Jane was feeling left out of such largesse, even though the gifts were clearly in the nature of terminal payments.)

Jane retreats to her old room, actually half a room, which ends in a nothingness, for she vaporizes Carla's bed, desk, and night table, as she used to do with Carla herself when Carla still lived here. She does not flop on the bed or slide from the chair onto the ugly yellow ink-stained carpet, novel in hand, as she would have done when she was in high school. (As for that carpet, her parents had bought the cheapest, prophesying that Jane would shortly ruin it, and she had.) Instead she stays at her desk, trying to be a whole new Jane. For if she should happen to, if she should have to, stay in Baltimore and should find herself acting like her old self in here, holing up, fundamentally, she could admit it now, hiding from the grownups, dosing herself with novel after novel, lying down on the ink-stained rug once a week or so to write her life story and never, not once, getting beyond the first paragraph—really it would be better to die and get it over with, to join the WAC's and let them send her to Viet Nam, or to court some other equally senseless and punishing finale.

So Jane sits at the desk, repossessing herself—she picks the word as if she had been a used car, for she has to sneer at herself for coming home at all. She already knew that when you pass through your mother's front door you automatically become half the woman you were; whatever bag of powers you're hauling deflates by half like a leaky balloon the minute you enter that atmospheric depression euphemistically called home.

And if you are reckless enough to come home in an already weakened state, and if you have only $3.19 left and by now are smoking your mother's cigarettes without even complaining about them, and your mother is making noises about how her friend Sybil has a friend at Creative Placefinders who could place you in a minute, and you know that, in your place, a good child would be plotting on money, big money, to make her mother feel secure, then you are in real danger of disappearing altogether.

Having been the happiest of infants, Jane had realized early that as long as she stayed in the city of her parents, her joy would always be sneaking away from her. One day she was walking home backwards from school—backwards along the grassy strip to the corner of Pinkney, squinting at the pock marks the sucker cups on her sneakers made in the stiff, rich mud. For so far the dirt showed only a few pale strands of grass. All at once it came to her that she was entertaining herself in this narrow and hunched-over fashion because she could not bear to look up and notice it was spring. "I'm not ready for it," she told herself. She was barely twelve. She raised her head, having sniffed something in the air, and then she felt something warm and fragrant, but distinct, brush her as it passed by. It was her spirit, which had seemed so beautiful to her in the beginning. And it still did, but it was going on without her. Jane, amateur of horror, saw what had happened. She was the opposite of possessed; she was vacated. And when escape began to beckon to her during this period, the idea was always to catch up to the happiness she had been born to.

Five things sit on Jane's desk: four telephone messages, which she is ignoring, and her notebook, in which she is trying to write something new. After three weeks there is more written on the telephone messages than in the notebook. They say:

JANE—CALL JIMMY BEFORE SUNDAY (714) FA 8 4589

JANE—JIMMY CALLED HE'S IN THE DESERT TILL SUNDAY CALL HIM (714) FA 8 4589

JANE—JIMMY CALLED AGAIN, WANTED TO KNOW IF I GAVE YOU THE MESSAGE. I SAID YES AND JANE, WHY HAVEN'T YOU CALLED HIM BACK! (714) FA 8 4589

OH JANE! JIMMY CALLED AGAIN! WHAT IS THE MATTER
WITH YOU! YOU'RE TREATING HIM HORRIBLY & YOU'RE
EMBARRASSING ME! (714) FA 8 4589

Jimmy is beyond the rufous Sierras. He has started school at
Chouinard. Though this is coping, he has a fat scholarship and
they are making much of him. He has sent six drawings that
prove (and this is a point in his favor) he has not gone down
without Jane. He has flooded her with letters that say (since
Jane's letters have been few and noncommittal): *I can't believe
you don't love me.* Only a soul far clearer and more beautiful
than Jane's could think up such a line, much less inscribe it in
swashbuckling pantaloons of black ink that leap and spark
across the white paper.

Now she remembers when they were drowning together all
July, when rather than face the police, they spent whole days
and nights in the bedroom, in the bed, since that was one place
to do nothing, know nothing, and be nothing. They rolled
around each other, slick with sweat, two eels in the abyss, meaning not hell but the Marianas trench, under seven miles of water,
having found each other by means of eerily glowing lures in
their pineal glands. You may ask yourself when it came down
to that, when love boiled down for Jane to pursuit of the invisible counterpart in the blind abyss, forgetful of beauty, higher
intelligence, personality, and even particular gender, if she did
not wake up again scared out of her wits and eager to put love
away in its proper place, in some closet out of sight. Scared,
yes; but Jane is not yet at all convinced she has more important
work to do in the world than to track down that greenish lure
in the abyss. In truth nothing has ever made a deeper impression on her, and she must fight the impulse to fly to it at once.

But Jimmy is still the shrewd and able changeling who makes
the world feel uneasily for its wallet, or its bloomers, or both.
Philip Turner hates him lavishly even sight unseen—the old
man can just imagine. And as for Jane, who sees in part with
her father's eyes, there will always be something fishy about

the man she loves. He is all Jane is not, an artist and a whore, thrilling because he made Jane his meal ticket without thinking twice. What is independence compared to that iridescent air, that sheen of a fountain into which some girl will always want to throw her lucky pennies—or anyway will do so, whether she wants to or not. That's what Jane fears: that his claim might be higher than her claim, his claim to anything whatever.

Think, he is a boy who has no fear of the rufous Sierras. But there's something about those big mountains inhospitable to one of her stripe, the stripe down a winding bumpy highway in, say, southern Ohio, banked with common deciduous trees. And why is Jimmy so airtight in the claim he telegraphs to the gods? Because he has no fear of parents either—in fact, that's where he learned it, how to be a holy bully for art's sake, from Pete and Ernestine, living forebears who are scared to death of him. Whereas Jane—egad, she shudders at the notion of trying, unsuccessfully of course, to bully her parents into anything. What she fears, in short, is that she will go to California and Jimmy will still be golden while Jane will be beating the bushes for a measly job within a week.

So Jane, as best she can, ignores the four messages on her desk.

In the open notebook next to them, she is trying to write a new version of the life story.

THE BEARD ENVY CURE
Old Family Recipe

In which three sisters sue their father for a share of the power that reposes in his beard, and being laughed at by him for their clumsy tactics, and having realized that they possess no external sites for the attachment of beards, they resort to parricide, cutting off the coveted part, divvying it up, and eating it.

Jane is taken with this idea, but now for three weeks she has been sitting here staring at the thing, first patiently, then angrily, and at last with a strange sleepiness that tries to push her off her chair onto the ink-spotted rug. Nothing comes. She gives up, closes and pushes the notebook to the back of the desk, and there are the telephone messages staring up at her again on pastel squares from Sasha's memo pad:

OH JANE! JIMMY CALLED AGAIN! WHAT IS THE MATTER WITH YOU! YOU'RE TREATING HIM HORRIBLY & YOU'RE EMBARRASSING ME! (714) FA 8 4589

Jane sighs. Why can blood never be thicker than water with Sasha? Why is she taking up the end of a boy she has never even met? Why couldn't at least one of Jane's parents believe she could do no wrong, for so empowered she might be able to murder her father in verse without inhibition. Jane clutches her forehead. Really, she can feel the two of them up there, each one squatting in the hollow of a temple like mismatched salt and pepper shakers stuck in two niches over a chimneypiece, the demonic miniature estranged parents that she, Jane, will never get rid of.

"And Jane!" Sasha suddenly shouts up the stairs. "Have you called Jimmy back yet?"

"Damn it," Jane mutters. "No!"

"Oh Jane! For God's sake—"

"I'm waiting till after eleven."

That shuts her up, for the present.

It is not as though Jimmy and Jane have not connected already, coast to coast, and more than once, over their parents' telephones—just wait till Sasha gets the bill. And if Sasha only knew what a saboteur of parental interests in general and of hers in particular she is supporting here, in the name of impartial justice and charity, why, Jane thinks, wouldn't she be thunderstruck.

"What are you doing there?" Jimmy asks Jane over and over, sometimes gently, sometimes in that more importunate note between a sob and a bray that means he is near a refrigerator full of beer—his parents' refrigerator, this has to be, down in

Cathedral City, in the desert, where there is also a telephone, for the hole in the wall by MacArthur Park where he is living has neither.

"I came to see my mother," Jane replies.

"Oh. How is she?"

"She's okay. Scared of being broke."

A pause.

"She should be as broke as Pete and Ernestine," Jimmy proposes, alluding to the parents whom he allows to support him in L.A. "Then she'd just thrash through the daily shitpile as best she could."

Jane thinks this over. "That's probably true," she admits. "But she hasn't, so she can't."

"She will."

Silence.

"I mean, what can you do for her, anyway?"

"I could stick around, get a job."

"What madness! What are you doing there, Jane!"

"I came to see my mother," Jane says tightly.

"Well, you've seen her. What are you doing there now?"

"I'm figuring out what to do next."

"Life's too short," Jimmy says. "We should be together."

Jane says nothing.

"Do you think you'll know any better next week? There's a war going on, you know. Any minute now, bombs could start raining down, and where are *you*?"

Jane says: "Anyway, I'm broke."

"Oh. What else is new? You could be broke here just as well."

"Even better, I bet," Jane replies, slipping poison into the well. Not that Jimmy is scheming on putting Jane to work in L.A., any more than he is scheming on putting himself to work. He simply imagines the two of them balled together down a shady hole in the sand, a pair of small scaly creatures of the desert, living on nothing more substantial than seeds and dew.

"Far better," Jimmy agrees, failing to perceive the fatal taint in Jane's last remark. "It costs nothing to heat here. I know a grocery store that sells three pounds of hot dogs for a buck. Also ten pounds of spuds for twenty-nine cents. The beaches are free. You don't need a coat. You can see the Sierras at the end of the block when the smog dies down a little."

"And there's always the desert with Pete and Ernestine," Jane says, adding more poison, "if you need a turkey dinner."

"There's always the desert," Jimmy echoes, again not tasting the poison, "if you can stand it! It's madness at this place. Mother is with Tubby every night. That's the boyfriend. Pete cooks her dinner and off she goes, cussing the lot of us clear to the end of the driveway. Not one dollar of her paycheck does she turn over to the old man. Pete's supposed to be taking it easy, but he drives down to El Centro—it's 130 in the shade there—to work on magnetos for Kaiser every couple days, he says as a favor to the foreman, but I think he needs the money."

Jane does not ask how much of the money Pete needs is finding its way to Jimmy in L.A. Pete has bought Jimmy a car —even if you're broke, you have a car in Los Angeles—a mint-green '61 Valiant with a mint-green bagel on the back and push-button transmission.

"It's not so bad out in my shack," Jimmy is saying. "They wouldn't dare bother me out there. I wouldn't let either of them in."

Jane says nothing.

"I can't believe you don't love me, Jane! What are you doing at your mother's, for God's sake?"

"You know something?" Jane says. "It's not a good idea to bully me by asking me that question over and over."

"To bully you! I'm telling you I love you," Jimmy says. "Life's too short. Is that bullying you?"

"Yes," Jane says, in a small, hard voice, and Jimmy crashes the phone down on his end—not hangs up, throws it on the floor, so that there is a boinking clatter out of the receiver, which flattens suddenly into the tense monotony of a dial tone.

"Don't answer it," Jane yells downstairs to Sasha when the phone rings a moment later.

"I'm not going to play that ridiculous game!" comes Sasha's voice. The chair at her telephone table scrapes back. She answers the phone.

"It's for you, Jane!"

Jane leans over the banister. "I'm not here. I don't have to be a slave to an ugly gadget made of black plastic. I don't have to talk to anybody."

"Oh Jane!"

"I'm not coming."

In two minutes, Sasha comes into Jane's room. "Don't ask me to do that anymore," she says. "You're going to have to argue with your boyfriend in a civilized fashion. I need to answer my phone! What if it's one of my children in trouble?"

"It is one of your children in trouble," Jane says. "She's sitting right here telling you not to answer it."

"That's different," Sasha says.

Jane, broke, trapped, unable to write a line, is hurrying upstairs with a pack of her mother's cigarettes, out of reach of her mother's next remark, whatever it is going to be, when the doorbell rings. It is the mailman with a letter for Jane, Certified Mail, Delivery Restricted to Addressee, from Turner, Wiener, Blum & Taliaferro.

September 29, 1965

Dear Jane:

Pursuant to our verbal agreement of last March, my book-keeper Miss Toohey assures me that a check in the amount of $79.16 will be ready for you in time to accompany this letter.

Let me remind you that a starting date for a repayment schedule was never determined between us. Since you did not give me a current address, common sense dictated that I await further intelligence before ordering the first check to be mailed. Such intelligence, of course, was not forthcoming.

Starting with this one, a check will be remitted to you on the first of every month for the next twelve months, provided I receive a current address for you on a timely basis, since I suspect your present domicile is a highly momentary arrangement. Under no circumstances will I permit this or any other check to be mailed to you in the care of a second party.

Regarding all the money you are generously sparing me by leaving that goofy school a year early, let me remind you that no law requires me to pay so much as one dollar of your tuition at any school, so that the generosity, insofar as there has been any, has been all mine. Moreover, I have just received a bill from Harmonia College for $800.00 for "Non-Attendant Extra-Academic Registration Charges" for the academic year 1965–66, which I interpret to mean that it will cost you, or rather me, eight hundred dollars for you not to be studying at that institution until you graduate in June 1966. And if that is the last of the miscellaneous bills and charges I see from that screwy school, I will be very much surprised.

Indeed, the bill for "Non-Attendant Extra-Academic Registration Charges" was followed immediately in the mail by a separate bill for "Miscellaneous Telephone Charges" in the amount of $38.73, which went on to itemize a number of calls from a Harmonia Springs, Ohio, number, to Baltimore, Far Rockaway, and Mozart, Saskatchewan, on the night of August 3, 1965. Since I am certain I did not initiate any of these telephone calls, I have of course returned the bill unpaid.

Finally, leaving aside the other crude and naive remarks in your letter of September 15, I will tell you that your characterization of yourself as my cheapest daughter was most insulting, and by no means true.

Your father,
Philip F. Turner

PFT/aw/ck enc

Jane notices that this letter has been typed by a new secretary —*aw*—one unknown to Jane, giving rise to a host of unpleasant speculations. Between "Your father" and "Philip F. Turner," the word *Dad* is scrawled in blue ballpoint, in his great-fat-looping uppercase, tiny-crabbed-knotted lowercase, backwards slanting hand.

Nevertheless, as stated, a check for $79.16 is enclosed.

Jane cannot help thinking: three thousand miles at around twenty miles to a gallon, 150 gallons or fifty dollars, plus oil, and stay off toll roads and don't eat—motels being out of the question. Looked at in this way, $79.16 is an exact amount. Exactly the right thing has happened to her. She has travelling money in her pocket, but only, owing to the smallness of the sum, if she leaves right now. Ah, the tissue of coincidence, tightening around Jane's heart like the first, gratuitous brassiere of a twelve-year-old. When she thinks that she could leave tonight, when she compares the lugubrious piety of becoming the ex-queen's retainer to the giant emptying wrench of a getaway, then she rushes to sweep everything else out of her heart. And as for whether Sasha could or could not paint, once in ten years, the slightly smaller house where she will end up now that both her husband and her psychiatrist have forsaken her—that she, Jane, has almost taken this cross for her cross is madness. She should run from such a budget like plague at her age, by crackey! And when she finds it at last, the bare floor of her heart, she does not even have to think it in words. I am free, free to go, it says, for the truth is, I don't care about any of them. At the very bottom I don't care about anyone.

"Could you cash a check, Mom? For seventy-nine bucks?"

"Oh Jane." The voice from the black cloud. "Oh Jane, I could, but I wouldn't have anything left. Couldn't it wait till tomorrow?"

Jane nods and turns for upstairs, noting coldly that, all the same, if the case is urgent, the cash is there, in her mother's familiar, black, quadruple-flapped, rather terrifyingly well-organized purse.

At six Jane eats a hamburger with Sasha. At six-thirty, to get out of the house, she goes for a walk along Western Run, crossing the stream here and there on rust-smeared stones, now and then sinking into black stuff up to her shinbones. She has a horror of the water left over from a period when she was nine or ten and this whole tree-lined bank from Green Spring to Falstaff was posted with paper typhoid warnings from the Department of Health. Then Hermine and Jane had been drawn to the brook day after day, for both believed that even one drop of this reddish black water on the skin would cause you to die of a dreadful disease, and neither of them ever left the brook without having felt the chill pinprick of at least one drop on the ankle, elbow, or forehead. In bed at night, Jane would wait for symptoms to set in.

Above Jane, the twilight darkens to cobalt, full of glancing clouds like the inside of a mussel shell. A wind springs up. Jane walks back up Pinkney Road barefoot, carrying her tennis shoes, as the first teacup-sized drops of rain begin to stain the sidewalk. By ten the rain, straight up and down, hangs in long gray beards on the storm windows. Jane paces the living room, glancing out its glass door now and then at a world that has turned into pure geometry and rain. At eleven Sasha, heading upstairs to the shower, passes Jane and mentions the time. Jane has no intention of calling Jimmy; she need only decide whether to lie to Sasha about this. At 11:05, the telephone rings, and Jane, letting it ring, hoping Sasha cannot hear it in the shower, kneels in front of her parents' liquor cabinet—the same one she used to hide in, behind the ranks of bottles, until she was eleven—and pours herself a big tumbler of Wild Turkey. She gulps down half of it, gasping, before the phone stops ringing.

A moment later the phone starts up again. Jane strolls into the kitchen, lazily picks up the receiver. "Good evening, James," she says in an oily tone, affecting to be more drunk than nature requires.

"Who is this?" says Philip Turner.

Now Jane feels, probably is, drunk in earnest. Things begin to burn at the edges, to bulge, soften, at the center. "Who wants to know?" she says.

"Jane?"

"Jane."

"Where are you?" Philip Turner barks, as if she has called him.

"Where are *you*?" she asks, sipping thoughtlessly from the glass in her hand. "I am in Baltimore, Maryland, at the erstwhile family manse on Pinkney Road."

"What are you doing there?" At least Jane thinks he asks her that.

"That question!" she erupts. "Are you two in cahoots?"

"Let me speak to your mother."

"I can't."

"What?"

"I can't."

"Get me your mother!"

"I can't."

"What do you mean you can't!"

"*Can not.* Auxiliary of ability, negative form."

"You can't."

"Can't."

"Why can't you?"

"She's in the shower."

"Don't lie to me. Tell your mother I'm calling."

"Can't."

"What kind of craziness is this!"

"Can't."

He hangs up. Jane means to tell Sasha he has called as soon as she hears her mother get out of the shower—she is dimly aware, as she hangs up the phone, of the appearance of conspiracy, indeed she finds a drab insult in the suspicion, she has reasons of her own to wish to offend her father—but by the time the gurgle of downflow in the plumbing dies away, she is no longer listening. She is lumbering through a glassiness, a sudden rigidity of air and object as though the interior of the house on Pinkney Road were turning into a flat color photo of itself with Jane the only thing in it left alive, barely alive, and lurching from place to place.

She begins lugging her stuff out to the Buick through the straight up-and-down rain. Dragging her metal footlocker down the front walk—she doesn't even know what is in it anymore, having stuffed it with dirty laundry, books, dishes, whatever came to hand, when she left the house on PCR 601 in haste, and never having looked inside it since.

When she comes back inside, streaming wet, Sasha stands at the top of the stairs in a brown robe, blinking down at her.

"I'm leaving, Mom."

"Oh Jane." But this is a hushed voice, not even a murmur, a voice gathering back its premonitions, its thoughts too desolate for even the black cloud to whisper out loud. "Where are you going?" she asks.

"I'm not certain," Jane says, looking at her mother's small white feet on the landing. She waits until Sasha steps back, then walks past her, averting her face, turning quickly into her room so that her mother won't smell the liquor on her breath.

"Did you talk to Jimmy?" Sasha asks, from behind her.

Jane does not answer.

She stands, trying not to sway, in the doorway to her room, a paper carton of books in her arms, watching her mother a few yards down the dark hall. "I'm sorry, Mom," she says.

"What about money?" Sasha says in a flat, dead voice.

"I'll find some job," Jane says. Halfway down the steps she remembers, stops, turns around. "Mom, I have to cash that check."

"Oh Jane." Beaten now, and getting it over with. "Just take it out of my purse. By the telephone table."

Jane's fingers pick the clean bills out of her mother's wallet. It is impossible to do this without feeling like a criminal.

"Jane!" Sasha's voice, with Sasha coming down the stairs behind it, is finally angry. "Why do you have to go in the middle of the night like a goddamn thief? If it's the right thing for you to do, won't it still be right in the morning?"

"No," Jane says. "I have to go *now.*" Without explaining why. For of course that is why. If she waits till morning, she may never be able to leave.

She blunders out to the car again and again through slats of vertical rain, packing the Buick in complete disorder. Only her typewriter she bothers to cushion a little, packing loose clothes around it on the floor of the backseat. After Jane's third or fourth trip, Sasha disappears, the light off in her bedroom.

When she is finished, Jane goes to the doorway of her parents' room. The door, as it always has, as long as Jane can remember, stands half open. Jane knows her mother is not asleep, for she cannot hear it, that low, slow skidding in the throat, more familiar to Jane, she suddenly realizes, than her own breath.

"I'm going now, Mom," she says into the darkness.

Sasha says: "I'm angry at you for leaving this way."

"I know," Jane says. "But I have to. I have to go."

Sasha says no more, and Jane runs down the steps and out to the car, without even—because of the stink of the liquor, or anyway she tells herself that is the reason—kissing her mother goodbye.

○
○
● **Jane**

drove

without

stopping

not, of course, in the world of gas pumps, roadside diners, and
highways like Route 50, by Romney, West Virginia, where she
pulled over at dawn to puke yellow-green bile into a ditch; not
in the literal world, but in that other world of endless serpentine blacktop parting the trees, down which Jane tracked her
missing spirit by the white broken line of a ghostly lane divider,
trying to overtake her in the land of the free.

Even in the world of thick white diner crockery, stained and
chipped, of pyramids of oilcans next to pinging red airhoses,
speed zones in Pleasantville, Unincorporated, Pop. 782, and
disconnected warnings, END DIVIDED ROAD, FALLING ROCK,
WRONG WAY, she hardly stopped, midnight to midnight, for the
first twenty-four hours, and yet she did not get far, for at first
she was not going anywhere, but rather away from every place
she had ever been. Jane was not used to hard liquor, though in
the West she was soon to deepen her acquaintance with firewater, cheaper firewater than that which fueled her desertion of
her mother. She left still drunk, and the effect of this, in the
monsoon through which she steered the moneygreen Buick with
hunched shoulders, gripping the steering wheel with both
hands, squinting through rain-cratered glass swept now and
then by old-fashioned suction windshield wipers, was to raise

the elemental ante of this departure. For the first six hours all she could see was a cave of road the size and shape of her headbeams, through which swam diverse electric eels, unidentified spiny balls and bars of light, all moving fast.

At the same time, she knew she was on the Baltimore Beltway going south, and saw herself pass Route 40 West, Frederick, Old National Road, before she understood what she meant by this. The thing was to stay off Route 40 and out of the state of Ohio, and to be in a state whose name had always been sheer disconnected vocabulary, before she stopped. Looking for the green glow of exit ramps over steamy asphalt, she headed vaguely for Richmond, then, shocked and blinded by glittering traffic on the Capital Beltway in the rain at two in the morning, turned west on Route 50 instead.

It was a road she hadn't seen before, and it wasn't Route 40. Traffic died away. Soon it became a two-lane country highway, and Jane, hung over now rather than drunk, not in a hurry, drove without stopping. Somehow unable to stop, she entered a habit of mind anciently familiar to her, for the cave she navigated, full of the random kinesis of rain and endlessly repeating itself, now became the hollow cave of other people's sleep, and she the only one left awake in the world—save for, out of nowhere, low, dark and fast, some mystery car that now and then swam by her left shoulder like a shark with other prey on its mind. And now she had no thoughts at all for a hundred miles, being obliged to keep only a tiny pinpoint of consciousness alive, no more brain than a lizard would require, aware only of motion, of cool, of damp, and at last of a gathering malaise, ending with Jane retching into a ditch by Romney, West Virginia—which a sign told her had changed hands fifty-six times in the Civil War—thinking, All right, now I can fall apart. I'm on the road and my mother can't see me. Though she knew she had not gone far, though she was well aware she could get hopelessly stuck in some town like Romney, Home of the West Virginia Schools for the Deaf and the Blind, with seventy-five dollars to her name. But she didn't get stuck or fall apart. She threw up, stood awhile resting her forehead against the cool roof of the moneygreen Buick, climbed in again and drove without stopping.

Jane drove without stopping over the mountains of central West Virginia, a frame of dark timbered slopes with gashes bleeding red mud, mud-laden creeks in gulleys below the road and loaded coal trains winding slowly beside them. And what did she see inside this frame? Mostly two broad lanes of pearly asphalt, a U.S. highway, its grade as old as the hills. She thought of her mother, now that she was getting away from her, with waves of shame that stayed to one side of the central task of road.

She drove without stopping for twenty-four hours, midnight to midnight, except for a hypochondriacal consultation at a run-down one-pump station halfway up the east slope of some mountain. She asked the attendant, lank, grizzled, wearing a Boston Red Sox cap and working a plug of tobacco between two broken fences of teeth, to tell her the odds on the Buick making it to the Mississippi; for now she began to worry about the moneygreen Buick, now her faith in her heavy car was wavering as it lagged on steep climbs up the ungraded highway.

He replied: "This buggy? Maybe she will and maybe she won't. Depends what ails her."

"It's slowing down a lot on these long hills, and now it's making funny whistling noises . . . "

"Ah heck," he said. "You can't figger from the mystery moans and groans these lizzies make, ek-specially on them hills. Long as she's running, don't listen."

Jane recognized this for sound advice, the very same theory with which she had held off Dean Lucorne and Sasha, and the Zwillings for whom they were advance guard, camp followers, and procuresses. She agreed. Nevertheless, she drove off warily, trying to overtake her happiness now by sheer perseverance instead of velocity, allowing the Buick a top speed of fifty-five miles an hour, dropping to twenty over the steepest grades. Thus she drove, rather slowly, without stopping, trying to get to the end of West Virginia (for West Virginia was *known*) to Kentucky, a state whose name was pure folklore, unsullied by experience, trying to get somewhere she had never been.

Oh every three hours or so there was a stop for a five- or a ten-cent cup of coffee, she could afford that, and once, under the sign of OLD 50 PIKE TRUCK STOP EAT, she ordered the cheapest thing on the menu, a fried egg sandwich that looked like a tulip bulb run over by a truck and laminated in plastic—but it was edible, good even, and she decided she could live on such fare, if she did nothing else but drive, until she reached California.

Not that she admitted she was driving to California. She did not admit she was going to Jimmy, to the great disbeliever in her unlove, to Los Angeles, California, to sex, to a job, to her base destiny. She was driving west, just west, west to the Mississippi. That was what she told herself.

In her thirteenth hour on the road without stopping, Jane saw a broad and shining river, the kind that has to be the boundary of something, sliding under a bridge and a B&O trestle like some gorgeous reptile on a royal progress in its spangled train. She was elated, and as quickly dejected, for she realized this could only be the Ohio. So she turned south on the meandering river road, knowing she would waste four or five hours simply avoiding Ohio, but after all, she thought, barely able to focus on the map in front of her face, what was her hurry? Only, why did she feel so ashamed, so compressed all the length of her spine like a dog waiting to be kicked? Why, now that she was on the road, did she feel as though she had committed every crime? And so she went on to her eighteenth hour without stopping, except for gas, until she came to U.S. 60 and crossed the Big Sandy River into Kentucky—a road and a state she had never seen before.

Now she could stop, but she didn't. Oh, maybe on the literal, asphalt, colloquial highway, the one that lazily parted two broken lines of autos whose airstreams boiled into each other's open windows in the warm twilight, she was pulling into a diner whenever she saw one, trying to cut through the fog in front of her eyes with burnt, acid diner coffee. The hour soon came when every car going the other way was brandishing two headlights like a pair of fiery tusks. Jane's eyes began to close. A tractor turnaround, a gravel patch beside a generating station, a dark dirt road with a wide shoulder—that was what Jane needed. Was she looking? Time passed, seamless beyond the hook of memory. It dawned on her she had seen no shield for U.S. 60 and hardly another car on the road for a long time. She no longer cared where she was.

Around midnight she was in the ladies' outhouse behind a low, gray, plankboard establishment called the Union Star Bar & Grill somewhere in northern Kentucky. She was peering through a crack in the outhouse wall at what seemed impossibly bright light, trying to figure out what it was, one hard white bolt that striped the seams between raw pine planks, when suddenly the train whistle behind this light blew, causing Jane to levitate a foot in the air from the jigsaw-cut wooden seat where she sat uneasily, her underpants around her ankles. And the freight came clattering slowly forward and passed broadside to the outhouse in the weeds, almost near enough to touch on the other side of the wall. And all at once Jane realized where it came from, that sense that she was getting nowhere, just beating through dusty bushes like a dog about to be kicked. It was fear of the ancestress, of the restless ghost of one undead. Her mother. Sasha was after her, and it had to do with a train. A train. It was that ruptured appendix Jane had had when she was eight, which had given her a feeling of having wormed her way out of her proper doom. Sasha had saved her, and saved her on a train.

For this had not happened at home on Pinkney Road, this ruptured appendix. It had happened at a girls' camp in Ossipee, New Hampshire. Presumed homesick, Jane had lain four days in the camp infirmary before anyone thought to take her to a hospital. Meanwhile, as though she had crawled into bushes to die, all day she had gazed at sunlight with the heliotropic incuriosity of a lizard. This time she had given up on grownups completely. She forgot she had parents. They had sent her to this place and deserted her and she erased them from her mind.

And so, the day Sasha appeared in Ossipee General Hospital in a blue cord suit and smudged white high heels and took Jane away and saved her, the case went to Sasha, and forever. Jane pardoned her for the crime of motherhood, and would never again unpardon her, no matter what happened.

So Jane remembered, sitting in an outhouse behind the Union Star Bar & Grill in northern Kentucky, where a train had just passed. For a week Jane had Sasha all to herself. Then they started for Baltimore on a train. And now Jane dared to remember how she had loved her mother then, how she had vowed if Sasha were ever in danger, she would go to the end of the earth to rescue her, how in a sudden passion of love for Sasha, she had longed to do so. But then they had been back in Baltimore, in the spongy heat, the white, freighted sunlight, the lowering haze. Jane was cross because she was not allowed to go swimming all summer, and her mother became again that other sort of grim little locomotive, shuttling between downtown and Pinkney Road, between Dr. Zwilling and Philip Turner, her pretty face set, her jaw firm as an iron cowcatcher.

Still, that was how Jane became the daughter who used to sit at the kitchen table and listen. But she had broken her vow to go to the end of the earth to save the mother who had once saved her. By now this vow stood on its head. Since her mother loved her, Jane was able to let her go, to desert her. She was almost far enough away already.

So tired she sees a different pink neon scribble of *Union Star Bar & Grill* in each eye, she rolls out of the dirt parking lot and turns right on the first gravel road she comes to. The shoulder slopes towards a field overhung by tall trees. She parks here, intending to sleep, but it's not going to be so easy. The road she steered the moneygreen Buick along looked flat at first, but now she sees it tilts up rakishly. Her emergency brake won't hold. The Buick rolls slowly backwards, and Jane, wanting so much to sleep, has taken a wrong turn and is in the green tree-tops, having carelessly driven up a branch. What is more, Sasha is below, standing between the muscular welts of tree roots. Her worried voice floats up through the dappled leaves, but Jane, embarrassed, hopes Sasha has not spotted her yet. Perhaps it's not too late to appear to know what she's doing. She climbs out of the Buick in a hurry and, thinking fast, heaves it up under her arm as though it were a dress box. Now she tries to look self-assured, as though this was how she'd intended to travel all along, with her car under her arm, and so starts down the branch the way she came, glancing around like a tourist. She shouts to Sasha, Don't worry, Ma, here I am. Here I come now. But just as Sasha's eyes meet hers, the branch begins to soften under Jane's foot. And here she is, sinking into quicksand, quicksand at, there is no getting around the word for this, at the crotch of this old Kentucky horse chestnut, and down at the bottom is her mother, sadly shaking her head at her, for Jane is in up to the waist now, the Buick under her arm.

So she had parked in a graveyard—a mercy she hadn't seen where she was last night—and there she had slept, just slumped over the steering wheel with her glasses still on her face. Now in the sunlight she opened the car door and slid down onto the Buick's beautiful green-edged black rubber running board, stared at the tilted and broken gravestones and tried not to piss on her bare feet. Then a thrill of fear—she heard men's voices, all but next to her. The treetops were full of telephone men. Had they seen her with her pants down? Probably not, she thought, or they would have hooted.

Then she was a telephone man catching sight of herself, a young woman asleep in a car in a graveyard, on a lonely road, with one window rolled down and her doors unlocked. No one knew where she was! What kind of tramp is this, she asked herself with a thrill, propped senseless behind a steering wheel, unknown, homeless, broke, and by now more than a little unclean? She rose to her full height, blooming in this role, but the telephone men in the treetops took no notice of her. She stretched and off she drove.

Still on the slowest east-west road in Kentucky, U.S. 60, which a sign said was once a meandering buffalo trail, and Jane could well believe it, Jane drove without stopping until she saw the Mississippi for the first time. And then it was behind her. And so across Missouri, always on U.S. 60, all the way over the Ozarks into Oklahoma.

By the time she turned the Buick onto the Will Rogers Turnpike at Vinita, she was tunneling again through the mineshaft of other people's sleep and very nearly of her own. She was tired, so tired that a sign swam up, suddenly, in the greenish film of her headlights

DO NOT DRIVE
INTO SMOKE

and sank away again like the enigmatic counsel one sometimes receives in writing in dreams. She was tired as a stone must feel tired if someone tells it to roll uphill; above all she was tired of looking at the road. And yet she could not decide to stop driving as long as she was able, on the particle of consciousness left to her, to keep on driving. She had now driven halfway across the country in two days without admitting, if you discount one glance over the side of a bridge at the Mississippi, she was going anywhere at all.

DO NOT DRIVE
INTO SMOKE

She worried about driving into smoke. And wasn't that smoke, she asked herself, that danced in scarves and rolled in weightless bubbles over the asphalt? But the air through her open driver's window smelled like nothing but cold wet leaves.

It was now necessary for Jane to see that, whether she meant to go there or not, her road ended in California. And now that she travelled on an empty turnpike through vast invisible country barely dabbed at by her headbeams—two tremulous cottonballs, these, in outer space—she had to admit it could get tedious, very tedious, this life of going on to the end of the road or your money, whichever came first. To jolt herself awake, she stuck her head out the window, into the cold windstream. And in the stamp pad of black space at the top of her window, she saw, to her astonishment, almost to her terror, a *comet*, an inverted snail of white light brighter than any star, its shape, unlike that of a star, suggesting its direction, which happened to be the same as her own.

It was the last thing she expected to see, and to say that the apparition seemed pregnant with meaning would be too hesitant, too merely figurative, an interpretation of the case. It was to Jane the secret message itself, the unique and fatal beauty of this trip. For the more the order of the past sank behind the prolix liberties of navigation, the endless trivial choice of roads, the less resistance she put up to sexual love as an organizing principle, a zone where she would believe in at least one thing. That, Jane admitted under the tail of the comet, was what she was crossing the country for—for one night of love. The trouble was, she already knew it would last *one night*. Already the body of the future was clamped in an awkward embrace in the backseat of the Buick, like some lost, dazed, adipose teenybopper the boys know will go for a ride with anyone rather than face one night alone with her pimples and 42 D-cup bra. Jane knew too much to be going to live with Jimmy, that was the trouble. Jimmy was not the face of love; good God, Jane thought, he's not even my type! He was not her type because, she realized suddenly, under the tail of the comet, no man was her type. Every man stood in the way of some vague, fantastic, solitary adventure. He reminded her, by standing in her way, of the fantastic, vague, solitary adventure she was missing, of the adventuress she once had been who was now receding before her—who would, however, circle back after a night of love to repossess the body of Jane. But then she would be on her speedy way again and gaining a league on Jane for every repetitious kiss, leaving behind her fishy tire tracks, tracks that would still be there, silver-puddled and empty, in the morning.

From now on it was nothing but interstates. For the small heart Jane had left to feed to this trip, it would have been too creative, too editorial an act to unfold a map and pry out of it a private route. She held on, that was all, held on to the steering wheel, and meanwhile she hallucinated a barely audible din of violins, as though some lonely pensioner were watching Lawrence Welk on the other side of the wall in a cheap hotel. In the middle of the Texas panhandle, on asphalt that absorbed rather than reflected her headbeams like dusty velvet, she saw without excitement a phantom cobra strike at her windshield, a tribe of empty shrouds roll lazily, gauzily, along the blacktop in search of bodies, and a Frankenstein rise out of the roadbed over and over to throw himself perfunctorily under her wheels. Cartoon Gothic. She would have expected her unconscious, erupting through the frayed screen of reason after so many hours on the road, to do better than this, but she was too tired even to scare herself properly. Now if she slept it was not on deserted country lanes but in the parking lots of mile-square truck stops hemmed by pure dark that could have been anywhere. She learned to feel mothered, in her sleep, by tractor trailers nosing around the Buick, giving huge sniffs to her bumper like gentle, inquisitive brontosauruses as they rolled slowly back to Route 66. The seams between waking and sleeping were so loose and indistinct by now that there could be no question of locking her doors.

In the Painted Desert, on the fourth day, with nineteen dollars left, Jane began to believe she would make it to Los Angeles. Elated, bored almost blind with driving, slapping herself in the face to bring her eyes back to the road in the hot glare, Jane suddenly, without warning, pulled over to pick up a hitchhiker.

In the rearview mirror she watched him drag a beat-up duffel bag towards the Buick by a rope. Blockhead, what are you trying to prove, she asked herself, and she remembered she could still drive off. He looked beyond having his mood ruined by a vacillating benefactress. He was blond, emaciated—far, far from her type—his long hair blew over his face like loose straw from a scarecrow, he wore jungle shorts much too big for him, a T-shirt gray with road dirt, and sandals. Oh well, Jane told herself, it will probably be all right—when he settled in the seat next to her, crammed his bag in front of his feet, and turned on her eyes like two pellets of Coke-bottle glass ground dull by the sea, so flat and empty that they seemed to be stoppering holes drilled through to the back of his head. A wave of fear washed down the gulley between Jane's shoulder blades, but she drove off anyway.

His first words were: "*I* understand the language of animals!"

My luck has run out, Jane thought. It's happened. From now on every stranger I pick up will be loony, because my radioactive plasma makes madmen come out of their holes.

"Do you?" he asked.

"No, I really don't," she replied hastily. "Not one word."

"They don't talk words," he said.

"Oh," Jane said. "Well, I only understand words. If that." She glanced over at him, he smiled shyly at her and she dared to ask him: "What are they saying?"

But the hitchhiker had lost interest in that subject. He turned to his own window, staring out of it for some time without opening his mouth.

"You're a strong person, aren't you?" he asked, turning to her suddenly.

"I don't think so." For some reason she did not want him to perceive her as a powerful figure.

"Oh yes you are. You're strong. Look at those arms. Look at this machine. But I'll tell you one thing. *I'm true.* The animals know who's true," he said. "At least I'm true!" he reiterated.

"Would you like a cigarette?" Jane whispered.

"I saw an angel ninety feet tall, with a sword!" he suddenly shouted.

Jane sneaked a look at him. He was gazing at the tar-patched, bone-white road in front of them, expressionless.

"Were you afraid?" she asked.

"Sure," he said. "It asked me if I was queer. I said hay-ull no. But it was looking at me that certain way, like it might know something I didn't."

"Then what happened?"

"I made a run for it. I jumped in bed."

"You figured you were safe *in bed*?" Jane asked, shocked at this idea.

"No," he said. "But to come in there with me he would have to get a lot smaller."

Jane laughed a little. "What did he do then?"

But again the hitchhiker had lost interest in the subject. He crossed his stringy, birdlike legs tailor-fashion on the seat and began rooting through his bag. Jane watched, from the corner of her eye. He seemed to own a lot of striped undershorts. State issue, perhaps.

"I'll take that cigarette," he said. "Say! You know, I don't get rides from girls too off-ten."

Jane handed him a cigarette and saw that, in the well of his folded legs, he was trimming his toenails with a Bowie knife.

"I just did it," she said unhappily, for that was the truth. "I didn't think much about it."

"Know what the Buick said?"

Jane looked hard at the road, pretending she was deaf.

"Here's what the Buick said. Where to, chief? I'm a magic car and don't nobody pass the Buick."

Jane did not stop to admire the demented pun. *Where to, chief,* she noted with furtive hope, for they had never discussed destinations. "By the way, I'm just going to the next exit," she informed him.

The hitchhiker craned his neck around at the lamps and frying pans in the backseat; and perhaps he had already noticed Jane's unwashed face and tangled hair, her bare feet, exotic license plate and, in short, the nomadic and hard travelling style of this whole outfit. Unfortunately, he wasn't stupid.

"Next exit?" he asked. "What town is that?"

"I don't care what town," Jane said stiffly. "I'm tired and I'm going to stop for a while."

"Hey!" the hitchhiker said. "I can stop for a while."

She squinted into the distance, trying to persuade a highway exit sign, a square of that green seen nowhere in nature, to bloom at the disappearing point of the white road. Not that she expected the stranger to stab her, though that was, of course, a possibility. At least she was wide awake now, the better to scour the pastel, shimmering conflation of desert and road for a way out of this fix. She glanced at the hitchhiker. The knife had vanished, the unlit cigarette dangled from his dry lips like a disconnected valve, and, eyes closed, head drooping on its thin stalk, he dozed, or seemed to. Jane nervously lit her own cigarette and stared at the road.

Suddenly there was an exit sign, a real one, not a mirage, but tucked off to the right, only a road number on its small green face, the short ramp it labelled already in full view, and Jane veered down it and braked at a stop sign. She was looking at a nameless crossroads that must once have tried to be a town. Its tiny shack of a post office was closed, the U.S. flag had migrated one hundred feet to a filling station that was open but doing no business, though some human appeared to be in its office, hidden behind a newspaper. Next to it was a bar in an ugly formstone building, with a sign in its one small window: CLOSED. A pickup truck with a home paint job, chalk blue, sat tiredly in the gravel parking lot between the two deserted enterprises, and across the road was a failed commercial property with a giant sheet of white paper falling down in its front window, EVERYTHING MUST GO! And that was all—no people, no traffic, nothing except a shuttered hamburger stand five hundred yards down the road.

Jane had been hoping for Main Street with a small police station in view. But having arrived at this desolate place, she decided all the same to blunder ahead, that is, to talk the hitchhiker out of her car, maybe with the help of the station mechanic-postmaster behind the newspaper. And so she rolled up in front of the high octane pump and covertly poised the heel of her left hand against the horn. Meanwhile her right hand was lighting the end of the hitchhiker's cigarette as he blinked awake, trying to figure out where he was.

"I'm going to California," Jane blurted.

"That's a nice place." The hitchhiker nodded approvingly.

"I've never been there," Jane said. "I've never been there, and this may seem odd to you, but I have to go on alone."

The hitchhiker stared at her. Jane got ready to blow that horn. Then a woman about ninety years old, maybe a hundred, came rocking out of the gas station–post office and made her way to the Buick, an odd scintillance about her mouth. Jane realized it was sunlight dancing on a few white whiskers.

"I shouldn't have picked you up," Jane hurriedly said to the hitchhiker. She wanted to own up to that much.

"These youngsters are from Ohio!" the aged postmistress announced to the air. "How long y'all been here?" She was lifting down the gas nozzle with both hands; it hung about level with her forehead. "I declare I never heard you two come in. I was reading that Dear Abby on premarital sex and has times changed! I'm for it a hunnert percent."

"Did you see anything about a comet in the paper?" Jane asked. "Uh, just fifty cents worth if you don't mind." She would be lucky if the tank took that.

"Fifty cents! You won't get fur on fifty cents in that old gas-eater."

"We're going to California," the hitchhiker said.

"Not on fifty cents you ain't!"

Jane handed her two quarters.

"That comet was first seen in Japan," the postmistress said. "And it's ten times brighter than the moon."

"Thank you so much." Jane started up the Buick, then asked a little desperately: "Are you really all alone there, ma'am? Don't you have a mechanic at that station?"

"Nope. Just me myself and I. And my old shotgun."

"Your shotgun?" Jane said.

"For snakes, because there is enmity between her and the snake!" the hitchhiker shouted.

"Two-legged snakes," said the postmistress, peering at him for a moment. But then she hooked her wrinkled little hands over Jane's window and said: "I want to wish you two kids a lotta luck gettin to California. Yer gonna need it."

Jane rolled slowly into the parking lot where the chalk-blue pickup glowed dully in the sun. "I have to ask you to get out now," she said. "I should never have picked you up. Please don't be insulted."

The hitchhiker looked at her; she felt sweat roll steadily, copiously, out of her armpits.

Finally he said: "Say, I sat there quiet, didn't I? I didn't take no money off you or nothing?"

"Please," Jane said. "You were perfectly nice. I just want to drive to California by myself."

The hitchhiker's eyes swarmed over her excitedly. "I bet you think I'm crazy," he said.

"Do you want a cigarette?" Jane said weakly. When his hand reached out, she said, "Take the pack."

He did. "I used to be crazy. But now I been certified sane. It's not everybody can say that! Here, I'm going to prove it to you." He unzipped his bag.

"I believe you," Jane said hastily.

"It's in here," he said, pawing through his underwear. "Now why do I have to prove I'm not crazy? Go ahead. Ask me why."

"Why," Jane said reluctantly.

He found a frayed pink paper and waved it at her. "I'll tell you why. Because of you! Because you can't understand nothing! Lyndon B-for-Bacteria Johnson! Queen of the Ice Capades! At least I'm true. The universe is a germ, and you're the carrier. But I will not harm you for you know not what you do."

"I'm sorry," Jane said. "Please don't be hurt. I'd just rather be alone."

The hitchhiker threw open the door, yanked his duffel bag out after him, and savagely kicked the Buick in the rear fender. "Because of you, Germ!" he shouted.

Jane leaned over and locked the door after him—she was getting to be a slightly more competent coward now—and then she rolled the passenger window up to an inch from the top and yelled through the crack: "You shouldn't have scared me with that knife."

But it had been a superior instinct not to name this object at all. Suddenly it was flashing through air in his hand, making a great cross, or perhaps it was an X to X her out. "Disappear, Germ!" he said, "in the name of the Father, the Son and the Holy Animals."

Jane stamped on the accelerator before he could think of slashing her tires. She was passing the boarded-up post office in wide-open second gear when she remembered the postmistress —what if the hitchhiker should cut her throat? Surely he was not lucid enough to be mad only at Jane, even if she deserved it. She threw the Buick into reverse and backed up with a roar into the gas station lot, almost running over the hitchhiker, who was trudging resignedly towards the highway ramp, dragging his duffel bag along in a long gray molehill of dust—that is, until he had to dive out of the way to save himself from Jane.

And then Jane slammed on her brakes, mesmerized. For the postmistress stood a little hunched in the doorway of the filling station office, her jaw a lump like a boxing glove under her shrewd eyes, the shotgun in her hands aimed straight at Jane.

Thus Jane experienced the revelation that the postmistress looked on both driver and hitchhiker as undesirables without prejudice. Then a rock bounced off her windshield, gouging a greenish pit and a tuft of cracks like the tail of a comet. Jane pressed the gas pedal to the floor as the hitchhiker bent for another rock. He seemed to know who had offended him after all.

Something clunked off her rear fender, but a moment later she was gathering speed up to 55 mph, alone in the Buick with a very full tank of gas, the windowglass between her and the highway only slightly marred, wide awake to the point of surrealism, even able to swerve deftly to avoid a chuckawalla crossing the warm road on some private mission. She picked up no more hitchhikers. She was ashamed of herself, but glad to be alive, ecstatic to be out of a fix, zealous to lay hundreds of miles between the Buick and the seat of her folly. And so, tracking with new single-mindedness on the assumption that she would make it after all, she drove without stopping the last five hundred miles (except to sleep a few hours in the parking lot of a radio tower near Barstow) over the rufous Sierras, across the Mojave Desert, into Los Angeles.

The 1951 Buick never did break down, but coming into the city at eight in the morning on merging lanes of the San Bernardino Freeway, with younger engines in longer, lower bodies cutting in and out of six lanes to pass it on four sides simultaneously, it labored. Its horn quit. The handle that rolled the driver's window up and down fell off. Jane understood it would never be quite right again. Pete will make it young, Jimmy said later, but Jane didn't think so. Now that she could see why you needed a car to live here—out the windows were strips laid end to end for seventy miles—she thought she would be almost glad if it died. She would move into some hole in the wall across the street from her job when she found one, and would clamber into the Buick only late at night for expeditions to the grocery store—and otherwise Jane bid goodbye to that way of being alone.

The
one
night's
entertainment

began, then, at 8:45 in the morning on a Thursday, an ordinary Thursday, when everyone else was going to work. Jimmy leaned in the doorway of a white apartment building near MacArthur Park, saying, "I knew you would come. I knew you would come." And Jane did not argue the point, not now. Here was her lover, his muscular legs spotted with morning light, one hand lazily on the doorjamb, one bare foot crossing the other, a lithe male under a long, tight, paint-spotted T-shirt, looking rather like the faun in *L'Après-midi d'un faune*. The music he was not dancing to was the drawn-out foamy syllable of rush hour traffic only two blocks away.

And Jane stood below him on the front stoop studying his eyes, where sunlight was collecting. Was this really the color of the Pacific, which she had never seen? You could say this airy blue-green admitted the sun as the Atlantic never did—it kissed back. Thinking of aquamarine waves and tidal pools, aware of the low throb of trucks and cars along Wilshire Boulevard, four nights and days of highway still ringing in her ears, she belly-flopped into Jimmy's bed and he climbed in after her; but she did not get lost so easily. She did not sink straight to the bottom. "Wait, wait," she was murmuring, afraid of being left behind. "Oh well," Jimmy said with a soft laugh, gathering her into his arms. "I'm only a man, alas! But we have all day" —which was true, for outside, ordinary people were going to work. And when Jimmy fell asleep for some minutes where the waves had left him, naked in midcrawl on her belly, knees half buried in sand, his mouth on hers, there came that lull, that melancholy lull, in the traffic and only Jane heard it. A half million cars had just found parking spaces. Now secretaries were locking their purses in their bottom drawers, claims adjustors poked sourly through their in-baskets, electrical repairmen lounged in a ragged queue before the dispatcher's window, the shift coming on suddenly emptied the diner behind the meat-packing plant—and Jane lay in a white room, her thighs clasped around her sleeping lover like waterwings, for this was their one night's entertainment.

They were not the only two unemployed persons in Los Angeles. On the other side of the building, a couple, male and female, tirelessly harangued each other. Through the walls it was hard to hear the exact words. From time to time there came an accelerando; then they went quiet; and soon after followed a series of dense skids or thuds as though they were using the truce to drunkenly rearrange the furniture. At last something fell over and the woman vented a prolonged horrified shriek, as if she were trapped beneath a toppled piano or bookshelf. "Jesus Christ," Jane said, stiffening. "Huh?" said Jimmy, waking up. "I think someone's being killed." "Oh, her. Don't listen," Jimmy said sleepily. "They never stop, never."

Was it all she expected, the one night's entertainment?— which she had greeted as one should a wild creature, taking care not to alarm it by staring it straight in the eye. It was more than she had hoped, and less. For in being more than she had hoped, a banquet for a glutton, a low trull's throne at a Feast of Saturnalia, it was automatically less than the golden flake she had hoped to prise from the eyelid of the creature when he wrestled with her, which she meant to pocket slyly as he ran away again into the bush. Jane didn't know what to do with an endless supply. Though she whispered urgently to Jimmy, "I never want to stop, never," perhaps she lied.

Once, in some book or other, Jane had seen an image of Isis riding naked in triumph into a city of her votaries on the back of a lactating pig. Jane had laughed out loud at this frank syndication of goddess and unkosher domestic animal. A bit shocked, in fact, she had tried to apply the old puzzlebook caption, What is missing from this picture? But the answer was: Nothing. The smiling goddess presenting her own round breasts, one in each hand, the huge and pacific sow whose feet could barely touch ground for the grog-shop of swollen teats on her underbelly, were saying, Follow us—there is enough here for everybody, forever. All was amplitude, plenty, never a shortfall, never out of season. One had to applaud such a scene with the multitudes, and yet it was so far from Jane's hope of love that she could only shudder at it in the end. Jane wanted to follow a solitary and possibly dangerous animal that had never been seen before, deeper and deeper into the wild. *I knew you would come*, Jimmy had told her; they were the first words out of this mouth. That he should dare to know this better than she knew it! She closed her eyes and felt herself reeling, shambling in circles after that wild thing that knew its way in the woods. That knew, too, though she thought herself lost, exactly where she was.

If only the coming into this wood, the last stop of all that driving, the conversion into heat and light of all that motion in one direction without stopping, were also without stopping, would go on exploding delicately like the spring rain over Ohio—if only the moment of coming were a philosopher, a philosopher queen instead of a scheming charlady—but Jane thought of all that later, in the coagulated darkness after actual midnight, not now, in her one night's entertainment, with late summer sunlight flooding the bedsheets with milk and honey from the open window, heating the purple roses on the trellis below until these panted such prodigal scent that Jane leaned out the window to stare at them. They were very nearly ugly, those roses, their petals so fat and oily in the absence of rain and cold they reminded Jane of some kind of preserved meat. She said so to

Jimmy—"They're grotesque, like roses made out of prosciutto"
—and he leaned across her naked back, looked too, and said
in a sad and dreamy voice: "To tell you the truth, when I look at
them, I think primarily of your cunt, if it can be called thinking."

Could it be called thinking, what the cunt did? All for the
best that this Czarina for a Day was not too intelligent, at least
not this day, this sunlit night of nights, but rather gorged herself without reflection, then rolled over shamelessly and snored,
woke up again to the same uncluttered banquet table and, shoving picked carcasses out of the way, fell to again, up to her
elbows in pig grease and spilled wine. "I never want to stop,
never." (By midnight she would have nothing, but Jane won't
think of that now.)

In the morning of their night of nights, Jane slept the longer
of the two, while Jimmy pulled on shorts and did something
useful, for instance, dragged her footlocker from the Buick by
the shortest route between white stucco units over a bed of ice
plant and a small oleander, and up the front steps, bang! bang!
bang! waking Jane, who was upset at the sight of her old trunk
coming to rest in the tiny apartment as if permanently—also
rousing the quarrelers on the east side of the hall. "What in the
something," the man shouted. Glass crashed to the floor and the
woman moaned like an agitated phantom. "I don't think I can
stand it," Jane said. "Believe me, they deserve each other," Jimmy
said. "Anyway she never looks any worse than usual when she
comes out."

October was hot in Los Angeles. The sheets twisted into a
canyon of deep gray pleats under their sweat. Jimmy and Jane
grew thirsty and the subject of money arose. She had arrived
with six dollars and change; Jimmy had four dollars and three
quarters. This was enough to make it to the desert if no check
arrived on Friday. Which reminded Jane to write her father a
note with the MacArthur Park address. Jimmy left to mail it,
Jane slept, Jimmy reappeared with eggs, day-old bread, a jar of
jalapeño peppers and a twelve-pack of 102 Beer, the cheapest in
Los Angeles.

They leaned on the windowsill, drinking beer. There was no view. If you could see the rufous Sierras above the low skyline on a good day, then, despite the lavish sunlight, this was not a good day; and indeed there was some bitter principle abroad in the blond aura of the one night's entertainment that made Jane's eyes smart and tear if she kept them open too long. Nearer by, two more white duplexes were crammed into what had once been the front garden of Jimmy's apartment building. A palmetto at the corner of the lot looked to Jane like the leavings of a party joke, an immense exploding cigar upended in a spittoon. She did not know how to read what she saw. The crowded yard would be squalid in the East, but some sort of silver spangle had been added to the stucco paint, giving the complex the air of a cheaply fantastic resort, and meanwhile along the cracked concrete drive and over the dented lidless garbage cans hung the sort of blooms she associated with the greenhouses of the very rich. And in the next apartment, the woman was sobbing some word heartbrokenly, over and over. Jane thought it was "Please, please, please." "She's begging for mercy," Jane said, clapping a hand to her temple. "I wish he would kill her," Jimmy said. "Then he'd have to disappear." "Is this a slum or what?" Jane asked. "Hey, I live here, don't I? What do you think?" "But it's so *white*," Jane said.

Towards evening of their one night's entertainment, Jimmy slept longer, as mortal man will, even the most adoring, even the most goatish, if his woman has not spared him, whether or not he has asked to be spared. I never want to stop, never. But now the traffic picks up. The ordinary world comes home from work, and Jimmy, having labored after his fashion, sleeps. Jane sat on her foot locker, drinking the soapy beer out of a coffee cup and looking at his maleness spilt sideways across the gray sheets, very like a faun some goddess had exploited and dumped, half dead but still shining, by a river. It was true, the light fur on his rump, his shanks, was of the purest gold, and the sun sliding behind white buildings on the other side of Hoover Street sought him out, touched the muscles of his back, his curls, played his advocate before the darkening female who appraised him. All right then. He should be visited just this way, from a great distance, plucked up from his woods, all his ripe seeds shaken out, and thrown down again in the grass like so much golden straw. But Jane, more mortal, if anything, than he was, having visited Jimmy from a great distance, could not now retreat like a goddess. She sat on her footlocker, stuck in one place like a lump of clay, waiting for the bill to be delivered for her latest adventure.

It came with the dark, as might be expected. She sat there, no longer watching her lover change from a particular human being to a mere whiteness, a gleam of anonymous bones in the dark. He had been a perfect lover—whatever that meant. For nevertheless she was glad to be relieved of his particularity, though this, she knew, was a symptom of all that was wrong with her. She welcomed his disappearance.

Her pleasure over, she was dull, maybe a little drunk. The moment arrived when, like Adam and Eve, she wanted to cover herself. To rise and look for clothes she had to unglue herself from the footlocker where she had been sitting for a long time in a small pool of seminal fluid—plasm of Jimmy that had leaked from her own sexual parts. She suddenly saw herself stuck fast to her old trunk by the superepoxy of sex, deposited here by her own ungovernable sexuality—on top of the trunk in which all the rubbish she owned, and what exactly this was she could not even remember, had been moldering unlooked at for months —and the idea was laughably grotesque, but Jane did not laugh. She lurched to her feet, spilling the cup of beer over her pubic hair, which dripped foam oafishly, like the beard of an ale-guzzling corporal. She stood there staring down at it in disbelief. She was disgusted with herself.

Now then, wasn't this exactly what she had been seeking, the solace, perfectly undeceived, of one night's entertainment? What was the matter with her, then? She felt marooned at the end of the world, and not the least bit free. It was only bitter to have crossed over alive in her body to the other side. For God's sake, this wasn't a covert prude's study in remorse, was it? She rifled her shipwrecked mood for any taint of sexual revulsion, and seemed to hear quite a different tune: *I would do it again,* said her body, and not only her body. But what do you suppose you have pulled off here? she interrogated this credulous pilgrim. What god do you serve, and if this is everything, why do I feel as low as the ground?

Think rather, *At least I have this,* said the body. Oh give me a break! Jane muttered under her breath, smacking down her empty cup on the footlocker so hard that its handle broke off in her hand. This is Philip Turner's daughter you're talking to. It was not written that I should live for love of my human male counterpart. My father early liberated me from that schoolgirlish hobbyhorse, or did me out of that sweet and just patrimony, depending on how you look at it.

How did you look at it? She got to a blank place in her ruminations and became aware—perhaps it had been going on a long time already—that the couple on the east side of the building was doing, what? whatever they had been doing again, playing at killing each other, or killing each other in earnest, who knew? First came loud knocks against the wall, as though some goliath were banging flies with a human head; then the woman's voice seeped through in an impossibly drawn-out moan. Jane listened carefully, for there was a precision to these modulations she had not heard before. That was because the traffic was dead on the streets. Gradually the moan mutated into a syllable uttered over and over but always changing: "All, all, all, all, la, la, la, la, lo, lo, lo, loa, loa, loa, loa, allah, allah, allah, lah, lah, lah,"—on and on while something wooden and heavy scraped by inches across the floor.

Jane pulled on Jimmy's T-shirt and stepped out in the hall. She intended only to bang on their door, but somehow her hand closed around the doorknob, it turned as if by itself and she pushed the door open.

And blinked, for the room was white, brightly lit, and despite all the noise, there was hardly any furniture. The man sat naked, sideways to Jane, on a chair in the middle of this space. He was hairy, thick and muscular, and his two fists were knotted around the woman's dark hair, which was a taut rope above them, an inky cataract into his lap below. She wore flesh-colored bra and panties that looked slightly soiled, and she was curled backwards over the back of his chair in an inhuman, rococo posture like the opening stroke of a *K* in ornate penmanship—bent so far backwards by his yanking on her hair that she offered her gibberish to a chandelier on the ceiling. And even now with her eyes rolling sideways towards Jane, she wobbled on: "Ha ha ha ha hell hell hell hell, hole hole hole hole oh oh oh . . . "

The man saw Jane and, after what seemed a rather long time, let go of the woman's hair. She straightened up, he put his hands over his penis. Then there they were, looking at Jane, the woman standing in her slightly discolored underwear, he sitting with his hands folded chastely over his crotch, their faces a little dazed, as though she had rousted them out of their marriage bed, as in a way she had—Mr. and Mrs. Blank and child, a baby of about two, big head, round belly, fat legs, rubber pants, sitting up sullenly in a crib behind them, sucking on a bottle.

"I can't stand it," Jane explained.

They only stared at her—but perhaps there is no fit answer to such a remark.

"You have to stop now," Jane said.

The man looked at Jane a while longer, then replied: "All right, but get out." The child's bottle rolled out of the crib and bounced with a seasick noise across the floor. The child began to cry. "You scared my baby," the woman said. "Who are you?"

Jane backed away from the door and shut it carefully. Leave them out of it, she instructed herself in all haste. But nevertheless they were there, Mr. and Mrs. Blank, the other two unemployed persons in Los Angeles, when she sat down again on her trunk at Jimmy's.

For their loathsome sexual practices, she condemned them to death. Maybe they were great explorers, Mr. and Mrs. Blank, in the service of the human race, cancer researchers or antiwar tacticians on furlough from overwork. All the same, she wished them death, not only death but falling down a long, long hole forever in sight of, but out of reach of, one another's bodies. She did not care if this punishment were just. Rather, having had their fun, why should they get off any more lightly than she had? Loathing steadied her, but there was no getting around it, sex had taken her to this bottom. It was getting what she wanted, or at least what she had asked for, that had left her here.

But she had thought this syndrome confined to men!—to that squeamish order of Don Juan in a barn-green bow tie who found himself, he knew not how, in yet another perfumed bed, and five minutes later was bolting the swamped vagina in panic. If that were Jane, she was her father's daughter, she was as bad as her father, she *was* her father. This was, to be sure, a disaster for her as it had never been for Philip Turner—and now conclusions dropped out of one another like Dixie cups in an employees' washroom:

She was a mutant.

She was a weird hybrid, luckily sterile.

She was a sex criminal, a loveless psychopath.

She was the wrong sex, or, like an account with two mutually cancelling transactions, she was no sex at all.

Deformed in her sex, she bred monsters.

She cared for no one, even if her first act as a woman of the world appeared to be the flight to the arms of a lover, and therefore qualified for the annals of high romance, and was something to tell to the grandchildren in a creaking anile soprano, to the granddaughters in particular—except there would be no grandchildren, for the thought of such issue filled her with disgust. Never mind her sentimental pardon of her mother once she had put a thousand miles of distance between them. The idea of motherhood struck her as such a defeat she could only imagine it as an act of revenge. She felt she could lie back right now and be delivered of a plague of vermin, her parting gift to the world.

As if to hasten this birth she bent over her bare thighs and wrote, or rather carved, across them the name of the child she expected, in three-inch letters, with the broken cup handle that happened to be in her hand. At first dead white, the script washed up a moment later in a fine crimson thread, the name of her future heir in four characters: PEST.

Now in some dismay she watched the letters lose their tidiness, saw the lines waffle and pucker into broken necklaces of small, ill-matched, bright red beads. Fat drops began to roll at the spine of the E where the three rungs crossed it. She stared, beginning to understand what she had done.

She had inscribed a curse on herself as obtusely as a metermaid writes a parking ticket, as officiously as a bank factotum stamps a check RETURNED UNPAID. Was she out of her senses? A wave of dense heat rose from her shoulders into her face, the room bulged like black dough, she lowered her head into her hands so she would not faint. My God, how could she? How could she do such a thing to her own body? She had a crude scar from that appendectomy, summer, 1952. In 1965 it still curled in a fat silvery arc like the trail of a slug from her navel into the dark bush at her crotch. Her family scarred easily. It was Sasha's face she was seeing, the welts and craters under the ex-queen's mask that, whether she left them alone at the next family gathering or not, were there for life.

Often she had tried to pardon Sasha for the crime of motherhood, not only to pardon but somehow to free her from its shadow of death, to find the inner value of this thankless mission, its intelligence, if it had any, its will to be what it was, even deprived as it was of all glamor. But in the end those self-inflicted scars got in the way. You were willing to justify your mother only up to a point; then you wanted her to fight back, to live for her own sake, for the sake of living.

Now Jane began to pace the room, clutching her temples, wishing childishly, even magically, she had not done what she had done. She considered wildly if there were not some way to reverse it, started for the bathroom, then stopped herself, recognizing the helpless bystander's impulse to clean up the blood.

But then she went and washed anyway, for she began to see that such fanatical standards would require her to be inconsolable. She remembered that she had been happy once. It was all right, it would do her no harm, to be like the rest of the world in most respects! She calmed down a little; at last she forced herself to understand the thing was done and she had done it.

And so she had come the whole route. She was squeamish like her father, had his little retractible chicken wings for flying the face of love, the instinct to screw (copulate) and screw (disappear). And she had her mother's gift for self-mutilation, for forging the signature of the world in her own flesh. She had run three thousand miles away from the two of them to find this out, to have them at last step down from their separate niches in her chimney piece, the old hideous mismatched salt and pepper set, and clink a glass over her and her damned and blasted one night's entertainment.

She was careful in spite of her frenzied pacing not even to stub her toe in the small room in the dark. She was through with hurting herself. There had to be some other way to pay for her shortcomings, and besides, what she really wanted, she remembered, was revenge—or at least not to have to pay—to get some of her own back. For she had been the happiest of babies, though now she was either a freak, or on the verge of disappearing. Even so, she knew her life story better than most, the fruit of all that wandering from a solo perspective, knowing the right thing would happen to her. And though she had been wrong about the right thing happening to her, she still believed that if she peeled away all the dead skin of opinion she was wrapped in (for all that merely happened to you amounted to that, an opinion) at the bottom would be her life story, which would save her.

If she set to work at once, it would save her now. No progenitor could do her in, no assailant could X her out. As for Jimmy, she saw clearly that her lover had no power either to save her or to ruin her. He could not shunt her into any garden of earthly entertainments, its rosebeds mined with pitfalls of service to the former prodigy, unless this digression coincided with wanderings of her own. Therefore she had no call to be afraid of golden Jimmy. Let him sleep.

And now, hurriedly, she turned to a whole new enterprise. Good. She had made a mess of herself. But she did not have to stand in the sleazy proximity of a Peeping Tom to this bloody vision even one minute longer. She wrenched down the blind.

She found her purse, last seen when she and Jimmy had pooled their crumpled bills and small money and counted eleven dollars, of which five were left. She cleared forks, beer cans, broken pieces of cup from the top of the foot locker. She dressed in her own clothes, laid out her pens and notebook, and turned to the page she had been stuck on for weeks in her old room in Baltimore.

She wrote big, in the dark, like a blind person, tacking across the invisible blue lines like a blind drunk behind the wheel until her pen fell off the page. It was so dark she could not look back at her work; or anyway she didn't, for once in her life, look back. She bumbled ahead, hanging from the top of her own pen like a bit of rag clinging to a derelict mast. She knew the words she was writing down were queer, crabbed, hostile. She trusted the invisible book in her lap in the dark was taking down her life story, down to the code word on her thighs, and therefore she might live.

O King of the Time and unique one of the Age and the Tide, I am thine handmaid, and this one night and a night have I entertained thee. May I then make bold to crave a boon of thy Highness? I crave that thou release me from the doom of death!

I take the Almighty to witness against me that I exempt thee from aught that can harm thee.

But when the room began to lighten, so that she could no longer help reading what she had written, she closed her notebook, climbed into bed with Jimmy, and went to sleep. So ended the marvels and wonders of the one night's entertainment.

Book V

Her

True

Adventure

○
○
● **The**

Grandview

Whether Jane caught up with her footloose spirit in the West, and, shocked at its worn face, put it deeply away, whether she lost track of it here on the footloose coast altogether, she ceased to think of such things. She could not afford reproaches from the unimprisoned creature she might have been. In Los Angeles everything was different, for now she was really lost. She hoped the rest of them would not find out.

The day after her one night and a night's entertainment, she drove south on Hoover Street in the moneygreen Buick, into an even cheaper district, and left their last five dollars as a deposit on an upstairs apartment, sixty a month, in a white building on West 22nd Street, eye to eye with the Santa Monica Freeway. The building was called the Grandview — every apartment had a picture window. And in Jane's apartment, late at night, the lights of cars themselves invisible on the elevated freeway moved across this picture window like foamy whitewash in front of a squeegee, and in its center pane there floated, clumsily by day, eerily by night, a great rectangle of that green found nowhere in nature:

Harbor Fwy 1½

Jane was going to live alone. That way they might not find out. Of course Jimmy would sleep at Jane's more often than not. The apartment had a Murphy bed in a fake mantelpiece and other datedly genteel appointments. But West 22nd Street was a slum, even Jane could see that. She was the only gringo on the block; the rest were Indians, gypsies, and blacks. Here and there a black pensioner held a green hose to a tidy plot of roses, but most of the yards were bald, dry, and choked with broken toys and trash. Old magnolia trees as well as garbage cans lined the sidewalk, and on the north side of the street, where only a few houses still stood, alleyways petered out in a brief wasteland of rubble and weeds almost rural until it was lunar, until it touched the elevated freeway and rose into flanged ramps of white concrete, where one heard day and night the deep and self-absorbed vibration of unseen traffic rolling towards outer space.

Her landlord, who called himself Cochise, claimed to be a full-blooded Kiowa. She did not know what to make of him at first—a huge old man, six feet four or five, heavy-set but fit, with a ledge of stiff white hair overhanging his forehead and, on top of that, a big white golfing hat with metal eyelets over the sweatband. He had an ex-bravo's flattened nose, on top of which he wore such thick glasses that his eyes seemed to be swimming in jelly. She thought, but was not sure, she recognized an idiosyncratic hustler on a bigger scale than Willie Usher, and more ruthless. On the way downstairs from her apartment, he pounded like a gangster on the door under hers—where the nameplate read, improbably, *Romanoff*—and demanded back rent in a terrifying bellow.

At the office of Cochise Realty on Magnolia, just around the corner, he raised his white golfing cap and showed Jane a pink bald track a half-inch wide across his crown.

"This is from me and Mama's honeymoon in Denver in nineteen and twenty-five. Which is where I learned don't ever stick your head out a hotel room during a shooting scrape to see who is shooting who."

There was an old rolltop desk, and otherwise the large room was empty except for a mountain of used neckties about four feet high.

"I bought them off a ragman cheap," Cochise said. "One of the richest men in Los Angeles sleeps there."

Jane stood gaping at the bed of ties.

"J. T. McNeil—he's a bum," Cochise added. "I knowed him from the other bums used to work on my truck, but he don't even work." He whispered loudly: "I'm trying to save him from the priests."

At the rolltop desk, he wrote Jane a receipt for five dollars.

"I wish I could say exactly when I'll be back with the rest of the money."

"Don't matter," Cochise said. "I'll trust ya."

"You will?" Jane asked uneasily, thinking of his violent pounding at the door of the Romanoffs.

"In fact lemme give you back your fin, here—"

"No, no," Jane said. "I'd rather you kept it."

"Well, let's go have a drink on it. A young thing like you don't come around here every day."

"Are you asking me for a date already?" Jane said.

"I should hope so," Cochise said. "You're a purty young girl, ain't you?"

Jane smiled.

"You haven't got a boyfriend, have you?"

"I'm afraid so."

"I bet you're not even old enough to drink."

"Barely."

"Well, I'm old enough to be your great grand-pop. I guess they can't take me to jail if I just look at your purty face."

And he blinked at her, the eyes enormous, diffuse, behind lenses that might have been coated with Vaseline.

On the way to the bar, Cochise nearly ploughed into the back of an Animal Control van double-parked in the narrow street.

"What was that went by?" Cochise said, when the van pulled away just in time with a flicker of taillights.

"The dog catcher."

"I'm going to complain to the city they don't paint those wagons bright enough."

"It was silver," Jane said, "and big as a barn door."

"You'd have to have a microscope to read what was wrote on it."

Presently they parked—they had gone just four blocks—in front of a saloon on Hoover Street that had no name out front. It was, in decor, the lowliest dive that Jane had ever seen, much less set foot in. There wasn't even a door, but rather a lopsided, lumpy purple curtain you had to punch a few times to find the opening, while dust flew in all directions. The tarry floor was exactly on a level with the street.

"This is Walter Moley," Cochise said, introducing her to the bartender. "Walter come from Red Wing, Minnesota, and paid cash to buy this dump." Walter shook her hand. He was another giant, younger and fleshier than Cochise, with a big round body and short legs and a puff of damp hair on an oversized pate. He looked to Jane like an enormous baby.

"Jane is moving in upstairs at the Grandview and Mama and me will take over the deadbeat gypsies' apartment," Cochise said proudly.

Walter clapped his hands together in happiness. "Look at that hair," he said. "A woman's hair is her crowning glory."

Jane sat down on a barstool and Walter put a draft in front of her. "Do you need a job?" he asked her.

"That's a fifteen-cent glass of beer you're looking at," Cochise whispered in her ear. "Walter takes care of these miserable juice-heads in here, don't ask me why."

"Well, yes, I do," Jane admitted.

"I need a girl Saturday nights, three to three. Can you come in tomorrow?"

"Ask her how old I am," Cochise interrupted. "She don't believe I could be her great grand-pop."

"I've never tended bar," Jane said.

"How old is this redskin, under a hundred?" Walter asked.

"Sixty," Jane said, flattering Cochise only a little with this guess.

"He's seventy-four," Walter said.

"It isn't true," Jane said.

"Lookee here." Cochise handed Walter his wallet. "Show her my driver's license. I don't have my glasses in my pocket."

His glasses were on his face, but no one said anything about this. The driver's license—Robert Alki, born, it said, in 1890—had expired in 1962.

"Gosh," said Jane.

"It's that Spanish athletics what preserves you," said a toothless little man two barstools down, "but you have to do it every night or it like to give you a heart attack instead."

"Oh, Billy! Don't talk like that in front of this nice young lady." This from a crumbling old dame maybe twenty years older than Billy, and overdressed for this establishment in a white straw picture hat and powder blue suit with a bunch of wilted rosebuds pinned to the lapel.

"Jane don't even listen to that dirty talk," Walter announced. "She is going to work Saturdays for me."

Everyone crowed at this news.

"I'm Marie Gammerman, also known by my stage name, Marie G. Night."

"She ain't never heard of you," Billy said.

"Marie was once a recording artist," Walter said.

"She almost was," Billy corrected. "She won a talent show oncet which they was supposed to give her a contract, but when she got to the place, it was boarded up."

"Of course this was during the Great Depression," Marie said. "But I had work. I sang behind many of the greats."

"Marie still sing a little," said a small, neat black man in front of the jukebox.

"Thank you, Sam," Marie said gravely.

"I've never tended bar," Jane told Walter again. "I don't know how to mix drinks."

"Mix drinks!" There was laughter up and down the barstools.

"All's you do is pull that pump handle there," Billy said, "and stay sober enough to count change. We'll do the rest."

"They're all beer drunks in here," Cochise said, "dying a slow death for a buck fifty a night."

"I like a nice Grasshopper every once in a while," Marie remarked delicately.

"Give the lady a Grasshopper," Billy said, throwing a five-dollar bill down on the bar. "Then she'll do the hootchee kootchee when we get home."

"He's showing off for you, dear," Marie whispered to Jane.

"I thought you was getting it every night," said a pewter-haired black man in a brown pin-stripe suit.

"Who, me?" Billy said. "I said it preserves you. Do I look well to you, Leroy?"

Leroy laughed. "You don't look no worse than usual."

"I'm going down the drain," Billy said.

"Ask Marie the secret of eternal youth," Walter said. "She's the looker in this crowd." He was turning pages in a tattered book. "I don't see a Grasshopper in here," he declared. "What about a Sidecar for the lady?"

"A Sidecar!" Marie said, beaming.

Billy smacked the bar. "What the hell kind of sorry joint is this! Don't the lady deserve to get what she asked for? Tell Walter how to make a Grasshopper, Marie."

"Why, I'm sure I don't know," Marie said.

"Marie won't take nothing but a Grasshopper," Billy insisted. "It's a green drink."

Marie, embarrassed, searched through her purse for some object. Walter placed a cocktail in front of her without touching Billy's money. The cocktail was not even faintly green.

"Self-respect is the secret of a happy old age," Leroy announced. "You remember my Uncle Wilberforce. When he didn't care no more if his pants was pressed—mind you couldn't see nothing wrong with him—three weeks later he was dead."

"Sure I remember Wilberforce," Walter said, drawing Leroy a beer.

"He had his will wrote out on a dry cleaner's tab in his wallet," Leroy said thoughtfully. "Got himself cremated in a two-hundred-dollar suit."

"They can burn me in another twenty years," Cochise said.

"Anything to beat them priests to the draw."

"You're gone to hell for that," Marie threatened.

"Not me," Sam said.

"Well, you fellows aren't Catholics," Marie said. "You can go to hell whichever way you want."

"I mean they ain't burning me when I'm gone," Sam said emphatically. "You think them stiffs don't hurt when they burn? I rolled hundreds of em up on the roof of Hyacinth Hospital. That's where they burn em, in a little brick house where the chimney is at. I used to watch through this little glass window they got."

"Man, you can't get no privacy nowhere," Leroy said in disgust.

"Did you know when they get good and hot they sit up at they waist like this"—Sam suddenly sat erect, his neck pushed up high out of his spine, and bugged out his eyes—"and say one last word?"

"What is it?" Jane asked.

Sam looked at her solemnly. "I couldn't always for certain make it out," he said. "But I think it was *Help.*"

Jane burst out laughing, and Sam laughed too, shyly.

"It coulda been *Heck,*" he said, and added, "No offense, Leroy, but they wasn't wearing no two-hundred-dollar bags either. They was naked."

Leroy nodded. "Self-respect isn't only in the clothes," he said. "Look at Cochise there. He won't loaf in no saloon without a girl on his arm."

"I'm too busy," Cochise said. "It's the opposite of self-respect. I never struck it rich yet."

"Why don't Cochise give up like the rest of us?" Leroy asked.

"He's the oldest geezer in here," Walter pointed out.

"I am somewhat over eighty," Marie objected discreetly.

"I never give up," Billy said. "I never give up, I don't let my woman out of my sight, particularly not in a low-down ginmill, and I got no self-respect whatsoever."

No one at the bar took issue with this statement, and Billy rose slightly in Jane's estimation on account of it.

"The secret," Marie suddenly proclaimed, in a clear but quavering voice, "the secret of keeping your looks as the ma-toor years overtake a person is the care, ouch, quit it, Billy, why can't you act nice!" "You shut up," Billy told Marie. "Nobody don't want to hear that old *Ladies Home Journal* stuff. This is all men in here." "No it ain't," Marie said accurately, her teeth clenched. Billy gave her a sharp prod in the ribs, she swung her round blue purse at his head. A moment later it was dangling lopsidedly from the loose string of its handle. "See that, you broke my best pockabook." "You broke it your durn self," Billy said, a hand over his eye.

"The secret, as the ma-toor years come on a person," Marie began again doggedly, holding the small blue purse in the air away from Billy. Billy snatched at the purse, Marie jerked it away, went over backwards off the barstool, and then Billy was hauling her by a shoulder pad towards the purple curtain up front. And the two disappeared onto Hoover Street.

Walter sighed. "Why does the sweetest old gal always have the meanest old cuss for a boyfriend?"

Leroy said: "They like them bums who ask for the moon."

Having found a job of sorts without even trying, Jane decided to work no more than would keep the two of them half alive, and if Jimmy would not do the other half, let them sink side by side, rather than be hoisted aloft on the flimsy strap of any footgear of Jane's.

She would be a poet the rest of the time, or even if she didn't succeed at that worn excuse for a non-career, she made up her mind she was not fit for service to the ex-prodigy, and she would not do it even if she had to starve too. In fact, they usually had enough to eat, thanks to Little Jack's Cut-Rate Market at Vermont and Jefferson.

Walter's was a public house in such deplorable condition that it seemed to be vying for distinction in this regard. Walter, who never left, must have loved not only its broken-down clientele, but even the worm-eaten purple curtain, the malignant and sticky black flooring studded with cigarette butts, the barstools all mended with black plastic tape and still leaking dirty white batting. Its prize was a wooden latrine set in a small junkyard out back. By what special dispensation an outdoor privy, which saw a steady parade of customers, as one would expect of the sole toilet of a beer bar, was allowed to exist a mile from downtown Los Angeles, Jane did not know.

So Jane was proud to work for Walter those long Saturday nights and a few more hours on Friday and Sunday, and for this she collected thirty dollars in cash from Walter and a few bucks more in tips, and all the beer, hot dogs, and potato salad she wanted, and she considered herself well paid at that price.

At that price they never had any money, Jimmy couldn't even paint, and you might think he would grow cross on their diet of hot dogs and boiled spuds and it would all come out that Jane wasn't doing her job. But no, the less Jane worked, the more Jane and Jimmy were blood brothers, and he never gave her any argument at all. Instead Jimmy began to scheme on big money.

Meanwhile he fit right in at Walter's on the other side of the bar, between Marie and Billy at one elbow and Sam and Leroy on the other. He gave up his old apartment near the school and took a storefront on 22nd Street, one and a half blocks from Jane. He painted the place white and put in one corner a hot plate, an air mattress and a sleeping bag. But these were never used. Jimmy slept in the Murphy bed across the street with Jane. He went to school less and less. Since he could not paint, he made fantastic machines, fifteen feet high, from rubbish he found behind Walter's: odd pieces of tube lighting, whirring pulleys, melodious broken glass.

He said it was useless to get a job in L.A. because it would never lead to big money. He needed a lot of money. He needed paint and then he needed more than paint. He needed a place of his own in the desert in sight of the rufous Sierras, and Jane needed a place of her own on the sea. He needed a Sears credit card and tools. He needed a jeep. This big money lay in the future, not all that far, to hear him tell it, for there was always the desert down the road, gleaming with hidden fertility—just add water. There was always Baron Moritz, decorator to the stars, who had a heart condition and sciatica and wanted Jimmy more now than ever.

Jane said to Jimmy: "Is is true that everybody can have what they want? That any woman can have what she wants? Then what happened to my mother?"

Jimmy said: "You are what I want."

Jane said: "How dare you be so sure?"

Cochise and Mama moved in downstairs, taking over the deadbeat gypsies' apartment. (The Romanoffs moved in with their cousins, other Romanoffs, two doors down.) Soon Mama began to ride with Jane and Jimmy to the Piggly Wiggly or to Little Jack's or wherever the spuds were going for fifteen pounds for twenty-nine cents that week. Mama was a big, dilapidated gray-blonde, a girl of the Wild West who had not so much aged as weathered to the shade of a fence post. For a large woman she had a surprisingly small voice, high and reluctant like the squeak of an old screen door. Her father had been a not too prosperous rancher near San Antonio, Texas, who had many children running about the place, riding half-wild ponies and eating with the cowboys; she was not sure how many children, except that she had fallen somewhere in the second half dozen, from the second wife shortly before she expired to make room for the third wife. In 1925 Clara—that was her real name, Clara Mayfield—had run away with a carnival barker, a tall dark Indian twice her age. No one, as far as she knew, had ever come looking for her.

For some reason she and Cochise never married. Jane and Jimmy found this out one evening when they knocked on the door of the downstairs apartment, which still said *Romanoff*, to offer her a ride to the Piggly Wiggly. She called, "C'mon in if you want," in a voice more creaky than usual, and they found her wandering barefoot in a dirty slip falling down at one shoulder among the paper boxes, stuffed brown bags, piles of old clothes, blueprints and metal money boxes that were their furnishings.

"Been drinking for a week—gotta quit—Cochise is mad—says he's gonna leave me high and dry if I don't quit and he could do it, you know we ain't married."

Jane supposed Cochise had left a legal spouse, or she him, without further inquiry somewhere in his wandering carney days, those happy days which lasted, according to Cochise, until a humorless reinterpretation of the conspiracy laws put an end to entertaining the farmhands by shearing them once a year of their overgrown capital. After that, Cochise became a snooker hustler, and Clara stuck with him. She was never a mother—she attributed this to a fall from a horse at the age of twelve. So she had gone everywhere with Cochise over the years, even to his fly-by-night building sites and unlicensed demo sites, and on day trips over the border where he peddled used building materials from the demo sites in yet another shady sideline. For all those years in the cab of the pickup, she had never learned to drive, but now that innocence was coming to an end. One day the corner bodega on Magnolia sprang for a small green neon sign, and the next day Cochise drove his big truck across the intersection on a slight tack and through the front window.

The morning after, a dented Corvette appeared in front of the Grandview. Cochise had bought the car on a deal from a USC student who was leaving town in a hurry. (Jane noted empty pink capsules all over the furry carpeting and doubted the student had been packing them with vitamins.) This car Cochise would on no account drive himself, not because he feared the police, but because he had tried it once and its break-neck takeoff scared even him. "I fired her up in one of them mile-long parking lots up the college and she was over the curb before I remembered about second gear." Nevertheless, he ordered Mama to learn to drive in this vehicle and gave the job of teaching her to Jane and Jimmy.

They returned to the mile-long parking lots, which, unfortu-nately, were spiked with parking meters from end to end. The

Corvette wouldn't tame down for Jane or Jimmy either, and with Mama behind the wheel it was a return for all three of them to the mustang ponies of her youth. "Whoops—whoa —hee-hee—why you no 'count son of a jackass, now you listen what I tell you, omigosh, what was that—" Meanwhile they sideswiped parking meters right and left down a hundred-foot swath, Jimmy yelled, "Clutch, clutch, clutch," and Jane hid her face in her hands. "Cochise will never leave you if you just learn to drive this goddamn worthless automobile," Jimmy lectured desperately when they finally came to a stop. "It ain't fair," Mama lamented in her disused screen-door voice. "I can't learn proper in no rich boy's showoff car that Cochise wouldn't drive it his own self. He's fixing to get us kilt." However, these lessons took place regularly twice a week or more, if Jimmy's nerves were up to it, and in the meantime Cochise went on driving his pickup, more cautiously now, often getting out of the cab at an intersection to walk up under the green light and peer at it a second or two to make sure it really was a green light before he climbed back in and drove all the way across.

Jane sits sideways to the picture window, her notebook open in her lap. She is composing, at a speed of two words an hour, the history in verse of the Fall of Mousetown to an invisible invader whom Jane alone knows to be the cunt from outer space. She sees, cannot help seeing, in the corner of her eye, a field of that green found nowhere in nature, with glowing letters on it that she knows say *Harbor Fwy 1½*. But she cannot see to Jimmy's. She places Jimmy's storefront at her back.

What is she doing in Los Angeles, California? Where will she wake up next? As for how she got here, she cannot even think —only that it once glowed yellow-green in the distance, and later she saw that mothy light bleeding on wet asphalt and looked up to see a thousand yellow-green electric bulbs—the garish canopy of a Washington Boulevard used car lot. She does not really view sex as a human practice. One feels murderous as a lion, temporary as a moth, and one does not question the deep recuperative stillness that has wrapped one in its fur, and which appears to be the decorum of a female animal a week beyond the breeding season. Yes, she has been beside herself, and now she has returned, but from what? She shakes her powdery wings, her great yellow head. Some state of being beyond credulity, beyond recall.

In the afternoon she will be visited by Jimmy all the same. They will get into the Murphy bed, and now it is Jane who is peevishly offering lessons. Not like that, like *that*, she may say, demonstrating. This is the death of sexual conviction, and Jane is so forgetful that she replaces headlong appetite with engineering. If Jimmy falls asleep before she does, she gets up and stalks around the apartment like a disgruntled chambermaid, bumping into things, breaking dishes, dropping ashtrays, making as much noise as possible. And yet it has to be admitted (not that she admits it) she is the distractible one. Things have come to such a pass that she can lie along the golden body of the former prodigy and think of something else.

An ice cream truck comes down West 22nd Street three times a day, driven by an enterprising Mexican who has taken on a huge route and knows its hot spots by heart, but has to race between these points to get to them all, which he does without bothering to turn off his music box, which happens to be hot-wired to his generator. So that for twenty minutes three times a day, Jane and Jimmy hear *Sailing, sailing, over the bounding main*, at tempos variable from *allegro assai* to *frenetico*. Jimmy is talking about destroying the ice cream truck with a homemade bomb. But one afternoon Jane raises her head from the Murphy bed at that plink plink of *Sailing, sailing* at 45 miles an hour, and suggests they have an ice cream instead of maintaining their mouths in their present employment.

"You want an ice cream! And you'd buy it from that demented Aztec? Jane, you act so incredibly cold sometimes that I think you're either some kind of machinery, or one of us is making a great mistake somewhere."

"I prefer to think of myself as machinery," Jane says, "of

a simple and unreliable sort." And she starts to laugh.

"You laugh too much."

Jane laughs even harder.

"Also in your poems you laugh too much."

She stops laughing. "What do you mean?"

"When did you ever go all the way mad? You never go any-where without smuggling your brain along in a violin case. Crazy? You could be a gangster packing a tommy gun with your nerves."

Jane stares at him. "It doesn't matter," she says, feeling for the basest part of his thought. "I only started to be a poet so I wouldn't think it was my duty to pay your rent."

"You don't mean it," Jimmy says, shocked.

"I wouldn't put it past me."

"You can't be a fake."

"I think I am."

"Art is no joke," Jimmy says suspiciously.

"Well then, how about an act of revenge? It's got to have some use, doesn't it?"

Jimmy shakes his head. "Maybe you are a fake," he says. "I mean, what is a word to a color?"

"You know why I write? I don't know what else to do with myself," Jane shouts.

"You're all I want," Jimmy tells her.

"I'm so jealous of you I could kill!"

"Stay with me and write. We'll have a house in the desert."

"I'm not crazy enough to write."

"I shouldn't have said that."

"I'm not mad. I can't afford to go mad. I don't believe that any-one is there to take care of me. I'm the opposite of you—you're rooted in the dead bodies of your two parents. You're a cannibal."

"What are you talking about?" Jimmy says coldly. "Pete and Ernestine are fine, thanks. I just talked to them this morning."

"Are they sending money?"

Jimmy doesn't answer. Jane pulls on her shorts. "I'm going downstairs," she says.

"What is a word to a color!" Jimmy shouts at her.

Jane tells him gravely: "I think I'll have a fudgsicle."

"Have one for me. That should last about as long as my dick."

She starts out the door. From the stairwell she hears him say: "I'm a fake myself, but I have my sights," in a loud, sad voice.

The ice cream truck is just whipping around the corner onto Vermont, its hot-wired hurdy-gurdy an incoherent blur, a melody with a gun to its head. Jane jumps into the Buick, makes a U-turn and chases after it, but the driver turns west and disappears into the grid of short blocks between Budlong and Normandie. She drives slowly up and down those streets, now and then catching snatches of the manic sea shanty, but no longer thinking of ice cream. She has forgotten to bring any money.

Jimmy has his sights, but Jane also has sights, and now, cruising aimlessly up and down, reluctant to go home, she sees two of them on their routes.

The first is a dog, a muscular yellow mongrel, what Cochise calls an Indian dog, one brown eye, one ice blue. Making the rounds, she comes to the Grandview garbage can every day around three. On her wide intelligent forehead is printed a peculiarly intent expression, for she sees the world through the lens of one unchanging idea. If she were human and approached you across a lobby with such a face, you would think her about to give you a hortatory lecture or to shoot you with a gun in the name of some cause, and you would make haste to go the other way if there was still time.

On the street, however, it is the dog who goes the other way. For Los Angeles, or at least the flat central plain of it that Jane has come to know, its rundown streets and avenues as tightly woven as a patch of window screen, is a great town for dog-catchers. They are numberless as postmen, restlessly predatory as old-time whalers. Jane sees their sinister Gray Maria glide down West 22nd Street at least twice a day, and though now and then she thinks she hears a desolate yelp behind the silver mesh, there are hardly any loose animals on the streets in her neighborhood, for the patrol has done its job all too well. But they never get that yellow dog, and this is where the dog's idea comes in. Simple and concrete, as a dog's great political idea must be, it has to do with human beings and a distance, in human terms, of about five yards. She never lets anyone nearer her than that. Never.

Now she stands beside a mailbox at Budlong and 29th on four straight yellow legs, her muscular neck drawn out at an angle of inquiry, reflecting on an oil-stained brown paper carton whose stink is of interest, but insufficient to warrant any violence against it. Jane steers the Buick to the opposite curb, some twenty feet away, and whistles softly at her. As always the dog looks up at the human without curiosity and continues at her work; Jane lets the Buick roll a yard closer, and she trots off at once without looking back.

She gives Jane a queer feeling, very queer. With a wave almost of love, Jane watches her disappear into high weeds along the foundation of a burned-out elementary school.

A little closer to home, she sees the tattered coat of J. T. McNeil, millionaire, flapping along the rim of a dumpster in the fish store parking lot. The spine, the flesh inside the ragged cloth is distinguishable by its quality of not being there at all; and his gray trousers look equally vacant. The man has no ass to sit upon, Jane realizes, and thus he wanders hither and thither about the world until at nightfall he lowers his bones onto a bed of neckties at the offices of Cochise Realty. And that is his life, either he walks, or he lies down, and meanwhile he drags home empty boxes from the trash. Cochise, for all his vows to butter up the millionaire incessantly until he can rest perfectly sure the old man's downtown parking lots are safe from the priests, will fly into a rage and throw out all the boxes again as soon as McNeil leaves in the morning.

"You know if I didn't know he owned five acres on Flower Street I'd say he was the most pity-full old bum I ever saw," Cochise has told Jane. "By Jesus, his personal habits is non-existent! I tried to get him a reglar bed in the office but he wouldn't have none of it. And he don't really sleep, he just lays there with his eyes cocked open practicing to be dead. It gives you the willies. He don't sleep, he don't hardly eat, he don't wash, he don't say two words a week, he don't even drink!" Cochise shook his head in disgust and bewilderment.

Here then is the other daily sight on its route. It is useless to speak to it, though you can come quite near, much nearer than to the dog, but as soon as he sees your mouth begin to work, unless you are Cochise and sometimes even then, he scurries away. Unlike the dog's, the millionaire's seeking lacks all practical usefulness. It's empty boxes he loves, most of all shiny boxes of waxed cardboard, still damp from crushed ice, that he finds in great numbers in the dumpster behind the Louisiana Fish Store, and which put Cochise in a frenzy. His blueprints, his contracts, even his white golfing caps stink of fish, thanks to that degenerate millionaire who is still going to Saint What's-His-Face every Sunday.

The yellow bitch who moves ever at the center of thirty feet of humanless space, the millionaire who makes such love as he makes to empty boxes—to Jane, who watches them daily from her second floor window, who spies on them now in their wanderings rather than hurry back to her lover naked in bed—to Jane these two stand by the gate of her new life like sentries, sentries profoundly uninterested in all who pass. The dog with the theory of humanless space, the derelict millionaire who walls himself round with empty boxes—these two she recognizes, she looks for them every day, every day she is relieved but also upset, shamed, chastised when they reappear in the flesh, for where they cross, the dog and the millionaire, where their solipsistic routes unknowingly intersect, there stands Jane herself.

Jane has her sights and Jimmy has his, and while she is gone, he decides to show her one of his.

She comes back up the stairs of the Grandview in no hurry, lets herself in, stops—the Murphy bed blocks the door. Jimmy is not in it, so she lets it clap shut with a slapstick *boing*. One corner of the pink sheet now hangs out of the fake fireplace like a tongue. She goes to the table by the picture window and sits down. And starts to look at her notebook, but her eyes slide to the wall instead, a blank white wall when she left.

There lifesize in black crayon is Jane, naked, on the Murphy bed, her legs wide open, a runny ice cream in one hand, a lighted cigarette in the other, an open notebook on her stomach, a pencil over her ear, a radio on the mantelpiece pouring out cheery quarter notes, an ice-cream beard on her chin. And there is Jimmy—this little fellow on his knees between her legs, blond, skinny, cartoon drops of sweat leaping from the back of his head like bicycle spokes, must be Jimmy—there is Jimmy kneeling between her legs, performing an office of bliss.

On one of those rare days when Jimmy goes to school, Jane finds taped in the window of a filthy laundromat near USC:

G. R. O. P. E.
THE GLOBAL RAG OF PSYCHEDELIC EMERGENCY
(A Monthly Sloughing of the Hypothesis)
SUBMIT NOW!
GROPE wants poems & stories of hallucinatory clarity!
KNOWN & UNKNOWN WRITERS WELCOME
No Depressed or Suicidal Puke.
No Jaded Sameness.
No Brutality.
No Haiku.
No Ivory Tower Masturbation.
Send s.a.s.e.—Payment in copies
GROPE
Annette Z & Melvin X, Editors
Box 138
Venice, California

Jane rushes home to stuff "The Beard Envy Cure" in an envelope. The flyer for GROPE looks so silly—a cheesy mimeograph with a crudely drawn logo, some sort of ball wearing a pirate's eyepatch—she is sure they will take her poem. But as soon as she drops it in a mailbox, depression overtakes her. She suddenly remembers that hitchhiker she picked up in the Painted Desert: "I saw an angel ninety feet tall, with a sword!" That, she perceives dispiritedly, is hallucinatory clarity. Could "The Beard Envy Cure" in fact be ivory tower masturbation? Good God, a clearer case of it could scarcely be imagined. So there she is, hanging upside down again on the same old jungle gym, caught in its delusion of invisibility with her red hand in her underpants. Jane cringes with shame.

Two weeks later she receives a letter.

Dear Jane Kaplan Turner,

"Beard Envy" is a strange trip! Who are u? Send GROPE a Contributors Note. Do you really want to be one of those 3-name authoresses? (Forgive us if yr a granny, but u seem too hip for that.)

Sad to say GROPE Number 2 temporarily constipated due to lack of funds but we should be back on the pot after XMAS. Beam GROPE yr new poems and if yr flush send $.

Pax et Coitus,

Annette Z & Melvin X
Editors
GROPE

Jimmy, Jane, and Roger Booth sit three across the green backseat of a donkey cart. The pink seat facing them is reserved for the ghost of Fred Blood. Seven weeks ago, Fred dumped a backpack of marijuana over the roof of the central parking ramp at O'Hare Airport, then jumped down after it. His body was separated with difficulty from the top of a Veterans Cab waiting for fares outside TWA.

Roger brought the news about Fred, along with five joints for Jane, from Willie, hidden in a road atlas with *Come home to Willie* scrawled on the cover. Strange to say, Roger is now a movie star. As soon as he arrived in Los Angeles he got a one-line part as a victim's date in *The Corpse Who Loved Women*. He hasn't gotten a paycheck yet; they haven't started shooting. Meanwhile he has his usual room at a certain remove—he sleeps, inscrutably enough, in Alhambra.

For Roger, Jane, and Jimmy to have themselves driven over the rutted streets of Tijuana in this pink and green buggy in broad day as Fred once drove them weightlessly up and down the hills of Pocahontas County on roads only he knew, under a full moon with the headlights turned off, seemed a good idea thirty minutes ago. However, Jane imprudently gave the donkey man five dollars in front, and he disappeared on the pretext of fetching his donkey a bucket of water. The she-ass left behind is trained to stand at the curb through riot and earthquake. She is not even tied. She may well be drugged, they think. Her eyes, under half-lowered eyelids, are lakes of small iridescent green flies. Her tail, far from swishing, is encased in a studded leather thong like a sinister sexual toy. Only a tremor passing occasionally over one flank tells them she is alive at all. Her owner is doubtless watching the three of them from an upstairs window, hoping they will grow tired of waiting and disappear, but they have been passing a pint of tequila and one, then another, of the joints from Willie, and they have forgotten all about the missing driver.

Jimmy says: "To Young Fred!" And they all have a slug.

"He must have been trying to go home," Jimmy says. "His old lady loved him."

Jane says: "It's always a mistake to go home when you feel weak."

"Who knows if he was trying to go home or trying not to?" says Roger. "Either way I don't get the feeling it was a great comfort to the kid."

"So how's Mrs. Blood?"

Silence. Jane repeats the question and Roger says: "To be perfectly candid, I heard the news, packed my stuff, and left the house by the back door." Roger is never wishy-washy about moves of this kind. He has *contramadonismo* (allergy to the madonna role) as does Jane, but unlike Jane's, his impulses are his convictions and he has the courage of them.

"Willie probably took care of her," Roger adds. For some reason this speculation sits on Jane's heart like a stone.

A few doors down, American sailors lurch out of one cabaret and stumble into another: ESPECTÁCULO BRAVO! GIRLS GIRLS GIRLS. They cross a doorway alcove where children are poking a lump wrapped in rags with a stick. Sure it is the corpse of something, Jane looks away. She yearns for someone to say, Oh Jane, let me take care of you, even though she wouldn't allow anyone to take care of her. A Shore Patrolman following the sailors from bar to bar stops in front of a poster full of girls, blinks at it, and idly spits on the sidewalk. Jane is dazed, dazed; too lit up by tequila and grass either to absorb Roger's news or to ignore it.

"Look!" she says, pointing. She has just noticed that the donkey is not connected to the cart at all, but only standing under a tangle of reins inside the shafts.

"Why, that bandito," Roger chuckles. "We've been had."

"I don't think Fred's coming," says Jane. "Why would he hang around with a bunch of patsies like us?"

"I beg your pardon," Roger says. "Speak for yourself. Maybe you didn't bring him good fortune. I have reason to think Fred was always quite partial to me personally."

Jimmy says: "Let's take Fred to a strip show. There used to be a place around the corner where the girls shaved their pubic hair in the shape of a keyhole and sat on men's faces."

"You think Fred would go for that? I want my five bucks back," says Jane, who is supporting this excursion with a week's pay.

"That's what Fred needed," Roger pontificates. "Sex. Hashish and the swamis got him first so he never knew what was eating him."

"You don't think he was a virgin, do you?" Jimmy asks worriedly.

"Definitely."

"Oh no! Wow! We should have turned him over to Jane."

Jane looks up in amazement.

"Come, come, you would have done that much for the lad if you knew he was doomed, wouldn't you?" Roger asks.

"Maybe," Jane says. "What makes you think it was me Fred wanted? I always figured it was you."

Roger and Jimmy look at each other.

"What do you think, James?" Roger says.

Jimmy says: "I never saw him looking at *my* ass."

Roger says: "That's because you don't have eyes in your ass. He worshipped you two. Both of you." He points an accusing finger at Jane. "He shot up that car in your defense, woman. His last stand."

"God, don't remind me." Jane buries her face in her hands. "I know it's true. I shamed him, too. Let me see that tequila." And she drains the bottle of its last half inch.

"There's more where that came from," Jimmy reminds her.

Jane hands Jimmy her wallet. He takes a few bills and sets off to buy another pint.

As soon as he rounds the corner, Roger leans across Jane's body and insinuates a mothlike hand under her skirt. This is their affair so far. When all three of them are together, they ramble noisily down the street with their arms about each other's waists. And as soon as Jimmy is missing, Roger enters the fragile claim on Jimmy's girl you see here. Though Jane has never been one for the tremulous approach before, now she gives as good as she gets, which is to say as little. She meets Roger in small and dirty public parks without winding footpaths where she might come to the fevered pitching of her underpants to the four winds; she takes that ghostly kiss over and over, and these pianissimo fingerings upon her skin. "Kiss harder," she sometimes says through bared teeth, "so I know you're there."

As he nibbles, Roger sometimes breathes through her hair: "Don't forget we're all bums except Jimmy." So Roger is an innocent, making love, after his fashion, to Jimmy, whereas Jane is only making trouble, releasing little slivers of glass into the eye of the world.

Now Roger's long fingers dip into her blouse without even making the buttons go taut, and slide over her nipples as weightlessly as a pickpocket's. Jane knows this is careless. To hell with it, she thinks, shutting her eyes, taking the kiss, letting the little goldfish take a furtive, nervous swim an inch behind her teeth.

A moment later blows are bouncing off their heads and shoulders, oddly undamaging blows, fists pouring down on them like snowballs in a dream. Even so Jane almost bites the goldfish in half, and now Roger sits there holding his tongue between his fingers, checking for blood as Jane and Hermine used hopefully to do when they had been horsing around and one of their chins got bumped. And Jane may be presumed to look almost as foolish, feeling her buttons to make sure they are buttoned—sadly, they are. "You two—you could do this to me!" Jimmy shouts.

Roger recovers so quickly that Jane sees this was the point all along. "Don't you see what love there is for you in this?" he says to Jimmy.

The line is canned, Jane thinks bitterly, but no less sincere for all that. She is jealous, jealous—that he could be so sure! She is one of the creeping things of the earth, but Roger is elated. He has been wicked but only for Jimmy's sake. He has loved Jane but only in God, as it were.

And Jimmy—when his fists were flailing he had looked touchingly like a little boy playing the drums, and he had meted out about as much pain. And now he looks altered and impure, as if he has found out something he didn't know before. Jane springs with dangerous pity at the sight. His misery is contingent, suspicious, wired to the outside world—to her, in fact. He throws himself into the pink seat, the one reserved for Fred, and looks angrily sideways at Jane.

Fighting off shame, she becomes afflicted with sincerity. "Not me," she croaks. "I have other ways of saying I'm in love. I don't know what I meant but it wasn't that." Her voice is the wicked stepmother's and both men look at her uneasily. Instantly, she feels relieved of some antique hunger, damned yet satisfied, as though infamy were bread. "Yes I do," she says. "I wanted you to feel the quicksand too. I'm sick and tired of being the only one."

"Congratulations," says Jimmy.

Suddenly the donkey-man appears, waving her five-dollar bill. From his upstairs window he has seen fisticuffs break out in his pink and green buggy, and he has one thought: to clear out these crazy gringos who have wasted his whole afternoon before they bring the police.

"Carro is no go today," he shouts. "I am pay you back all de money."

"We want a ride!" Jane demands. "Uno rido . . . ahora, you brigand!" She stands up on the seat and shakes her fist at him. "We have a ghost to amuse."

The driver stares at Jane a moment, then appeals to the men. "Hombre, mujer histérica, no? I sink ees dronk," he remarks, dismissing Jane with a gesture. "No go Sonday, absolutamente no." He holds up the money in both hands like a placard. "I am pay you back everysing."

"Okay, okay," Jimmy says, taking the bill. "We're going." He jumps out of the cart and starts down the street alone. Roger follows Jimmy and a moment later Jane runs after the two of them.

Already they are turning into a club with a green awning, EL CHICAGO. It has the usual lurid signpainter's work beside the open front door: GIRLS GIRLS GIRLS in Day-Glo chartreuse, Polaroids of current stars mounted on sunbursts of glue-on spangles —La Sultana—Anita—Marilyn—Jane is always amazed at the candor of these shots, the strippers always too young or too old, underfed or waffled with bulges, looking either like your Aunt Yetta surprised in her garter belt or the teenage victims of a hypnotist. She has seen posters like these up and down the Block in Baltimore, but has never been inside such a place.

This one is pitch dark. Blue smoke eddies over the stage, which is roped off like a boxing ring. Men crowd around it, more of them Mexican (a thick plate of shiny black hair, a ruffled short-sleeved pastel shirt) than Jane would have supposed. Roger and Jimmy go straight to the bar, but Jane is rooted to the spot where she stands from the moment she sees what is going on onstage. Four middle-aged women recline, back to back, against a silly paper volcano, and their cunts are smoking cigars! They puff round smoke signals to a mambo beat out of the ends of four fat panatelas, which look as one-hundred-percent as the box of Havana El Presidente Número Unos her father got from a client once and hoarded like gold between two bricks of frozen ground beef in Sasha's freezer. The cigars between the legs of these artful hags stink authentically—an El Presidente used to keep the women out of Philip Turner's den for an entire day.

Jane can't stop looking. None of the women is pretty, and they don't seem to be deluded about this. They leer, jiggle their breasts, each stickered with a pasty like a supermarket item, and make dirty cracks to the men. The men howl with laughter, but in fact this is a horror show in place of a come-on. They are menacing, those cunts with cigars in their lips—if the mysterious pharynxes behind them can yawn and constrict and belch smoke rings at will, my God, what else can they do? No one dares come close enough to find out. And Jane thinks of Bernardine, of mythical vaginas in general, of vaginas that can mimic Crater Lake and the Grand Canyon, the self-immolating Krakatoa and Mount Rushmore, complete with the heads of four *El Presidente Número Unos* turned to stone at a single glance. Jane has a hermit's dank cave to compare with these national monuments, and even so its darkness is nine-tenths unexplored.

Suddenly this scene is swept away. The women disappear, the four cigars are left feebly smoking themselves in a row on the edge of the bar. Somewhere a scratchy record is put on and a stripper climbs onto the platform. Now Jane is really shocked, for compared to those four weirdly potent and untouchable beldams draped over their volcano, everything about this performance is fugitive and maladroit. The deadpan girl runs up and down the stage in something like black gauze shorty pajamas and a little cape, a skinny, dark, very young person, hardly any hips or breasts, looking in that get-up like a mascot to a funeral. The music is a kind of retarded mariachi, and the girl runs ahead of it, knock-kneed, not even trying to dance, only listing from side to side like a sick colt. And in very little time she throws aside the brief garments one by one, a repetitious, irritable gesture—a housemaid culling stained tea-towels into the trash.

What is she, thirteen, fourteen? She is inexpert, artless, but knows what she knows. She knows what is required, and that is what she gives—nothing less or more. She never smiles. Soon enough, there it is, the keyhole-shaped pubic hair. She is so young, Jane is surprised she has any pubic hair at all. It could be glued on: It is black and discrete as a cheap toupee, and shaped like a knife blade tapering down into her crotch, not a keyhole. Before the music has quite ended, she steps across the ropes nearest the bar and bows her knees out over the men's faces, offers a lick, calmly getting it over with. This must be easier than dancing, for she is no longer in a hurry. There are plenty of comers. Her air of complete neutrality does not discourage anyone; they are not looking at her face. Jane sees Jimmy in the vanguard, getting his turn, not overexcited, just being a man of the people.

Jane pulls her eyes away, looks around the room. Who owns this girl? Half the pastel shirts at the bar probably belong to pimps, and then there are the bartenders—and her stomach lurches at the thought of the grid of connections between all those black pompadours gleaming with hair oil, the slow-lidded eyes and licorice wax mustaches. She feels sick—the tequila probably—imagines one of the bartenders is gesturing roundly at her, beckoning to her—and sees her wallet in his hand.

"Ees of the lady?" he says, with almost affectionate irony. The only other ladies in El Chicago are working the bar and tables and clearly have business on their minds. They are not losing their wallets. The bartender, unlike the donkey-man, is pleased with Jane, for she has acted like a stupid gringa exactly in accord with his specifications—a daughter should be so pliant, so mild, so predictable!

A moment ago Jane was dizzy, sick, but tequila is a drink that leads through immobility to transparency, and Jane instantly understands everything that has occurred in the girlie bar El Chicago. She gaped at the floorshow, more taken in than any yokel or john in the place. She had a straw pocketbook over her arm, traffic brushed by, men together and alone, whores with their customers, a kid selling papers. Her wallet, lying in the very lips of her bag, levitated into one of their palms. Maybe the bartender saw, maybe he didn't, but soon he jerked, with a deeply educated gesture, one of those wires of connection, and the wallet, empty, appeared in his proffered hand.

"Ees of the lady?" "Thank you," Jane says, reddening as she is supposed to. "De nada," says the bartender, and a grapevine of smirks curls along the bar, under the fat black mustaches. She does not look to see if there is any money in the wallet. She is lucky it amuses them to give it back to her at all. Of course it may be that outside of his career as a thief and a pimp and an exhibitor of his daughter's flesh (for she has begun, for no very good reason, to think of the stripper as the bartender's daughter), the bartender is quite a decent fellow.

Jane turns for the exit. Jimmy and Roger join her. They have watched the whole affair. Ghost or no ghost, they are 140 miles from home, in a mean cruel border town on the Mexican side, and flat broke.

At such a turning the males of the human species divide cleanly into two sub-sexes, those who instinctively cry out *You incompetent cunt!* and those who wouldn't dream of it. It is not a question of temper—anyone is entitled to a cross mood at this pass—but of whether a sexual slur rises to the lips.

Jimmy wouldn't dream of it. He roars with laughter. "You should have seen yourself," he says, "in outer space. You were so gone you forgot your pocketbook."

"I'm going to Uranus later," Jane tells him sheepishly. They come out into the sunshine. Jimmy takes her arm.

"Did you really cuckold me with my oldest friend, you hussy?" he asks her under his breath.

"I was thinking about it," Jane says.

"WHAT NOW?" Roger inquires from a step behind them. Jane looks over her shoulder at him. *You incompetent cunt!* is engraved in cipher all over his handsome face.

Nevertheless, Jane can read it. "I don't think he's really my type," Jane whispers.

"Let's take Fred to the desert," Jimmy proposes. "If we run out of gas in El Centro, Pete will come get us."

"What say we leave Fred out of it," Roger snaps.

Jane is on the stoop of Jimmy's old place near MacArthur Park. She is killing time until the mailman comes, with her back turned to the house where, in the dark night of her one night's entertainment, she encountered that catastrophic nuclear family, the Blanks. She faces a fat, red-faced little girl who rides her tricycle around and around a square of broken sidewalk like a fugitive dwarf from some belfry clock in Bavaria. But soon enough, down the stoop around Jane comes the dark, famished bride of the nuclear family in its catastrophe. Jimmy is right. Though last seen in her discolored underwear, yanked over backwards by a thong of black hair into her husband's lap, by day Mrs. Blank looks no worse than usual. Her hair is in a bun that could be a second, shrunken black head on the back of her neck, and her deflated thighs hardly whisper as they scissor by in short shorts, behind a stroller. From inside the stroller the larval Blank looks back at Jane and, as little cheered as Jane by what it sees, explodes in sobs.

Jane is waiting for the postman for the third straight day. A check from her father is due. Having sent Philip Turner a postcard with the MacArthur Park address the day she arrived, one day later she moved, forgetting postcard, address, debt, checks, everything.

But now, because she has lost a whole week's pay in the girlie bar El Chicago in Tijuana, the wolf is at the door. Suddenly she really needs that seventy-nine bucks, although now to collect her money Jane must really grovel, get down there in the dirt with those meaty roses and ambush and sweet-talk the post-man in person.

Moreover she has detected a humid and runtish sentiment under her skin. She is hoping her father will write her a letter. She knows that his bookkeeper sends the checks and there won't be any letter. She knows she can use this fact to harden her heart, and she does. It isn't hard to harden your heart, not if you are Jane. But when you are lost, really lost, you think all at once what a father could be.

For it's true every woman can have what she wants. If your heart is hard enough, you can do all the unrequiting in your life and call your exes crybabies if they complain. No, if you are Jane, it's softening your heart that is the problem. For even an adventuress cannot choose her father, her first lover, the one least liable to be forgot. And what if a girl's father never liked her? Where is the bottom of that mystery? Who to blame? *How to get over him?* To wrench a thousand bucks out of his pocket only reminds her how far she is from getting over him.

"It's a check from my old man," she has told the mailman, "but I don't live here anymore. He *owes* me the money," she was careful to add, on the chance the mailman has some grudge against remittance cases, as she would in his place. He has a thready beard, the postman has. He will give Jane her letter, for these are still the days when the bearded trust the bearded, the barefoot the barefoot, the longhaired the longhaired, and every-one under all that hair is young. Jane's shoes, such as they are, are stuck in her pocketbook, she's wearing purple tights, her hair is out to here, and she is supposedly headed for an antiwar rally at UCLA later in the day, while the postman will still be pounding his route. The better to get her hands on that check, Jane has inspired him to think of her as his deputy at the march and maybe even in the station-house tank.

But Jane isn't sure she needs to spend the night in the station-house tank. For her education, that is. And yet a trip to Westwood could be highly educational. And Jane will surely go west, when Jimmy picks her up, to the Hollywood foothills, green as funny money, of Wilshire Boulevard at the other extreme from MacArthur Park. But Jane keeps thinking, not of war and peace, but of her mother's old psychiatrist, Manfred Zwilling. Her mother said to her on the phone not long ago: "Oh Jane! You remember Dr. Z! He's in Hollywood. Do something for me—stop by and say hello." Never in her life has Jane completed such a mission from a relation to stop by and say hello, but for some reason she feels a powerful urge to look in on the doctor in the character of a spy. She imagines herself rafting by Dr. Zwilling's shingle again and again as if some secret message might be culled from the mere facade—though that is the sort of thing a disgruntled mental patient would do, she knows that by instinct.

A male shape she recognizes comes around the corner—not the mailman but Roger, with a white bag in his hand. "Tarts for the tart," he says, thrusting it at her.

Jane smiles at this escalation of his disrespect. She takes a Danish with a gory hole in it. "What are you doing here?"

"Oh I don't know," he says. "I was passing by."

"Jimmy is coming," Jane tells him blandly, hoping to incite God knows what with this bulletin. She has thought about it. She sees now that she, not Roger, was the guilty backslider in their snail-paced tryst, and that adds fresh envy to her bouquet of resentments against the paramour.

"Gosh, he is?" Roger says, and sits down beside her.

"We're going to the antiwar to-do."

He puts his hand on Jane's knee. And his other hand circles her waist, a more definite tension, at last, than the sketchy, ghostly touch of the late past. Nevertheless she says, "What are you trying to do, prove to Jimmy what a trollop I am? He knows that already. Hey, I'm capable of learning from experience."

"Let's go in the garage and take off all our clothes," Roger says.

"I can't. I'm waiting for the mailman."

But the mailman suddenly arrives. He gets a certain look on his face while he fishes out Jane's check, as if he's going to say *Don't say I never gave you anything*, like Philip Turner. "Don't spend it all in one place," he says.

He adds: "And I wouldn't take a lot of dough to the march. Something's going to happen."

They all believe this. Something's going to happen. Even Roger doesn't scoff.

"Peace and love, children," the mailman says, shouldering his bag. "Hell no, we won't go."

"As a matter of fact," Roger tells him, "I work for Aeronutronic."

The mailman nods tolerantly. He understands what it is to be a pack mule for the enemy. "Just wait till you're drafted," he says.

"Hey, they won't send me. I'm the sole support of my mother till my four brothers get out of the penitentiary."

The mailman stops smiling. "Do you know this guy?" he asks Jane.

"Slightly."

He departs, looking troubled. Jane is glad he gave her the check first. She holds the envelope up to the sunlight. There's no letter, just a check.

"I loathe these smug innocents," Roger says to his back.

"Did you make that up?" Jane inquires. "I thought you didn't have anything to do with your family."

"My mother is the port of last resort," Roger says.

"What else have you got in the works?" At his physical, Jimmy simply told the examining doctors he was a fruit, and since through no fault of his own he is a boy spun out of golden silk, he was believed.

"Come in the garage and I'll show you," Roger says.

"I can't."

"Can't what? I'm trying to show you a freak of nature, for God's sake. Who'd have thought you'd turn out to be such a tight-ass."

"It's true," Jane says. "I'm a failure as a hot tamale."

Roger pats her knee. "Keep trying," he says. "You're certainly an overachiever as a plain bitch. Now come on." He leads her behind a palmetto, unbuttons his shirt and drops his trousers a few inches.

Jane sees only a slender, elegant torso and nipples like old British pennies, large and almost black.

"You don't see anything wrong?"

Jane shakes her head. Roger points to his nipples, then to a set of birthmarks halfway down his ribs, then to a smaller pair in the whorling sea wrack at his navel. Slowly Jane wakes to the symmetry.

"Eek, what is it?"

"Even Jimmy doesn't know," Roger says. "I'm a dog, and not only that, I'm a female dog. If you tell a living soul I'll never speak to you again."

If this is courtship, it is an inspired attempt, for Jane is fascinated and deeply touched to have this confided to her. The face of love, she thinks.

"Wow."

"You see who's the real bitch around here," Roger says gallantly. "A doctor in Teaneck told me I was one step up from a duck-billed platypus. Are they going to let this in the army?"

Jane considers. "Why not? They let it in the movies, didn't they?"

"Oh come on! Uncle Sam wants men, not dogs. I'm going to tell them I sometimes get down on all fours and bark uncontrollably."

Jane starts to laugh.

"Let's face it, in any other age they would have left me on a hilltop for the buzzards. That's why I like the twentieth century, even with the wars—as long as I personally don't have to go." He draws Jane's hands to his naked chest. "So," he says, "you can bear to touch me."

Jane squints at him suspiciously, starts to back away, but he holds her hands tight.

"Speaking of wars and of not having to go personally—I think you just missed your ride."

Tires squeal, and a small car speeds backfiring around the

corner. Jane sees the chrome-trimmed bagel on its mint-green rear end.

Roger laughs uproariously.

"You did that on purpose," Jane shouts at him. "What are you up to? Did you ever really want to fuck me?"

He shouts back at her: "Who knows! Maybe. Did you ever really want to fuck me?"

"Don't you have any consideration for Jimmy's feelings, if not for mine?"

"In the short run, no. You deserve each other."

Jane does not wish to curse him, for every malediction only inflates his self-esteem. She heads for the Buick, stumbling over aloe spears, crushing ice plants to pulp with her bare feet.

"I'll bet Jimmy knew you had dog breasts the whole time," she yells back over her shoulder.

"Maybe. Why don't you ask him when you see him? I'll just never speak to you again. Small loss."

"I might do that," Jane shouts.

Roger shrugs. "You know what you're doing," he shouts back.

In the Buick, Jane chases Jimmy's Valiant west down the Santa Monica Freeway, then loses him in the tangle of interchanges at Exposition Boulevard, where his more acrobatic vehicle suddenly dips down an exit ramp and the Buick lumbers by. *Lost him*, Jane says out loud at the time, and would be charmed by the wistful music of the phrase, except that it might in the greater sense be true. How much can the poor boy take? Why is she trying to drive him away, and how long before, in her half-witting manner, she succeeds? At first she ploughs on in the moneygreen Buick towards the antiwar rally at UCLA, wishing she had a PEACE NOW sign to hold in front of her guilty face. But at last it strikes her as berserk to pursue Jimmy through a crowd of ten thousand, trying to explain.

Manfred Zwilling, M.D. dangles at the bottom of four dentists and an astrologer in front of a modest pink apartment building

—modest for Beverly Drive. Jane observes that the presence of an astrologer gives this carte du jour a slightly disreputable air satisfying to a spy. She sits out front in the moneygreen Buick trying to ripen into a real mental case, the kind who will darken her mother's old psychiatrist's door with a look in her eye that liberates at least the fancy, *This woman may have a gun in her purse.*

She feels like a dangerous person. For once in her life she could almost admit that to lay her head down on someone else's office furniture and say "Fix it" would be good, but consult a quack like Zwilling? She would die first. And yet she feels —what—garrulously out of control, like a child playing with a wireless set, a clever child but too lazy, shiftless and excitable to read the directions, hence sending messages that nobody, not even Jane, understands. *When did you ever go all the way mad?* She sits in the moneygreen Buick in front of Dr. Zwilling's pink stucco building, trying to feel deranged enough to go in.

She would like to know how a woman should act, how a woman could face the face of love without erupting to her own shock and chagrin in a currish snarl. For as far as she can see, there is no way to face the face of love but hind end foremost, an unbearably endangered position. Sasha of course never faced the face of love, never came face to face with her own butt end, but chased her tail around and around, never quite offering it to either male, her husband or her doctor, as though she had no idea what was under it. And this is the question Jane wishes to take up with her mother's former psychiatrist—why he never told her mother what was under it. Perhaps her father Philip Turner was just a male, but these doctor guys are supposed to know better. How in fifteen years could he possibly avoid telling her?—unless he was a charlatan.

A woman walks out of the building in oversized, scrap-iron jewelry, jingling like a drayhorse. This could have been Sasha in the early days, who, Jane has to admit, would have left Dr. Zwilling in just such jewelry, in just such a mood—lathering along above the thoroughly earthbound, thoroughly female *squink, squink* of her high heels on the concrete sidewalk. Nothing could hurt her now—at least not for thirty minutes, until she ground into the driveway of the house on Pinkney Road.

A second woman pushes through the glass doors in a black sheath, bosomy and funereal. Her eyes are wet inside green wings of eye makeup, and she mashes a handkerchief back into a silver purse. Jane has seen her before—a movie actress of the third or fourth magnitude, cheekbones as wide apart as tire tracks, plenty of room there for the contortions that make horror films horrible, now giving one of her most human and affecting performances. Jane knows that the astrologer might beam out two such satisfied customers as easily as Dr. Zwilling, and of course they could be having affairs, one ecstatic, one miserable, with two of the dentists, or even with the same dentist. All the same, the sight of these two handsome females engulfed in contradictory catharses from male healers is not bracing Jane to her task, and so she lurches out of the Buick before she can lose her nerve and runs for the pink stucco vestibule.

His waiting room has been done, as they say, in one color, the noncommittal but self-assured gray-brown of the ash of a good cigar. Jane sniffs a change of heart, or at least of style, remembering Zwilling's old office in the Latrobe Building, where the furniture was recklessly mismatched and a rather sinister green-tinged aquarium bubbled in one corner like a houkah.

No one is waiting and there is no secretary. She sees a plain closed door, behind which a bell pinged discreetly when she came in. She sits down. Even the fan of magazines on the glass coffee table is subdued, colorless, glossless, supremely unseductive—newsletters from Whole Message, virgin copies of *The Nation*, and what looks like a stack of PTA minutes, mimeographed and stapled. She picks this up. Something about the linty, broken lines of the title banner catches her eye. She has seen that patched up globe before.

It's *G.R.O.P.E.: The Global Rag of Psychedelic Emergency* (A Monthly Sloughing of the Hypothesis) Volume One, Number Two—already three weeks old. She forgets to be astonished at finding this pretentiously slovenly tabloid in Zwilling's waiting room. Instead she is staring at the masthead, at the patched globe, for suddenly she is pained to understand the crudely drawn ball is the planet Earth in a sanitary belt and Kotex. Now how can she ever send copies to her parents?

She flips the corner-stapled pages and there is "The Beard Envy Cure" spread over pages three and four like grit under a carpet. The mimeograph machine seems to have suffered some crisis while her work was in its mangles. Still, you can make it out. Line six reads "His mysterious bear of origin" instead of "His mysterious beard of origin," and the typewriter that cut the stencils must have been older than her own, or anyway every *s* is halved to a tiny *c* floating above the line. But all the same her heart chugs up, up, up, and she wishes Jimmy were here. Short of that—she rolls up the magazine like a spyglass and thrusts it in her purse.

"May I ask what you're doing?"

It is Dr. Zwilling himself, his head poking around the door from the other room. Changed, but still theatrical—now he looks less like a Latin second lead who might jump up at any moment and start doing the rhumba in Rio, and more like the stock physician who would try to sell you milk of magnesia on TV. Not that he wears a white coat or has a round mirror strapped to his forehead. He is wearing a conservative business suit; there seems to have been some rapprochement over the years between his taste in clothes and that of her father. All the theater is in his face, the caterpillar eyebrows, the big thumb-latch nose, the wide, firm, closed but flexible mouth. The slick wormy mustache Jane remembers from the old days is gone, along with the shiny suits.

"I'm taking this magazine," Jane explains, but she is no longer cramming the thing into the darkness of loose change, broken cigarettes and decomposing sales receipts. She lets it rest, gently unfurling, on top.

"Do I know you?" Dr. Zwilling asks after a time. "What do you want here?"

"In what sense know? You gave me a Rorschach test when I

was five," Jane replies. Then her mouth falls open, for she is as shocked at this news as if she had heard it from Zwilling and not the other way around. Do they put some kind of dope in the air conditioning in psychiatrists' offices, so that a charlady can't push a vacuum cleaner through the waiting room without being bombarded by long lost memories? Think of it, a Rorschach test. But what on earth were they—Sasha and her psychiatrist—trying to find out? What *did* they find out?

Dr. Zwilling seems unperturbed at the news that he gave her a Rorschach test when she was five. Either he does such things every day, or he doesn't believe her for a minute. He says nothing. She knows what is going on. He is waiting for her to speak, has not even had to will himself to be quiet, as Jane would in his place, but simply steps behind the mask of his profession. And when the urge to explain sets in a moment later, she is ready for it. She thrusts out her chin, wires down her jaw. Let him wait.

She thinks about that Rorschach test. One plate she remembers: Mr. Pain, a bogeyman from the Ben-Gay advertisements in the funny papers, was turning a somersault with no clothes on, his green penis, which needed a shave like the rest of him, pointing the wrong way—which is to say, up. Jane eyes Zwilling, still standing with unfriendly patience in the angle of his office door. No wonder he once told Sasha, and Sasha in due course told Philip Turner, this little girl was aware, maybe too aware, of sex. It hardly took a genius. But great snakes! the concatenations of grief that one throwaway line of Zwilling's had set off over the years.

"This magazine," Jane says recklessly, "is more mine than yours."

Zwilling's head cocks slightly sideways.

"I have a poem in it," she declares.

"Really?" Zwilling says. "Congratulations. Does that make all the copies of it belong to you?"

"I don't have any copies of it," Jane replies.

"I see. Well. I paid ten dollars for a subscription to this magazine under duress from my daughter, who also insists I display it in my office."

A silence. Jane is thinking, His daughter! Then—If I died, Philip Turner still wouldn't show this thing in his office. Jane returns the magazine to the coffee table, smooths it out.

"Can you tell me why a baseball is wearing a sanitary pad on the cover?" Zwilling asks icily, as if Jane were the genius of this design.

"It's not a baseball. It's the planet Earth sloughing its monthly hypothesis."

"Then why does it have seams?"

"That's the polar ice cap and a little bit of, uh, Patagonia."

Zwilling's eyelashes flicker. "I suppose you're a friend of Annette's."

"No."

He retreats to an earlier, stonier plateau of suspicion. "Do you mind telling me your name? What makes you think I gave you a Rorschach test when you were five?"

"I don't know what you two, you and my mother, were trying to find out, but you decided there was too much sex going on up there under the baby bonnet. Oh, and you said I had artistic tendencies. So you see why you owe me this magazine." Jane picks it up again. "You were the voice of doom. Doomed to GROPE. You shaped my whole life."

He squints at her. "Are you from Baltimore?"

"Yes. Actually, my mother asked me to drop by. That's why I can't understand what I'm doing here."

"Your mother?"

"Sasha. Sasha Turner. Sasha Kaplan Turner."

And now Jane sees something that really shocks her, that pushes her down below the ballast of stale indignation she was prepared to discharge here and grinds her face along the bottom. Before Zwilling's chin sinks in a small nod of recognition, it tips back a hair, to free the action on some contraption he thought he'd gotten rid of, and there Jane sees it: a rusty landscape and a little grayish pink ghost it frames. "How is Sasha," he says quickly, to cover this over, for she was a good girl, a very good girl who gave him no trouble, but—now Jane sees it—she was not one of his successes. She depressed him too.

"Sasha. How is Sasha?"

"Her divorce is pending," Jane says. "At least she can't afford a shrink now. That's one consolation."

Jane sits very still. That her mother adored a humbug Jane has been ready, even eager, to swallow, but that her love was unrequited—it's intolerable. That it went on for fifteen years, that weekly revival of the corpse of her marriage in Dr. Z's more perfect maleness, was the doctor's crime, a crime not of vanity and cheap self-love, as Jane has long pictured it, but of mild neglect! All the while he had not even loved her—he had hardly noticed her. It went on for fifteen years because all the while he was thinking of something else—his mistress, his daughter, his tomato plants, God knows what—and had allowed Sasha simply to use herself up.

"Sasha. How is her potting?"

"Now that she needs to do it for a living, she thinks she's developed an allergy to clay."

Zwilling barely nods at this. Jane sees that unless the news is good, he will not engage. He should be safe from Sasha, no longer a patient and three thousand miles away. He does not need a headache from her daughter—he has his own daughter to give him headaches. He peers tiredly at Jane: Why are you here?

"How could you let my mother stay in therapy for fifteen years?" Jane shouts at him. "You know she used it to keep from doing anything else."

"You might be right," Zwilling says mildly, after a short pause, his eyes gliding towards the outer door he hopes Jane will make use of presently. It is not agreement, just a refusal to take her on.

"She might have got out of that marriage while there was still time," Jane persists.

"Perhaps her marriage was more important to her than you realize."

Jane narrows her eyes at this smarmy commonplace. "Then what do you think it means that she finally left my father before you were out of Baltimore a year? You were the ersatz husband, that's what. And don't tell me you weren't trying to please the ladies with those glitzy Ricky Ricardo suits you used to wear."

This insult to his former taste in clothes has some small success, since the doctor has come to agree with her.

"Psychiatrists make mistakes like other people," he says with a shrug.

"Do you think it's true that everybody can have what they want? Then tell me what happened to my mother. She started out so beautiful. Why couldn't she figure out anything in fifteen years that she really needed to know?"

Zwilling makes no reply. His face says, Don't you see the audience is at an end? For this hostile girl is not his business. Nothing has happened, but Jane understands there is nothing further she can get him to do, short of calling the cops on her, and she is not going to break his glass coffee table.

But she's not going to let it end either. If he won't save her, he'll have to throw her out. She sits there in silence for about two minutes and at last he says: "Do you really think I'm the one you're angry at?"

"I hope you're not sending me to my father," Jane says. "I'll never get anything I need out of him."

"I'm flattered that you think in five minutes you could get anything useful out of me."

"Oh no," Jane says. "All I want to know is why you couldn't save my mother in fifteen years."

He shrugs.

"I'm taking this magazine," Jane announces.

"It doesn't belong to you."

"Well, I can't give it up right now." She is thinking: Having come here was worse than a waste. It was whining and beggary. I should have paid him for his time.

"All right," he says. "I would like you to return it."

Knowing she won't, feeling more naive than deranged, Jane rushes out of his office.

Why wasn't there ever a comic called *Her True Adventure*? A monthly rag with a circulation of 50,000. All girls like Jane. Jane asks herself this as the moneygreen Buick inches west on Wilshire through the floating wreckage of the antiwar march. She doesn't mind that no psychiatrist will ever cure her. She's sick and tired of feeling like the only one. Along Wilshire she looks without hope for the Valiant, or for Jimmy's golden head. Small groups trail through late afternoon traffic, here and there torn pants or a bloody forehead, they find cars and funnel into them, nose into traffic with the parking tickets still flapping under their windshield wipers. They are stunned by their adventure. Jane, a less virtuous piece of wreckage in a moneygreen Buick, yields. *Missed it*, she thinks. *Lost him.* And at the same time, heading back to Jimmy, she pictures herself on the cover of a comic book called *Her True Adventure.* Ten years ago she would gladly have sprung for a copy, even if the pretty, gritty-faced heroine in pointy sunglasses on the cover, driving a fast, outdated, unreliable roadster at sunset down a deserted highway in the rufous Sierras, under a thought balloon like I'VE GOT TO GET TO JIM ON TIME! had turned out to be fundamentally living for love like every other pulp heroine. She sees that no psychiatrist will ever cure her heart, which hurts for good reason. It has been folded the wrong way as many times as the crumpled map in her glove compartment. All that crazy driving in the service of love or to flee it—for that's what it means to have been born the happiest of female babies, that she lives for love like every other girl, only with a lot more zooming off in the contrary direction. Anyway she's sick and tired of being a freak. She wants *Her True Adventure*, and what she gets is *GROPE*, in an overconfident printing of 150 copies, and heaven knows she would never buy one.

I'VE GOT TO GET TO JIM ON TIME!

She pushes through the purple curtain into Walter's at five, two hours late, and looks straight into the face of her lover, Jimmy, larger than life on TV. He is in profile above a PEACE NOW sign, a foot across from nose to earlobe, for some reporter has noticed his beauty.

The face is a still behind the titles on the evening news. No one asks Jane where she has been. They assume she was at the march too. "Where's the star of the show?" they ask her. "We got separated," she replies, trailing a gray rag down the bar. Everyone is wondering if Jimmy got beaten up or thrown in jail. And now that Jane has shown up without him his martyrdom is complete. "He sure was a good-looking boy, your hubby," Marie says, as though he were already dead. "Bet he got his purty face messed up good," Billy rasps. There follows a chorus of Shaddaps along the bar, at this carelessness of the feelings of the ladies present.

Billy has been in poor standing at Walter's since Marie showed up lately with a black eye. "Aw, Billy can't help himself," Marie says thickly. For Marie's sake Billy is tolerated, barely tolerated, by the regulars.

Jimmy does not appear in the actual news, but such is the suggestive power of that still, it is as if all that happens at the march happens to that luminous, familiar, poetically missing face. The moiling clouds of tear gas, temples streaming black blood, limp bodies stuffed like corpses into a paddy wagon —even Jane begins thinking all this is Jimmy, though not quite with the rapture the barflies are experiencing.

"Those are some cold modern-time gorillas," Leroy observes, looking at the riot troopers in their gear, and Marie, almost in tears, tells Jane: "Good Lord. I hate to think those goons took your hubby away." "Oh yes," Sam says, "they done took him. He was in it, or why'd they show his pitcher up front like that?" And the tension of frustrated fellow-feeling in the bar is terrific. Walter tells Jane to set em up, and have one herself. Leroy stands everyone a beer, and Jane has one of those too. Billy grudgingly orders a round. Jane draws beer after beer and in between she drinks it as fast as she can. She lags behind the others, but not by much, and when Walter sets her a little shotglass of some clear orange fluid next to the toaster oven, she throws that down too.

For Jane, black sandbars are already rising at the far ends of the bar. She struggles to count change, all the regulars whistle, blubber, and applaud, and at last Jane is swept away. She too believes her lover is being bandaged in some emergency room or on ice in some jail, so that she is the last to see him punch his way through the purple curtain up front and take a barstool, unaware, for the moment, that the commotion is in his honor. He stares ill-temperedly at Jane, and when she approaches he leans across the bar and informs her: "From now on, love, I think of you as more a bitch than a beauty."

She gathers him into her dwindling focus. His skin and clothes are all there, no more holes in anything than when he left, but his eyeballs are threaded with rose, his voice tends to bray. She sees he has stopped in a bar on the way home.

"Can you stake me to a few beers?" he asks Jane. "I wish to be drunk."

"You don't need me," she says, gesturing towards his public, and now he notices. "We just saw you on the TV," Marie is telling him. "I never knew such a handsome young gent. And brave!"

"Who, me?"

"You just missed yourself. Your face was all over the pitcher tube. Sorta sideways."

Jimmy looks incredulously at Jane, who nods.

"Well, I declare. Fame is a capricious mistress, isn't she?" he says, smiling sweetly at Marie. Marie snaps open her round blue purse whose strap is secured with a safety pin.

"I would personally like to buy you a drink on me," she says, laying a dollar on the counter. Her fingernails rest on top of it, painted a chalky pink, one raised in a gnarled coquettish arabesque.

Jimmy takes up the hand, kisses it. "I'm pleased to accept your offer, mademoiselle."

While the dollar lies neglected on the bar, Billy snatches it away. "You ain't buying no durn hippie no drink," he spits. "I've had about enough of you, old lady."

"Gimme that back!" Marie wails.

"Making eyes at that pipsqueak cause he's too chickenshit to fight like a man."

Jimmy laughs at this.

"For his country," Billy adds hastily, lest he seem to have offered to fight himself. "What's so funny, you pretty-face boob?"

"At least I don't hit girls," Jimmy says.

"Oh, Billy wouldn't hit a *girl*," Marie says, in all innocence.

"I said I had enough of you!" Billy screeches.

Walter comes over, as placid as a bathtub in flood. "What seems to be the trouble?"

"Marie was hoping to buy Jimmy a drink," Jane says.

Walter reaches down a bottle of Old Granddad and cascades a tumblerful over two little pieces of ice.

"How's that?" he says. "From the lady. For our hero of the night."

"Jane was a hero too," Marie points out, loyally but inaccurately. Walter pours another, smaller bourbon.

"For Jane."

The second Walter turns his back, Billy yells at Marie: "You made a monkey outa me for the last time." And he punches her, with confusing speed, in the eye—the same black eye that Jane has been thinking looks like a wrinkled, sun-deadened bit of tank-cover, so many spots of lizard green and brown.

Marie vanishes under the bar. She has to be dead, Jane judges, leaning over to see. Then Jimmy is helping her off the sticky floor. A gold-filtered cigarette butt clings to her waxy permanent; Jimmy brushes it off. Behind them Walter is half pushing, half dangling Billy toward the curtain up front by a handful of flannel shirt at the back of his neck.

"You shoulda threw me out before I had to bang her," Billy whines. "I'm going, I'm going. Y'all take that slippery broad's part every time."

While no one is looking, Jane's hand steals around Jimmy's deserted, hero-sized bourbon. She inwardly plugs off her nasal passages and drinks it, most of it, down.

Afterwards, pictures float on platforms in black space. Marie leans back on Walter's arm and suddenly he lowers a mercy killer's pillow into her face. But no, it's a bar towel stuffed with ice. Jimmy peers down at his empty whiskey glass and up at Jane. "It's a good thing you know what you're doing," he tells her, and spins away on his barstool to talk to Leroy. Then Jane is splat across the bar from her breasts to her chin, and Sam is looking away in embarrassment. "See don't you have thirty cent on you for this child, a corder and a nickel," he is saying to someone. "A corder and a nickel." He digs in his pocket. "She can't count change no more." "I can too," Jane hears herself say very faintly, then, "I CAN TOO," at the top of her voice. Whereupon sadly, resignedly, with dignity, Sam hands her a five-dollar bill—certainly he never saw that again.

And a disconnected view of Marie holding a white rabbit-shaped thing over her eye. Then she is at the deck rail of an invisible ocean liner singing goodbye. "N.O.," says Walter's fluty voice, "N.O., Billy can't come in here anymore, period, that's it." Something is shining in Marie's one good eye. Then bon voyage! she croons. Goodbye forever! Black billows close over her.

There is a spot of gold in all this murk—the back of Jimmy's head. Thank God her golden changeling has not left her. Jane thinks of that head bending over Marie's hand to kiss it and recalls the gallant cowhand of their first meeting. *May I ignite your cigarette? Do you think I'm just a male?* And suddenly she longs to kiss him on the mouth. I'VE GOT TO GET TO JIM IN TIME!

She comes out from behind the bar for the purpose, but can't get a fix on the mouth behind the golden back of his head. Jimmy won't speak to her, won't even look at her. She circles him like a moon; he revolves away on his barstool. It is Leroy, the astonished Leroy, she kisses, and then rather than explain, she is passing down the long bar, kissing all of them one by one, except Jimmy. She kisses Leroy, Sam, Croaker, Indian John, and a half dozen men of assorted shapes, ages, colors, before she comes to Walter. Whose hand closes firmly around her upper arm. He does not wish to be kissed. "Time to take her home," he announces, in a big clear voice.

The golden head swivels around at last. Appears. All the light in the long dim bar, as if it were a church collection plate, flows into it. "She knows what she's doing," it says, and turns away again.

A comfortable blank. This must be where Jane has her head down on the bar, until car keys are jingling in the dark like bells on a troika. She is hoisted up, handed over to Cochise and Mama, who, though she won't remember this, take her home to the Grandview. Cochise carries her upstairs, lays her flat on her back on the Murphy bed, fully dressed with her tennis shoes still on her feet and her key ring and purse placed carefully beside her.

She wakes up in this corpselike pose some little while later, a body and its identifying possessions alone in the dark, in her own bed, having no idea how she got here. She sits up, finds the floor with her feet, and begins to wander aimlessly about the apartment, only a little less drunk now than when she, oh no, she clutches her head, can I really have done it, french-kissed the whole bar, Leroy and Sam and ten or twelve others, pressed hotly into the laps of a whole platoon of old men who should have been left in peace? But now her drunkenness is of the quality of a glass paperweight in which the snow has settled, the inner landscape sparse, drowned, slow moving as a glacier, but exceedingly clear, or better say relatively clear. In the front room, set into the curtainless onyx of the picture window, *Harbor Fwy 1½* glows like something radioactive, a slab of that green found nowhere in nature, a dashboard indicator from outer space, telling her exactly where she is. Her pockets are completely clean, one hundred percent empty of tips—even the small change she arrived at Walter's with is gone. Remembers prying that five-spot out of Sam, its further history untraceable, and cringes with shame. Then fear zips crazily up the keyboard of her spine—her father's check! No, here it is in her purse, fleshpink in its torn envelope. And why is she swaying in the front window, clinging stupidly to her purse, her keys? Because her car is missing. Under the magnolia tops, beyond the garbage cans, is no moneygreen Buick. So with exceeding, better say relative, clarity, she stumbles out the door and down the front stairs, and starts up 22nd Street towards Hoover to retrieve it.

The red light at Hoover shines at the distant intersection like an appliance left on in an ugly kitchen. Even in her condition she knows better than to be walking this street at this hour, whatever this hour may be. She tries to see all of 22nd at once —under every fluted streetlamp, the same dusty pollen of light over sidewalk and curbstone, eternal broken colonnade of garbage cans, nothing human except, in the next block, a man and woman slowdancing together in the middle of the street, draped over each other as if either body would fall down alone, their voices stoppered in a kiss. Somewhere a door slams with a rattle of loose glass panes. When a pair of headlights pops into view at Hoover and swells down 22nd, Jane launches heavily over sagging chickenwire and ducks behind a plyboard doghouse. On all fours she waits for the car to pass, then stumbles on. Another car comes and she squats behind a hedge, curses when it snags her hair. It does not occur to her to wonder at herself. She might have been staggering around dark streets in a low-down city all her life, clinging to lampposts and crouching behind garbage cans. She knows what she's doing. No one can possibly show up in this place at this time who would have her best interests at heart. The slowdancers don't count. Their tongues coiled in a long kiss, they have inserted all their power of menace into each other for the time being. Not hiding from them but watching them carefully, Jane treads unsteadily by.

Now she is standing in front of Walter's, the moneygreen Buick forgotten by the curb at her back. To persuade herself she can walk upright she is gripping the frayed curtain with both hands. The place is still alive. The jukebox is playing. She tries to peek through holes in the curtain without being seen. Jimmy—it is Jimmy she wants—but now she loses her balance and stumbles inside. Stands there blinking. Jimmy is gone. Walter, wiping down the bar in slow, morose orbits, steps back at the sight of her and gets that fixed look under the eyes as if the whole great baby face had been done in wax. This face, Jane knows, precedes ejection of a regular. Okay, okay, I'm going.

Except it is worse than that. Not only Walter but Sam and Croaker, Leroy and Indian John are all looking at her funny with that hard inscrutable gaze of your public in exhibitionist dreams—the kind where you show up at work without any clothes on, and think if you just act normal, maybe people won't notice. And in fact people stare, yet don't react. From the men at the bar comes just such a look. Jane sees she has vexed these gentlemen in a very particular way. When she was their little girl they were safe from themselves, but when she was bad they were horrid. All at once she was that free-of-charge, any-dick-at-all jane of myth and legend. They, knowing themselves to be any dick at all, are dazed and affronted.

Propelled by the shame of the four along the bar, Jane backs out of Walter's again while Walter is still forming his words. She knows Walter would never fire her. To be stuck up or violent are the only crimes around here. She fights her own silly shame, slams the door of the Buick on it, but she knows already she will not be back.

Muttering to herself, trying not to be unhappy about it, even rather droll to get the heave-ho for acting like a hot tamale, she drives down 22nd a little faster than she should, bumps over a brown grocery bag lying in the street that makes a sickening crunch as if it had a dead cat in it, swerves wide around a six-pack of empties standing on the pearly blacktop where the slowdancers were, slides through the stop sign at Magnolia. When she passes here during the day, all the gypsy men pour off the Romanoffs' stoop and swarm around the Buick in the intersection, offering to do her body work. *Risible rates*, they say, rolling their *R*'s. What body work, Jane asks indignantly. There's not a dent on this Buick, just a few pock marks. We fix, they insist cheerfully. *Risible rates*.

Afraid she is going to be unhappy after all, Jane spots something that may save her—Jimmy's Valiant parked in front of the Grandview. She does not see that Jimmy is in it until it lurches away when she pulls up. Confused by this but unable to part with her happiness so soon, Jane makes a U-turn and follows him.

Now even more so than when she was tacking on all fours from doghouse to garbage can, you may well ask what Jane thinks she's doing, flying through stop signs at 45 miles an hour, taking corners up one five-inch curb and down the other, tossing garbage cans out of her face like rodeo clowns, pushing WRONG WAY signs to strange angles with her swirling rear-end. Jane bounces after the ghost of an ice-green fender around and around a three-block square until it dawns on her—maybe this isn't a joke. Why wouldn't he want to see me? Now she might be unhappy, but instead, gazing at a streetlight throwing phantom snow across the garbage can lids, lost in the Arctic now, she only wants, terrifically, to sleep. She drives, all slumping mildness at last, to the Grandview, numbly climbs the stairs. Could easily puke, but it would be too much work. Find bed, fall down on it, is her plan.

She pushes the door, door is standing, she sees without curiosity, a little open, angling into the dark, dark alive and glinting incoherently, flecked, unfamiliar, pondlike. Door sticks against Murphy bed, ouch, how did she get out with the bed down, who cares. She crawls into the apartment on hands and knees over the mattress, swamped bridge, hisses and bubbles under her kneecaps like a wet. And penetrating, a sponge of cheap soup, wild garlic, wicking into her skirt—piss. Someone has pissed her bed.

Who. Don't ask, difficult, very perplexing question. Might even have pissed it herself, hand to crotch, no, baby is dry. Arrives at length at the far end of the mattress, slaps at light switch on the fake mantelpiece and tumbles off the bed into upside down light, flock, debris, pages, bread mold, ransack. Shut the light! Jane's pursuing foot locker has exploded, regurgitated, torn its paperback books in half, smashed its tarry ashtrays, spat out mildewed bras and panties and blown the sky-blue sheets formerly of the master bedroom of the house on Pocahontas County Road 601 half out the open window. Jane crawls to the window—more down there. Underwear in the scrawny hedge, pages blowing away. WHAT HAS HAPPENED.

Jane can't think. There are no suspects, only Jimmy. So don't ask. Sleep. She lurches onto two legs, fumbles out the light, gropes for the chair in the front room, drops into it and sleeps.

"Here I am, white girl."

Jane opens her eyes.

"That's my shank in your neck."

The point of something sticks in her clavicle, and now a glimmering minus sign floats before her eyes, licked greenish by *Harbor Fwy 1½*.

Jane sees it. Already her heart is off and running like a wild goose cross country, but behind it, the mind refuses to move, says to itself: I'm tired of this. Not up to it. So this is what it means to learn from experience. Her mental wings unfold, then slump in the grass. Last time it was so much work, it went on so long, and all for what? This time she is already used to it.

"Who are you?" she whispers.

"You don't know me, white girl, but I know you."

The voice, soft and ringing, she is certain she has not heard before. She tries to see the face. He must be very black, because it isn't there—only a shadow darker than the dark, a stripe of colorless light outlining the flare of a nostril.

"I eyeballed you a hundred times up Hoover by that old juice-head bar you work in."

"You did," Jane says, recalling no one.

"Every day you walk by me like you blind, and I say to myself, there's something else I want that I can't have. I know I could get you any time I want but I let you be a while. Give you a chance to see. Only you don't see, so I felt I should sense it into you. I don't argue with people. I show them."

This speech is long for the purpose. Despite its actual words, despite her wings gone flat, it is a speech, as surplus as an aria, art for art's sake. Jane begins to hope.

"I am blind," she says.

"Something wrong with your eyes?"

"Blind," Jane says. "See for yourself." She dangles her glasses at the ends of her fingers, having had the good luck to conk out in her chair with this mask on her face. Metal clunks against wood—he's put the knife on her desk. The glasses levitate.

"Whew," he says. "You blind, baby." Jane reaches out her hand. Her glasses fall gently into it.

"You should have talked to me on the street," she says. "I would have talked to you."

He doesn't answer this silly remark. The sad part is, it's true. She is one hundred percent civil to strange Negroes. Later, when she ceases to see them as Negroes, she's as rude to them as to anybody else.

She is not the soul of tact now. "If you wanted to fuck me so bad," she blurts, "why did you piss my bed?"

"Why I did what? Say what?"

"PISS. MY. BED."

Pause, then: "You funny-time, girl. I never piss no bed."

A note of disgust and even, if she is not mistaken, of alarm. Jane believes him, but she is a woman with blame to distribute, and he is a man who is inching backwards before it. Let mere justice impede no telling accusation once it is underway.

"I'm not FUNNY-TIME," she shouts. "LOOK at this place."

She jumps up to pound the light switch, her chair collapses in shock behind her. The two of them blink at the wrecked apartment.

"So where do you want to lie down!" She presents the mattress, a slumping relief map half off its frame, with a dark continent of piss in the middle of it. Shreds of pink nightie hang from the ceiling fixture, splashes of blood (which later turns out to be shoe polish—who would have thought Jane owned shoe polish?) are coagulating on the inlaid mirrors of the fake mantelpiece and brightly spot the piss-wet sheets.

Jane passes a hand over her eyes. I'VE GOT TO GET TO JIM ON TIME!

"He's gone crazy," she says aloud.

"Somebody hot at you, baby," he says.

"I guess so," she says wearily.

"Got no place to hide."

Jane looks up at this, remembering whom she is with. "Hide from who?" she says. "I wasn't trying to hide."

"Yes you was. Can't hide from the Rayman."

"Are you the Rayman?"

Silence, and Jane stares at her partner in conversation, a man after all concealing a knife on his person.

He is elegantly shaped, slightly long of face, and very black. He wears glasses himself, horn-rimmed, that are a little askew; they make him look intelligent and puzzled. He is dressed all in black like a prince in a classic comic, leans on the back of one arm against the wall, easy and familiar in his bones. His draped fingers make a black swan.

And he says to Jane: "What you staring at?"

"I can't believe I walked by you without seeing you," she says. "Was I with a blond guy?"

"I never saw you with no old man."

"Oh no," Jane says. "Please don't tell me that." For that could scare her to death, to think she's wearing a radio beam on top of her head that tells every idler who doesn't have her best interests at heart, COME GET ME I'M ALL ALONE.

"Tell the truth," she says, "please. You saw me somewhere tonight making a spectacle of myself." She trembles, looking sideways at the shapely head, the face closed and aloof rather than twisted by any obvious intention. And he is looking silently down at her. She might even have kissed him tonight, she realizes, might have shoved her tongue into his silent mouth—for she had pushed herself on every man along the bar at Walter's —but she feels sure that this one she would have remembered.

"I saw you," he says, "but you wasn't with no man."

"Oh yes I was," Jane says weakly.

"Naw," he says, "you wasn't. I saw you."

"What was I doing?"

He is slow to answer. He might be embarrassed for her.

"Scrooching down back of Horton's doghouse," he finally says.

Jane cringes. He even knows whose doghouse, Horton's. She recalls loose chickenwire, cracked earth under her fingernails.

Two headlights wobbling by. And now she sketches in this face watching her from between buildings, masked in its own blackness.

"You live in this neighborhood," she says.

"The Rayman don't live nowhere."

"You know this neighborhood."

"Too good."

"Don't say you never saw me with a guy on Hoover Street."

He reflects for a time, then declares: "That little gray who dog you around is invisible to me."

And he adds slowly, returning to business: "I done watched you a long time."

Jane goes empty, balloons enormous, loses all track of words. This is what it is to be somebody else's face of love. She wonders if he plans to kill her since he doesn't bother to hide his own face. At this point, she doesn't even care. She can't stand it any longer, this feeling that she's sending out some secret message that everyone can read but her. Which made her father gallop away in a sweat, his football under his arm. So that Willie Usher saw her coming a mile off. *When you going to be my freak?* And pretty soon she was his freak. Is she wearing her sexual organs on top of her head—not simply that wiry brown fright wig that so distressed her father, but a pink cunt smack in the middle of it? Which will never be safe until it puffs on a big fat cigar.

"You've got to tell me," Jane says. "Am I going around with something-I-shouldn't hanging out of my clothes? Why did you pick me?"

"You ain't doing nothing wrong," he says slowly. "Take it easy, baby, don't go funny-time on me."

"Please, please tell me," Jane says. "I have to know."

He's silent for some time, looking at her, and Jane suddenly sees: He likes me. He likes me now. He won't hurt me.

"Because you one of them," he says at last. "Ain't you one? Ain't you one?"

"One of what?"

"Ain't you one of Raymozo's—one of *them*, man. I done watched you a long time."

"I wish I'd seen you," Jane says.

"Don't matter no more."

Silence. Jane feels sick, deeply sick, like the inside of a well whose walls some creature is clawing its way up.

"Gotta sit," she says, and they sit, delicately, on the edge of the mattress. Her forehead sinks to her knees.

Comes his voice, low, hushed, a fogbound shimmer: "Remember, he looking at you."

"Who is?"

"The Rayman."

"Listen," Jane says. "I don't think I know the Rayman. Tell me. Tell me who the Rayman really is."

"Nobody know that," he says. "But I tell you. His daddy wunt black. And he wunt white. He was like light, man. You could see right through him. His name was Raymozo the Rayman the First. My mama, she was always funny-time. But the Rayman, he cared for her. He come from far away. He come at night when she couldn't see him. The Rayman did her like a man. That was before me. You see what I'm saying?"

Jane nodded.

"She up Camarillo now."

"Your mother told you?"

"No, man. She don't understand nothing about it. I heard it from the Rayman. I done told her. All she knew was a bunch of voices telling her I love you.

"And I said, Hey, that ain't bad, is it? Mama? A buncha folks saying I love you? And she say, Naw they ain't bad, it ain't bad, but it, you know, get on your nerves."

Jane says: "So your dad was from outer space."

"Who! The Rayman! He wunt from nowhere. In the can, man, he come in and out the walls. Like a wave. Like X rays. But wayever he see something he care for, he stick onto it."

Jane says in a low voice: "What makes you think he cares for me?"

"Because," he says, "he see you down here where life swobble off life so bad. He see your old man done cut you loose. And look, you still going around, ain't you? You ain't scared."

"I am, too, scared," Jane whispers. "I don't know what to do with myself I'm so scared."

"The way life swobble off life around here, you get scared. But the Rayman is looking at you now. Nothing can harm you. Say," he says. "What I come for—what I say I come for—you can forget it. *You with the Rayman.* You don't have to do nothing."

He gets to his feet and walks to the picture window, stands in the dark in front of that green glow found nowhere in nature, with his back to Jane.

And a swooping gratitude lifts her in turn from the mattress, wraps her in its wings like a vulture. And now she is staggering towards him. "But I want to," she tells him, "I want to," and touches his elbow, which is startlingly hot and dry. He whirls around and pushes her off, she reels, grinds along the bottom of black waves, and the next moment is hanging onto the back of a chair and the windowsill, vomiting onto the floor. She retches again and again. Nothing comes up but a thick clear string of yellowish gall. Finally she stands up, shaking.

"You sick, baby," he points out.

"I'm all right," she says. "Drank too much last night."

"Gone get you some milk. Glass of milk what you need."

Jane thinks, I'm so pathetic, I've fallen so low, that a rapist instinctively takes care of me.

He moves in his black clothes like something written in smoke to the little kitchen in back. The refrigerator door opens, closes. He comes back.

"We gone get you some milk," he says.

"You mean out there?" Jane says. "On the street?"

"Dairy Dreem up the Boulevard."

Jane looks at the window, trying to comprehend. Outside the sky is the color of soaked ash, shot with little rills of molten solder. Almost dawn. They start down the stairs. So he, not Jane, is finding a way for this night to come to an end.

They walk two blocks east in silence. Then Jane remembers: "I'm broke."

"I take care of it, baby," he tells her.

The two turn north on Hoover. In the caked darkness under the freeway overpass, their shoulders brush. He walks fast, Jane realizes, like her. The gait of a stranded nomad—you walk like this from childhood or not at all. This is the way she always went before Willie Usher sold her a car.

They reach the Dairy Dreem. The shack, on a small pad of broken asphalt, is astonishingly alive at this hour, cars parked every which way or rolling up and down the crumbling curbs, windows open, soul music pouring out. Jane hangs back while Raymozo the Rayman threads his way to the window, a tall, sober, even ascetic figure in faded black, and as he passes, women stare after him, bosoms in sequins or scooped-out jersey swinging in his direction, their hands clutching their purses or hair or the lobes of their décolletage. A few people peer at Jane, her white face, dun cloud of hair and baggy purple tights, with hostile curiosity. She slumps, to look inconspicuous, but what is the point? Better to concentrate on feeling out of place, to get that by heart—for this, to be out of place anywhere, Jane knows, is the egg she sits on, the future she is hatching.

He comes back with a half pint of milk and a straw. They walk slow so that Jane can drink the stuff.

"You feel better, baby?" he wants to know.

They are on the north side of 22nd, where a few last houses back up against the freeway embankment. The new light is gray and the world still colorless. Even the streetlights poke only small yellow holes in it. Now Jane and her guide are standing in front of Jimmy's storefront. Jane's feet simply stop here. She is holding a small, red, half-empty box of milk.

"This is my boyfriend's place," she says.

The Rayman glances at the building, says nothing, but Horton's doghouse is right across the way. He knows whose place this is as well as she does. *That little gray who dog you around is invisible to me.*

She points at the streakily whitewashed windowlight. "I just want to peek in and see if he's there."

He still says nothing, looks down at her with half-lowered

eyelids. She backs away a little, towards the storefront.

He says: "Is that right talk, when you with one man, to ask him can you go pink in on another?"

"Is that right talk?" Jane repeats dumbly. She begins to weep.

The Rayman says: "Aw, pink on him if you want to. I didn't mean nothing by it."

But Jane doesn't want to. They tack across the deserted street, and walk on, slowly, the last half block to the Grandview.

Jane puts out her hand, and the Rayman shakes it. "Well, goodbye," Jane says. "Thanks for the milk."

344

He starts digging in his pocket. Going to give me something, Jane thinks in despair. *I take care of it, baby.* She stands still, holding the red carton of milk.

He pulls out a bit of yellow pencil, and a dollar bill. Writes a telephone number under FOR ALL DEBTS, PUBLIC AND PRIVATE. Hands it to her and walks briskly away.

When the front door closes behind her, she runs upstairs to watch him from the picture window, to see which way he goes. But by the time she looks down through the magnolias, he is out of sight. Probably eyeing me from some hole in the wall across the street, she thinks, and steps back from the window too late. For it is this feeling, that he can see her effortlessly and at will, while she, no matter how hard she looks, remains blind—this is the feeling that will not leave her.

○
○
● **Contra-**

madonismo

It is the next day around noon, and Jane is staring out the picture window. In the empty sky over the freeway, a flat sun keeps rolling sideways in and out of silver clouds like a quarter flirting with the coin slots on a public washing machine. Cochise and Mama are behind her, squeezed up to the rickety breakfast table. Jimmy sits on the floor, broom and dustpan by his knee.

Jane has just offered to whip up a mess of pancakes for the lot of them. Having heard this with her own ears, she turns to the window, squinting with disbelief. But already Cochise is ransacking his pockets for enough bills to cash her father's check, and Mama is scratching up a grocery list with the butt of a pencil. Only Jimmy shakes his head. He knows Jane is an alien in the cozy realm of pancakes and syrup and butter and the rest of it. She doesn't know how to make them, never has made them, just prods one dry pancake with a fork when Jimmy makes them. I for a fact hate pancakes, she confides, under her breath, to the coin machine sun. How then has she come to this pass? Why ask the crew behind her to break half-baked bread together?

Some half-baked motherly gesture of conciliation, that must be what Jane had in her mind. The day began with an argument.

"You know who this person is and you won't go to the cops?"

"I sort of know who he is." Jane has told Jimmy no names,

much less a telephone number. "There's no point subjecting myself to cops, since he didn't hurt me."

"You're going to let this guy walk around until he jumps some other broad?"

No answer.

"Some other white girl who's stupid enough to take an apartment in this neighborhood?"

Jane does not point out that she appears to be uniquely stupid in this regard. Instead she says: "Look, if it comes to that, he did less damage around here than you did."

"I'm sorry, but I swear it would drive possibly the sanest man on earth to desperate acts, living with you."

Jane turns to look at possibly the sanest man on earth. "If you had just hauled me home like a real comrade," she says.

"Sorry. You've trained me to think you always know what you're doing."

"Couldn't you have just taken me home like a blood brother instead of a silly, outraged boyfriend?"

"Blood brothers don't french-kiss every bum in the barroom!"

Jane shouts: "You realize your secret mission is to be a million miles away whenever I'm in danger."

"What can I do when you're broadcasting TAKE ME to every joker who applies?"

After which, silence descends, except for the noise of Jane and Jimmy, cleaning up the apartment. Jane dumps another dustpan of broken glass, trampled underwear, and torn pages into a Piggly Wiggly bag. A puff of dust rises into her face and she coughs a little cough of accusation. And Jimmy glances up at her, having just shoved a wad of wet paper towels, good for scrubbing at shoe polish, into another Piggly Wiggly bag. His face says the state of disgrace is too familiar; he isn't cowed. "It's disgusting," he suddenly snarls, "to live in and out of a grocery sack. Can't we buy a goddamn trashcan? It makes me think of goddamn Pete and Mother, who never bought a kitchen trashcan in twenty-five years!"

Jane gazes at him. Jimmy has gone over the edge. She has

driven him over the edge. But what lies south of the edge is not madness—it's kitchen trashcans, a Sears credit card, and a tab at the lumber yard. Order. Solid construction. Big money.

Soon Cochise sticks his head around the front door. He addresses Jane, pointedly ignoring the male. "Has that young feller of yours plumb lost his reason? I brung you home last night and he jumped out on the stairs at me and stuck me with a cooking fork."

Cochise shows his torn sleeve and a small red scratch under it. Jane looks at him blankly. She has no recall of Cochise's role in the previous night's cracked dream. "Where was I?" she asks.

"Passed out." Mama's creaky voice floats up the stairs behind Cochise. She appears in an oddly twisted housecoat; Jane sees it has three buttons left and Mama has used whatever button-holes came to hand. "Walter called up and we come get you," Mama explains. "Cochise hauled you up the stairs. I done the driving," she says proudly, "in that old rich boy's machine with the headlights on."

"Oh, you got your license," Jane says dumbly.

"Heck no. I can drive good now, what I need a license for? That Jimmy," she adds, "he's such a good-hearted young feller. Why, he took the time and showed an old girl like me how to drive. Now I reckon he had one too many last night and figgered you and Cochise was pitching woo, hee hee! If that ain't the beatnest thing I ever heard."

"That boy stuck me with a cooking fork," Cochise repeats in a hurt tone. "This ain't going to be an everyday thing now, is it? If he means to take up scrapping, you better learn him to throw a punch like a man."

"Don't worry," Jane says. "His job is to be a million miles away at the first sign of danger."

"Say, is you two having a wrangle?" says Mama.

"No," Jimmy says.

"Yes," says Jane.

Jimmy whispers: "Just tell me it's what you want and I'll never leave you again. Never."

Cochise and Mama are drifting into the room from the landing, and Jane winces, thinking of the pissed mattress—she and Jimmy simply flipped it over—steals a glance at the cracked mirror in the woodwork over the Murphy bed, the web of fine lines where the shoe polish bottle bounced off it. Also the blond stain of the hardwood floor isn't looking so good where Jimmy lost patience with paper towels and went after the spots of shoe polish with a scouring pad. Then again, Cochise is three-fourths blind and Mama oblivious to housekeeping. Jane decides it's safe to let them in.

Cochise squints into Jimmy's face and says: "A cooking fork, by Jesus."

"Well, I wasn't going to carry a knife," Jimmy says. "I might hurt somebody."

All four of them start to laugh. This is where Jane conceives the strange idea of making a feast of pancakes for those gathered here on the slightly damaged premises. "Come in, sit down," she hears herself say. "I'll make pancakes for everybody, if someone can just cash this check so Jimmy can go get groceries."

Now Jimmy peers at her in amazement. He catches her eye, shakes his head no. His eyes inquire clearly, Are you sure you know what you're doing? Jane turns to gaze out the picture window.

"Write down butter, flour, eggs, milk, syrup . . . "

"Whoa there, how you spell syrup?" Mama says.

"I'm going to the desert," Jimmy says, "tonight. To see about a job"—offering Jane an excuse.

"Eat first," says Jane. "What else do we need?"

"I'm in no mood to cook," Jimmy tells her sharply, to remind her how such things usually get done.

Jane ignores him. "Excuse me, I'll be *in the bathroom,*" he then tries, and tiptoes off theatrically to that destination. He wishes Jane to recall that, in his fury over the intruder's rubber-soled footprints across the bottom of the bathtub, he has rigged a burglar alarm on the window above it, which has no lock, by stringing up half their kitchen utensils. Even Cochise could not miss the iron frying pan, cheese grater, and rusty colander poised to clatter on one long shoelace into the bathtub at the first quiver of the window frame.

But this warning makes no impression on Jane. Sullenly Jimmy goes off to Jack's Cut-Rate. Soon Roger appears in the open doorway, carrying a fifth of cheap vodka.

"What's going on?" Roger says. "I know you two don't indulge in housecleaning for the sheer fun of it. What happened to this little mirror? It smells sort of funny in here."

"Shut up," Jane says through her teeth, taking the vodka.

A little later, she is swigging vodka straight out of the bottle at a kitchen counter that could be a scale model of a lime quarry —hardened hills of flour in all directions, stagnant milky pools of groundwater, white dust clouds of TNT. Jimmy squeezes behind her through the tiny kitchen on his way to the refrigerator for a beer. "You know you don't knead pancake batter, Jane," he says. "Don't you?"

"What was that?"

"That should be a batter, not a dough."

"Are you telling me how to cook?" Jane shouts. "I'm going to thin it with vodka."

"That sounds like a great idea," Jimmy says after a long pause. He disappears.

"You can't put too much vodka in these things!" Jane calls after him, slopping vodka into the bowl. Presently she yells: "Where's the frying pan?"

No answer.

"Where's that damn frying pan?" she repeats, louder, swaying in the archway.

"I seen it," Cochise says.

"Well, where the hell is it!" Jane barks, and Cochise looks alarmed.

"Weren't that a big black frypan standing on its neck in the bathroom window?" he says timorously.

"Oh for the love of Pete, I despise men," Jane bursts out,

and, lowering her head like a bull, she tramps angrily and unsteadily into the bathroom.

"Weren't that a frypan?" Cochise asks, looking around for a sane person.

"What you got a frypan in the bathroom for?" Mama inquires.

The iron pan, grater, colander, a whole trolling line of pie plates, odd pots, and silverware come crashing down into the bathtub.

"Goddamn it!" Jimmy bursts out. "Because it's a goddamn burglar alarm. Because some guy broke in here last night, but don't worry, he ended up buying Jane a milkshake instead of raping her."

"I can't get this damn thing loose," Jane hollers from the bathroom.

"Leave it alone," Jimmy yells back. "You can't cook that strange shit you mixed up anyway. Are you trying to poison people?"

Now Cochise is shouting louder than the other two. "Who was it? I'll find out which of them no 'count punks it was and rip him to pieces."

Jane appears in the bathroom door, the frying pan in her hand. "That's right. I'd like to poison everybody. Every single one of you."

"Now, Jane. You just got yourself drunked up," Mama points out. "We're gone home, ain't we, Cochise?"

"I'm going to bust that punk's head for him, that's what. I'm going to hang his black hide on a fence. Wha'd he look like?"

"Okay, go home. EVERYBODY GET OUT!" Jane yells.

"He didn't harm her," Jimmy tells Cochise. "Don't get so excited."

"Didn't harm her! Lookit that sweet girl gone crazy as a bedbug!"

"She's just drunk."

Jane sees Roger laughing. She slings the frying pan at him. It bounces off the wall, gouging a fist-sized crumbly hole in the plaster.

"WILL YOU GET OUT!" she shrieks. "I CAN'T STAND TO LOOK AT A MAN'S FACE ANOTHER MINUTE!"

Jimmy stands in the open door, crooks his finger urgently, and everyone edges by him and down the stairs. They speak to him in low voices as they go.

"AND QUIT WHISPERING BEHIND MY FACE," Jane adds. As soon as the door is closed she yanks down the unmade Murphy bed and flops on it, staring at the ceiling. Jimmy lies down beside her.

"This place is ruined," Jane says.

"Maybe so," Jimmy agrees.

"Aren't you going to the desert?" she asks him.

"Do you think I'm just a male!" Jimmy says. "I'm not going to leave you here in this condition. Go to sleep. I swear I don't know how you stay on your feet." Jimmy reaches down Jane's book from the fake mantel over their heads and begins to read. *Island Life*. Jane sleeps.

About two hours later, Jane completes the destruction of her apartment at the Grandview by her own act, but this act she knows only by report, that evening, from Jimmy. She gets out of bed and wanders into the kitchen, where Jimmy supposes she means to draw a glass of water. Instead she lowers the oven door, pulls down her underpants, sits, and before he can jump up and stop her, pisses all over it. By the time he gets there she is rising stony-faced, pulls up her drawers as though nothing is wrong, and returns to bed with her eyes straight forward and unblinking—a somnambulist's.

"A terrorist act of *contramadonismo*," Jane suggests at the end of this account.

"Huh?" Jimmy says.

"You know, a protest against woman slaving over a hot stove." It is dusk now, and Jimmy is getting ready to go to the desert.

"I doubt it," Jimmy says. She doesn't dispute this, since around here Jimmy has always done ninety percent of the cooking.

Jimmy is in the desert. As the sun sinks under the picture window, Jane orders herself to act normal. Walk to bodega for bread. As she passes Horton's doghouse, she knows she isn't walking properly, knows she has popsicle-stick legs, gimp arms, metal kneecaps like a polio victim. She walks as if touched by slippery eyes; her own eyes drive a fixed, moveable point down the sidewalk five yards in front of her.

On the way home, when she gets near Horton's doghouse, someone says her name. *Jane.* She glances left and can't make out his face in the dark. He is sitting on a stoop with others. Could it be the way he holds his jaw close to his chest, so that light falls by it like water dripping from eaves?

Raymozo, she says, stopping.

They all nod, and she walks on. No remarks fly after her as they would have done from that stoop in the past. She is under his protection.

In front of the picture window, Jane rolls a blank sheet of white paper into her typewriter. She had better hurry, that's what she gets out of all this. She had better write her life story at the speed of light—when there comes a crash from the bathroom, tinkling silver and the gong of the iron frying pan as it bounces around and around the bathtub. She sits very still, listening to the rapid plink, plink, plink, of someone's black playground hightops down the long xylophone of the fire escape, going away. Now probably Raymozo is insulted—the frying pan was not welcoming—but is he intending to pop in the bathroom window whenever he craves a word with Jane, at any hour of the night or day? She tells herself she is disrupted rather than scared, but her fingers are shaking so badly they can't find the proper keys on the typewriter. She stares doggedly at the empty page another moment, then runs to the bathroom and sets the frying pan and colander, spoons and pieplates on the windowsill over the tub again.

Next day, at his insistence, Jane drives Cochise in the big truck to look for J. T. McNeil. He is telling her about every fight he ever had.

Starts with the daily battles at St. Patrick Mission School in Anadarko, where his father's brother dumped him with the padres at the age of six. "Hell, in a week I lost count. They learned me to take care of myself good there—I don't mean the padres."

Jane jams the brake pedal and far, far away, the blue International slows down from six miles an hour to five, rolls off the blurry end of a dirt driveway on 25th Place and into a pile of tarpaper roofing. Cochise climbs down, goes around back of a shed marked DE SALIS DEMO, returns with a piece of plyboard.

They inch up the driveway at Cochise Realty. Jane does not want to roll into the ashcans out back, though Cochise says that's what they're there for, to keep the truck from ploughing through a board fence. Inside the office, Cochise tears open a few pieces of mail and pretends to peruse them through the pink aspic of his glasses, then stuffs them in his back pocket for Mama to read him later. In the front room he inspects the necktie pile for any sign of McNeil. He is hoping for fish boxes, calls Jane in to look, but there are none. McNeil's trail has been cold for a week. "Could be he died on me and I ain't heard, if the padres got him." Cochise sounds resigned, even defeated.

"Maybe he's sick," Jane suggests. "Maybe he stopped over at the Catholic Mission for a few days."

"Naw," Cochise says, "he couldn't sleep with all them other bodies so close around him. He'd as soon kick first."

More a millionaire than a bum after all, Jane thinks. But she thinks it forgivingly, as from one millionaire to another. After all, a year ago—only a year!—it was dormitory life, bodies all around her in spiny pink hair curlers, nightmares of teeth crumbling to Roquefort cheese, and the shrunken white ring of a desk study lamp—it was hatred of life in a dormitory that drove her into the life so pregnable to mischance she is living now, the adventurous life she would have called it, what a joke, no heart is left for adventures, and even so she would not go back (not that they would have her back): Only she sees plainly that what she wanted all along was simply to be left alone! A small order? A pipe dream even for a millionaire, it turns out.

They roll up Hoover and down Vermont, looking in vain for McNeil.

"Lemme tell you how I bankrolled the move west—this is me and Mama and my partner Izzy in a Model A Ford. I'm playing pool, snooker, tonk, skin, anything for a buck." He passed through Anadarko, stopped by the Kiowa Agency, and who should stroll in but the same uncle who had dumped him with the padres twenty-five years before.

"He knew me," Cochise says with heavy drama, "he knew me." The nephew stepped forward, six foot four, nose like a hunk of spoiled dough, and the uncle donated three thousand in cash to his interests on the spot.

"But when we come outside, I still had to put my boot in that Ind-yun's face for deserting another Cherokee to save hisself a dollar. Only son of his dead brother!"

"I thought you were Kiowa," Jane says.

"That ain't the point. I'm a full-blooded Oklahoma Indian and proud of it," Cochise declares.

"Speaking of the point, what's this all about?" Jane says. "You seem to be putting a heavy stress on the warrior aspect."

Cochise glares blindly at her for a time, then out the windshield. A small flock of priests from St. Boniface is strolling on the east side of Vermont; with their cassocks belling out behind them, they remind Jane of a pirate ship in full sail, and suddenly they duck into the Louisiana Fish Store. Jane sneaks a look at Cochise—thank God he can't see them.

Cochise finally says: "I heard that rascal pounding down the fire escape last night. Why don't you tell me who done it to you?"

Jane says: "Nobody *done it* to me."

"You think I can't put a stop to it? Why, I could take his black ass and wrap it around his head. I could—"

"You could," Jane says wearily, "if you could find him."

"I could find him with these," Cochise growls, "but you ain't helping." He is holding up his very large work-bleached hands, the calluses yellow like parchment, the nails ringed and scored.

Jane says: "You're not going to get yourself hurt over me. I'm not that kind of girl."

"I could find him," Cochise repeats, wounded and even a little suspicious now.

Jane sighs. *If you could find him,* she is saying to a blind man who always found his enemy. Who is Jane to protect a common rapist? And if she never quizzed Raymozo the Rayman on his qualifications for that title, in all candor she assumed the worst. So why does she save him? The truth is she negotiated her destiny with a private individual who did not have Jane's interests at heart, and they came to an agreement that Jane was to have her freedom, and to live. Against the smoking plain of her private relations, every inch of it disputed territory, with this small treaty she is content. So what if her hands are shaking, her nerves no party to the agreement? And she could wish the guy weren't still trying to break in her bathroom window. He had no right to put her life in question, no more than anyone else does, and yet she believes or deludes herself that it has always been in question, and upon the whole she has come off in the judgment many times worse than now, without exacting punishment.

Her own father, for example, would have found the planet Earth a better place if she had never landed on it. He, Philip Turner, might have sacrificed himself for her. Now it is too late. She will not accept Cochise nor any other man in his place.

"Please." She puts a hand on Cochise's shoulder. "The best thing to do is nothing."

Cochise says: "Don't pay me no more rent if you won't let me help you."

Jane says: "I couldn't do that."

"Then you're going to quit me, aincha?"

Jane shakes her head No or I don't know, pushes the faraway brake and feels for the road.

A

golden

gun

Now to the gun. Jane will always remember it as a golden gun, a foot long from the hammer to the end of the barrel, a cowboy-looking, pearl-handled six-shooter just like in the Westerns, its grip long and arched like a horse's neck—a COLT SINGLE ACTION ARMY .45 LONG COLT (this redundancy appeared in fine print on the barrel, and Jane was the type to read everything, even a gun). But above all she will remember it as gold, almost as gold as the two-inch brass cartridges looped side by side in its belt.

Only, there are no golden guns, and never were, for the gun was already old when Pete took it for a bad debt in the middle of the Depression and hung it high on the wall of the shack that later became Jimmy's, a curio of the Wild West that no one ever dreamed of taking out in the desert and shooting. So it had to be one of those nickel-plated .45 long Colts the Army issued to Indian scouts, which turned yellow in the hands of devotees of tobacco—must have come from the kit of some pariah brave in the pay of Ft. Dodd or Ft. Sill, "a friend to everybody," wearing buffalo-strip earrings and a greasy plaid gentleman's waistcoat, a mashed silk top hat with a cavalry bugle pinned smack in the middle of it—a figure at once adroit and clownish, squatting by a rock over the Canadian River, his nickel-plated, never-cleaned gun ripening to greeny gold in a cloud of tobacco smoke.

So there you are, Jane thinks. Another orphan Kiowa or debased scion of the Cherokee Nation, a wandering outcast, an ur-hustler like Cochise whom the padres never got, must have owned this old equalizer. But Jane and Jimmy do not ask Cochise if he ever ran across a gun like this in the late days of the Indian Territory. They do not let on to Cochise about the gun at all. Instead they let down the Murphy bed and stuff the thing under there nervously, in a heap.

"You've got to get rid of it," Jane says. "Even if it won't shoot."

At this point neither of them believes it could shoot. An ancient princely toy, it seems more likely to blow up, or—Jane's thought—to attract criminals magically to the spot rather than to repel them.

"But he would still get out of the way if I pointed it at him, wouldn't he? I mean, if that guy opens the window again and doesn't run, I'll kill him! If it shoots, that is."

Jimmy suddenly yanks the gun back out from under the bed, loads it in fumbling haste, and points it at the bathroom window.

"Hold it right there. Blam," he says.

"I'm going to have a nervous breakdown," says Jane, clutching her hair in a wad.

Jimmy unloads the gun and looks up at her, his hand full of golden bullets.

"I have a job in the desert," he says, "if I want it." He slips the bullets into the gun again, click, click, click.

"Will you put that down?" Jane retreats to the front room. "My God, someone could get shot any minute. You, or me."

"It's with the Baron," Jimmy adds. "Starting next week. If I want it."

"If you want what?" Jane asks, puzzled, from behind the archway.

"If I want the job! I'd have to go back to the desert!"

"You're going to leave me alone here with that gun?"

"That's the whole point. I'll take the job, you'll come with me, we'll be rich and we won't need the gun."

"What job?"

Jane hears the weighty, gritty noise of six-shooter and belt sliding under the bed again. Jimmy comes through the archway.

"With Baron Moritz, the decorator. The guy is such a bandit, Jane! He takes these terrific mark-ups, he has more work than he knows what to do with, and the contracts start, *start*, at a hundred grand. I'd get salary and a percentage—"

"Is that thing loaded?"

"Of course it's loaded."

"But of course. Why ask." Jane whirls and stares out the picture window into the vapid blue over the freeway.

"That guy could be through the bathroom window in three seconds," comes the voice of reason.

"Jimmy! Just get it out of here."

"You wouldn't rather have a—"

A knock on the door, loud. They run through the archway. Jimmy opens to Cochise, who is carrying tools and the piece of plyboard from De Salis Demo. Jane posts herself at the foot of the Murphy bed, lest their landlord glance underneath and see the golden gun.

But of course he can barely make out the bed. His foot bangs into the metal frame—Jane jumps two feet—then he squints down at the mattress; touches it to make sure.

"Didn't mean to bust up your party," he says, embarrassed.

"Oh no, oh no," say Jane and Jimmy. Jane computes. In five days, since the night of Raymozo the Rayman, they haven't even kissed. "We were just—" They trail off vaguely, looking at each other without inspiration.

"Reading," Jane finishes.

"I mean to fix the window but good," Cochise says, turning into the bathroom.

"You can't just board it up," Jimmy says. "That's the fire escape."

"So? I ain't calling the fire chief. Are you?"

"We could at least try a lock first."

"You mean it ain't got a lock?" Cochise slides his big hand along the top of the lower sash. "Well, I'm a born fool. Them gypsies beat me for the rent and pinched the brass too."

"I'll go to De Salis," Jane offers hurriedly.

Cochise is entrusting her with certain passwords that will stir his front man into combing through the junkyard for a window lock, when Mama appears.

"Ain't it the beatnest thing? Cochise wanted to borry a shooting iron and plug the varmint," she reports.

Is this clairvoyance or only an epidemic of lower logic? With her shoulder Jane steers Jimmy to the end of the Murphy bed, positions him between Mama and the golden gun, glowing (or so Jane imagines) in its dark cave.

"With them eyes I reckon he'd get hisself kilt. Or get lucky and wind up dying in the pokey."

"I always been lucky," Cochise comments.

"Oh no," Jane says. "Don't even think about a gun." She gives Jimmy a look meant to paralyze his jaw, not that he talks much in situations like this. Thank God for sensible, yellow-bellied women, preservers of the race, she is thinking.

"Now if he left me charge of a decent six-shooter, that's diffurnt," Mama says. "Time was I could shoot the whiskers off a barn cat—"

"Me give a lady a sidearm! What kind of knucklehead idee is that!" Cochise bellows.

"No guns," Jane says faintly.

"I never got my hair parted crossways in no hotel shooting scrape," Mama wheezes.

"Why you lying old newsbag," Cochise says. "You was right behind me and I guess that's the thanks I get for gone first."

No point in arguing. Jane knows what to do next. She grabs her purse and the keys to the moneygreen Buick and starts down the stairs. At the front door she hears Mama, Cochise, and Jimmy clattering down the steps behind her. Cochise is going to telephone De Salis, then they'll all have a beer. Jane breathes easier. This gives her a little time.

Next to Horton's doghouse she lets the Buick nudge the curb (she burned out the handbrake chasing Jimmy around and around the block), slides over to the passenger side and rolls down the window. Finds the others lounging on the stoop where she saw Raymozo the Rayman the other night, but Raymozo is missing. They eye her in silence.

"Does Raymozo live here?" she whispers at them, too low.

"Say what?"

"Who you want?" from somebody else.

"Raymozo," Jane repeats a little louder, looking nervously back over her shoulder at the Grandview. "Raymozo."

Someone bursts into short gasps of laughter which she instructs herself to ignore.

"Don't know nobody called, what-you-said, Ray-mo-zo."

"You know who I mean," Jane dares. "I saw him here the other night."

A doubtful *"Yeah?* What you want with him?" "Can I show you something, baby?" "No, she don't want you, jack, she want *Ray-mo-zo,"* all of this with laughter, as though Jane has picked some ridiculous name out of air. She sees now she shouldn't have stopped at all. She has only invited another visit by asking for Raymozo, since she can't tell this bunch anything about a golden gun. Angrily she kicks the throttle and drives off—a big mistake, she sees, because she has already left him a message. Now she has to find him before he sees them first.

She drives by Walter's more circumspectly, surveying the black men loafing on the corners, peering at the few lone wolves who hang in doorways with a view of the traffic in and out of Walter's (*I eyeballed you a hundred times up Hoover by that old juice-head bar you work in*) but she can't see him, not even after she starts to have that eerie feeling he has long since seen her. At last she must break down and use the telephone number he gave her. She makes a U-turn into the Dairy Dreem parking lot. Then she is standing in a telephone booth, squeamishly fingering the frayed garrotter's cable of the vanished phone-book, dialing.

"Hel-low?" says a child's voice slowly.

"Claudette, go way from that phone!"

Deep in Jane's ear a pool ball clatters across a concrete floor. "Hello?" she says. "Hello?"

A TV voice says, *But, Doctor, my son has a brilliant future as an aviator.* A door slams. "Hello?" Jane shouts. *I'm sorry,* says the TV.

"Hel-low?" The child's voice again, small and surreptitious.

"Is your mother there?" Jane says quickly. Not that she wants to talk to anyone's mother.

He has his whole life, says the TV. "No," the child says.

"Claudette, what I tell you!" A whack, a shrill wail, and the pool ball in Jane's ear is bouncing across the floor again. "Hello!" Jane shouts as loud as she can.

"Yeah? Who you want?" A woman's voice, suddenly big as a house.

"May I speak to Raymozo?" Jane says.

"WHO?"

"Raymozo," Jane says. "Raymozo the Rayman."

"Ray-mo-zo the Rayman." Incredulously, mountainously, starting to laugh.

"He gave me this number."

"Huh? What number?"

Jane repeats the number.

"WHO you say gave it to you?"

"Raymozo the Rayman," Jane enunciates dully, for she is beginning to have her doubts.

"Lord have mercy!" The receiver clunks down. A static noise rises—something frying busily in a pan.

"A white girl and she want to speak to Ray-mo-zo the Rayman!"

"To who!"

"Ray-mo-zo. The *Rayman.*" The women are shrieking with laughter; Jane pictures them falling over each other, mopping their eyes.

"Shut that doggone TV, Yvonne. Y'all quit that fool cackling." A small old voice, sharp as a stick—the laughter falls at once to exhausted titters. "Who is it and what do she want!"

"A white girl and she want Raymozo the Rayman."

"Must mean Raymond," the old woman snaps.

"But he done told her Ray-mo-zo." Laughter resumes, more slyly.

"Gimme that phone. Shut up now. Who is this!"

"It's Jane," says Jane.

"You must want Raymond Buttons. This is his grandmother, Edwina Buttons."

"May I speak to him?" Jane says.

"He ain't home and I don't know when he's coming home. Never know nothing about that boy cause he don't tell me nothing."

"He comes home sometimes, doesn't he?" Jane asks.

"Maybe he do and maybe he don't."

"If you see him, would you tell him," Jane says, *"please stay away?"*

Silence.

"Would you please, please, tell him?"

"I tell him."

On her way to De Salis she pulls up in front of a liquor store, runs in and buys a pint of Spanish brandy, the cheapest. Back in the Buick she throws down one hot, spiny mouthful and hides the bag under her seat. She does not wish to be drunk—oh no, never again!—but rather to make her way through the world with a civilized anesthetic at hand, a mild balm decanted from a small, private supply.

Back at the Grandview they are playing cards. The door to Cochise's, still marked *Romanoff*, stands open a crack for Jane. She places the two halves of a window lock on a pile of hardware catalogues. No one asks what took her so long.

A gray metal money box is open on the floor by Cochise's mud-dried work boot. It gleams with thousands of red pennies, and Cochise is in his glory, learning these children how to trim a sucker at Spanish Monte.

"Say, girlie," he says when he sees Jane. "You look lucky to me. I'm going to trust you for fifty little ones just like I done for my pal here." He points at Jimmy, who has a heap of pennies in front of him. "The boy is killing me, but I can't complain because I always like to see a young feller do good. Now dotter. What will you ride on this here . . ."—Cochise leans down until his nose is an inch from the table—". . . queen of hearts?"

Mama says: "Who is gone to trust a dealer has to lay his whole shirtfront down on the table to see the cards?"

"These two greenhorns will, that's who."

"They ain't stupid, Cochise. They know you're fixing to cheat em. You told em you was."

"Are you in, Mama?"

"Heck no!"

"Then in the name of goodness, leave us in peace." Cochise cleans a tooth with his fingernail and says behind his hand, "These two has a little while to win yet, ya see. What you want on this here queen, dotter?"

"Fifty," says Jane.

Cochise is disappointed in Jane. "Your entire poke on the first go-round!"

"You said I was going to win for a while."

Cochise turns over a queen and rakes away Jane's coins.

"I can't let you win if you jump in with real money. That ain't the way it's done."

"I can't think of this as real money," Jane complains. "How can it be real money if it isn't mine?"

"Dotter, things is seldom as they appear. I'm trying to learn something into you. Use your imagination like this young lad. Now what do I see on the jack and the eight? You're getting greedy by now," he prompts Jimmy. "Put down plenty on that top layout."

Jimmy pushes pennies across the table. "Another ten and a twenty. Purty sure of yourself, ain't you, youngblood? Ouch! I wish I was home and my dog was here."

"You are home," Mama says.

"That's your opinion. I just live here."

"Home as you'll ever be," Mama says.

"Okay." Cochise rubs his glasses with the back of his hand. "The bets is all in. Watch careful now. Make sure nobody's standing in the door. Get ready to disappear." He slides a queen off the deck, flashes it and scoops all the coins off the table. "Thank you, gentlemen. Dollars is more portable," he adds.

"Where'd that queen come from?" Jimmy cries in frustration.

"Wasn't you watching?" Cochise bangs the deck on the table and belches complacently.

Mama says: "If that ain't the beatnest thing I ever saw, showing these two well brung up younguns how to cheat at cards."

"Now Mama, this is for their protection. They ain't actually gone to go out and do it."

"That's what you think," Jimmy says.

Jane glances at her lover. Only now it sinks in—an hour ago he told her he has a job in the desert if he wants it. *You'll come with me. We'll be rich. What a bandit that guy is. I'd get salary and a percentage. . .*

"Them was golden days," Cochise says. "Now my partner Izzy was a gentleman. He might starve but he would not work. Used to say Don't nothing work but a fool and a mule."

"It's a good way to get your head stove in, that there," Mama says. "Once we had to lay out all night in a frog ditch. You think what people mean to do with you if they lay hold of you. Life is as low as the ground."

Cochise says: "I always looked at it like this. You are teaching the sucker a useful lesson. When his luck starts up, that's when he ought to smell something funny. Here is this clyde what never played before, and suddenly the feller is hot as a pistol. But no, he just figgers this is what he always had coming to him since he was at his daddy's knee, his mama's little darling, and he's finally getting his hooks in it. And which is why he's your fool, ya see."

"Let's see that trick with the queen again," Jimmy says. "Where did it come from? Up your sleeve?"

"Up my sleeve! What you take me for, a rank ama-chore?" Cochise starts to lay out the cards again.

"So you're going back to the desert," Jane whispers in Jimmy's ear.

He hisses back: "If you say so. Aren't you coming with me, Jane?"

"It comes from the deck, you young fool," Cochise says. "Now watch this time. What do I see on the king and the trey?"

Jane hears it first, a soft rubbery skid along the ceiling. She closes her eyes.

"Ain't you in it, dotter? You asleep?"

"I'm busted," Jane says.

This time a distinct gritty scrape along the floor upstairs —everyone hears it. Cochise looms up from the box he's been sitting on and flies right over the table. Coming to earth he stumbles against Jimmy, who topples sideways with a pile of newspapers. Cochise is half out the door.

"Cochise, there's a gun up there and he's probably found it," Jane yells.

"Oh my gawd," Mama says, and runs with a queer paddling motion into the hall.

In a second all four of them are on the stairs, Mama halfway up the dark flight behind Cochise, Jane and Jimmy behind Mama, and Cochise already twisting onto the landing. He rams Jane's door with his big shoulder, the unlocked door pops open weightlessly and sticks against the Murphy bed, Cochise goes tumbling through. They hear a giant wheeze of the bedsprings, and muffled scrabbling—two bodies falling together. A *fump*, and Mama starts to charge up the last of the stairs. Jane grabs at the checkered housedress. "Leggo," Mama squeaks, pawing at her. Jane clenches her jaw, expecting a shot. She pictures the two on the floor with the gun between them. How long before it goes off? Maybe it won't go off.

The Rayman rolls through the bottom of the doorway and unfurls at the top of the stair. Poised to fly he looks down into the populated stairwell—draws back, his face unreadable, and drops out of sight in the dark corner of the landing. Cochise thumps through the door and staggers against the banister, a heavier man now than when he went up. He too sways over the stair, unsure of what human shapes he is looking at, and Jane hopes the Rayman will spring up behind him, through the apartment and out the bathroom window. But Mama yells, "Back of you." Cochise turns and crumples into the corner.

Cochise's belly hangs down like an old mare's; the Rayman is curled on his back, churning with his knees at this hammock of gut, and in between their hands are woven together. Jane realizes they are both trying to slide a hand under Raymozo's black blouse. The gun must be in there.

Cochise finally shovels in one hand, while the other pushes at the Rayman's face. The slighter body whips around like a scorpion, to kick, to knee, to grapple Cochise about the neck. Cochise raises his chin a little, tries to shout something down the stairs, but his famous bellow is pinched to a gargle. At last the tension of the dark neck breaks like a hinge; the throat arches back, the skull thuds against the floor. The golden gun appears, bubbles up in the air a little—but then it has never looked real —and bounces, pointing randomly, goldenly, this way and that, down the rubber treaded stairs.

As she watches the golden gun bump from step to step, its barrel describing a big slow arc like the lazy floor pointer over an old-fashioned elevator, Jane is still thinking the gun is dead —she thinks this more confidently than ever, now that two men have struggled over it without anyone getting shot—when it hits the fourth stair and goes off with a bang as big as the world, the frosted transom stenciled 1320 over the front door explodes, and the gun itself flies, really flies this time, into the air. Jane shrinks as small as possible against the wall and Mama tries to flatten herself down on one stair. Cochise scrambles heavily to the back of the landing on all fours. Only Raymozo the Rayman sits quiet at the front of the landing, his bony shins drawn up, looking out over the stairs. But no, he's not dazed. Jane sees his face in that dark hall as well as she has ever seen it. The retracted angle of his jaw, severely dignified rather than cocky, happens to catch the light from below, or perhaps it's that he looks directly down at her. His face is clear, not dazed. And he is pointing to the eyes behind his twisted glasses and slowly mouthing words Jane can't hear, but she can see them. *He looking at you. The Rayman looking at you. He looking.*

And she mouths back, Go. Run. Pointing at the open door to her apartment. And Jimmy is rushing up the stairs behind her, trying to repossess the princely toy as it rolls in air. He crowds her stair—Jane makes room. Together they hold out their hands like supplicants.

But the thing falls onto the step above Mama with a dull chock. Mama says: "All right, you low-down yellow-eyed sidewinder, you run out of luck when this gun fell in my hands. Think pure thoughts, yer time has come." She picks up the foot-long golden gun as if it weighs nothing at all and holds it way out at the end of one arm and draws a bead and cocks it—and Jane yanks her dress, the gun goes off and, wide of the landing, something falls over like a tree.

Raymozo the Rayman runs into the apartment, and Jane hears that melodious, hollow, *plink, plink, plink* of oversized sneakers running down the fire escape. Then Cochise's face blooms white, blind, and enormous around the top banister. He's missing his glasses and his golfing cap and is groping for something in back of him. "I think my ass is shot up," he says. "I ain't dead." But then he slumps down two steps to the landing and his forehead bounces on the floor.

"Good gawd, I've kilt him," Mama says.

"I'll call an ambulance," Jimmy says, and runs down the stairs into Cochise's apartment.

As Jane squeezes past Mama's fleshy arm with the .45 long Colt, still hot, dangling at the end of it, Mama begins to cry and says to her: "Why was you gonna let that nigger do for my Cochise?"

Jane says contritely: "I don't know."

Now Cochise is on all fours on the landing, swaying like a sick ox. In the dim light the seat of his white work pants is black with glistening blood.

"Aw Cochise, look what I done to you," Mama sobs.

Jane says: "It was all my fault."

Cochise says: "Now, Mother, a lot worse could of fell out. You can thank Jane here they won't have to take and put you in the pokey for murder."

"What you mean?" Mama says. "Ain't that self-defense?"

To Jane Cochise whispers: "That punk could have had me four time over. Why didn't he shoot me? I weren't nothing to him. He taken that gun."

"I don't know," Jane says. "I don't know what he wanted."

Three or four sirens from a distant boulevard clarify out of the quiet.

Jimmy pries the revolver out of Mama's fingers. He says: "Jesus, I'm going to have to tell them it was my father's gun."

Cochise says: "Well I never heard such a bunch of crybabies. They're just gone to ask a few questions. Janey'll put us all in the clear! They'll sew up my ass and we'll come home and I'll show you children how to lose at—"

"Who, me?" Jane says.

And then she sees what's going to happen. It's all going to come down to Jane. How did things go so wrong that this canny old shyster, well known to the police, should be shot in the ass for a young girl's sake with a golden gun? Why Jane? The right thing not having happened to her for quite some time, this is where she comes in. *Janey'll put us all in the clear.*

"I'll be right back," Jane tells her friends, as the sirens get louder. "Wait right here."

She sincerely means to gather her notebook and pen, but once inside the apartment she turns towards the bathroom, not the picture window, to stare at the distinct print of the Rayman's black playground hightop in the bottom of the bathtub. It's a flat peanut-shaped fossil, filled with squiggles, tic-tac-toe boxes, and stars. No—something too queer has happened, she thinks, to be discussed with a mind as invulnerable to paradox as a policeman's. And finds herself balancing on the rim of the bath-tub, climbing out the open window onto the fire escape, descending it rung by rung, past Cochise and Mama's moldy pink shower curtain, without noise—so why did the Rayman always make such a racket? She drops to the ground, gropes in her skirt pocket for car keys. And she is already halfway to the light at Vermont, the Buick blotting up asphalt as guilelessly as a milk truck, when an ambulance and three police cars whip around the corner. They swerve around her; in the tilted lozenge of her rearview mirror, their miniature vehicles veer to the curb and uniforms swarm out. And she turns left, left, left on trashy, quiet streets until she has circled back to Hoover and is idling in the shadow of the freeway overpass, twenty feet from an on-ramp. Across the concrete median is the wide sunken plain of the Dairy Dreem. It is deserted. A yellow dog is inspecting the telephone booth where Jane stood earlier. Her yellow tail sticks out stiff as a pencil, haunches high, head low and out of sight inside the glass.

It occurs to Jane that she could make a U-turn and call Raymozo the Rayman, to tell him: *I'll never give the cops your name, but you've got to disappear from my life.* Now there is a truly criminal idea—to try to make a deal like that with a doomed man, loony besides. Where's the percentage for him in getting over her? She's the only one of them who has room to disappear. Besides, he wouldn't do it even if she did ask him. And anyway he won't be home.

She drives up the on-ramp, whirls in its concrete tilt-a-loop, and heads south on the Harbor Freeway towards San Pedro.

○
○
● Harbor
Fwy 1½

I sat in a green park at the bottom of San Pedro, looking over a
brick balustrade to the Pacific. It was too dark to see, but I knew
the ocean was there below me at the foot of a cliff. Its noise
rushed into my ears without hurry, without intention, and filled
them. I smelled its lean perfume. It played by itself, a model of
self-possession.

I was at a picnic table. The pint of Spanish brandy was open
on the bench beside me, hidden between me and the wall. There
were few other people in the park. At another wooden table a
Mexican family was having its dinner, the littlest one upholstered in a snowsuit. It must be winter, I thought—how odd. I
hadn't noticed. At the table next to me were two teenage girls,
their eyes ghastly with eyeliner, looking around for whoever
might appear.

I had left the moneygreen Buick on the street. In case the
cops were looking for it—though I was beginning to see that
was a crazy idea. What would they want with me? But already
a patrol wagon had driven along the circle of picnic tables and
stopped to have a look at me. I had heard the crackle of a police
radio and glanced over my shoulder. The deputy at the wheel
was observing me with a wise-guy face. "Everything all right?"
he asked me.

I told myself: A woman alone in a park after dark, that's why they're talking to me. No other reason.

"Everything is fine," I said. They ground slowly off on the gravel.

I fingered the sleeve of brown paper my brandy was wrapped in, then took a swig before the cops were quite out of sight. I was not sure whether the possession of a bottle with a brown bag twisted around its neck was illegal or not. Either way, I probably looked too young to drink. And I was not drunk, or so I told myself. I was having my first experiment with a civilized anodyne decanted in moderation from a small, private supply. It seemed to be having the right effect.

I was calmer. Things looked simpler in the clarified dark under the park lights; questions were bearable once rinsed in the white noise of unseen water. Tomorrow I would get my friends out of trouble. Then I would have the rest of my life to think about what had happened to me.

For that was the strange thing. I felt it had happened to *me*. I had not been raped, not lately, I had not been sacked from a job, I had not been evicted. My boyfriend hadn't left me. No one had shot me in the ass. My mother's psychiatrist had not had me arrested—though any of these things might easily have occurred. I had gotten off light. But I felt low, as low as the ground. And this was the real reason I would not give the cops the name of Raymozo the Rayman, not even the crack-brained science fiction nom-de-guerre he had given me. The Rayman and I were equals. I would not say anything about him, not one word, to people who did not have his best interests at heart. I was certain he would do the same for me.

On the other hand, when I thought of going back to 22nd Street and facing that frying pan burglar alarm in the bathroom window, I felt a low, boiling rage, bubbles of pitch in the gut, something I had never felt before. I wished that Raymozo the Rayman, rather than be allowed to bother me one more time, be cut in half by a train. However, I put this idea out of my mind for the present.

I became aware of a commotion behind me. I glanced around. One of those mammoth tow trucks that come out of their caves to ply the roads in eastern snowstorms was idling on the gravel path, which it occupied completely and then some. Its headlights drilled two conical holes in the picnic area. A snaggle-toothed tire was denting the grass.

Its present mission was not humane. An old Plymouth was wrenched up on the tow hook, carelessly, it seemed to me. It even swung a little, like a wrecking ball. I was sure the old Plymouth had not broken down but had only been left too long in some spot of problematic ownership, like the parking lot of a public park.

As for the driver of the tow truck, I hated him on sight with an excited hate that might have tipped me off how drunk I was, except that I did not think myself drunk at all. A beer-fatted mercenary for small-time politicos, I thought with a snarl, and I stared at his shiny cheeks, low forehead, little eyes, fleshy chin, with a smack of satisfied disgust. I especially loathed his mouth, which was twisted to one side, ever ready to pour out abuse or a come-on, though his voice was only a leaky little toot. Right now it was a come-on. He was talking out his window to the two teenage girls.

" . . . take you dolls anywhere you want to go," I heard. They had gotten up from the silvery picnic table, but hung back in the dark away from the swirling cones of headlights.

" . . . too cold," one girl murmured.

"I don't want to ride in a dirty old truck," said the other distinctly. She smoothed her skirt and gazed with ruby eyes where the headlights were shining, as though she might see something better coming down the path.

"You girls are going to pass up something terrific," said the driver. He reached into a pocket with an insignia on it, pulled out a pack of cigarettes.

The first girl walked nearer the truck. The second sat down again, crossed her legs and looked pointedly the other way.

A short, polite beep came from behind the tow truck; at once

I realized I had been hearing those apologetic beeps for some time. A dented Chevrolet was waiting at a discreet distance. One of its headlights was a single glowing wire, and even the good one looked small and wan beside the truck's brilliant beams. It was the Mexican family. They had finished their dinner and were trying to leave. The driver of the tow truck did not seem to hear them.

He was leaning farther out the window now, offering the first girl a cigarette. When she reached up for it, he pulled her to the truck. She struggled. In a fumbling, complicated gesture he lit two cigarettes with his free hand and tried to push one into her lips. She turned her face to the side. The cigarette rolled away in the grass.

Now she brushed off her dress, and she too sat down primly at the picnic table and looked the other way.

"You ain't even going to thank me for the cigarette?" he yelled.

Behind him the old Chevrolet beeped again.

"What is this, you floozies ain't talking to me now?" He flopped back in the cab, smoked sulkily, then suddenly pressed his own horn, one short impatient blast. It was three times as loud as the Mexicans'.

"Come on, girls! Make up your mind!" he shouted at them.

"Go on back to your garage, ape," one of the girls said icily.

"Hey! I don't have to go nowhere, never, nohow, for nobody!" he announced.

The Chevrolet beeped.

In a flash the tow truck driver was halfway out his open window, shaking both fists. "Just cool it, you asshole greaser. Wait your goddamn turn or back up, you uglyface taco. Or I'll back you up, comprende?" He revved his engine and the tow truck lurched backwards a threatening inch, the abused Plymouth swaying stiffly to either side like a carcass on a meathook.

His choice of terms suggested he knew the Mexican family had been there all along. They, too, suddenly seemed to grasp the meaning of the situation. The Chevrolet's gears ground into reverse and it began backing slowly down, down, down the meandering gravel path between the trees and isolated picnic tables towards a distant parking lot.

The tow truck driver smiled broadly. His good mood was restored. "Well—what's it going to be, ladies?" He drummed his fingers on the side of the truck. "Last chance for a swee-e-e-et ride."

I don't know if it was that smirk, or the way the Mexican father had silently, instantly obeyed his orders—and no doubt I was a little drunker than I thought. All at once I was on my feet, blood crashing thickly in my temples. It was that same low, boiling rage I had felt before. I went up to the window of the tow truck and peered in. The driver stopped drumming on his door. "Who the hell are you?"

"I just want to see who you work for," I said, and read the emblem on his pocket out loud as if I were memorizing it. "JACK AND BOB WRECKING."

"What's it your fucking business!" said the driver. "Look, I've had a rough day. I've been working since eight a.m.—"

"I don't care if you've been working since you were born," I said, suddenly out of breath. "You're a bully. You shamed that man in front of his family. You're supposed to be working for the public and you—you upset people."

I had no idea if the Mexicans were upset. I was upset.

"Well, what are you going to do about it! Huh? Huh?" He glanced at me and suddenly pounded his horn with the heel of his hand.

I jumped a foot, leaned in, and said: "I'm going to make sure you get in terrible trouble. My father is an alderman and my uncle is a judge and my other uncle is the . . . the dog catcher. They're going to line you up and shoot you dead. You'll never work in this town again."

I whirled around in a kind of ecstasy. From the picnic table the two girls stared at me with suspicion and disapproval. Behind me the tow truck driver blasted his horn one more time. I picked my way carefully along the grassy fringe of the gravel path. I knew I was in the tow truck's way, but I was trying to look unafraid. Then the driver stamped on the gas, bars of heavy metal clanked into place, and I saw in the corner of my eye his angry face and the dark gleam of the truck sweeping past. Something tremendous hit me from behind. I fell to my knees, dazed, heard the truck screech to a stop and saw churning legs—the two teenage girls, running in wobbly high heels down the hill.

"You stupid girl!" a voice was shouting. I looked up into the driver's round white face. "Now you really did it to me, you stupid, stupid girl."

Then I felt terribly sick and let my head sink down, just for a moment, to the dark, wet grass.

They were the same two cops who had checked on me before. I blinked, trying to clear my eyes. Beyond was clear inky air, motion denoted by rushing, furry balls of light, and the heads of these two policemen, whom in a wave of depression I recognized. My head ached powerfully at the sight of them. The deputy who wasn't driving held his glossy head cocked towards me and wore the slanted smile of a city cop who is hearing just what he expects to hear.

I sat up in rigid alarm in the backseat of the police car. What exactly was he hearing? For I had the feeling I had been babbling about something without knowing what it was.

"What was I saying?"

The dark-haired cop shrugged tranquilly. "Something about your uncle the dog catcher."

"Oh." I had only been lost, then, in one of the trash-strewn industrial lofts of consciousness; I had not strayed into the guilty cellar. I relaxed.

We were on a freeway. Night was sweeping by. They were taking me home, I decided. I had been drinking and had shrewdly omitted to mention my car. Still, I could not recall their picking me up. Suddenly I flashed to a giant tow truck, a Mexican family in a dusty Chevrolet, and a blow, a sifting downward of powdery stars, sickness, and laying my face peacefully in the cold grass.

I touched my head, felt a tender, spongy bump on the back, and straws of grass in my hair.

"I'm all right," I said, hoping someone had asked me.

"So why don't you tell us your name, miss," said the dark-haired cop, as though repeating the question for the tenth or eleventh time.

I looked away and out the window. The freeway could only be going north, back to the city. The darkness grayed over an endless plain of other people's houses; stars slowly appeared in the gray, like flecks of lint clinging to washed-out flannel. If they didn't know my name, they couldn't be taking me home. And I was in a police car, hurtling through the night. The case was serious, for the possible destinations were not many.

"I don't need to go to a hospital," I said, putting, for a moment, the happiest construction on the matter.

The deputy scratched inside his ear with a ballpoint pen. "Your name?" he said again.

"Jane Turner. Middle initial K. I'm not hurt and I left my car in San Pedro."

The policemem looked at each other. The dark one wrote something on a sheet on a clipboard. "What's the K stand for?"

"Nothing."

I described the moneygreen Buick and gave its license number. "I can show you where it is," I added hopefully.

"She wants us to take her to her car," said the dark one. They smiled small wise-guy smiles at one another—ten-cent misanthropes the pair of them, I thought. I could see they were not going to turn around.

"Do you know what happened?" I began to explain. "There was this guy in a tow truck. And two teenage girls sitting at a table dressed to—"

"What kind of rotgut were you drinking up there?" asked the blond cop.

"I wasn't drunk," I said impatiently. "There was a Mexican family in a Chevrolet trying to get out of the park. And there was this big wrecker with an old gray Plymouth hanging off the back—"

"I thought you said a 1951 Buick, dark green."

"No, that's my car, this was—"

"How intoxicated would you say you were, miss?"

"I was drinking," I said, "not drunk. I saw . . . *you* know there was a tow truck in the park, don't you? Don't you?"

"Well, uh," the dark one looked down at his clipboard for my name, "there could have been a tow truck, Jane. I don't see where it makes much difference to you."

Slowly, as I sat there looking from one to the other, it came to me what this meant.

"Do you know the kind of guy you're taking care of?" I burst out.

Both of them smiled—discreet appreciation, this time, of a private joke. They knew what kind of guy they were taking care of.

"Where are you taking me?" I finally asked.

"Somewhere safe. Sort of a hotel. Clean, not your deluxe establishment. Not your top class of people."

"Somewhere you can think." These commonplaces were delivered in a bantering tone.

"You're not taking me to jail, are you?"

Two soft gusts of laughter.

I sat back on the seat, determined not to speak to them again. My excitement was profound. It was happening, and *to me*. I was going to jail.

The city began to appear beneath me, familiar intersections laid out, from this angle, under a mad seamstress's basting of electric wires. A coldly festive traffic light asserted a meaningless dot of red or green, and then toy cars bulged slowly into spaces where they had not been, like schematic cartoons of invasive diseases. The gray roof of the Piggly Wiggly, from where I looked, was a space station, an airfield riveted in giant plates by a robot boiler maker, and the earthlings being dragged across the supermarket lot by tiny gleaming shopping carts were in a deep sleep, fitting for slaves on Uranus. This was my neighborhood, I noticed, myself in a deep clarified sleep. Walter's was three blocks away, and if I was carried west at the next interchange, whose loops I could already see, I would gaze down at the Dairy Dreem, teeming with sinister gaiety at this hour though perfectly silent to me.

But the police car turned east, to the San Bernardino Freeway, and I ceased to be the stunned tourist of my lot. I remembered being driven to the hospital for a "pelvic" by Patrolman Dickey, how I had slid down so low I couldn't see out the window, sure that everyone in Harmonia Springs would know the worst if they saw me in a cop car, especially in the front seat. Now I was in the back, clearly a prisoner, and I sat upright, eyes forward, posing stonily for the stares of passing motorists while I let my own mind go black.

The police car was snaking up a wooded drive to a receiving dock; the two cops delivered me inside a set of glass vestibules, turned and left, their buttocks jingling with hardware. I had already decided they were not worthy of my hate, nor even of my attention. I let them go. A clerk in shirtsleeves asked me to empty my pockets, then scrutinized the paltry heap. Where was my wallet, my ID?

"Not on me—I only decided to go to jail at the last minute," I said sweetly. He picked through the stuff and pushed back at me a lipstick, a beaten-up pack of Pall Malls, paper matches, and sixty-three cents. Another clerk took my picture, another rolled my fingers, one by one, in a patch of tarry ink, then in boxes on a sheet of stiff paper. Thus I was booked. A woman guard as tall as a basketball player felt under my arms and between my legs and led me to a large, empty cell lined with stainless steel benching and walled with glass in which chickenwire was drearily fossilized. On the back wall was a black coin telephone. The guard ushered me in and left without a word, pulling the steel door shut behind her.

"How long do I have to stay here?" I shouted after her. Through the glass wall, I watched her white legs flicker away down the hall under a green uniform. I sat down on the metal bench, stared at the phone and instinctively clapped my hands over my ears.

My head, this reminded me, hurt, my hair was bristly with grass cuttings, I was dirty, butt-sore, and sick to my stomach from drink. And though I had sixty-three cents in my pocket instead of the dime an arrested man gets in the movies, so that hypothetically I could make six phone calls instead of one, practically enough to open up a bookmaking operation, I had nobody to call.

I mean, who do you call? Your lawyer, if you are one of those who can threaten to call your lawyer without thinking *My lawyer —what a joke*. Or a bail bondsman, but that meant a debt, with interest, on the installment plan, collateral—doubtless you had to own something besides a junk car or produce someone who did—and besides, what was I charged with? Interfering with a tow truck on public business? More likely, those two cops thought the less said about the tow truck, the better. Drunk, then—drunk and disorderly at worst—how long could they keep you for that?

Or you called your dearest friend to go your bail. If such friends as I had were not lying in cells themselves at this moment, it was through no good office I had done them. Anyway, I was not about to call the Grandview and find out.

Or you called your family. Mom, Dad. Come get me. Take me home.

I began to walk about, to look for something to look at, but this was a mistake. It was a sign of *Her True Adventure* I was hoping for—fifty thousand women just like Jane. I didn't want to be the only one. But every sign of previous human occupation had been mopped, scoured, or sponged away. The stainless steel benches gave the place the air of a veterinary examining room. I looked under the benches and found no bit of paper, no frayed cigarette butt, not even a wad of chewing gum. On my knees I examined the drain in the middle of the tile floor; it was dry, gleaming, mute. I told myself that I was alone by accident. By sheer chance, none of the thousands of drunken and disorderly women in all Los Angeles had displayed themselves to police at the right place or time to end up here with me.

Only an accident—all the same I was alone, a freak, the last of my kind on earth. This time the others really were sneering at me around the corner. And having been the happiest of babies, I had begun without fear of immobility and solitude. I had even found bliss in that combination. After all, what could go wrong? But that was before I understood all the things that could happen to you, and probably would. And now I was thinking: Life gets no lower than this.

I should never have seen that gun, never have learned how easily you can have, have if not manage, that power to make others pay attention. You should never find this out, unless you are the type who, once seated in the train of outrage, would be sure to kill yourself a stop or two ahead of the junction where you embark upon the idea of killing someone else. Having been the happiest of babies, I had never, not once, thought of forfeiting my sweet life to clarify some point of argument with those who did not have my best interests at heart. I was not the happiest of babies now. I might even be, by now, the unhappiest. But where had I gone wrong? Who was to blame?

I pictured myself with a gun, not a golden gun, any gun. I could see myself doing it. That was the difference between now and five minutes ago. I already knew I was capable of complete secrecy, that I would not have to fight the miserable human urge to whisper my crimes to another of my species, for I alone on earth did not have such urges. No one would ever know.

I would find another Jane Turner in Los Angeles—easy enough, large city, ordinary name—and when she travelled to some hair stylists' or dental assistants' convention, I would fly straight to Ohio under some other name. I would rent a car. In a blond wig and contact lenses with four rolled-up pairs of nylons stuffed in the bottom of my bra, and a low-cut dress, something with polka dots, I would drive into the Sunoco in Xenia, fill up my tank, and make a date with Homer Stamm. I was sure he wouldn't know me, sure he would leap at a date with this tootsie. I would pick him up when he got off work, drive him out to some dirt road near Harmonia Springs—there at least I knew what I was doing—saying to him all the while, Gosh, Homer, I guess you know what *you* want—and then I would show him the gun, tell him who I was, study his reaction, and shoot him through the head. I would stop for a minute to look at his face, a face not yet wholly dead, convulsed around a small distinct point of inquiry, as if just here had finally penetrated, into a brain of remarkable denseness, a burning question impossible to answer, while the power to think of anything but this question drained blackly out the back of the skull. *Was this what I really wanted? Where in the world did I go wrong? Why would anyone want to do this awful thing to me?* Now I have pushed him out of the car, I am staring down at his face in the grass, and I shoot him a couple more times since I am no expert in that part. But none of my victims would ever get up again or manage to say one word.

As long as I was in Ohio, I killed Sheriff Staples too. This man, having a better brain than Homer Stamm's, inside even thicker battlements, was even more in need of surgical implantation of that unanswerable question, *Why would anyone want to do this awful thing to me?* All it would take to rouse the sheriff out of his house in his pajamas was a damsel with car trouble at the end of his driveway. But then I remembered the sheriff was a public figure, an elected politician no less, whose shooting was automatically an *assassination*. I would be one of *those*—and I caught an alien glimpse of myself, a small sleepy face in a wire-photo, one of those structural irrelevancies in the design of society who suddenly explodes to the bafflement of everyone else—no, that wouldn't do. Nevertheless, I stopped to savor it, what it would be like, the sheriff spinning away backwards by the force of that deeply lodged but unscratchable itch of a question, into the vestibule of his suburban house, splattering red drops across the pastel bathrobe of a wife whose helmet of bobby pins connotes a woman the jury always like better than Jane. I could look at this for hours.

As long as it was so easy, why should any of them be spared? The sickly, etiolated little troll of a polygraph inspector; the fatuous bully in his tow truck; and never mind my earlier dispensation of them, that pair of sneering cosmopolites, the two cops who had brought me in—every one of these men was in need of a big surprise, a drastic piping through his thick skull of that final question, *Why is this awful thing happening to me? Where in the world did I go wrong?* This was not a bad question for anyone to put to himself, and in fact I now recalled that just such a question, put to myself, had set off this wave of exhilarating slaughter.

Where did I go wrong? I had never expected anyone to make me happy. I was happy from nature. I had had a lucky birth— such a fine and thrilling ride. No doubt it deceived me into thinking that only the right thing could ever happen to me, that I could play at being scared, ride with my pink sex forward, and come out none the worse. As Doctor Zwilling pointed out long ago, to my very great trouble, I had no choice in this matter. Such was my nature that I knew a man from a woman with no instruction. But also I had no fear. Now, at the age of twenty-one, I had fear—oh terrible fear, though not fear of being alone. I had been insulted in my pink and conspicuous sex, and I was sure that the wrong thing would always happen to me. Who was to blame?

Only one person could have held his hand over me and saved me from everything, repelled even golden bullets, and kept me happy in my sex, where I am most betrayed. Far from shielding me from the world, he had been the very burgermeister of its wish to confer invisibility upon a girl like me. No sooner could I walk than he had not liked to see me at all. This was my father Philip Turner—my blood boiled like pitch at the thought of his many insults to me—and now he would have to pay.

This is what I have travelled back to recollect: how I could have sat in a jail cell three thousand miles from Baltimore, and projected onto its glass-and-chicken-wire walls, next to my own reflection, the murder of my father, not once but again and again, as if nothing else would make me happy.

I bought a ticket to Philadelphia, where no one would recognize me. Magically equipped with a whole gin hand of credit cards made out in phony names, I rented an inconspicuous car. Or sometimes I took a chance and flew straight to Baltimore, disguised as a business woman in nylons and a conservative suit. My father now lived in a high-rise apartment building on Park Heights Avenue. The doormen at such places were mainly decorative. I could slip in dressed as a female menial of some kind—a maid or a nurse.

Five or six floors up I unsnapped my bogus uniform and rolled it in a ball. I needed no disguise to be admitted to his presence. My father would let me in, I was sure of that. But I never imagined going farther than the front entrance. Even more so than Sheriff Staples, who plausibly would come to the door buckling a holster over his bathrobe, my father seemed capable of terrible reprisals if I showed him my gun without shooting him right away. I was certain that, unlike Homer Stamm, he would never beg me for mercy, even if he had time. I could enjoy his shock only for an instant—then I fired straight into his face.

The face was more crudely demolished than the others had been. Why this unnecessary gore? I went over and over the scene, and each time my father's handsome face had to be wrecked, cloven, butchered, a gypsy scarf of blood thrown against the beige wall, broken pieces of cranium soaking into the carpet. I could look at this, I wasn't horrified at the sight, but naggingly disappointed. Even in the most unhinged fantasy I could not make that fatal question stick to my father's forehead—*Where did I go wrong?* There was no limit to what I could do to his head, his body. He alone of all the men on earth would resist the point of this interrogation to the end, and beyond. In his white tennis clothes, in his green MG, stopping only to take its top off if the day were fine, he would zoom off headless to be safely dead before he would allow this question to be introduced to him.

I could not believe I could make my father face what he had done to me, not even to save his own life, or to explain his terrible death. I, sitting in a drunk tank in some women's prison in Los Angeles, California, had to know everything, even that I was capable of murdering my father—and I still meant to do it, never mind that my satisfaction would be less than perfect, it was better than nothing—but he was going to escape without ever seeing me at all.

Now I am standing in front of the black coin telephone. I am calling collect, the blood thudding in my throat as though I had a gun in my hand instead of a receiver.

Hello? A woman's voice, half asleep. I roll my eyes—Elizabeth Marcus. I had forgotten all about her.

I have a collect call for Philip Turner from Jane Turner. Will you accept the charges?

Good lord, what time is it?

It is 4:20 a.m. in Los Angeles, ma'am.

A pause.

Is there someone there to accept the charges, ma'am?

Sure, sure—wait a minute. PHILIP! Another pause. I think he's out running. I'll talk to her if she wants. Do you want to talk to me, Jane?

I—

Will you accept the charges, ma'am?

Sure, go ahead.

Go ahead, ma'am, the operator says.

No, wait a minute—here he is. The phone clatters down.

Operator? I say. The operator is gone. A door closes with a remote but solid woof. The same door I had come through so lately with a gun in my hand.

Philip (shouted), it's Jane. On the phone. From Los Angeles.

I could hang up now, start over, but I don't.

Jane? My father, breathing hard.

I'm here, I say.

Jane? Where are you?

I'm in jail.

He laughs. This is a good start, for through history my father laughed at my jokes so seldom that, as long as we lived under one roof, we both could easily believe I made no jokes at all.

I am, I say, but never mind. I called . . . why did I call? I called to see if you would accept the charges.

Why shouldn't I? says my father, in an expansive, gubernatorial tone. I'm always glad to hear from one of my daughters.

He has just come back from running; he is going to live forever, and can afford to be generous. It's the right answer, but I don't like that *one of my daughters*.

Supposing, I say, this was 1955 and you were destitute, Dad, completely without prospects, and your only way of keeping yourself—here I lose my nerve a little—keeping the family alive was to sell one of your daughters into slavery. You follow me?

Silence.

Your *only way*, Dad. Would I have been the one?

I'm not going to answer that ridiculous question!

Okay, okay. In fairness he still has credit to spare for accepting the charges, even though Elizabeth answered the phone.

Dad, you like being married, don't you? I say.

What is this!

It's a serious question.

What did you do, marry that—somebody?

He is not going to say *marry that bum* in front of Elizabeth Marcus, and this shows progress. He never made concessions to the civilizing influence of Sasha, if indeed the thwarted Sasha could be called an influence in any shape.

No, no, I say. I'm not marrying anybody. This is something I really want to know about you.

Marriage to the right person has much to recommend it, he says cautiously.

Elizabeth is the right person, I can see that, I say. Now Dad, there's something else I have to ask you. Are you still—do you still need to—you know, go with other women. Now that you're with the right person.

Silence. Then: What's this all about!

Dad, I swear I'm not judging you—not about that. Be brave, answer the question.

I don't need to be interrogated by a daughter I hear from once a year.

Yes you do, I say. You don't have to like me, Dad. I'm through with that. But you have to answer my questions.

What about you? he says aggressively. Do I get to ask you a lot of exceedingly personal questions?

Aw Dad, you know you don't want to know anything about me unless the news is good.

But you want the bad news about me.

Yes, I say, because I can take it. Now listen, Dad. You've always been an important person—

No I'm not, he says abruptly, dismissively.

I mean to me. Do you realize that I could tell for years and years you couldn't stand to look at me?

That's not true.

Don't deny the obvious or I'll get crazy.

A pause.

I know I've expected too much from all my daughters.

Stop calling me *all of your daughters*. Could you ever imagine, Dad, that all by yourself you made someone angry enough to kill you? I mean to murder you with her own hands.

What are you, threatening me? he says, panting like a little boy ready to fight.

Of course I'm not threatening you, I say slyly. I just wonder how far you go in seeing yourself the way other people might see you. How do you think I look at you, for instance? Do you ever wonder, where did I go wrong?

Another pause. Then: Is this some kind of test?

Yes, it's a test.

And what if I don't answer.

Please answer.

What if I don't?

A long silence.

Then I'll think the worst of you.

My dear Jane, he suddenly cries out, in shrill, even passionate sarcasm, I couldn't care less what you think of me.

And he hangs up—not pushes the button down, but in his temper, three thousand miles over the hills and far away, throws the vitrified fetus which is the shape of a standard desk-telephone receiver at its pronged cradle, where it lands with a sharp clunk. Then there I am, back in jail, staring at glazed wall tiles the color of frozen dust on either side of the pay phone, the buzz of a dial tone in my ear. I am looking at something—along the dead-white grouting, not quite scoured away, are scales of dark blue. Someone once smuggled a ballpoint in here and stood at this phone idly defacing the wall tiles. Idly, meaninglessly, but full of meaning for me. *Her True Adventure* in an edition of 50,000. The moment I stop asking if it has any message for me in particular, everything in the world has eloquence.

I fish my dime from the coin return, reinsert it, and start to place a second call to Philip Turner from Jane Turner, to give my father a chance to refuse the charges—he would certainly cooperate in his present mood—but suddenly this strikes me as a tedious, rather didactic drama, long since played out. In truth I got rid of my father shortly after birth. My sluggishness only matched his precocity in grasping that fact. Then providence, whose witty ploy it is to give the disbeliever whatever she asks, showered me with fathers better than my own—Willie and Cochise, and even Pete's son, Jimmy, were the proper sex for the job, steeped in inventive virtue, immensely brave where Philip Turner was chicken, and they all loved me very well. But I would have none of them—not in *that way*.

I am curiously elated, for I seem to have stumbled upon some proof of my own existence. Only think where I am! I'm in jail, in jail at last. Even my father, who can be depended upon to think the worst, was unwilling to believe it of me. What matter if I got here by none of my many crimes, but on the wings of human folly and bluster, through the abuse of public institutions, to placate a dull-witted tow truck driver's fear of a lawsuit? To be thrown in jail as nobody, for nothing, is all the more an accomplishment. I might as soon bless them all as curse them all, for leaving me no one to thank.

I have escaped into bareness, into immobility, into the blind unreflecting bottom. Whatever I see from now on must be in some way free of my weight and imprint, safe from my designs for it, and I in turn will go free, having no choice in the matter.

In this transfigured state I sit for perhaps ten minutes—about as much transfiguration as I personally can stand. Then the guard reappears in the steel door, to lead me through more steel doors, sliding electronic outer space affairs this time. She takes my clothes, squirts up a pink cloud of institutional flea and louse powder, and delivers me to Wing C, Awaiting Trial, well within the gray heart of the building.

The courtroom is airy, full of smoky late-afternoon light, and almost empty, but for the untidy queue of female prisoners —all alcohol cases—in the dock, an island of public defenders slumped in the deserted spectators' seats, and, far away and up front, the judge. One after another he gives them thirty days, the women I have spent the long morning with—toothless Daisy, whose husband and pimp brought her here from Albuquerque, then dumped her for a younger moneymaker; a crazy old woman named Cha-Cha, who flip-flopped up to me in her jail-issue thongs and hissed in my ear, "Glasses make your eyes stink"; and Ruby, who lives at 30th and Budlong, not far from the Grandview, and who cautioned me to conserve my cigarettes and split my paper matches up the middle. But I have plenty of cigarettes, having spent my last sixty cents on two packs in the cigarette machine outside of C Wing. "Yeah? Well, don't be so free-hearted, girl. These leeches in here won't leave you with nothing." I gave Ruby my lipstick and told her I didn't think I'd be here very long, but now I am not so sure. Whatever their story is, they get thirty days, thirty days, thirty days. The bailiff asks how do you plead; they say guilty; the judge asks them a question or two, listens sleepily to their narratives, then says thirty days. Now and then the judge recognizes one—Cha-Cha, for instance. He asks her how she's been. "Can't complain, suh," she says with a leer. He gives her thirty days. "Thankee, suh," she grins, "and same to you."

At last I hear my name read, and the charge: DRUNK IN PUBLIC. I step up front. After my thirty days is up, I am thinking, I'll say goodbye to Jimmy. I'll borrow money from anybody who will lend it to me and drive back east, but not to Baltimore —to the country. I'll stop and see Willie. And after that, rivers, fields, and forests. I'll live alone for awhile, far from other humans. To manage my fear, I'll get a big dog.

"How do you plead?" says the bailiff.

I say: "I don't know."

The judge, who has been shuffling papers, looks up, takes off a pair of heavy black-rimmed spectacles, and squints at me. He shakes his head as if refusing to believe the evidence his eyes deliver.

"What are you doing here?" he asks.

I stare back at him for a time. Suddenly, with a soft crash, I bump into his mirror. I see what he is seeing—a young woman, possibly his daughter's age, white skin, glasses, curly hair, a small sharp face. The judge is an urban demographer, a little careless in the fine points (thirty days, thirty days, thirty days), but he does not need the fine points to read in me a child of the upper middle class. His class.

"What are you doing here?" he repeats.

"Do you want me to explain?" I ask, since this is the same judge who has snored with open eyes through all the stories, long and short, of the others.

"Explain," he commands.

I open my mouth, look around me uncomfortably, but the other prisoners are behind me now, out of sight.

"I was alone in a park in San Pedro, drinking brandy and listening to the sea."

(Already a sentence so tendentiously poetic I grind my teeth. But I go on.)

I explain about the tow truck driver, the two girls, the Mexican family, the mysterious blow from behind.

"I stuck my nose in it," I confess, with disingenuous humility.

The judge shakes his head in grave disgust, but not at me. He puts on his glasses and holds up a paper in front of his face.

"Gannon," he reads, "and DiBiasio." These are the names of the cops who arrested me. I hope, but doubt, I've gotten them in trouble.

"Get out of here," the judge says. "Case dismissed."

I stand there.

"What is it?" says the judge, looking up again.

"I'm not sure where I am," I say. "And I don't have a cent."

The judge crooks his finger at me. As I approach he reaches into his robe, leans over his desk and holds out his palm. In it are a dime and a quarter—thirty-five cents.

"Carfare," he says. "Don't mention it. Just get out of here."

I take the money and walk slowly, poker-faced, concealing my joy, out the open double doors.